Praise for the Dune s

"The magic lingers, even when the final chapters have already been written."
                                    —*Kirkus Reviews* on *Mentats of Dune*

"A fun blend of space opera and dynastic soap opera."
                                    —*Publishers Weekly* on *Sisterhood of Dune*

"Delivers solid action and will certainly satisfy."
                                    —*Booklist* on *The Winds of Dune*

"The saga continues to embroider the original works with intelligence and imagination and also a stronger role for women."
                                    —*Booklist* on *Mentats of Dune*

"Fans of the original Dune series will love seeing familiar characters, and the narrative voice smoothly evokes the elder Herbert's style."
                                    —*Publishers Weekly* on *The Winds of Dune*

"This sequel to *Paul of Dune* is an important addition to the Dune chronology and will be in demand by Herbert fans."
                                    —*Library Journal* (starred review) on *The Winds of Dune*

"Characters and plot are beautifully set up, the timing is precise . . . The universe . . . is so vast, complex, and fascinating that the magic lingers."
                                    —*Kirkus Reviews* on *Sisterhood of Dune*

DUNE
THE HEIR OF CALADAN

Brian Herbert

and

Kevin J. Anderson

TOR PUBLISHING GROUP

NEW YORK

DUNE: THE HEIR OF CALADAN

A Tor Book
Published by Tom Doherty Associates / Tor Publishing Group
120 Broadway
New York, NY 10271

www.tor-forge.com

Tor® is a registered trademark of Macmillan Publishing Group, LLC.

The Library of Congress has cataloged the hardcover edition as follows:

Names: Herbert, Brian, author. | Anderson, Kevin J., 1962– author.
Title: Dune. The heir of Caladan / Brian Herbert and Kevin J. Anderson.
Other titles: Heir of Caladan
Description: First edition. | New York : Tor, 2022. | Series: The Caladan trilogy ; 3
Identifiers: LCCN 2022034289 (print) | LCCN 2022034290 (ebook) |
ISBN 9781250765161 (hardcover) | ISBN 9781250765178 (ebook)
Subjects: LCGFT: Science fiction. | Novels.
Classification: LCC PS3558.E617 D892 2022 (print) | LCC PS3558.E617 (ebook) |
DDC 813'.54—dc23/eng/20220721
LC record available at https://lccn.loc.gov/2022034289
LC ebook record available at https://lccn.loc.gov/2022034290

ISBN 978-1-250-76518-5 (trade paperback)

Our books may be purchased in bulk for promotional, educational, or business use.
Please contact your local bookseller or the Macmillan Corporate and
Premium Sales Department at 1-800-221-7945, extension 5442,
or by email at MacmillanSpecialMarkets@macmillan.com.

First Tor Paperback Edition: 2023

Printed in the United States of America

0 9 8 7 6 5 4 3 2 1

When we think of dedicating any book we have written, we always think first of the incredible women who have dedicated their entire lives to us, Janet Herbert and Rebecca Moesta. As part of our commitment to them, we lovingly dedicate this book to Janet and Rebecca.

And, in special gratitude for his extensive work in the Dune universe, as well as his constant support of this trilogy, we also want to dedicate this to Christopher Morgan of Tor Books for his constant support of this series.

The dream becomes more real each time I experience it. In my waking moments, I long to return there, though I sense great danger.

                         —PAUL ATREIDES, private journals

In his dim bedchamber, Paul lay awake on an unusually warm evening, his covers thrown aside. He felt very alone in Castle Caladan and adrift, uneasy that Duke Leto and Lady Jessica were far away and separated from each other. Gurney Halleck was gone, too.

But he was the heir to noble House Atreides, and he had to think like a Duke. He was about to turn fifteen, and Caladan was his responsibility, at least temporarily while his father was gone.

He knew that the Duke's mission was of utmost importance, and he recalled the recorded message his father had left for him. "Watch this only if I don't come back," Leto had said, placing the shigawire spool in the young man's palm. "I hope you never need to view it. You know why I'm doing this, why I'm taking such a risk." And in the Duke's expression, Paul saw a genuine realization of the danger to which he was exposing himself—willingly, for the sake of the Imperium.

Now, Paul tried to sleep in the uncomfortable heat, feeling sticky sweat on his skin. The day had been unseasonably hot without the sea breezes that customarily skimmed over the water and moderated temperatures along the coast. As bad luck would have it, the castle's mechanical air-cooling system had failed at just such a time. Caladan engineers had inspected the mechanism, consulted manuals provided by the Ixian manufacturer, and apologized to the young man that repairs could not be completed without securing parts from off-planet.

Paul was not a delicate noble child, so he could deal with such discomfort, preferring to adapt to the weather and ignore it as much as possible, a human surviving the elements. Open windows and sea breezes were welcome to him. With the wilderness excursions he'd made with his father, the young man felt relaxed without being enclosed within a structure.

For security reasons, as well as the expected decorum of a ducal heir, he couldn't be footloose and aloof. He had to play the part of a young nobleman residing in the ancient castle, ready on a moment's notice to rule in Leto's place. It was what his father expected of him, the same as old Duke Paulus Atreides had demanded of his own son a generation before.

To make his father proud, Paul would meet those expectations, but he rather liked the idea of doing things people did not anticipate.

The boy tossed and turned in the darkness, wiped perspiration from his brow. Finally, he swung out of bed and carried a sheet and pillow out onto the small balcony of his bedroom, where he lay down in his thin nightclothes. The tile balcony was hard and warm, still radiating heat from the day. With a sigh, he gazed up at the gently twinkling stars in the crystal-clear night.

Across his field of vision danced stars whose names he knew, the ones his father and Dr. Yueh had taught him—Seille, Ikam, Jylar, and many others, all part of the vast galactic Imperium. But none of the brightest stars overhead at this time of year belonged to powerful noble families. Caladan did not have a particularly favorable location—not physically close to the capital, Kaitain, and not on any major Heighliner shipping or passenger routes. Other Landsraad Houses had equally unfavorable locations, but some managed to excel even so. Paul wondered about the future of House Atreides, and what his part might be in that unfolding story.

As he lay there, he heard a fluttering of wings. One of his father's trained hawks landed on the stone railing of the balcony. In the low light, the magnificent creature looked sidelong at him, then took up a sentry position, turning its head first one way and then the other.

Paul realized that the bird had not come here by coincidence. The head of Atreides security, Thufir Hawat, somehow knew that the young man had gone out onto the balcony, and he'd sent the hawk. The old warrior Mentat and his staff had been working with these birds in recent weeks, part of the falconry group maintained by the Duke. These specialized birds had surveillance equipment secured to their bodies.

Thufir worried constantly about young Paul's welfare, complaining about the "unnecessary risks" the fourteen-year-old had been taking, such as climbing steep cliffs and flying aircraft into dangerous storms over the sea. Duncan Idaho had accompanied him on such risky endeavors, calling them maneuvers to stretch the young man's abilities. He had sworn never to let Paul come to harm, but even Duncan had been concerned. "Perhaps we're going a bit too far," the Swordmaster admitted to the boy. "Thufir wants you to train, but within limits."

The Mentat watched the Atreides heir like a hawk, figuratively and now literally.

Paul extended his hand to the bird on the rail. It watched him, then looked away, continuing its sentry duty. Paul could see the small lenses on its feathers, a transponder at its throat. No doubt, the old Mentat was reviewing images right now.

"Thufir, I am perfectly capable of taking care of myself on my own castle balcony."

The transponder emitted a small, but discernible voice. "It is not possible to concern myself 'too much' with your welfare, young Master. If harm were to befall you under my watch, my abilities would be worth nothing. Now, I want you to have a restful sleep."

Paul lay back on his pillow. "Thufir . . . thank you for your concern."

He used a Bene Gesserit mental exercise his mother had taught him to remove troubling thoughts, so he could open the doorway to sleep. His body was exhausted after another long day of training with Duncan.

With warm sea breezes around him and the hawk standing sentinel above him, Paul drifted into a slumber of darkness and solitude . . . which shifted gradually into a desert landscape, bright sun on hot dunes. He stood on an expanse of sand, squinting at a rock escarpment baked in the sun. In the dream, it was morning in that distant place, but already warm, portending another hot day.

A figure made its way down a trail on the great rock, moving athletically in a desert costume. At the bottom of the rock, opened a burnoose to reveal the elfin features of a young woman with skin darker than his own and hair matted with dust.

He'd seen her before in dream after dream, and the voice was familiar as well, drifting over him like a breeze from the desert. "Tell me about the waters of your homeworld, Usul."

Having experienced this in many haunting variations, he felt it was more than a dream, and he always awakened in the middle of it. This time, he managed to remain in the other reality a little longer, but as his dream-self struggled to speak a response, to ask questions, the landscape and the intriguing young woman faded from view.

Much later at night, when the breezes turned damp and chill, he lay awake on the open balcony, again resorting to thought exercises. He counted the nobles in the Atreides line who had preceded him. The castle had stood for twenty-six generations on this commanding spot overlooking the sea, originally constructed by Earl Kanius Atreides. Not the first Atreides to rule Caladan, he had envisioned a great fortress on this rocky promontory, commissioning the grand blueprints when he was only nineteen years old, not much older than Paul was now.

Earl Kanius had seen the mighty castle completed in little more than a decade, along with the gardens and a thriving coastal village. Paul recalled a filmbook image of his ancestor's face, and then thought of the successors of Kanius, counting each one all the way up to Paulus Atreides, his own grandfather, whose painting hung in the castle's dining hall.

But when Paul tried to summon the next image in the line, his father, he could only summon a fuzzy, undefined outline. He missed the man so much and hoped he would come home soon.

He felt the weight of all the work done by Kanius and the other Atreides, all the planning they'd had to do and the decisions they'd made to empower their Great House. He finally drifted into a deep, troubled sleep.

In the Imperium, everyone masks their secrets, and the more damaging are
not merely concealed, they are buried deep—along with any witnesses.
—COUNT HASIMIR FENRING, private note to Shaddam IV

The planet Elegy had lovely forests, rivers, and lakes, but it was not Jessica's true home, and its beauty was not the same as the ocean world of Caladan. She tried to console herself with the thought—the *hope*—that she was merely a visitor here, and that she would return soon to Duke Leto and their son, Paul. But each day away from them made her more settled here, increasingly immersed in the life of Viscount Giandro Tull as his bound concubine, on orders of the Bene Gesserit Sisterhood.

Troubled, she sat now in the compact but nicely appointed office that the handsome Viscount had provided for her. His small administration building was concealed from the manor house by a grove of lichen trees. Giandro's own office was down the hall, and she watched a steady flow of functionaries hurry past her own, including a surprisingly large number of uniformed military officers. Despite all the appearances and the trappings of daily business, Jessica had now learned the nobleman's true plans.

Only a few days ago, prowling secretly through the forests to watch Viscount Tull as he rode off on a fine thoroughbred, Jessica had spied him receiving a mysterious weapons shipment into a hidden underground bunker. That was how she'd learned that Giandro Tull was a silent supporter of the violent Noble Commonwealth rebellion.

That revelation changed everything about their relationship, but since he had arranged for her to go on her own mission to save Paul, Jessica owed the man a great deal. After she confronted Giandro, he had taken her into his confidence, but still did not reveal the deeply personal reason he had decided to support the overthrow of the Corrino throne. The two were still understanding their new roles, and alliances.

Jessica busied herself completing paper order forms for lichenweave fabrics, filling in a ledger book by hand—an outdated system, but she found it refreshing. Duke Leto had done much of his administrative work by hand as well.

Trusting her, considering their shared deep secrets, Giandro had expanded Jessica's role in his household, asking her to help with the ordering of supplies. She considered the assignment an excellent camouflage role, and he gave her the freedom to procure whatever she wanted. Out of nostalgia, Jessica tried to order a shipment of moonfish from Caladan, only to learn that the product was no longer available. She wondered what might be going on back at the place she still considered home.

Giandro Tull had thriving business dealings, some surreptitiously connected to the rebellion. And now that Sardaukar had searched and cleared his operations, he had grown bolder. Apparently, his overt support of Jaxson Aru had begun soon afterward. Jessica still didn't understand why.

In the short time she'd known the nobleman, she had come to respect him, had even grown fond of him—within the limits that she herself had set up. Though he had publicly announced her as his concubine—which satisfied the Bene Gesserit and other observers—he displayed no romantic or sexual interest in her, or in anyone.

It was not the relationship many people thought it was, but it worked efficiently for both of them. Let others assume what they wished. Meanwhile, she would do anything necessary to change her assignment and go back to Leto and Paul.

She sighed. Under other circumstances, she might have accepted remaining with House Tull. But not after knowing Leto. In him, in the Duke of Caladan, Jessica had found as close to an ideal partner as she could imagine . . . even after the terrible quarrel that had broken them apart. Though she knew that Leto doubted her, her love for him remained strong. She had already stained herself in the eyes of the Sisterhood by choosing to give birth to the son Leto wanted, instead of the daughter she'd been commanded to bear. . . .

In the corridor outside her office, she heard something fall to the floor as a uniformed military officer rushed by. Glancing up, she saw him kneeling to gather papers he had spilled, stuffing them into a leather case. He was one of the soldier bodyguards who had joined Giandro out in the hills to receive the illicit weapons shipment. After snatching the papers from the floor, the man hurried to the Viscount's office.

Jessica noticed that one of the loose papers had slid under her door, a technical drawing of some kind. She retrieved it, but the officer had already ducked into the Viscount's office. She felt a chill as she glanced at the drawing—it appeared to be related to the hidden weapon shipments and a new military design.

Remembering the flustered urgency on the man's face, she walked briskly down the hall to give him the missing document. She pushed past the clerk who guarded the Viscount's office, who called after her, startled, as if he didn't recognize the new concubine.

Hearing the commotion, Giandro opened the inner door, caught her eye. "Jessica! What is it?"

Inside, standing before the broad wooden desk, the flustered officer was arranging his documents.

Jessica held up the technical drawing. "I assume this is something important."

The officer looked up from the desk, horrified. "I'm, I'm s-sorry, my Lord! An inexcusable lapse on my part."

"But fortuitous." Giandro ushered Jessica inside as he gave a reassuring nod to the confused clerk in the outer office, then closed the door for privacy. "We are lucky Jessica is the one who found the document, rather than someone who would do us harm."

She looked down, playing demure. "I am not here to serve a political role." She noticed the blue-spiral Tull crest in the middle of the old desk, partially obscured by papers.

"Spoken with the wisdom of a Bene Gesserit," he said. "But of course I value your wisdom and opinions. This is Lef-Major Zaldir, one of our experts on a new project." He gave the officer a meaningful glance. "Jessica is fully aware of our plans, and I trust her implicitly."

Zaldir was both alarmed and surprised. "Even . . . even about this, sir?"

"Even about this."

Jessica had glanced at the drawing. "I am not familiar with this design. I saw the previous weapons delivery, though I wasn't supposed to. Were these devices among them?"

Giandro gave her a warm smile. "It's distressing that you spied on me, and more distressing that you succeeded, but in the end, it was serendipity. Having you aware of our efforts makes many things smoother for us."

Zaldir took the paper back, inserted it into proper order. He looked anxious. "The first prototypes of the shield nullifiers are packaged and ready to be shipped off." When he looked up at Jessica again, sweat beaded on his brow. "Does she . . . does she know about . . . ?"

"Yes, she knows the new shipment is bound for Jaxson Aru."

Jessica covered her reaction. She hadn't, in fact, known that. She lowered her voice. "That man's penchant for grand and bloody statements is not to my liking." On Otorio, Leto had been one of those innocent bystanders who barely escaped from the massacre. So many others had been killed, and the incident had greatly shaken him.

Troubled by her obvious reticence, Giandro gestured Jessica to a seat beside the Lef-Major. The antique chairs also bore the crest of House Tull. He frowned and said, "Though I support the Noble Commonwealth—for reasons that I consider sufficient—I don't always agree with Jaxson's tactics. I would prefer a less violent, yet more effective, approach. Hence, this new weapon design is for *defensive* purposes, rather than aggression." He glanced around his private office, as if to double-check his own security. "This room is blocked and shielded. We may discuss freely. Lef-Major, tell her about the nullifiers."

Though the officer still seemed uncertain to have Jessica brought into the circle of extreme confidence, Zaldir pulled the technical documents toward him. "These devices level the playing field and give our allies equal standing against a far superior Imperial foe." Clearly more interested in the technical details than in military protocol, he grew more animated as he talked. "Our ingenious new nullifier can short out personal shields within a certain radius. Once such a device is activated, our opponents will be vulnerable to simple projectile weapons, needle guns, antique pistols—a vulnerability they will never expect. Imagine the invincible Sardaukar suddenly mowed down by mere bullets!"

Grasping the implications, Jessica nodded. The invention and use of personal shields had rendered all projectile weapons obsolete in major combat for thousands of years. No one would think to defend against such a thing. The introduction of Tull's shield nullifiers would impose a fundamental change in warfare—again.

The Viscount scanned the report. "Of course, much more significant pentashields and house shields would not be affected. But, oh, what a surprise in personal combat!"

She nodded. "The Sardaukar won't realize the rebels possess such defenses. If they ever do track down Jaxson Aru or his Noble Commonwealth base, they'll charge forward in force." She allowed herself the smallest smile. "Thus exposing themselves to destruction."

During her recent secret trip to Caladan to save Paul, she had spoken with her son, but Leto was gone on a mysterious mission of his own. Bound by a promise, Paul had not revealed to her what his father was doing, but Jessica had gleaned hints from Giandro Tull that Leto might have made overtures to the rebels as well. It did not seem possible . . . unless Leto had some other reason for doing so.

Looking up, she saw the nobleman's eyes dance, and he said, "We will send a shipment of the prototype shield nullifiers to a rendezvous point, where Jaxson can retrieve them for distribution to the rebels. I will include a message for him, so that he knows the true importance of these devices."

Lef-Major Zaldir gathered his papers. "The unmarked crates are ready outside your stables, my Lord. Security will clear the area, so that you may record your message. We can encrypt and encode within a bonded ridulian crystal so that no one but Jaxson Aru may activate the recording."

Giandro rose from his seat behind the antique desk. "Jessica will stand with me as I record. I want my new concubine at my side."

Jessica felt a sudden flare of alarm. What if Leto did see the message, in his dealings with the rebel leader? "I would prefer not to be placed on public display, my Lord."

He chuckled, not understanding her concern. "Not to worry, this will be the most private of communiqués." He donned a brown military jacket with silver-and-gold epaulets and ribbing, then prepared the words for his message.

Measure us not by our words, but by our actions—and even those may change with circumstances. From the outside, no one can ever know the secret intent of our hearts.

—Bene Gesserit *Azhar Book, Training Commentaries*

U r-Director Malina Aru was not convinced that even the security of the CHOAM stronghold on Tanegaard could protect her, especially now that Jaxson was convinced that his mother supported his cause. He believed that she endorsed a violent, chaotic overthrow of the Corrino Imperium, rather than a controlled reshaping of the government.

After leaving Jaxson's secret rebel command center on isolated Nossus, Malina traveled here to Tanegaard to meet with her other two children, the reliable ones. Together, they could discuss what to do about this frightening radical faction. She hoped she wasn't alone in her doubts.

Her private transport emerged from the Guild Heighliner over Tanegaard. Because Malina was the Urdir of the Combine Honnete Ober Advancer Mercantiles, she could divert space travel according to her own priorities. After what she had heard and seen on Nossus, she didn't care about inconveniences to others, not even the most powerful Houses of the Landsraad. After delivering her ship, the enormous vessel left orbit, the prescient Navigator folded space, and the Heighliner was on its way. The passengers aboard likely didn't even know about the detour.

Frankos and Jalma were also en route. As CHOAM's figurehead President, her son Frankos would pull similar strings to rush to Tanegaard. Jalma, as the lady and powerhouse behind House Uchan, could also arrange swift transport. When their mother issued her summons, she had used a code word that this was a call to arms. Malina had no doubt they both would come running.

Jaxson needed to be controlled.

Having served her for a long time, her private pilot knew not to make inane chitchat. Cool and professional, he guided the Urdir down to the cyclopean buildings on Tanegaard, great blocky structures that looked as if they could withstand a supernova. Malina stared out the window while absently stroking the silver fur of her two spinehounds, Har and Kar. The pets lay on the deck beside her, content to go wherever she did.

Tanegaard's armored, encrypted vaults contained secret financial, business, and personal records that others in the Imperium did not have access to, not even the Emperor himself. Such information was utterly confidential, revelatory, and even damning, but CHOAM dealings were secure. Without confidence in complete privacy, many Landsraad Houses would cease to conduct business. Should Shaddam try to make a power play and subpoena such information for some shortsighted political purpose, any Ur-Director would simply vaporize the records rather than relinquish them.

In the early days of the Imperium, administrators of Combined Mercantiles had purchased Tanegaard, an obscure planet with unremarkable natural resources. There, the Company built their corporate headquarters into an impregnable citadel. The bureaucrats who lived here had served CHOAM for multiple generations. Very few had ever left the planet, nor did they express any desire to do so. They lived in walled enclaves and absorbed the business of a galactic empire that spanned a million worlds.

Her ship descended smoothly through calm skies. As Urdir, she would be obligated to take meetings with her primary secretaries, division chiefs, and commerce commanders, but she could not reveal the real reason for meeting Jalma and Frankos. Malina's long-standing involvement with the broader and more circumspect Noble Commonwealth movement was a well-kept secret, and if that connection were ever revealed, not only would her own position be ruined, but so would CHOAM's standing in the Imperium. Any support of Jaxson would be a thousand times more toxic.

Her ship landed on an exterior receiving port of the gigantic central building, twenty stories up. The Ur-Director emerged from her craft with the alert spinehounds at her side. She gazed up at the sheer cliff face of the citadel building, impressed. The stone was smooth and unscalable, and the armored walls were strong enough to withstand even the impact of a crashing spaceship. Or so she had been told.

The citadel building was riddled with vaulted conference rooms, audience chambers, and private offices, as well as data libraries of compact shigawire spools and reams of thin ridulian crystal sheets. The vaults extended for miles across the surface, and only armies of cooperative Mentat librarians could begin to understand the organizational structure and find any information stored there.

A military cohort of corporate aides and majordomos stood under flags with the black, red, and yellow circles of the CHOAM Company. A high-powered aide-de-camp—Holton Tassé—stepped up to her and gave a sharp bow, pretending not to notice the pair of fierce spinehounds. Though he was considered a minor functionary of CHOAM, this man alone controlled more power than much of the Landsraad. She had relied on him a great deal in the past.

"Ur-Director, when we learned of your unexpected visit, we adjusted our schedules and will block out as many meetings as you desire. We have calendar ambassadors available to negotiate blocks of time with you. We are willing to narrow them down to five-minute increments."

"Keep them to a minimum," Malina said as she walked past the aide-de-camp, with her spinehounds at her heels. "I will do what is required for the good of the Company, but I am a mother as well as the Ur-Director. Jalma and Frankos must take priority. When they arrive, send them to me and cancel anything else on my schedule."

She strode through the warren of offices, administrative depots, and meeting chambers. The immense corridors were wide enough to accommodate slow suspensor carts that drifted along, making deliveries and bearing passengers from office to office. She turned to Tassé. "Set up my first conference in half an hour. We will do what business we can."

On Nossus, Malina had seen Jaxson's eager smile as he bragged about his dangerous plans. Pleased to have her seeming support, he had made a great show of introducing the members of his radical inner circle. All of them had been previous supporters of the overall Noble Commonwealth movement, but she had not known them to be impatient enough to join her son's violent fringe. The other prominent inner-circle members included the heads of House Londine, Fenimer, Mumford, Myer, Vok, Ellison, and even the newly recruited Viscount Giandro Tull.

Jaxson had been proudest, though, of his fresh alliance with Duke Leto Atreides of Caladan, a man known for his adherence to a code of honor. The fact that the Duke would join not only the Noble Commonwealth, but Jaxson's extreme efforts, spoke volumes about the general hatred for the Corrino Emperors. . . .

Malina was able to compartmentalize her feelings, though. For the next several hours, she sat through six back-to-back meetings in an ultra-private conference room with no windows and only a single thick metal door, her business associates never guessing that she was distracted. The Urdir gave them her apparent full attention, and they left satisfied. At any other time, she would have considered such business to be significant, but now everything paled with her other priorities. The spinehounds, sensing her uneasiness, were alert, their ears pricked.

Malina ate a fine dinner and conducted more business throughout the meal, then attended more meetings, and she finally had to sleep. The next morning started with a series of rapid-fire consultations in her large office, no more than five minutes for each of her aides, as Tassé had promised. She found herself growing increasingly tense, impatient, and concerned.

After the lower-level aides departed to follow her commands, Holton Tassé stepped forward and said, "We learned something disturbing in your absence, Urdir," he said, placing a document on her desk. "I ordered this report on it."

Malina scanned the summary, then looked up at him. Her face felt hot. "A security breach in the central vault? Our black archives?" She could not cover her alarm. Those were the most explosive, damning records, which CHOAM kept only as a last-resort hammer to control intractable Houses, even the Emperor.

"I ordered this investigation the moment we found out, although the breach likely happened some time ago." Tassé was quite tall, with curly blond hair thinning on top. "The crime was well executed and concealed, but we have a new forensic system that burrows into deep data better than before."

"Who did this? How did this happen? The black archives!"

Tassé looked around to make sure the other aides had all left. A number of business executives were waiting in the outer office for their turn to address Malina.

"Someone bypassed security codes, Urdir, while being clever enough not to leave any clues about who it was. Data appears to have been copied, not stolen or eradicated."

"Those should have been our most protected records in our most secure central vault." She fumed, knowing what the black archives contained, the favoritism and corruption in the Imperium, the most damning blackmail secrets, the explosive clandestine dealings—the system by which some Houses were kept at the top tier, and others at lower tiers.

She drew a deep breath. "I already had enough on my mind. If the black archives are released publicly, there will be a bloody civil war. What can their intention be? Have we received any threats or ultimatums?"

"No, we haven't. It is most strange."

Malina rose to her feet, and with this new matter unresolved, she canceled all further conferences for the day, much to the disappointment of those who believed they had urgent business. Tassé was dispatched to continue the investigation.

By the end of the afternoon, Frankos and Jalma arrived at Tanegaard. Seeing Malina's mood, they looked alarmed but dutiful, ready to do whatever their mother—and Ur-Director—asked.

Malina claimed the sealed conference room as her own, and she sat with daughter and older son. The spinehounds took their places by the door.

Though she had not seen her children in a while, she didn't move to embrace them, did not offer the usual demonstrations of maternal warmth. The Aru family did not have that kind of relationship. They were powerful, wealthy, ambitious, and content, but not filled with laughter, hugs, or kisses. Instead, the Urdir faced them, met their inquisitive gazes, and remained silent for a long moment.

Frankos was tall and lean, with a youthful appearance despite his poise and steel-gray hair, while Jalma had short, dark hair and wore the conservative attire of Pliesse. As the figurehead CHOAM President, Frankos had learned how to master his emotions and play delicate political games, but Jalma did display some of her younger brother's impatience, such as when she'd arranged to kill her doddering old husband, even though the man had been at death's doorway for years.

"Why are we here, Mother?" Jalma asked. "I was in the middle of crucial hederwood negotiations, and Frankos was chairing a multiplanetary summit at the Silver Needle on Kaitain."

Instead of justifying herself, Malina simply folded her slender hands in front of her on the table. Until she had more information on the black archives breach, she would not mention it to them. For now, she limited herself to her original purpose for summoning them here. "Indeed, and I would much rather be back home on Tupile, but this is about Jaxson. I've just met with him and his group of dangerous rebels, so I know exactly what they're up to." She narrowed her eyes. "And I know you both privately claimed to support him. So, are you truly that dissatisfied with the behind-the-scenes workings of the Noble Commonwealth? Can you not wait for the dissolution of the Imperium in a manner that we control?"

Fuming, Jalma sat back, brushed at the front of her prim, conservative dress, and avoided answering.

Frankos looked embarrassed. "He came to us, Mother, individually, and explained his plan for an accelerated timeline. I heard him out, but I didn't exactly endorse him. He is quite . . . overwhelming."

Jalma looked upset. "We merely humored him, Mother. You know that it's dangerous not to listen to Jaxson. We pretended to agree with him." She let out an exasperated sigh. "I just got control of the entire government on Pliesse—do you think I wanted him to bombard us from space in some other grandiose statement?"

"Jaxson might believe we are interested, if not sympathetic, but we did not encourage him," Frankos insisted.

"Of course we're interested—if I believed he could succeed," Jalma said.

"He'd reshape the Imperium a century sooner than our other plan. The Noble Commonwealth would become real, rather than theoretical."

Malina looked slowly and carefully from one to the other.

Frankos furrowed his brow and asked, "How did Jaxson bring you to his new hideout world? He keeps its location extremely secret."

"He came to me with the same proposal he presented to you," she said, then gave them a forgiving smile. "And I, too, heard him out. I'm not blind to the fact that his fringe group is gaining support, and power. If I could snap my fingers to be rid of the Corrinos and free a million planets, then of course I would do so.

"But Jaxson is dangerous. I have denounced him in front of the entire Landsraad, both as an official statement from CHOAM and also as his mother. Yet I am wise enough to use his exuberance for our own purposes, if he could help our movement. That's why I went to Nossus and pretended to endorse his extreme efforts. I have seen the extent of this violent splinter group." She narrowed her eyes and skewered them with an intense glare. "Where do you stand on this?"

Malina was relieved to see that their indignation and denial were not feigned.

"The fact is, Mother, we're afraid of him," Frankos admitted.

Jalma straightened. "He's a wrecking ball, and I don't want to get in his way. I couldn't stop him if I tried."

"The question is whether we try to stop him, or wholeheartedly endorse his alternate solution," Malina said. "That is what we must decide."

The planet Nossus looked peaceful and bucolic, with open meadows, tall clumps of spiky grasses, and wandering herd animals. The sky was blue and clear, deceptively empty of threats.

Leto knew it was all an illusion.

Jaxson Aru and his passionate revolutionaries had chosen this out-of-the-way planet for conceiving the violent overthrow of the Imperium. Leto had pretended to join their splinter group, though it went against his core personality. He played along with Jaxson's obsession and determination, pretending to agree with their vendetta against House Corrino.

And Jaxson had believed his sincerity. He considered the recruitment of Duke Leto to be the most potent affirmation of his own goal. Now Leto felt trapped in the lion's den, but he needed to continue this charade, to build their trust, to take them down. The Emperor's Sardaukar had failed to root out the rebellion, but Leto just might be able to accomplish it. No one else was in the same position.

Across an empty swath of landscape, Jaxson had built an estate house that included an adjacent hangar and acres of crops tended by supposed farmers, who were actually his private army of fanatics. At first, Leto had been treated with some suspicion by this core group, but Jaxson's wholehearted endorsement had assuaged most of the doubts. The rebel leader seemed to need validation, and a friend.

Malina Aru had recently departed after meeting with the small core of determined insurrectionists. Leto had been astonished to see that the tentacles of the Noble Commonwealth extended all the way up to the CHOAM Ur-Director herself. He remained alert to glean any detail of their plans, but kept his words to himself.

Jaxson's mother was an astute businessperson, cautious in her assessments, capable of hiding her true thoughts and emotions. Even so, Leto wondered if she truly embraced the actions of her black-sheep son. When meeting with the core rebels, she'd spoken cautiously, making promises that left a small escape hatch of vagueness. After the Urdir had departed on vital CHOAM business, the other conspirators remained on Nossus to finish their planning, though they, too, would leave soon.

Leto had been introduced to Jaxson's inner circle. After several days of enthusiastic late-night debates, the other rebels had slept in before the next scheduled arrival of a Heighliner. Jaxson, though, got up early and found Leto already awake and sipping coffee in the kitchen of the main house.

The rebel leader gave him a warm smile and an invitation. "Come with me to a very special place, Leto." He seemed to be trying to solidify their friendship.

Leto was on his guard. "Are we making plans without the others?"

"It's just something I want to show you. Something . . . very personal."

Playing along, Leto followed him outside. They walked past the newly constructed hangar behind the main house. Inside, a work crew used lascutters and welding apparatus to reconstruct the distinctive Imperial treasury ship, which Jaxson had somehow swapped during his attack on the palace. He had also stolen a fortune in solari coins, which had already been dispersed to fund rebel activities.

Jaxson paused on his walk to glance into the open hangar. "They'll finish refitting the vessel soon. It will have a new set of engines and be ready to fly—whenever and wherever I choose."

Leto stared at the odd vessel. "Is this what you wanted to show me?"

Jaxson made a dismissive gesture. "No . . . not yet. Come with me."

On a hill above the main house, he led Leto into a grove of scrawny olive trees. Jaxson touched their gray-green leaves with clear reverence.

Leto watched and listened, letting the rebel leader decide when to talk again. Jaxson was a man accustomed to fiery speeches and provocative suggestions, but now he spoke in only an emotional whisper. "On my family's Otorio estate, the olive grove was centuries old, with majestic trees that seemed to emanate peace and calm." Jaxson heaved a long sigh. "In our sacred olive grove, I understood my place in the universe. Everything was as it should be."

"And you're trying to re-create it here?" Leto asked as they walked through the grove.

"These trees are only a few years old, but they can live for centuries," Jaxson said. "My father was buried in our olive grove on Otorio. I would often sit beside his grave and think about all he had taught me. My mother and the rest of CHOAM considered him an embarrassment, but they just didn't understand him." He shook his head. "When he was gone, my mother dragged me into the CHOAM business. She wanted to indoctrinate me, just as she had trained Frankos and Jalma. She took me to the CHOAM fortress archive vault on Tanegaard and made me sit through interminable meetings in the Silver Needle on Kaitain. She gave me full access and made me understand the intricacies of the great galactic company."

"Did it work?"

"My mother underestimates my grasp of everything." Jaxson knelt beside a small tree, stroking its gray trunk. He seemed to be imagining the olive grove as large, ancient. "I was away from the family estate when Shaddam Corrino decided to annex Otorio. He uprooted and plowed over our beautiful grove. He desecrated my father's grave and built his museum on top of it." The bitterness in his words was like acid.

"My mother wanted to undermine the Imperium and gradually reshape the political system. That was when I decided to accelerate her efforts." He forced a laugh. "I'm glad she now believes that my way is the best path forward, to shatter the fossilized Imperium so we can be free in a new commonwealth." He clapped a hand on Leto's shoulder. "And you shall help me with it, my friend. We will do great things together."

"We already have," Leto said. "I consider our efforts on Issimo III to be proof that alternatives work."

The other man's expression tightened. "Yes, it worked to enhance my reputation. I'll grant you that."

Leto had been relieved when he talked Jaxson out of another painful "grand gesture"—instead of releasing a terrible blight on an already afflicted colony world, the rebel leader had provided food, equipment, supplies, everything that Issimo III needed. Now on that planet, Jaxson's name was celebrated instead of reviled, but Leto wasn't sure his companion knew what to do with those feelings.

BY THE TIME they returned to the main house, other rebels were up, most of them packed for departure. In the large parlor, Andros Fenimer and Bos Mumford were in a heated argument—not about any rebellion plans, but over some sporting tournament.

One of the rebels staying in the main house, Tuarna Vok, had already delivered her traveling cases to the foyer, still stewing about the previous night's debate. She gave Jaxson a cold look, which Leto didn't understand.

Though she was supposedly a devotee of Jaxson's extreme tactics, the lean, hard woman had been edgy, even hostile during their meetings.

The Noble Commonwealth leader saw her and offered a sparkling smile. "Ah, Tuarna, why not give us a little joy on your last day with us? You are going back to your own holdings—I thought you'd be happy."

Her expression darkened, and she didn't seem to notice Leto at all. "Home, perhaps, but still under your bootheel."

"My bootheel?" He chuckled. "After generations of oppression, you balk at a little encouragement to follow the right path?"

She sniffed, facing him directly. "I support your noble cause; have no doubt of that. Your methods of coercion were unnecessary, and insulting."

"I would merely call it a reminder, dear Tuarna. Not coercion."

"What does she mean?" Leto asked, trying to put the pieces together.

"Tuarna Vok leads a very powerful House with several prominent manufacturing planets. Some years ago, House Vok released a substantial shipment of power cells, which were found to be defective and would have contaminated all users. This flaw was discovered while the power cells were en route to a marketing transfer complex, too late to recall. The debacle would have been a terrible blow to the reputation and reliability of House Vok."

Jaxson held up a finger as Tuarna fumed in front of him. He continued, "To prevent widespread embarrassment, dear Tuarna had arranged for the carrier to be sabotaged, destroyed in transit. After filing the proper forms, she recouped all her family's losses through complex insurance claims. The contract transport company took the fall."

Leto narrowed his eyes, absorbing the information. Others in the front room had stopped to listen.

"Worse," Jaxson said, "in the convenient destruction of the shipment, a passenger frigate was caught in the backwash, resulting in the death of the only family heir of House K'Urunu. If such information were to get out, there would certainly be a vicious interfamily blood feud declared between K'Urunu and Vok, not to mention the fact that Tuarna's family finances would be ruined because of the insurance fraud. In short, House Vok would unravel if word were ever to leak out."

The woman looked like a statue made of ice. "And now you speak it in front of all these people?"

Jaxson looked around the room and clicked his tongue. "Let's keep this our little secret, shall we? Just by knowing one another's names and faces, we all have blackmail bludgeons to hold over one another's heads." He suddenly looked less aloof, becoming a firebrand again. "But that's not why we're here, is it?" He narrowed his gaze and looked again around the parlor, where many others were listening, tense. "I'm glad I can count on all of you."

He strolled off with Leto deeper into the main house.

The household staff seemed innocuous and attentive, but Leto knew they were all dedicated killers, defenders of this hideout. Even with over a hundred fighters here on the secret base of operations, though, they would be able to do little when a Sardaukar force arrived.

As soon as Leto managed to get away from Nossus, he would dispatch an urgent, secret message to Kaitain and expose the rebellion to Shaddam's justice. Imperial soldiers would sweep in and eradicate the violent heart of the Noble Commonwealth. . . .

❧

ON THE EDGE of the breakfast room, a familiar voice interrupted his tense thoughts, and he turned to see a lean, older man, who said to him, "Leto, my friend, I depart for Cuarte today, and I insist that you visit me there." Rajiv Londine had swept-back gray hair and dressed in intense orange and red garments, the traditional clothing of his people. He stood with his long-faced chief administrator, Rodundi.

Londine was an acerbic critic of Shaddam Corrino. Only a few months earlier—seemingly a lifetime ago—Count Hasimir Fenring had even offered to arrange Leto's marriage to Londine's daughter, on condition that he destroy the gadfly nobleman. Leto had refused as a matter of honor, long before he'd known the man had any connection with the Noble Commonwealth.

Leto tried to dodge the answer. "I belong back on Caladan."

Enthusiastic, Jaxson stepped between them. "The rebellion is everywhere!" He spoke loudly, for all to hear. "I approve of an alliance between House Atreides and House Londine." His thin lips quirked in a smile. "Together, you could establish a commercial network to fill the void left by the unraveling Corrino Imperium."

Leto remained noncommittal. "I have been looking into ways to increase the wealth and holdings of House Atreides. That's why I spent my recent time on Kaitain."

Nearby, several of the rebels made rude noises. Then Londine said, "And how did that work out, Leto? Count Fenring tried to make you betray me, dangling my lovely daughter as a reward."

"Vikka is indeed lovely, sir, but it was the holdings of House Londine that he considered the greatest bribe."

"Maybe we can achieve the same goal in a more honorable way." Londine lifted his eyebrows, but his expression became unreadable. "You and I already have certain common business interests, and it would be good for us to be open about them."

Leto chewed at the side of his mouth. "What common business interests?"

Chief Administrator Rodundi quickly interceded. "My Lord, we should be circumspect until we've had the opportunity to show Duke Leto our operations." When Rodundi leaned closer, Leto felt that the man was . . . off, somehow. His expression was bland and difficult to decipher, and he bore the faintest odd and unpleasant odor.

Londine let his chief administrator lead him away, calling over his shoulder, "Still, I insist that you come to Cuarte as soon as you can."

"For the time being, Leto will stay with me a while longer on Nossus," Jaxson announced for all to hear. "After our great achievement on Issimo III, we have further plans to discuss."

Leto was anxious to get out from under the man's thumb. From the time they had met at the rendezvous point above Elegy, he had not been out of the rebel leader's sight. Emperor Shaddam was certainly waiting to hear from him. By now, Gurney Halleck would have already traveled to the Imperial Palace with the hidden message crystal that explained how Leto meant to infiltrate and bring down the rebels.

But he could do nothing until he got away from Jaxson Aru. . . .

By midmorning, the other radical nobles departed in the transport shuttle, rising into the vast, vacant sky of Nossus. As requested, Leto stayed behind with Jaxson and his household security forces. He had to play his role well because if these people doubted him at all, he would not survive to ever go home.

A heaviness filled his heart. He knew Paul was fully capable of ruling Caladan, especially with the guidance of Thufir Hawat, Duncan Idaho, Dr. Yueh, and Gurney Halleck. Leto had been mentally lost for months, feeling he had little to lose with Jessica gone. Dearest Jessica. . . .

And so he had risked everything.

An unmarked cargo shipment was dispatched from the same Heighliner that arrived to take the other guests away. Leto and Jaxson went to meet the delivery, accompanied by estate workers who carried the stacked cases out of the small delivery vessel.

Studying the manifest sheet, Jaxson was perplexed. "I was not expecting a shipment from Elegy . . . Ah, from Viscount Giandro Tull! One of our most enthusiastic new recruits. Do you know him?"

Leto shrugged. "I know the name, but we've never had any dealings."

As he opened the crates, Jaxson let out a delighted sound. "A shipment of prototype weapons!" He pulled out a metallic inscribed cube with embedded lenses, each side about as wide as his extended palm. "These devices have not been widely tested, but knowing the quality of military items we receive from House Tull, the rebellion should make great use of them."

He turned the cube around in his hands, trying to figure it out. After rummaging in the crate, he found a sealed holo-crystal. Using his ID imprint and setting it to play, he leaned forward to watch a message recorded by Giandro Tull.

In the image, the handsome nobleman looked proud and determined as he stood by the crates of his new prototypes. He had filmed the recording from behind the stables for his prized horses. "Jaxson Aru, I am sending you fifty shield nullifiers, devices that will neutralize an opponent's body shield. Enemies will suddenly find themselves vulnerable to traditional projectile weapons."

Jaxson's eyes gleamed as he looked at Leto. "Oh! We could slaughter even Sardaukar if we get them in the right position!"

But Leto kept staring at the image, as if he had turned to ice. He couldn't believe what he was seeing.

Giandro continued, "My new concubine is a vital adviser and sounding board, and I value her opinion. We look forward to assisting the Noble Commonwealth."

In the image, her hair was shorter now, dyed dark, but he knew that oval face, the generous lips, the green eyes, the classically beautiful features that he had loved for so long . . . the woman he had held and caressed, the mother of his son.

Jessica stood at the side of Viscount Giandro Tull and gazed out from the image, as if mocking him.

In the final analysis, all answers can be tied back to the spice melange.

—VLADIMIR HARKONNEN,
operations memo, Carthag headquarters

I n the rubble of the Orgiz spice refinery, Baron Harkonnen contemplated his lost fortune. It was a necessary sacrifice, though, to throw Count Hasimir Fenring off the scent of his black-market smuggling operations.

Dark smoke roiled into a sky the color of fine orange dust. At the end of an isolated box canyon, the Orgiz spice silos, packaging operations, barracks, and landing pads had all been leveled by a swift bombardment from unmarked attack 'thopters.

His refinery workers must have felt betrayed when the ships attacked without warning. His nephew Rabban had been enthusiastic and thorough when the Baron secretly instructed him to scuttle the operations and leave no scrap for Fenring or his persistent Mentat, Grix Dardik, to find. Rabban was often a disappointment, but when given a chance to hurt, maim, or destroy, he excelled.

The inspection troops at the ruined site wore desert gear, nose plugs, and recirculating suits, but the Baron refused, saying it made him look weak, especially in front of Count Fenring. Given the incredible wealth that House Harkonnen reaped from these spice operations—both the Imperial-sanctioned wealth and his private smuggling income through CHOAM—he could buy all the water he needed.

As the Baron looked around the Orgiz wreckage, the heat and appalling dryness made his face, throat, and nostrils burn. He would rather be back in Carthag enjoying a steam bath, but this was a role he had to play.

"The attackers were well armed, and thorough," he observed. "Whoever they were."

A few days earlier, Fenring had somehow learned the location of Orgiz and demanded that the smugglers be detained for interrogation. Even as he feigned cooperation, the Baron had dispatched his nephew to destroy it all.

Now he had to maintain that fiction in front of the inquisitive Imperial Spice Observer.

Fenring glowered. "It's as if someone knew we were coming, hmm?"

Knowing that Rabban often had trouble keeping his mouth shut, the Baron had wisely sent him away from Arrakis. Normally, his nephew would have grumbled about being taken from the spice operations, but this time, he actually looked forward to returning to Lankiveil, so he could toy with their Atreides captive, Gurney Halleck. . . .

At the moment, under intense sunlight, the Count struggled to control his fury. As soon as the Harkonnen ships landed here in the wreckage, Fenring had bounded out as if he could salvage something. Fires still burned through the debris. Charred, twisted metal lay strewn among the rocks of the bottled-up canyon. Huge slabs of the cliff walls had been sliced off with lasbeams, and the resulting avalanche had buried anything that the bombardment hadn't directly destroyed.

"Likely a rival smuggling operation," the Baron suggested. "Those thieves have no honor and no loyalty."

"Hmm," Fenring intoned, but did not elaborate.

Grix Dardik scampered along beside his master, bobbing his overlarge head on a stalk of a neck, sifting through details with his wide eyes. Dardik was like a child's doll that had been stretched and tugged too hard in various directions. His large-knuckled fingers kept moving as if playing an invisible musical instrument.

The eccentric Mentat climbed over scorched rocks, hissed when his palm touched a still-hot lump of plasteel. When he kicked aside some debris, a metal flange scraped against a fallen rock, leaving a mark on the soot. Dardik bent over to inspect it.

Straightening, he turned to Fenring. "Years ago, these Orgiz operations were thriving, sir. The Baron's half brother, Abulurd Harkonnen, even expanded the refinery, but it was destroyed by a sandworm attack." Dardik chuckled. "Imagine a huge sandworm trapped in this canyon, thrashing around!" He chuckled again, then looked up at the curling smoke, the collapsed canyon walls, the clear burn marks on the rock. "I don't think this was a sandworm, though."

"Thank you for the Mentat analysis," Fenring snapped at him. As he trudged along, he mused to himself, loud enough for the Baron to hear, "Whoever ran this, it was a well-financed operation. The investment to create such a refinery would be far beyond the means of some minor smuggling ring. Ahhh, there is something more to this."

The Baron adjusted his suspensor belt to make him lighter on his feet as he walked over the broken terrain, lurching over a bent curve of metal that might have been the wall of a spice silo. "Melange generates wealth, my dear Count. Even smuggling a few illicit loads offworld would generate a significant profit. It would not be difficult for an ambitious person to secure a forward-thinking investor, someone willing to take a great risk for extreme profit."

"But who, hmm?" Fenring asked. "Such a sudden influx of wealth would be noted among the Landsraad."

The Baron shouted orders to his troops as they exited the scout vehicles. "Spread out! Comb through the rubble. Tell me if you find anything—we need to get to the bottom of this!"

The uniformed men fanned out into the burning destruction. In private, they had all received specific orders that they were *not* to find anything.

He turned back to Fenring as they skirted a pile of broken boulders. "One alternative occurs to me, my dear Count. There is a group in need of significant funds and willing to take tremendous risks." His plump lips formed a smile. "And such income would be entirely outside the purview of any Imperial records."

Fenring's feral eyes darted in his direction. "What do you mean?" His question sounded like a threat.

"Why, the Noble Commonwealth—the insidious, violent rebel movement. Jaxson Aru and his ridiculous cause have created an uproar and cost many lives. Imagine how much money that man could earn for his bloodthirsty campaign if he were to create an independent conduit for selling spice."

Fenring stroked his chin. "Hmm, you raise an interesting possibility."

Smiling, the Baron realized that he'd found a neat solution to throw Fenring off the scent, but then the Count's next question twisted it back again. "But if the Orgiz refinery was rebuilt by well-financed Noble Commonwealth terrorists, then who destroyed it?" He gestured around.

The Baron shrugged. "Some rival band, perhaps?"

"Unlikely," Fenring said. "It does not make sense."

"Such matters are far too complex for me," the Baron said. "We could always put the question to Emperor Shaddam."

Fenring paled and moved about quickly. The Baron smiled to himself, knowing he had applied just the right amount of provocation.

Count Fenring had prematurely told Shaddam that the black-market spice thieves were caught and executed—well before this incident—and now he could not let the Emperor know that the operations had been ongoing for all this time. "Ahhh . . . hmm, we should not disturb Shaddam with such things. You and I can figure this out ourselves."

"Don't forget me," Grix Dardik chimed in. Sniffing, he bent over a crevice between fallen slabs of rock and used all his strength to shove the stone aside. Pebbles and twisted metal bars skittered away. "I found something!"

The Mentat reached into the widened gap, rummaged around. Then in triumph, he tugged, wrenched, and finally pulled free the roasted skeletal arm from a buried corpse, broken off at the elbow. "I found an arm." He leaned closer, sniffed the charred flesh. "Is this useful, sir?"

Fenring scowled. "I would rather have taken the man alive." He gestured for the Mentat to carry his prize back to the ship. "Perhaps detailed genetic analysis will offer some answers. For now, keep looking."

The Baron turned to his troops and raised his voice. "Continue the search! Have you found anything?"

His men wisely shook their heads and looked even busier than before.

Around him, the smell of smoke, dust, and burned meat also had the sweet cinnamon undertone of melange.

Left to watch over Caladan in my youth, I felt like a baby thrown in a deep pool and forced to swim.

—PAUL ATREIDES, the ducal heir

E ach day was a mixture of uncertainties and questions. Paul made his way through the castle's rear courtyard toward the little-used Atreides stables, an amalgamation of old and new structures in varying states of repair.

On this very path, his father and grandfather had walked, and many Atreides Dukes before them. Now Paul was worried about his father secretly off with the rebels, and Gurney Halleck away delivering an urgent message to the Emperor, but far too late in returning home . . . and he had deep concerns for his mother, recalled by the Bene Gesserit.

As he pondered his ancestors, he surmised that each previous Duke had undoubtedly faced challenges that they considered insurmountable. Paul chastised himself for lamenting his own position, for wallowing in pity. It did no good to feel sorry for himself, or to regret the past. But the future, that was another matter. Some of it lay beyond his ability to control, but he did hold a portion of the future in his own hands.

He feared that his parents' long-standing relationship had been broken irreparably, the two of them pulled away to different parts of the vast Imperium. Tempering his concerns, though, was pride in his father's great confidence in leaving the young man to oversee an entire planet in his absence, albeit with excellent mentors and advisers.

The last time he and his father had spoken, Paul had sensed a despondency in the Duke. Whenever the subject of Paul's mother came up, Leto tried to cover his feelings, but Paul had been trained in Bene Gesserit powers of observation by Jessica herself. The Duke of Caladan was deeply wounded to be separated from his beloved lady.

Now as Paul walked toward the stables, he felt a sense of undefined, terrible purpose—and he could not run away from whatever it was, could not avoid the inevitable. Instead, he needed to face the trouble head-on. But what was it? He could not tell.

Yet he knew this: Only if he overcame a supreme challenge could he find the light. This hope shone as a distant pinpoint, like a star in the darkness.

The main stables were empty, and hadn't been used for some time. Walking on the hard-packed floors, Paul made his way through one of the tack rooms, smelling the lingering scent of animals, feed, and oils. Curious, he tugged open a rear door, yanking hard because it stuck against the frame. The rusty hinges groaned and squeaked.

A dusty corridor led to the oldest section of the complex, where his grandfather had once kept ferocious Salusan bulls. Paul pushed aside cobwebs and entered the shadowy building, remembering the story of how the Old Duke had been gored to death by a maddened animal. A long time ago, Leto had threatened to tear down the empty bull stables, but decided against it. Maybe he remembered how much his own father had loved the giant animals and the spectacle of the corrida.

The stables had a vaulted ceiling, and beams of sunlight streamed down through cracks in the roof. From up in the rafters, small hill birds fluttered their wings, and one of them swooped down toward Paul, as if guarding its territory. He ducked, and finally the bird veered off before flying back up to the vaulted area.

Hearing someone behind him, Paul whirled and instinctively dropped into a fighting stance—but found himself looking at a smiling Duncan Idaho.

"I knew you would eventually come here to poke around, Paul. I'm surprised it took you so long." He stepped forward into one of the shafts of light, where dust motes danced like tiny asteroids. "I brought this." With a flourish, as if he were a bullfighter himself, Duncan brought forth a banderilla with faded Atreides green and black feathers on it, a long dart that matadors would thrust into a charging bull. "This belonged to your grandfather."

The Swordmaster handed it to him, and Paul felt a hint of awe as he turned it over in his hands. He noted a dark stain on the feathers. "Is that blood?"

"From the very bull that killed the Old Duke. He stabbed it into a shoulder of the beast, right before it gored him."

Paul shuddered. He knew that story well. The head of the enormous bull was a mounted trophy now in the castle dining hall.

"After the tragedy, your grief-stricken father tossed the banderilla into a corner of this building. I was a stable boy then, and I retrieved it. I want you to have it."

Paul looked at the banderilla, imagined if it were one of his only weapons against a rampaging beast.

Duncan's face filled with emotion. "Your grandfather was good to me when I was a child, just escaped from the Harkonnen animals, and your father helped shape me into the man I am now. I owe everything to House Atreides." He grew grim and serious. "I will serve you ably and loyally until my dying breath."

Made awkward by Duncan's tone, Paul tried to break the tension with a small laugh. "I know you will, Duncan, and I appreciate that." He proudly lifted the banderilla, which felt both delicate and dangerous in his grasp. He wondered how his father would feel about him having it. "Thank you for this gift."

"Originally, I kept it for myself as a memento of the Old Duke," Duncan said, "because he meant a great deal to me. But now I think you should have it. You never had a chance to meet your own grandfather."

The teenager turned the object over in his hands, looked again at the ancient dried blood on its sharp tip. "In some ways, my own life situation is like a bullfight, thinking fast, facing danger, and sometimes it feels like some kind of performance."

"That it is, young Master." Duncan seemed to find the comparison amusing. "Speaking of that, you've been brooding around the castle for too long. That's not how to become a Duke! Caladan is quiet and can take care of itself for a few days. It's about time I took you out for some real training." He flashed an enigmatic grin. "Let's make plans, just the two of us."

"Anything except fighting bulls," Paul said, feeling a rush of excitement. "I have nothing to prove in the ring."

⸙

THAT AFTERNOON IN his father's office, Paul stood behind the desk that seemed too large for him, looking at paperwork arrayed across the refurbished burlwood surface. Thufir Hawat arrived to deliver his regular briefing, but this time, Duncan accompanied the old Mentat, which was unusual.

Before getting down to business, Thufir paced in front of Duke Leto's desk, obviously waiting for the young man to take a seat, but Paul just stood with his hands on the wooden chair. The office still felt imposing to him, and it didn't seem right for him to conduct the business of Caladan from his father's desk, even if there were no crises and the world seemed calm. Paul longed to have the real Duke back in his proper place, completing the tasks he did so well.

Thufir exchanged a cryptic glance with Duncan, then said, "Young Master, as your father arranged in his absence, you serve as the steward of Caladan, with the counsel of myself and other select advisers. I believe you have shown that you are fully aware of your responsibility and competent in your duties."

Paul felt warm pride inside, and he waved a hand. "Thank you, Thufir. Proceed with your report."

The Mentat gave a formal nod. "The business of Caladan continues as expected, with a few local disputes and weather incidents, but nothing that can't be handled by administrators and proxies." He seemed pleased that everything was running so smoothly, even in the absence of Leto and Jessica.

Impatient, Duncan advanced toward Paul and nudged him into the desk chair. "You must get used to this in your father's absence. Have a seat and act like a Duke."

Paul shifted behind the desk, feeling out of place. "I'm sure my father didn't find this comfortable either."

"Perhaps not at first," Duncan said, "but he grew into it. Because of the current circumstances, you will have to learn at a quicker pace."

Thufir continued, "Also of interest, young Master, within the next week or so, we expect our first data packet from the passive surveillance spy-eyes that Duncan and Gurney deposited on Lankiveil during their recent raid on Rabban's holdings."

"And a fine raid it was," Duncan interjected, grinning. "Surprised the hell out of the Harkonnens, caused a lot of damage. What a beautiful sight to see the filthy Harkonnens scurry about like rats, trapped in their fjords . . . all the fishing structures, outbuildings, docks, and secure facilities . . . up in flames. But not enough to make up for what those monsters did to our moonfish industry."

The Mentat gave a contemplative nod, his mind churning. "During the melee on Lankiveil, our forces used the opportunity to deposit spy-eyes that should be active by now. We will have an unprecedented glimpse into Harkonnen activities on Rabban's world."

The Swordmaster smiled. "Rabban's people were so busy fending off our frontal attack that they didn't look for the subtle part of our raid."

"And in careful tactics, young Master," Thufir said, "the least obvious part of an attack is often the more important. We will soon see what intelligence these devices provide for us."

Paul grinned. "Now we'll have an unexpected way to keep an eye on our enemy. I only wish we could have accomplished the same thing on Giedi Prime! Then we would be able to keep watch on the Baron, too."

"Good, lad," Duncan said. "Now you're thinking like a Duke."

The three of them laughed, until Paul felt a sudden chill, wondering if the Harkonnens might have planted similar devices on Caladan.

Seeing the young man's expression change, Duncan asked, "What's the matter?"

"I feel the weight of my responsibility."

People can be used as pawns by the ambitious or corrupt, but one must never assume that all pawns are innocent.
> —CHOAM report, *Business Strategies and Ethics*

When the Imperial engineers delivered their report to Emperor Shaddam IV, the good news inspired only outrage.

The Emperor leaned forward on his Hagal crystal throne beside his lovely new Empress Aricatha, who sat in an ornate seat created especially for her.

Standing nervously before the throne, Raf Neddick, a Captain-Major in the Imperial Corps of Engineers, wore a formal uniform accented in scarlet and gold. It had been some time since the engineer had actually gotten his own hands dirty. Two other officers stood on either side of him.

He cleared his throat, as if the distracting noise was part of his report. "Sire, your Issimo III colony is saved from the terrible ravages of solar flares and the severe blight on crops." A smile flickered across his lean face, but he averted his gaze and lowered his head as if in embarrassment.

Not liking the engineer's attitude, Shaddam's expression grew stern, though he struggled to recall any particular colony under duress. As the Padishah Emperor, he ruled countless worlds spanning the galaxy, and Issimo III was not one that he remembered. . . .

On the smaller throne beside him, Aricatha came to his rescue. "Ah yes, Issimo III. Those poor people." He was grateful for how she deftly refreshed his memory. "Half a million inhabitants, led by House Grandine, but they are suffering due to intense solar flares and a lengthy drought. A disease wiped out their primary crops." She glanced at him. "You sent your engineers to help them survive, my love. How considerate of you."

"Of course I remember. A truly tragic situation. Not every colony planet can be as verdant and beautiful as Kaitain."

The engineer looked as if he had been given a small reprieve. "Issimo III is a difficult place, Sire, though not as terrible as Arrakis or Salusa Secundus.

Still . . . the populace struggle to survive. With the worsening solar flares, they would have been doomed, despite our best efforts."

"But you say they've been saved? That is good to hear." Shaddam tapped his finger on the smooth arm of the Golden Lion Throne. "Yes, I seem to recall dispatching supplies and equipment there. House Grandine should have all the resources necessary to provide relief." He lifted his chin. "It is what I, as an Emperor, must do."

"Our engineering operation was only a token effort with minimal funding," said Neddick. "Certainly not enough to accomplish such a large mission."

Aricatha touched her husband's forearm to calm him. "Perhaps we didn't realize the extent of the problem, Engineer. If you had requested more generosity, we would have been happy to oblige."

Shaddam's face had gone stormy. "Of course . . . happy to oblige. But you say they have already been rescued? Why is this not cause for celebration?"

The engineer's shoulders slumped. "Because the success is not our doing, Sire. It was the rebels who saved them." He seemed about to collapse and abase himself before the thrones. "A convoy of supply ships appeared out of nowhere, hundreds of drop boxes filled with food, seeds, agricultural equipment, protective sheeting to withstand the radiation storms! Lord Grandine and his people called it a miracle, a rescue. The sheer magnitude of these relief supplies dwarfed any efforts the Imperium previously provided. It was . . . embarrassing for us, Sire." He sucked in a breath. "Jaxson Aru took credit for it all in a grandiose recorded message that everyone saw. And now the people of Issimo III revere him as a hero, as their savior."

Shaddam half rose from his chair. "But I am their savior!" The Sardaukar guards along the throne hall turned stony gazes toward him.

Neddick dropped to his knees, as if afraid of being executed on the spot. "Lord Grandine has been begging you and the Landsraad for the past year, without result. His entreaties never even made it onto the Landsraad agenda."

"Why didn't I know about this?" Shaddam demanded.

"You have so many things to worry about," Aricatha said. "Alas, this crisis slipped through the cracks and didn't get the Imperial attention it deserved. We will have to make amends, so the colonists understand who their true benefactor is."

Neddick shook his head. "I'm afraid it's too late, Sire. They already celebrate Jaxson Aru for what he did."

"But that man is a venal murderer, a terrorist, and a barbarian! Lord Grandine has to be aware of Jaxson's bloody attack on Otorio and here at the Imperial Palace. So much blood on his hands! He is not a hero. He's an animal."

The engineer flushed. "It is hard for a starving person to hate the man who fills his belly. The Noble Commonwealth sent all those rescue materials and took credit for them, so the colonists already know who their biggest benefactor is. Lord Grandine dispatched a message of gratitude to Jaxson at the Landsraad Hall."

Shaddam paled. "House Grandine cannot be allowed to celebrate terrorists in front of the Landsraad."

"It has already been done, Sire. An hour ago."

Shaddam turned to his Empress, then glared back at Raf Neddick. "Then send more relief supplies to the colony. Pull together another shipment larger than anything Jaxson Aru delivered. Machinery, shielded dwellings, sophisticated agricultural equipment. Make Issimo III into a resort planet! We have to counter this somehow."

"Jaxson has already won this engagement, my love," Aricatha said. "An attempt such as you describe would only appear weak and desperate."

Shaddam's mind spun. "Then we'll send Sardaukar to seize all those assets as illegal gifts from a criminal."

Though Aricatha averted her dark eyes, her disapproval was apparent. "That would turn the people of Issimo III entirely against you."

Shaddam knew she was right. Sighing, he looked up at the chief engineer. "You should have foreseen this, Captain-Major. You should have done a better job with the resources you had, and then Issimo III would not have needed another savior."

The man remained on his knees, pale and terrified. He spread his hands in supplication. "But I had only a skeleton crew and very little equipment, Sire. My team was . . . never meant to succeed."

Shaddam felt deflated, and further vindictiveness would only seem petulant and impulsive. "Send me all records of Jaxson Aru's rescue operations. I want to see images of anyone involved. Track down those relief supplies, that equipment, those ships. Where did they come from? Who provided the materials? How can we identify the rebels and trace them to other traitors in the Landsraad?" He ran a finger along his lower lip, pondering. "We have been searching for the rebel leader and their base. If these relief efforts help us root out the terrorists, perhaps we can consider this an acceptable loss."

Neddick shakily rose to his feet. "Thank you, Sire. My team has many images of the unexpected operations. Surely we will find something. Your court Mentats can dig into the data."

Empress Aricatha raised her delicate hand, then gestured for the engineer to depart. She turned to her husband. "Jaxson Aru is not a subtle man, my love. Surely he left some evidence behind."

Shaddam didn't want to talk about this anymore, and he started to get up from his throne.

Just then, a young runner burst into the throne room, her mouth open and eyes wide. She moved so recklessly that the Sardaukar guards took up defensive positions. The runner was flushed and skinny. Her mop of hair was mussed, her garments drab and dirty, inappropriate for court. She looked more like a street urchin than an official messenger.

"You must come to the Imperial stables, Sire! Your new purebred horses!" The runner looked around, brought up short as she noticed the intimidating Sardaukar, the imposing Golden Lion Throne. Startled by the immensity of the hall, she opened and closed her mouth, then broke down into sobs. "Your beautiful horses, Sire."

Aricatha rose to her feet. "What about the horses, child? Those are such remarkable beasts, so rare." Her dark eyes flicked back and forth as she faced the Emperor. "I always wanted you to take me riding."

Again, Shaddam tried to grasp the crisis. With his vast planetary concerns—the politics of the Imperium, the rising rebellion, interfamily feuds, and CHOAM trade wars—he barely remembered that he even had stables here on Kaitain.

Ah yes, now he did recall the prized thoroughbreds, some of the most valuable animals in the Imperium, only recently obtained. "My beloved horses. What is happening to them?"

The runner was sobbing, and she wiped her nose. "The prized horses are dead! Somebody killed them all."

Now Shaddam was on his feet next to the Empress, outraged. He gestured to his Sardaukar. "Escort us to the stables. I will see this with my own eyes!"

A security detail was sent ahead. Then, as guards rushed him and Aricatha through the vast palace, he realized the difficult logistics of just taking a trip to the stables. He wore full Imperial finery from the throne room, and the Empress was dressed in an ostentatious gown and enameled showpiece shoes, none of which was appropriate attire. Though the stable runner wanted them to hurry, they could not move quickly.

The horse facility was on the other side of the city, and one of the escort guards managed to arrange a shielded passenger craft that would whisk them through the streets. Normally, when Shaddam appeared in public, it was a formal procession with cheering crowds. Now—with rush security clearance received—the escort took a direct route to the stables, with no fanfare.

The large building had been built on the edge of open parkland reserved for the Emperor and his private guests. The Imperial stables had high ceilings and airy chambers open to the pleasant weather, with finer architecture than most noble landholdings.

As soon as the procession arrived, the young runner leaped out of the transport craft and bounded toward the stables, gesturing for Shaddam to follow. An emergency security detail had already checked the facility, but now four lead Sardaukar also inspected the area for traps and signaled an all clear. Shaddam and Aricatha walked together into the structure.

He wrinkled his nose as he inhaled the thick, moist animal smell, the heavy, sweet scent of hay and sour manure. Now he remembered why he didn't spend time with the animals. Though the stable was kept immaculate, he took Aricatha's arm. "Be careful not to step in something unpleasant, my dear."

Undaunted by the possibility of manure, she strode ahead, her expression drawn and urgent. "What happened to the horses, child?"

"They're dead! Poisoned—all the thoroughbreds."

Shaddam had been informed these animals were exceedingly rare in the Imperium, a sophisticated bloodline stolen from House Tull, a prize that no other Emperor had ever obtained. Shaddam was the only outsider who possessed such fine Tull horses, though he himself had not had the courage to ride them. Most of all, they were a victory for him to have, a point of pride. They were *his*.

And now they were dead.

Running into the line of open stalls, the girl stared with wide eyes, tears pouring down her face. She dropped to her knees in scraps of hay on the floor.

The powerful animals lay inside their stalls, each one stretched out and motionless, as if sleeping. They looked at peace, but all were dead, nevertheless. Euthanized in a swift wave.

"Poisoned, Sire!" the stable runner cried again. "All of them together. It was so quick, there was nothing we could do to stop it."

Aricatha went from stall to stall, clearly shaken. "How did this happen? How could they all be poisoned at once?"

"Deadly gas, my Empress. I was tending the horses when I saw a strange package. It exploded, and thick gas curled throughout the stables. I thought I was dead, too! I fell unconscious, and when I woke up, the animals were . . ."

Shaddam cried, "My thoroughbreds!"

Aricatha shook her head. "The poison gas must have been specifically toxic to horses." She looked at the young runner. "You're lucky to have survived, child."

"Lucky?" she wailed and gestured toward the motionless horses.

"I am as shaken as you are," Shaddam said.

Showing humanity and compassion, Aricatha placed a gentle hand on the girl's quaking shoulders.

"This is a personal attack against me," the Emperor said. "It took incredible effort for me to obtain these thoroughbreds—I doubt I can ever replace them." He ground his teeth, convinced that this was another attack from the despicable terrorist leader and his rebel movement.

~∽~

Do not misinterpret common interests and aligned goals as friendship. We Tleilaxu are focused on our own success. Supporting another party's objectives is merely a convenience.

—CHAEN MAREK, letter to Tleilaxu Masters

Approaching the secret barra fields deep in the jungles of the Southern Continent, the ship bore the markings of a local Caladan seafood company. Under the hazy tropical sunlight, Chaen Marek watched the craft come in, flying low toward the rugged mountain range, on the slopes of which he had established his growing areas of barra ferns. The shielded vessel transmitted a masking field that would foil casual scanners. Because this continent was so sparsely populated, the Atreides trade ministers paid little attention to intermittent commerce on the distant shores.

The Tleilaxu drug lord wore a grim smile as he waited for the vessel to arrive, knowing what it contained. He had insisted on this meeting with his superiors, declaring it worth the risk, and Master Arafa had taken extraordinary precautions to make this journey here.

Marek and his workers stood at the edge of the camouflaged fern fields in the jungle, behind which loomed the great mountain. Faint nets blocked the view from any overhead observers, but here at ground level, he could see rows of curling growths, fern shoots poking up from the rich soil. Some of the ferns were tall and speckled, others stubby and lime green. Different barra species yielded a spectrum of potencies of the ailar drug. The strains had been developed by Tleilaxu genetic manipulators, and Marek had learned which ailar subset led to many inconvenient overdoses—as he'd tested on captive Muadh primitives from isolated jungle villages.

Even with modifications, the ailar was dangerous, but Chaen Marek had no sympathy for the weak fools who addicted themselves to the insidious drug. No Tleilaxu would touch the substance. Nevertheless, he reaped great profits for the Tleilaxu cause, as well as the associated Noble Commonwealth movement.

Although Marek disliked Jaxson Aru personally, the rebel leader offered many opportunities. For their own reasons, the Bene Tleilax despised the Imperium, which had oppressed them for millennia. If the Noble Commonwealth movement succeeded, then the Tleilaxu race would have independence, too, a singular commercial empire that could impose rules and conditions on any powindah customers. It behooved Chaen Marek, and all the Tleilaxu Masters, to make sure the rebellion succeeded.

The disguised ship slipped under a camouflage overhang to a jungle clearing for shuttles that distributed the processed ailar. The supposed commercial vessel looked scuffed and unimpressive, drawing no attention.

Marek's work crews and mercenary teams were conditioned so that they would give their lives before being captured. Now, after glancing at the ship's arrival and seeing no cause for alarm, the workers went back to harvesting the curled nubs; others carried baskets and bins to the processing laboratories in mountainside caves.

After the ship settled in the clearing, a tall Caladanian pilot climbed out of the cockpit hatch, clad in old dungarees. He had a shaggy gray-brown beard and a squinting gaze beneath heavy brows. He tilted his head, studied the fern fields that rolled along the steep mountainside, then looked at Marek. "Are we clear?"

"These fields are secure," Marek said, wondering who this man was.

The pilot ducked back into the cockpit and worked controls to open the cargo door. The rear hold was stacked with sealed crates marked as containing live crustaceans. He gestured inside the hold. "The delivery you asked for, sir."

Wary, Marek narrowed his eyes. When he looked at the stranger, he realized that the pilot's gaze had changed. Something about the man was unnatural.

As if sensing the question, the pilot offered a knowing nod. He touched the crates, released a hidden catch, and swung them aside to reveal a shielded compartment, a hidden passenger chamber in the hold. Inside, a Tleilaxu Master waited in a comfortable seat with clean walls, small amenities, food, and drink.

"Master Arafa!" Marek bowed before the important man inside the shielded compartment.

The Tleilaxu Master scratched the thin scar on his face and leaned forward, but he made no move to emerge. "This chamber has not only been sealed, Chaen Marek, but it is also blessed, since you insisted that I travel to this outsider planet. You may have been contaminated, but I have not."

Marek placed his fingers together and bowed. "I am honored that you came."

Arafa was revered among the Tleilaxu, his position superior to Marek back on the homeworld. The man had narrow features, a gray pallor, long nose, and pointed chin—bodily characteristics the Tleilaxu had developed through breeding, even though other citizens of the Imperium found the distinctive physical standards to be loathsome.

"This way I can meet with you as you asked," Arafa continued, still remaining inside his private chamber. "But if I do not emerge from the ship, then I have not been contaminated by Caladan."

Marek was aware of the thorough cleansing rituals Arafa would otherwise have to undergo when he returned to sacred Bandalong. He sighed, conceding. "I wish I could take you through the barra fields and show you our operations in person. Then you would better understand the scope of our plan."

"I understand the scope well enough," Arafa answered in a curt voice. "I developed the plan in our laboratories. You merely implemented it."

The retort stung, and Marek diverted his annoyance by turning a suspicious glance at the pilot. "And who are you?"

Seeing his dubious expression, the pilot asked in a Caladan drawl, "You want to know that I am trustworthy? Not everything is as it appears." He squared his shoulders, brushed his scruffy beard. "We received guarantees of confidentiality when we rented this vessel, but that was not sufficient. Thus, I have also *become* the pilot, and all possible records and witnesses will die with him."

The man's distinctive Caladanian features shifted. His beard slipped away, his face went slack, and his tone became pale. The nose receded into a flat bump with only slits for nostrils. The eyes became dead gray.

A chill went down Marek's back as he watched the transformation, but he smiled. The revelation gave him cause for wonder, not fear. "A Face Dancer—unexpected, but perfect."

Arafa said, "Jaxson Aru believes that our people serve his revolution—and we do so, as long as he succeeds. But if his movement should fail, we have asserted other pressure points, other places of control. Face Dancers are in key positions in the Noble Commonwealth, ready to assume a more vital role if necessary."

Marek nodded. "Yes, I already detected one—the chief administrator of Lord Rajiv Londine, who is one of our largest secret distributors of the Caladan drug."

Master Arafa considered for a long moment. "Yes, our Face Dancer is in a prime position to guide Londine's participation in the rebellion, and he also has his fingers on ailar drug distribution. You will continue to supply the nobleman, and he unwittingly does our bidding." From inside his isolation chamber, the Tleilaxu Master craned his neck to see out of the cargo compartment. "Your new operations may be hidden in the jungles here, but Duke Leto Atreides will be a hindrance if he discovers them."

"Fortunately, he is off-planet," Marek said.

"Yes." Arafa smiled. "In an unexpected turn, our Face Dancer in Londine's court reports that the Duke of Caladan has joined Jaxson Aru and the violent rebels."

"That does not sound like something he would do." Marek scowled. "Leto Atreides ruined our ailar operations in the north. I have wanted revenge on him for a long time."

"The Atreides leader may be a fool," the Master pointed out, "but if he supports the Noble Commonwealth, then he is our fool now. We will see if Lord Londine can wrap him around his finger. For now, brief me on your operations here. I brought you new fern specimens." Arafa indicated one of the sealed "crustacean" crates. "We modified the genetics again. By making the ailar strains innocuous, we also made them less potent, but some thrill-seeking customers are willing to take the risk."

Marek opened the latch, and inside, he found racks and racks of barra fern specimens.

"These are the original subspecies," Arafa explained. "Continue to grow them for discerning customers."

Marek was surprised. "They will willingly take the risk of the dangerous potency?"

"Who can understand fallible powindah?" Still sitting in his padded chair, Arafa spread his hands. "They willingly pollute their bodies with all forms of drugs, some of which are deadlier than others. The risk gives them as much of an endorphin surge as the chemical itself."

Marek resealed the case. "I can test these on Muadh subjects from the local villages. They are primitive people no one will miss." He lowered his voice, conspiratorial. "I also captured a researcher, Dr. Xard Vim, a botanical scientist who came to study these jungles. He stumbled on things he should not have seen. Now he is my captive, and he serves a purpose. He has no choice."

"So long as he doesn't survive to tell anyone else." Master Arafa sniffed, showing impatience. "Hurry, bring me records and show me images of your operations on this mountain. Transfer a portion of the profits, which will be used to fund Tleilaxu efforts." He leaned back in his shielded cabin, making no move to get up. "I want to be away from this place. It smells foul, like fish."

Marek did as he was instructed, cowed by the Master's political power and influence. He removed the new fern specimens for immediate planting and then provided everything that Arafa asked. When they were finished with their business, he watched the Face Dancer transform into his routine, local appearance again. Before long, the seafood cargo ship flew away from the mountain toward the distant ocean.

Reveling in his own power once more, Marek strolled around his fields, then climbed the path to the mountain caves that held processing warehouses, barracks for work crews, and the isolated chamber where the miserable captive scientist was held.

A thin middle-aged man, filled with scientific knowledge but little practicality or survival skills, Dr. Vim had come on an expedition from Kaitain, naïvely believing he would just live among the Muadh natives or camp in the jungles with no one to disturb his business.

Vim had found and documented the extensive fern fields, then poked around the ailar operations. He'd been quickly seized, but Marek had been slow to decide what to do with him. The drug lord crossed his arms over his small chest and looked through the bars into the scientist's hopeless eyes.

"Dr. Vim, at last I have some work for you to do."

When we reach the crux point of a monumental decision, we will likely
have to forge ahead without any road map. We cannot know which route
might lead to success, and which to total disaster.
                                   —CHOAM Ur-Director CONKLA BELLAR,
                     Long-Term Strategies for Expansion and Consolidation

In guiding CHOAM's entangled web of alliances, treaties, tariffs, and repercussions, the Ur-Director knew not to make up her mind impetuously,
nor in a vacuum—no matter how urgent any matter might seem. The wheels
of business turned ponderously, allowing enough time for careful consideration and course correction.

Now, in Tanegaard's gigantic administrative complex, Malina had a great
deal on her mind. The apparent leak of black archives data was still being
investigated by Holton Tassé and his team of CHOAM Mentat accountants.
The fortress vault was now under increased security, but too late to mitigate
the loss of damning secret information. If it were to get out. . . .

At present, though, the wild actions of Jaxson were a more immediate
problem. She had to decide whether to join her notorious son or sabotage
him. Which would better guarantee the Noble Commonwealth plan? On
Nossus, she had met Jaxson's inner circle of radicals, those intent on destruction rather than careful manipulation. Those followers had initially supported
the meticulous plan, the gradual dismantling of the Corrino Imperium, but
now they had gone to such extremes.

Apparently, her son's fiery "demonstrations" had inspired the most impatient and dissatisfied nobles and illuminated many of the unforgivable wrongs
the Corrinos had committed. Malina felt pressure from other armchair rebels
who wanted to see change in the near term, not a generation or more away.

Now she had to decide whether to continue with her well-orchestrated
course, or to espouse swift change through fire and blood. No one could make
that choice but she.

Jalma and Frankos had discussed the matter and offered their opinions,
but those two had been conditioned to agree with their mother, not to

challenge her. While Malina valued their opinions, she didn't believe her daughter and older son were objective enough. No, she needed an unbiased assessment.

After Frankos and Jalma returned home to their own political struggles, Malina walked along the mammoth corridors, mulling her thoughts. Only one of her spinehounds paced at her side, its nails clicking on the polished floors as Malina glided along. The other dog, Kar, was getting treatment for a stomach malady due to an unknown cause. They were running tests. Finding an appropriate veterinary specialist on Tanegaard had proved to be a significant challenge, but she was the Urdir. A veterinarian had been provided.

Hovering transports flitted back and forth under the high ceiling of the citadel building, shuttling records to private rooms, carrying encrypted agreements, taxation treaties, shipping records, and private manifests. No one knew all the entangled business and secret alliances: commercial competition, unfair practices, price fixing, gluts, and shortages. Privacy was paramount, and only the CHOAM Company held all of the strings. The worst, most damning information was kept inside the supposedly secure black archives.

Malina had canceled all other meetings. She walked undisturbed for miles along the corridors, past enormous inner vaults that provided even more security than the Emperor's protective chambers. The success of the Noble Commonwealth movement and the reshaping of the stagnant Imperium would ensure free commerce across all star systems, and it meant the very future of CHOAM. Other urgent problems could wait.

Almost two centuries ago, dozens of nobles had initiated the long-term plan to break up House Corrino, intending to replace the Imperium with countless independent planets or consortiums—increasing competition and diversity, and more equally distributing resources.

At first, the scheme had been no more than a parlor game for bored members of the Landsraad and their business associates. Throughout the reign of Fondil III, then Elrood IX, and now Shaddam IV, the malcontents had worked to undermine Imperial monopolies and shore up interplanetary trade alliances—all without the Emperor's knowledge. For generations now, the secret members had laid a careful groundwork with the cooperation of the Spacing Guild and CHOAM, so that House Corrino would become less and less relevant.

Now Jaxson wanted to come in with a cudgel and smash the government apart.

Malina smelled the dry air inside the building and looked at the lights of countless floors above and below the walkway. A hovering courier flitted by on suspensor engines, passing close enough that Har growled. The courier didn't even notice the Ur-Director, streaking past with a cargo bin full of important documents to be certified and filed.

The powerful woman paused, looking at the central fortress vault, like a bastion within a bastion. The size of a small hangar, two stories high, it had one enormous blast door, and thick double walls separated by a narrow air-gap, only wide enough for maintenance workers to squeeze through. Inside the great chamber, teams of Mentats, along with clerks and trusted adminis-trators, worked on the most sensitive data. The fortress vault's very *implaca-bility* gave her pause . . . as implacable as CHOAM itself.

But in which direction did its future lie? As she pondered this branch point in time, a fork in the road to the future, Malina needed an objective assessment, just to be certain.

The Ur-Director summoned ten of CHOAM's best Mentat accountants. They were loyal, blood-bonded, and psychologically incapable of betrayal. While Malina waited for their attention, Har sat on his haunches by her side inside the secure conference room, letting out an occasional whimper as if he felt lost without his sibling. When the heavy doors sealed, giving her com-plete privacy, she presented the Mentats with her conundrum.

"Consider this a thought experiment, but a vital one. My son Jaxson is more than a gadfly. He's dangerous. His plan—to call it the first scenario—is to lay waste to the Imperium so that an egalitarian commercial common-wealth can be rebuilt from the wreckage." She watched the Mentats intently absorbing information. "All of the reports and damage assessments are avail-able for you to review."

They nodded, still waiting for more.

"Second scenario. The general Noble Commonwealth movement is also dissatisfied with the current Imperial government, and like him, they want to unravel the stagnant political structure, but they wish to do it in a method-ical way that could take centuries—and would not be so idealistically, and naïvely, egalitarian.

"Third scenario is for the Imperium to remain as it has been for ten thou-sand years, and we simply accept the corruption, unfairness, and inefficiency as unavoidable."

She crossed her arms over her chest, looked at the silent men and women.

"I want you to run deep Mentat projections, calculate forward assess-ments, develop possible scenarios of what is likely to happen should Jaxson's radical approach be supported. Then project the outcome if the more gradual movement is pursued." Her throat felt dry. "Finally, assess what would happen if the Imperium should remain intact. Which one is the best alternative for

CHOAM?" She almost added *and for the human race,* but decided that was not in her purview to decide.

She dismissed the Mentats, telling them to consider details and repercussions of the three scenarios.

Hours later, when they had made their projections, Malina met with each Mentat individually so as not to influence their separate conclusions. Each human computer stood before her, calm and silent; each with red-stained lips from the sapho juice they consumed. She sat back and listened.

The first Mentat gave the answer that she expected, and also the one she feared most. "After working behind the scenes for more than a century, the Noble Commonwealth movement has created numerous stress points in the Imperium." His piercing gaze was directed just past her left ear as he talked. "The government has multiple instabilities, and therefore it is ripe for a dramatic shift. Throughout history, there are known and recognizable signs that a large empire is nearing its end. I see some of these indicators now."

"Does that mean that what Jaxson attempts is inevitable?" Malina asked.

"A massive shift in political structures is inevitable, Ur-Director, and it will occur soon—likely within the next century or two," the Mentat reported. "Whether such a shift is swift and chaotic, or gradual enough to be adaptive, is a different issue." His eyes became more distant, as if he did not want to reveal his additional conclusions. "The alternative that your son presents might swiftly topple the Imperial throne, but would do so only with incredible disruption, extreme chaos, the loss of entire populations. I estimate the death toll to be in the tens of billions."

"Billions?"

"*Billions.* Perhaps as many as half a trillion."

A chill went down her spine. "Thank you for your assessment. I will take that under advisement."

The second Mentat delivered a similar projection.

Then the third, very like the other two. One after another, the Mentat accountants predicted the extensive destruction her son would cause if his radical activities were left unchecked, or if Malina actually supported him in bringing down the Corrinos.

Her gut tightened. She had reached the same conclusions in her heart, but wasn't willing to admit them. She could not allow her son and his handful of violent rebels to continue along their path.

Wrestling with her thoughts and emotions, Malina knew she could not simply leave Jaxson to fail on his own. She would have to actively bring him down, expose the fringe movement for the greater good—the longer-term reshaping of the galactic government.

She would have to give up her son.

Oddly, four of her Mentats added something unique to their reports. While they agreed on the original point, they pointed out one other anomaly. "We understand the motivations behind several of Jaxson's extremist recruits," said one of them. "But there is an outlier whose presence doesn't make sense. One of your son's noble supporters does not align with the established pattern."

"Which one?" Malina asked.

The Mentat stared straight ahead. "Duke Leto Atreides. His motives are unclear and mysterious. He . . . does not fit predictable patterns."

She remembered the handsome, dark-haired Duke among the rebels meeting secretly at the Nossus base. Jaxson was pleased to have recruited such a staunch adherent to honor, to law and order. "I'm certain he has his reasons. We do not know all of them."

"He is an outlier," the Mentat insisted. "We are missing a significant part of the data."

By the time a fourth Mentat said the same thing, Malina grew agitated and suspicious. Her decision about Jaxson was clear: neither she, Jalma, nor Frankos could ally themselves with Jaxson's movement, and she had to decide how to unravel his plans.

But what did Duke Leto have to do with all this? What was his involvement and his endgame?

She dismissed her Mentats after emphasizing the confidentiality of their theoretical projections. Then she made up her mind to return to Nossus, where she hoped to learn more.

Victory feels like flying, while defeat is a deep gravity well that crushes all hope. One feeling can switch to the other in the briefest of moments.

—Zensunni paradigm

On the images from Viscount Tull, seeing Jessica so close to the proud nobleman made Leto feel leaden inside. She didn't speak a word during the brief message, and kept her arms at her sides, though brushing against the other man as he described his shield nullifiers.

Oblivious to the crippling emotional blow Leto had received, Jaxson was aglow with possibilities, imagining how he could use Tull's new devices in a devastating surprise strike against even the Emperor's feared Sardaukar.

Eager to test the nullifiers, Jaxson took two of the ornate cubes from the crates and called ten of his house guards, asking them to don full uniforms and personal shields. Though Nossus was isolated and secure, Jaxson kept a significant armory in the main house, including numerous projectile rifles that were ostensibly for hunting wildlife in the hills, but Leto wasn't fooled. Now the rebel leader loaded two of his projectile rifles with gel bullets, soft spheres that would bruise a target without causing permanent damage.

"Come, my friend. We must test how well these work." Jaxson was smiling, filled with nervous energy, glad to share the activity with Leto. "My people will volunteer for the experiment."

Although hesitant, Leto accompanied Jaxson as they set up the prototypes on the edge of a grain field not far from the main house. The volunteer guards stood in a line, showing no anxiety. They were stony, as if willing to face a firing squad for Jaxson if that was what the rebellion required.

Leto's heart was heavy for personal reasons, but he tried to distract himself, remembering why he was here. He inspected the nullifier. "Did Tull send any instructions or performance specifications? Did he inform us about the efficacy?" He turned the object over in his hands, studied the smooth lenses. "Does the device work in a burst and destroy personal shields, or simply dampen them for a limited time? Fighters will need to know before they rely on these weapons in battle."

"These prototypes are breathtakingly new and untested," Jaxson said as if it were a good thing. "And so, we are about to find out how effective they are. We'll find the answers for ourselves." He was like an eager child with an intriguing toy. "Shields on!"

The ten volunteer guards activated their belts, and a faint watery ripple in the air indicated the protective barrier that would block any swift projectile. Long ago, Holtzman shields had fundamentally changed warfare and personal combat, effectively removing bullets and artillery from the battlefield. If Tull's new device neutralized personal body shields, then all of those old weapons would suddenly be deadly again. And few people possessed them anymore. . . .

His eyes shining, Jaxson activated the first of the lens-studded cubes. The device glowed, then emitted a bright white flash, like lightning. Leto expected the line of house guards to be bowled over in a shock wave, but the men stood apparently unaffected.

Jaxson picked up the nullifier, disappointed. "It did not work."

But Leto noticed that the near-invisible ripple around the guards had vanished. They touched their shield belts, pawed at the controls in puzzlement, but remained vulnerable.

As if on a whim, Jaxson swung up his projectile rifle, pointed it at the first guard in the line, and fired a gel bullet. The soft projectile splattered against the man's chest, knocking him backward as he grimaced in pain. He touched the stain on his uniform, and his mouth dropped open.

"The projectile was not deflected at all! It struck the target." He nudged Leto in the arm. "Try it yourself. We have to prove this."

Reluctant, Leto aimed for the leg of the next guard and fired—with the same result. The man dropped to the ground, clasping his bruised thigh. The household guards began shouting with concern and excitement. Unable to contain his enthusiasm, Jaxson fired off three more gel bullets, although there was no need for further testing.

"We have to inspect the neutralized shield belts," Leto said. "Are they destroyed, or will they reset?"

They jogged out to meet the mystified guards, who were also pleased when they realized this was exactly what the rebel leader wanted. After about fifteen minutes, though, one of the shield belts flickered, and a faint hum filled the air. Once again, the active shield shimmered close to the wearer. Over the next few minutes, all the personal shields were restored.

"Important data." Jaxson nodded gravely. "We'll test it a few more times, but we can assume the effect lasts a quarter of an hour. That's how long any attackers will be vulnerable, so we'd better be prepared." He raised his voice. "Make sure we have enough projectile weapons for a siege! Build up our armory!"

"It will only work once as a surprise," Leto said.

Jaxson chuckled. "That is true of most surprises."

❧

THAT EVENING, HE and Jaxson dined together. The rebel leader relaxed and confided in him, telling stories about halcyon days with his beloved father on Otorio. As he talked, Jaxson would subconsciously touch his face, his eyebrows, all of which made him look much like Brondon Aru due to the Tleilaxu facial cloning procedure he had undergone to conceal his identity.

Listening to the nostalgia, though, Leto felt far from his own home and impatient to go back to Caladan. He could not forget where Jessica was, but he focused his determination on finding a way to dispatch a vital message to the Emperor—so he could put an end to this radical movement. Once he was done with this dangerous, self-imposed mission, he could just go home. "When is the next Heighliner arriving in this system? I have to be—"

Jaxson cut him off. "I want you to travel to Cuarte! Londine is waiting for you there, as is his lovely daughter. Another ship will be here in two days, and you can depart then. I will make arrangements for you." He flashed a crooked smile. "And I'll be on my way, too—secret business of the rebellion. I must court a new recruit, someone nearly as impressive and influential as you, Leto Atreides."

Though he still felt deeply out of place, Leto forced a smile at the good-natured teasing. "I am not all that influential. Who is this new recruit?" He needed any information he could get.

Jaxson's expression turned mischievous. "That shall be my secret for now, Leto. If I convince him, then I can tell everyone. You will be as excited as I, once you see the big picture."

"I always try to see the big picture," Leto said.

After the meal, Jaxson led him outside, under the burnt-orange skies of twilight. They walked to the nearby hangar, where the engineering crews were mostly finished refitting the stolen Imperial treasury ship. By now they had switched out the hull plates, removed any identifying marks, and altered the lines so that the vessel was no longer recognizable.

Jaxson stood at the hangar door, inhaling deeply, as if he enjoyed the smells of hot metal and chemicals. "The new engines are installed. This ship is truly an unexpected asset. We will keep it as a special surprise, if needed."

Leto studied the configuration of the vessel, which was the size of a noble frigate, but with an antique feel to it. "Why is it so special?"

"This ship does not depend on the Spacing Guild. With it, I go wherever I like."

Leto considered the archaic-looking craft. "How can you travel between star systems without a Heighliner or a Navigator?"

"Just as the League of Nobles traveled the galaxy before the Butlerian Jihad." Jaxson entered the hangar, approaching the ship so he could stroke the hull plates. Leto followed him to where they both looked at the exhaust cones of the powerful engines. "It has an antique faster-than-light drive, the same kind of engine the Army of Humanity used when they eradicated thinking machines across the Synchronized Empire." He pursed his lips. "Not nearly as fast as foldspace engines—it might take us a week or more to travel to a destination instead of a few suspended minutes—but it'll work as a last resort."

Leto was taken aback. "Where did you find such technology? It's unheard of now."

"Not unheard of, just little known," Jaxson said. "Working with my mother in the CHOAM stronghold on Tanegaard, as well as my brother in the Silver Needle on Kaitain, I learned that CHOAM has several such FTL ships, a secret fleet to serve a commercial company that spans countless star systems. The Ur-Directors could not let themselves be entirely beholden to the Spacing Guild monopoly. So, CHOAM retained their own ships to use in extreme circumstances. I secretly copied the plans for my own use. Though the Guild has ironclad confidentiality agreements, my mother says we can't trust anyone." His smile widened. "Not anyone, my friend."

Leto stared at the engine, shaking his head. "I never imagined that anyone used that risky old technology anymore."

Jaxson nudged his shoulder in a comradely gesture. "I am not averse to taking risks—as you well know."

"That's why you do business with a man like Viscount Tull," Leto grumbled.

Jaxson did not seem to notice his sour tone, but the rebel leader was not a man to detect subtle nuances and emotions. "Giandro Tull was as brave as any of us. He only recently turned against House Corrino. Think of the emergency supplies and food that you yourself requested for the Issimo III colony—much of them were donated by House Tull. Didn't you know that?"

"You included pundi rice without my knowledge," Leto pointed out. "So technically, Caladan contributed, too."

"Then we are all three heroes." Jaxson laughed. "The people of Issimo III will probably build a statue for each of us."

Leto could only think how glad he would be to board the Heighliner tomorrow and be away from Nossus. He was exhausted from constantly hiding his tension, from pretending, and his skin crawled every day. He reminded himself of his plan. Once he was safely off-planet, when the Heighliner stopped at some waypoint transfer station, Leto would dispatch all of his findings directly to Kaitain. By now, Gurney Halleck should have prepared the Emperor for how the Duke had infiltrated the Noble Commonwealth ranks, and Shaddam's forces would be ready to act. Without reservation, Leto would reveal the location of the Nossus base as well as the identities of the other conspirators who openly supported violence and bloodshed.

Though it went against his grain, he reminded himself that he had chosen to undertake this task for the stability of the Imperium, no matter what personal price he had to pay. Though he had his own issues with Shaddam IV, the terrorists were far worse, and they sought to bring down the very fabric of society, the rule of long-standing law. He had made up his mind to put an end to the extremists. Though Jaxson Aru considered him an ally, Leto had hardened himself. He could never forget all those whom Jaxson had already hurt or killed. Shaddam would surely reward him—and more importantly, Paul would be proud of him.

But the direct involvement of Ur-Director Malina Aru added extraordinary complications. If CHOAM supported this rebellion, would Shaddam dismantle the enormous trading company? Did even the Emperor possess that much power? Such an action would create a terrific uproar throughout the Imperium, likely even a civil war.

Politics was a monster ready to devour everything in its path. Leto was glad that Caladan was isolated and self-sufficient. If need be, he would hunker down with his people, and they would withstand the upheavals. . . .

Glancing at his preoccupied expression, Jaxson led Leto away from the hangar, lowering his voice. "I can tell that you're worried, my friend. I worry about it, too."

Cautious, he asked, "What do you worry about?"

"I trust our comrades in this great effort—I honestly do—but with such dangerous activities, someone might make a tragic mistake, or openly betray us. I have had to take certain precautions, create an insurance policy of sorts. As a last resort."

When the two men had reached the young olive grove, well out of earshot from the hangar, Jaxson reached into his pocket and withdrew an oblong onyx object as long as his thumb, smooth on all sides like a river-worn rock. Conspiratorially, he leaned closer to Leto. His glittering eyes seemed out of place on his altered features. "This is a memory stone. Ancient technology that no one could reproduce today. Its storage capacity is vast."

"And what do you need to store?" Leto asked.

"Information." Jaxson smiled brightly. "CHOAM records, commercial transactions, illicit bargains, weapons shipments, forbidden technologies. When I worked in the CHOAM data fortress on Tanegaard, I had security codes—my mother trusted me to be a vital part of the family business, you see. When I learned of a terrible reservoir of blackmail data, called the black archives, I knew it was a weapon we could use for our cause. So, I copied the library of incredibly confidential information, business betrayals, noble schemings."

Leto's voice was cool. "You're going to have to explain this to me."

Jaxson turned the memory stone between his fingers. "This contains proof of secret Landsraad-CHOAM transactions for centuries, none of them openly recorded or made public. So many notable families, so many illicit dealings and commercial treachery. The Imperial family is not the only corrupt one in our civilization."

Leto observed the man, remaining noncommittal. "That goes beyond anything I ever imagined."

"Remember the story I told about Tuarna Vok, her sabotaged shipment of power cells, her insurance fraud, and the accidental blood on her hands? This stone contains a thousand times a thousand such nuggets of information, each one more damning than the last." He looked into the darkening dusk. "But the thorniest entanglements all twist back to House Corrino. They would suffer the worst . . . and some of it concerns you, my friend. And the stain on House Atreides."

Now Leto flushed. "What do you mean?"

Jaxson was deadly serious. "The Emperor's Sardaukar, for example, are not exclusively held for protection of the Imperial person, as you might believe." His eyes narrowed, and his gaze became razor sharp. "Are you aware of how your own father was coerced to take part in a dishonorable power grab of House Kolona? Why would an otherwise decent man like Duke Paulus spring an attack and wipe out a rival noble house, when he had shown no such ambitions before? Certainly, not to obtain the planet Boorhees!"

"I already had my suspicions of that, and some evidence, early in my role as the Duke of Caladan, I relinquished all those holdings from House Kolona. I wanted nothing to do with them."

"Yes, but did you know that Emperor Elrood provided *Sardaukar in Atreides uniforms* to so decisively secure a victory?"

A chill went down Leto's spine. "I suspected that, but could not prove it."

"I can prove it!" Jaxson held up the memory stone. "But House Atreides wouldn't want this information released, so the whole Imperium would know how your father was manipulated and duped . . . and swallowed it all."

Leto felt a strong flush of anger. "I do not want this known."

"Imagine how the other nobles in the Landsraad would react. How many powerful families would be pitted against other powerful families like dogs thrown into a fighting arena? Utter chaos! If we're lucky, maybe they would all turn on House Corrino . . . but likely not before they tore one another apart."

"You play a very dangerous game, Jaxson."

"Dangerous, yes, but it is not a game." The rebel leader mused as he stared down at the obsidian surface of the memory stone. "Spread out the cascade effect a thousandfold, and you can imagine the truly seismic consequences—if any of this were ever released."

The magnitude of this blackmail threat sank into Leto's awareness.

"But only as a last resort." Jaxson tried to sound reassuring. "This memory stone always remains close to my body, covered with a proximity film and a bio-field. It knows whether I am alive or dead. If my life signs were ever to disappear, the data packets would automatically be transmitted, widely dispersed to open receivers that I have set up in countless hidden repeater stations around hundreds of Imperial worlds. Some are carried aboard CHOAM vessels or Guild Heighliners. If this database were to be broadcast, stopping it would be like trying to catch the rain."

Leto paused to take a breath and center his thoughts as they stood together by the small olive grove. "Such a release of incriminating and disruptive data would send tremors throughout the entire Imperium, igniting countless civil wars, family feuds, and other squabbles. Our current view of kanly would look like a child's tussle. The destruction it would cause—you could never predict . . ."

"Of course, but the most intrepid and resourceful families would pick up the pieces and thrive, even if it were to take a few generations." He began walking back toward the main house as full dusk settled in. "That is not how I'd choose to bring down the Imperium, but it would certainly generate that result." Jaxson seemed proud of his cleverness. "It's a perfect fail-safe."

Leto had no doubt this man would do exactly as he threatened, with no concern about the consequences. This threw Leto's entire plan into a spin. If he sent out his secret report to Kaitain and Imperial justice swooped in, the fanatical leader would happily go down in a final flash of glory and release the damning information.

Leto growled, "We must make absolutely sure you never have to use it." He did not underestimate him. He had already known that Jaxson apprenticed at the Ur-Director's side, being groomed for a high-level position in CHOAM, but even with her tacit acceptance of the Noble Commonwealth movement,

Malina Aru could not be aware that her son had such a ticking time bomb! Surely Jaxson realized that releasing this dark data, these black archives, would tear CHOAM apart as well.

Or did he not care?

Though his expression did not change, Leto felt even more determined that the man must be brought down, along with his coconspirators.

Then the knot in his chest tightened as a new thought fell into place: Jessica was the new concubine of Viscount Giandro Tull, another rebel supporter. If Shaddam ever learned that Tull was one of the traitors, Leto knew full well what the Emperor would do to him and his entire world.

He had to find some way to resolve this, but felt like he was drowning in quicksand.

Not all secrets are dark, but the majority of them are.
—A saying from the days of the Butlerian Jihad

Drawing upon her Bene Gesserit training, Jessica remained Viscount Tull's concubine in name only. Surprisingly, the situation fit both of their purposes quite well.

On a damp, cool morning, she was about to set out alone on a horseback ride, feeling a freedom in her place here that had not been apparent before. She and Giandro had a clear understanding of their roles, which were different in private than in public. They held mutual secrets, each balanced on a tightrope of obligations.

She felt exhilarated and intimidated because he was letting her take one of his prized thoroughbreds out on a casual ride. The animals were among the most valuable assets of House Tull, with a renowned bloodline that had remained undiluted for centuries, never sold to any outside customer.

Though he wanted to ride with her, Giandro had been occupied with business matters, possibly work for the rebellion. A refugee incident had occurred the evening before, in which hundreds of people arrived on a Guild Heighliner, seeking sanctuary on Elegy after their planet was destroyed in a mysterious Sardaukar attack, just like what had happened to House Verdun on Dross. Jessica didn't know what other world had been attacked, but she did hear the Viscount lamenting the loss of a fellow nobleman, and tragically that there had been so few survivors.

As he buried himself in his political work, he had sent an order to the stable master to prepare for her a stallion of calm disposition. The charcoal-black horse, named Tivvy, had an unusual white blaze and stockings, and now as she stood outside the main barn, holding the reins, she stroked the neck, then moved her fingers down to pet the muzzle. She was pleased when the proud animal nuzzled against her palm.

The stable master, a wiry dark-skinned man named Darci, looked on. "You have some knowledge of horses, my Lady. I can tell."

She thought wistfully of the times she had gone riding with Leto. "Some knowledge." But she remembered that the main Castle Caladan stables had been closed down for some time, with most of the horses sent off to be tended in open pastures inland.

Hearing an indignant snort, she saw another stallion poking his head out of a stall, looking in her direction. He whinnied again and stomped his hoof, pawing the ground.

She turned to the stable master. "I could handle one of the racing stallions, too."

"I suspect you could, my Lady, but Lord Tull would never let you go riding by yourself on a steed such as that, and I have my orders." He patted Tivvy's side. "This is the best mount for you today, good disposition and calm, though you do have experience."

Despite her confidence, she supposed the feisty stallion might stretch the limits of her ability. Perhaps another time, with Giandro accompanying her.

Mounting up, she took a moment to settle into the saddle and get a feel for the horse. She adjusted herself, watched Tivvy's manner, considered the other mounts she had ridden. When she felt comfortable, she guided the thoroughbred away from the barn and into the sunshine. The magnificent animal seemed just as excited about having a chance for exercise, and she wondered if he was truly as calm as the stable master suggested. He walked fast and responded quickly and powerfully to a light touch from her leg.

Jessica found the main path that led up a slope through a lichen tree copse and into what Darci called "the riding hills." A few kilometers away, in the opposite direction, she could see the sprawling Elegy spaceport and remembered when she had first arrived here and met the Viscount to whom she'd been assigned. . . .

Behind her, another rider emerged from the barn and followed her, but far behind, staying in view but no closer. Jessica knew that Giandro no longer distrusted her, so she would put up with a minder for her personal safety, if only to maintain appearances. Not long ago, she had managed to outsmart her watchers when she wandered into the wooded hills, eluding them so she could surreptitiously watch the Viscount's mysterious dealings. That was how she had discovered his secret weapons shipments—and that changed everything between them.

Now, halfway up a grassy hill, a crumbly rock outcropping forced the trail to the right and down into a small swale, then across a meadow before winding back up and around the rocks to the top. Glancing over her shoulder, she still saw the rider following far behind, only a small figure.

When she reached the top of the slope, Jessica dismounted and gazed out across the rolling hills, lichen forests, wildflower meadows, and a blue-water lake. She found a faint path that would take her over to the calm lake, and she walked ahead, letting Tivvy follow. By the time she realized it was merely a meandering game trail, the slope had steepened. Broken rock from the out-croppings made the footing treacherous for the horse. She tugged the reins to turn around and go back, but stones crumbled and slipped away under the stallion's hooves, and soon he began limping.

She examined Tivvy's hooves, finding that a small, sharp rock had be-come lodged between the frog and the shoe. She patted the horse's neck again to reassure him, then rummaged in the small saddlebag, looking for a hoof pick, and was disappointed to find that the stable master had not packed one. She had only been going out for a short ride, but even so. She lifted the hoof again, tried to dig out the stone with her fingers, but could not pry it loose from the edge of the shoe.

Again trying to calm the animal, she stroked his muzzle. "Can you walk back?" She led him by the reins up the crumbling slope, trying to retrace her way. He continued to limp. Finally, reaching the top of the hill, she walked along the gentler trail through the copse.

Suddenly, she heard a rushing rumble—a skitter and roar of falling rocks. Precariously balanced boulders had shifted in the loose dirt, then slipped and thundered down the slope onto the trail that led back to the estate. Though Jessica was well away from the rockfall, the stallion spooked and jerked the reins out of her grasp. Despite his lame leg, Tivvy ran off trail into the lichen tree woods.

Angry at herself for letting him go, she called after the thoroughbred, to no avail. Then, resolving to make her way back to the stables for help, she found that the fresh pile of loose, unstable rocks lay across the main path. She picked her way over the debris field, trying to set her boots on the wobbling rocks, but the loose stones kept slipping and shifting. Halfway across the new rockfall, she heard a horse approaching.

Giandro Tull rode toward her on a black stallion of his own—apparently, he had replaced the rider following her and come on his own. "I'll help you down." He dismounted, and she kept working her way toward him. One of the lower rocks broke loose, and the large slabs slid down toward Giandro. He bounded out of the way as the rocks fell past where he had been.

After the secondary avalanche ground to a halt, he approached the loose pile as she made her way gingerly over the rubble. He reached up to her, still trying to help. Behind him, his own horse danced about as if anxious to continue on its way.

Although Jessica could manage on her own, she let him help her descend to the stable ground. She knew he had been raised and trained for courtly formalities, even if it was for show, although no one was here watching.

When finally she stood on firm grass away from the rockslide, he looked at her for a long moment as if expecting a show of gratitude. She offered a smile and a gracious nod. "Thank you, Giandro. Alas, we had no witness to your gallant gesture."

"You saw what I did, and that's more than enough."

He retrieved the racing thoroughbred and gestured toward the saddle, offering to let her ride, but she shook her head. "I'm willing to walk back to the stables, and keep an eye out for Tivvy. We need to get his hoof checked out."

Giandro seemed disappointed. "As you wish. I'll send Darci out to find him. My man is good at that, and all the horses love him. As for Tivvy, his racing days were long over before today, but I still want to keep him healthy and happy. He is a fine steed, from a good bloodline."

She strolled along the trail, and he walked at her side, leading his horse behind them. He explained, "These rare and beautiful animals have been exclusive to House Tull for many generations, until recently when the Emperor stole some of them. He is a wicked, oblivious man, and he does not deserve them. Unfortunately, the stolen horses all died, some kind of a tragic poisoning."

Alarmed, Jessica looked over at him. "Poisoning? Treachery among their stable crew?" She tried to read details from his facial expression.

"Who can say? An Emperor has so many enemies, and they will look for any way to hurt him. But Shaddam Corrino never cared about the horses anyway—except as a prize to take away from me." His expression darkened. "I . . . I just feel sorry for the poor animals. It was not their fault they were used as pawns for the Emperor's greed."

Unexpectedly, he reached out to take her hand. The gesture surprised her because they had come to an understanding about only maintaining appearances with her as his concubine, and no more. Nevertheless, out of friendship, she allowed him to hold her hand, and they walked on, with the horse following.

But when the trail narrowed and they moved close together, Jessica remembered times with her Leto on Caladan, the sweetness of holding hands like teenagers, the kisses they had shared—not just in the giddy rush of new love, but over the past fifteen years, too. Though there had been opportunities, and outside expectations—especially from the Sisterhood—Jessica had refused to sleep with Giandro Tull. He was a handsome man, sought after by the ladies of Elegy, but he showed little interest in a real romance.

For the time being, Jessica would play the role of Tull's concubine, giving him the cover he needed. Emperor Shaddam would think that House Tull had nothing to hide from prying eyes if he permitted a Bene Gesserit so close to him. But now she was inextricably connected to the rebellion herself, since she had stood at his side when he recorded his message to the rebels.

She dreaded what Leto would think if he ever saw that recording, if he was indeed in the company of Jaxson Aru. But would he *see* the real message, her finger movements?

Gently but firmly, she pulled her hand free. Though he had not tried to seduce her, Giandro Tull had clearly come to care for her. He appreciated her conversation and her advice, and Jessica respected him as well, despite his dangerous politics. She was also greatly in his debt because he had helped her to save Paul from extremist Sisterhood assassins. No one here knew about that, but she could never forget it.

Even if her situation on Elegy was tolerable, she longed to be back on Caladan. Jessica had done what Mother Superior Harishka demanded, but she doubted they would let her return home to her son and Duke. Would Leto even have her?

She set her jaw in determination. There was more she could do to make the Sisterhood feel their obligations.

As they continued back toward the stables, Jessica considered what she was about to say. Giandro would not like it, but ultimately, this would benefit both of them. "You—we—are doing dangerous things. I'm at your side, but the Bene Gesserit are watching both of us, and the Emperor is watching you as well, because of your connections with the disgraced House Verdun."

"And because of the new refugees I took in." His expression darkened. "Shaddam Corrino sees rebels in every shadow. He already sent his Sardau-kar thugs here, but they found nothing." His lips quirked. "I had nothing to hide . . . not at that time anyway."

"Though now you do."

He stared ahead as they walked. Behind them, the horse ground his teeth over the bit, making a squeaking metal sound. Giandro ignored it. "Quite right, now I do."

"I know a way to strengthen your cover, to allay any remaining suspicions the Bene Gesserit have. We can give them what they want, under your own terms."

Now he stopped, turning to look at her. "I want nothing more to do with your coven of witches. What more do they demand? I already accepted you into my household."

"They always want more." She didn't try to keep the bitter tone out of her voice. "Your father was a great financial supporter of the Sisterhood. After he died, not only did you expel his concubine from Elegy, you also cut off House Tull's long-standing stipend to the Mother School. That stung the Bene Gesserit more than any humiliation to one of their Sisters."

He seemed insulted. "I have more important uses for Tull money."

"And the Mother School wonders what you are doing with the funds that were formerly sent to them. Perhaps they are asking questions of Imperial accountants. We both know you diverted solaris into the war chest of the rebellion, but why give them the excuse to look?"

"So I should pay them off?"

"Consider the investment, from a business and personal perspective. If you restored the donation, at least provisionally, then the Bene Gesserit would no longer suspect you of hiding something—and the Truthsayer would whisper that conclusion in the Emperor's ear. And it would also convince the Mother School that I have truly accomplished my mission here."

Emotions warred on his face. "That would benefit you."

"It would benefit both of us. More importantly, they would leave House Tull alone."

When they finally reached the stables, warm and flushed from the long walk, Giandro turned his horse over to the stable master and asked him to send out a team of searchers to round up Jessica's horse in the woods.

When they were alone again, the Viscount said to her, "You are sincere, and I apologize for accusing you. The idea of paying more to the manipulative witches sticks in my throat . . . yet you are correct. The benefits outweigh my pride. Let them think I am their patsy again." He nodded. "I will renew the stipend, the same amount my father paid. Until I decide otherwise."

Jessica felt no victory at helping the Sisterhood, but perhaps she had increased her own chances to return to her former life.

Even when one trains to the extreme, physically and mentally, it is still possible to fail.

—SWORDMASTER JOOL-NORET, founder of the Ginaz School

P aul and Duncan sat across from each other in the library of Castle Caladan, facing opposing armies . . . at least in Paul's mind. Two sets of game pieces, jet obsidian and Caladan jade, were arrayed across the complex Cheops board.

Thufir Hawat stood behind them like a looming sentinel, concentrating hard and frowning as usual. Paul had not moved a muscle, as if he had fallen into a perfect prana-bindu trance.

Distracted by the sedentary scrutiny, Duncan Idaho was restless. "Are you ever going to move, lad?"

"Yes." Paul didn't lift a finger as he answered, but thought, *Not yet.* He continued to study the pieces. The old Mentat seemed pleased with his behavior.

"Pyramid chess is only a game," Duncan said after waiting another minute in silence, "and games are supposed to be amusing."

"But instructive as well," Thufir argued. "A test of mental dexterity."

Paul lifted a hand, about to touch the soldier piece, but reconsidered and withdrew, still thinking. Now, the Mentat's tone changed. "Due consideration is one thing, young Master, but paralyzed indecision will never let you win the game."

"Or a war," Duncan said. He and Paul gazed at each other across the board, which had a grid of game squares, some populated by pieces, an Empress, Prince, Princess, Truthsayer, Swordmaster, Suk Doctor, Mentat, and four Sardaukar.

"Battles are won or lost in the mind and military preparations. You and Thufir both taught me that." Paul lifted the jade-green Suk, raised his eyebrows, and took his chance. "It's best to consider obscure rules because they can be used to your advantage." He raised the Suk to the top level of Duncan's onyx pieces and swapped out for a Sardaukar standing just adjacent to the Empress. "The Mindcastle move. Allowable only with this precise arrangement of pieces, and now I am directly inside the Empress's vulnerable zone."

Duncan let out an annoyed grunt. "Mindcastle? What in the hells is that?"

Curious, the old Mentat stepped forward, analyzed the pyramid board, and then his red-stained lips smiled. "I believe the young Master has defeated you, Duncan Idaho. He is well within the rules!"

"Foolish rules like that teach you nothing about real life." The Swordmaster scowled and tipped over his Empress figurine, conceding the game.

"Regardless, I won," Paul said, grinning. "And I'll accept a victory even if it falls in my lap." He rose to his feet and stretched, rubbed the back of his neck. "But I do agree with Duncan's comment about real life. While this enjoyable exercise will improve my mental strength and agility, I'd prefer actual activity that pushes me to my limits. Ever since we visited the Muadh village in the north, I keep thinking about climbing the Arondi Cliffs. You know I've mastered the headwall and the sea cliffs here, and this would be a greater challenge. My grandfather did it."

"And many others did not survive," the Mentat chastised. "Too dangerous. Your parents would never allow it."

"And each day, I am pointedly reminded that my mother and father are not here. Should I not be the one to decide? I have been left with great responsibilities. I need to be ready for them."

Duncan stretched, then roughly nudged the Cheops board aside, knocking over a few more game pieces. "If you want extreme training, I have a better idea—a more rigorous protocol that you and I can do together. Think of it as another . . . game."

"More rigorous than climbing a high cliff?" Paul asked, already intrigued.

The Swordmaster smiled. "Dangerous enough—unless you are afraid."

Paul had already made up his mind. "I know you will keep me safe, but you'll also push me to my limits. That is what I need."

Duncan stood and crossed his arms over his broad chest. "It is a simple, primal exercise. A hunt—but in this dangerous game, the hunter and the hunted are the same. We will go to the wildest country, deep in the Southern Continent. Just the two of us. I will hunt you, and you will try to survive."

Paul was intrigued. "And I will hunt you?"

Duncan shrugged. "You can try, young Master. I can give you a wilderness experience like my own ordeal as a boy on Giedi Prime, when Beast Rabban hunted me."

"I don't like the sound of this," Thufir cautioned. "You should remain here, as the proxy Duke."

"As you know yourself, Thufir, Caladan is running smoothly with plenty of other proxies and advisers, including you, to handle the day-to-day business." He looked over at the Swordmaster. "How long would we be gone, Duncan?"

Duncan considered. "A week or so on the Southern Continent, and we will always have a comm." His dark eyebrows drew together, and he faced the Mentat. "You know I will keep the boy safe."

Thufir Hawat stood rigid, considering possibilities, but he could not contradict the other man's statement.

Paul gave a firm, decisive nod. "This training will be worth the risk, and the effort." He had visited portions of Caladan wilderness before, but he was not familiar with the deep jungles of the south. "What's down there, Duncan? Have you explored it yourself?"

"The jungles are sparsely inhabited, though isolated tribes of Muadh live there. But I'm thinking of an area far from their usual hunting patterns at this time of year." The Swordmaster had obviously been considering the details. "It'll provide exactly the challenge we both need."

Paul felt a flush of excitement. "Thufir, you can oversee any bureaucratic matters for a few days while we're gone, and Gurney should be home soon to help you with security." He looked hard at Duncan. "And hold nothing back in your efforts to defeat me."

"Oh, I won't," he said. "Within reason, I will pull no punches."

"Nor will I."

In any business transaction, one must balance protection against profit, risk against reward. However, if the consequences of a bad decision include complete annihilation on the downside, then the potential profit must be weighed on a different scale.

—CHOAM investment parameters

With the Orgiz refinery destroyed to keep his secret, now the Baron had to explain to CHOAM why the lucrative black-market spice channel needed to be stopped. And he did not want to meet Ur-Director Aru on Arrakis.

Fortunately, Count Fenring and his annoying Mentat had found no incriminating evidence, despite snooping into every cranny at the destroyed refinery. The Baron was confident in the skills of his crew, but mistakes could happen that might trigger explosive repercussions.

Leaving Fenring to keep digging and investigating to his heart's content, the Baron departed for Giedi Prime, citing House Harkonnen business. He had arranged for the Urdir to travel there—not so he could grovel or make excuses, but for them to determine how they might continue their profitable relationship even without their secret spice refinery.

Afterward, he would go to Lankiveil to see what Rabban had managed to extract from his Atreides captive. But first, business on the Harkonnen homeworld.

Giedi Prime was a civilized place with blocky administrative buildings, manufactories, weapons plants . . . a constant beehive of activity. Now he breathed the rich air, smelling only the scent of profits and technology. He drank in the flying craft, the gray smoke in the skies, the brute-force buildings. Then he entered his lavish suites, treated himself to a steam bath, an oil massage, and diversions with young pleasure workers of both sexes.

Feyd-Rautha came to see him, aloof, confident, and beautiful. His youngest nephew was lean and muscular—as the Baron himself had been at his age, before the bitch Reverend Mother Mohiam had afflicted him with this disease. Even though Feyd's older brother managed the spice operations, the Baron felt that this one might be a better choice for his own successor.

Oh, he realized Feyd was still immature, ambitious, and ruthless. Perhaps the young man didn't yet have all the patience and subtlety that a real Baron needed. And it remained to be seen just how Feyd would meet his uncle's challenge to inflict devastating harm on the hated Atreides. It was supposed to demonstrate his prowess. So far, the results had been disappointing and inconclusive.

The Baron couldn't help but smile when he received the young man in his suite. His nephew wore a feline grin and expensive clothes that gave him freedom of movement. He was not only a dashing lordling, but a deadly fighter as well who had proved himself time and again in the combat arena.

Now, he kissed the Baron's knuckles, giving the older man a brief rush of excitement.

"I did not expect you to return so soon, Uncle. Let me present a report of our Harkonnen businesses." His cocky grin widened. "And I'll describe other schemes that I have afoot."

"I am still waiting for results, my dear Feyd. I want to see the Atreides *hurt*. Your brother already caused great harm by spreading a biological plague that destroyed a large export industry on Caladan."

The young man's expression tightened. "True, and Duke Leto retaliated with a counterstrike that caused equivalent harm to my brother's Lankiveil holdings. Hardly a victory." He huffed. "Besides, your instructions were to inflict *personal* pain, not kill a bunch of fish." He lowered his voice. "I fear for the Imperial economy if my brother thinks he is capable of manipulating commodity trades."

The Baron chuckled at the response.

Feyd continued, "Mine is a long and meticulous plan, and it has already produced bloodshed, though not as much pain as I had hoped, so there is more to come. The blood and outrage will be worth it, I promise."

"Then I shall wait, my dear Feyd. I don't want to spoil the surprise."

He had surprises of his own in the works, plans that even his nephews were not aware of. Secretly, he had begun driving screws deeper and deeper into the Suk doctor of House Atreides, Wellington Yueh. No one could know about that, though.

He was aware, however, of Duke Leto's risky plan to infiltrate the violent rebels, pretending to be one of them. How could the Baron use that against him? So much potential! After meeting with the CHOAM Ur-Director, he would join Rabban in the interrogation of Gurney Halleck. No one else knew that the Duke's highly confidential message to Emperor Shaddam had been intercepted.

"Oh, there are so many ways to damage House Atreides," the Baron mused. "We need not limit ourselves to only one."

Feyd's eyes glittered. "Tell me about your plans, Uncle."

"Now, now, I must keep some of my secrets. You will see as soon as the plans come to fruition."

Their discussion was interrupted when the Baron received word that a private CHOAM vessel had arrived, and Ur-Director Malina Aru was on her way to the Harkonnen residence. He glanced at his nephew, considered dismissing him, but decided that Feyd should observe these complex dealings. After all, he might become Baron someday.

The Urdir arrived within the hour, formal and impatient, as if she wanted an explanation for being diverted from her own business. She wore trim, formal attire, without jewelry; her dark brown hair short and serviceable. "I came at your request, Baron, though I have multiple CHOAM priorities. I was en route elsewhere, but you said your message was important." She frowned. "I hope you don't make a habit of this."

She was accompanied by only one of her spinehounds this time, although even the one silver-furred predator seemed as dangerous as Malina Aru herself. The dog was obedient, though its molten copper eyes blazed with contained violence.

Feyd was both fascinated and intimidated by her pet. The young man's manner became more edgy. "Only one spinehound? What happened to the other?"

Her demeanor became instantly frosty. "Kar is ill and being tended right now. I expect him to recover completely." The other beast sniffed and let out a thin whine. "I trust your spinehounds are well? Few deserve such an impressive gift. Once imprinted, they are the most devoted pets."

"Mine were, ah . . ." Feyd looked away, embarrassed. "They were defective and had to be put down."

Malina turned her gaze toward him like cracking a whip. She looked both shocked and sickened. "Defective in what way? Exactly how were they euthanized? I used significant influence to have the Tleilaxu create those pups for you."

The young man squared his shoulders, indignant. "They were hacked to death by my Swordmaster when the beasts tried to kill me." He sounded as if he blamed her. "We were on a hunt. They tore apart my hunt master and then charged after me. I would be dead if not for my Swordmaster."

Malina was accusatory. "Did you imprint them properly?"

Feyd snorted. "You blame me for those vicious beasts?"

The Baron raised a hand. "Now, I'm certain it was Tleilaxu error. They are a venal race, unreliable. And a vicious beast is a vicious beast." He narrowed his spider-black eyes. "In fact, such deadly animals could have been part of an assassination plot against my dear nephew."

Malina reached down to pat her own hound. "It is acceptable to blame the Tleilaxu." She turned back to the Baron. "Now, about your urgent business? I must be on my way before the Heighliner departs again. I have to make a rendezvous before I can return and tend to Kar."

The Baron had called for refreshments—spice cakes, fine wines, candied fruits, and melange honey—but Malina Aru showed no interest in such pleasantries. "Unfortunately, Urdir, there has been a setback. Our illicit channel of spice had to be terminated, at least for the time being."

Her face tightened in a scowl. "Why? Has it not been profitable for you?"

"Indeed it has, Urdir, but Count Fenring somehow discovered the Orgiz refinery. Before he could find evidence against us, I had to take care of the matter."

"Take care of the matter?" She raised her eyebrows. "What did you do?" Beside her, the spinehound growled. "You didn't actually kill Fenring, did you? That would attract far too much Imperial attention."

"No, I didn't kill him," the Baron snapped. "I had no choice but to scuttle the Orgiz operations. They've been slagged, leaving no evidence behind. That also means I do not have the operational base required to continue our plan—at the moment. Until I develop an alternative channel, we have to place a moratorium on our spice distribution."

The Ur-Director sat in silence. Needing to distract himself, the Baron plucked a spice cake from the tray and popped it into his mouth. And Feyd, still staring at the tense spinehound, too, took one of the melange treats.

Malina said, "Count Fenring is like a ferret after a rat. He will keep asking questions. Are you certain he won't uncover our alliance?"

"I sent him chasing after a red herring," the Baron said, pleased with himself. "I made a compelling case that the Orgiz refinery must have been a secret base established by the Noble Commonwealth rebels! Perhaps even your son Jaxson." Seeing that she was startled by the suggestion, he continued in a rush, "An excellent diversion. It makes perfect sense, Ur-Director. We know the rebels need to reap great profits to pay for their terrorist activities. Why not melange? Thus, we sent Fenring chasing off in the wrong direction."

Malina clenched her jaw, then snapped her fingers so that her animal sprang to its feet. "I must be off. I have business to attend to, and I cannot miss my next destination." She reached down to scratch behind Har's pointed ears.

"As you wish," the Baron said with a glimmer of relief. He didn't relish the thought of entertaining this hard woman any longer than necessary.

He watched her stalk off, while his nephew couldn't pull his gaze away from the retreating spinehound. The Baron couldn't tell if Feyd longed for another pair of the animals, or if he wanted to kill this one.

After this, meeting with Rabban and his torture victim would be much more relaxing.

When all truly seems lost and hopeless, you may very well be right.
— A saying of the desert Fremen on Arrakis

Gurney Halleck was no stranger to pain or abuse. He swam in a dark sea of awareness, somewhere between the agony of consciousness and the escapes of unconsciousness . . . or death.

Though the troubadour warrior had fought many battles, he now experienced the worst physical torture of his life. Terrible pressure squeezed the sides of his head, compressing his skull. Pain screamed like ice picks in his ears, and his eyes felt as if they would explode out of his head.

It had not relented for hours, days . . . forever, it seemed.

On the periphery of his screaming nerves, he heard a guttural voice, toxically familiar. Rabban . . . Glossu Rabban. A reeking pile of excrement with a voice.

"I'm squeezing, Uncle. Squeezing! Just a little more, and—"

Gradually, Gurney felt the pressure diminish, or maybe he just lacked the capacity to feel any more and his end was near. But the intense pain lingered. It was no better, only different.

Another voice intruded on his awareness, basso and dominant, and Gurney knew it—the Baron Vladimir Harkonnen. "Keep him alive, Rabban. He is Duke Leto's man. You cannot kill him without my authorization, and I am not quite ready to give it."

Not quite ready, Gurney thought. *A stay of execution, but my sentence has not been overturned.*

"If you had not intervened, I could have squeezed his skull a little more without killing him," Rabban said in a petulant voice. "He might have gone blind, though."

Gurney still couldn't see through the red haze.

The Baron sounded angry, making a threat that rose like an intense flame. "Are you arguing with me?"

"I'm sorry, Uncle. You know what is best."

"Eventually, you will learn how to walk the fine line of extremes that dominate your mind. In truly painful torture, a subject must always believe there is hope. Take him to the brink of irreparable harm, but only to the brink."

Do they think I cannot hear this? Gurney thought. *Do they think the pain has driven me to unconsciousness?*

"There are steps below the threshold of permanent harm. In this lesson, Rabban, consider fingernails and bones."

"Fingernails and bones?"

"Violent harm and horrific pain, but not irreparable. You can rip out fingernails, and they grow back. Broken bones can heal. He will *know* they grow back and heal, and so he will cling to that hope."

The other man let out a deep grunt. "Very well, I'll break some bones."

"Ah, but not just any bones! Understand your subject's functional physiology. This is Gurney Halleck. Break a baliset-strumming finger or two, and you break his heart."

Rabban's voice came from the other side of the darkness. "I will keep him alive and make him suffer. And then we kill him. By degrees . . . one piece at a time."

"You aren't listening, Nephew."

Gurney wanted to leap out of this nightmare and slay both of them, but could not move. Maybe this was part of the torture.

Duke Leto had sent him with an urgent and highly sensitive message embedded in his arm. But his travel to Kaitain had been interrupted by an unforeseen Spacing Guild delay on Harmonthep, and during that interminable wait, Harkonnen agents had discovered and captured him.

Because of Gurney's failure, Emperor Shaddam didn't know that Duke Leto was merely pretending to side with the violent rebels.

And now he'd been dragged off here to Lankiveil! To Rabban's holdings, the same place that Gurney and Duncan had recently raided with Atreides troops.

But none of the Atreides knew he was here. The Duke didn't know. His message had not been delivered to the Emperor, and these vile Harkonnens had taken it out of his arm, viewed it themselves! What would they do with the damning information? He needed to get back to Caladan! But first he needed to survive.

He recalled a verse from the Orange Catholic Bible, clung to it. "Pain is only pain, and the children of God have many ways to shield against it, through memories, through loyalty, through love, and through faith."

Behind him, little more than a red blur, Rabban sounded surly. "We've already extracted any information this man has. How long must I keep him alive?"

"Until I decide." The deep rumble became a laugh. "Don't be impatient. It will be more painful for him that way."

The darkness grew deeper, and Gurney at last withered into unconsciousness.

❧

GURNEY AWOKE TO men quarreling out of sight . . . and a profound smell of blood and fish. He lay on a rigid stretcher, held up by suspensors, and his stomach roiled, but he fought back nausea.

Oddly, his body had no restraints, and he could sit up now. He lifted his right hand, flexed it in wonder. He had thought it was crushed, but although his joints throbbed, the fingers and knuckles looked intact. Nothing he couldn't tolerate. Dr. Yueh could fix it, if he could ever get back to Caladan.

Shaking off the blurred vision and the pounding thunderclaps in his head, he swung himself over the side of the wavering stretcher, resting his feet on the floor. Swaying with pain and disorientation, he looked around to find himself inside a chamber of horrors. The lights were harsh and white, and the shadows severe. When he blinked, his eyes throbbed. Terrible machines were all around him, horrific devices that included crushers, amputation blades, and pulleys and cables to stretch bodies apart.

On the far side of the chamber, a door stood open—tantalizing!

Vaguely, he remembered the Baron's discussion with Rabban about the exquisite pain of dangling hope in front of a victim. Hope . . . like an open door. Though Gurney was suspicious, he had no other choice.

Beyond the doorway, the voices continued to quarrel, shouts and insults, on the verge of a physical altercation.

Not knowing if this was reality or a dream, Gurney crept toward the doorway, ready to fight for his life, or at least to die here and end the torture. Breathing hard, he peered into a dim corridor, and his shadow cast by the harsh lights of the torture chamber looked ominous. The hall in one direction was dimmer, and the shouts came from the gloom, around another corner. He heard the noises of a scuffle, grunts and curses. Farther down the hall, he could see the commotion in low light—the shadows of two guards pummeling each other in a side room.

Were they his own guards, assuming he remained unconscious? They seemed to have forgotten about him for the moment.

The light was brighter in the opposite direction, fewer shadows to give him cover, but he had to go that way unless he wanted to kill both guards in his attempt to escape. He was too battered and weak to risk that.

Gurney had to get some message out, inform the Duke that he had been intercepted. Or he still had to deliver his message to the Emperor. He couldn't imagine how he might smuggle a note away from here and then through the highest security on Kaitain. Maybe he could get some desperate communication off to Caladan. Thufir Hawat would know what to do.

With his rolling, combat-ready gait, he prowled forward, and the brighter corridor led to a dead end with additional rooms on each side. He recoiled when he saw Rabban and the Baron seated at a table inside one chamber with their backs to him, attended by servants who moved as if they were afraid of their own shadows. They presented heaping platters of meat dripping with blood and juices. Gurney could smell the food, and it was like a siren song in his head.

Is this real? Or another twisted part of the torture?

A subject must always believe there is hope.

Gurney slipped into the adjacent empty room instead, careful not to disturb the occupants of the other chamber. He found a bank of equipment on one wall—transmitting equipment? Local comms? He couldn't possibly be that fortunate. And yet, after that surge of excitement, he realized that even a transmitting station did him no good. Who would hear him? No signal, no message could ever reach Caladan. Across the vast Imperium, couriers had to travel in person, on Guild Heighliners, to carry a message to the intended recipient. Any transmission from Lankiveil would fall on deaf ears. Knowing that was enough to crush his hope.

But he smiled tightly and felt the rough, hard scar on his cheek, reminding him that Rabban himself had given Gurney that mark.

He did have an alternative, one that no Harkonnen knew. During the recent punitive raid he and Duncan had led here, the Atreides strike force had not only destroyed Rabban's facilities, they had also secretly scattered countless small, camouflaged spy-eyes throughout the vicinity . . . surveillance instruments that would passively record Harkonnen activity on this bleak, cloudy world. And their signal packets would surreptitiously piggyback on outgoing shipments from Lankiveil, onto Guild ships, off to other vessels, transfer points, eventually making their way back to House Atreides.

At the comm controls, he selected a link and heard a small click as a line opened. He set the comm for the precise frequency of the passive spy-eyes, so his message would join the rest of the reconnaissance data.

Speaking in a low voice, his throat raw—from screaming?—Gurney identified himself and said quickly, "Tell the Duke that I never made it to Kaitain and was delayed on Harmonthep! Captured by Harkonnens! I am currently being held on Lankiveil. Couldn't make it back to Caladan!"

He was startled when the transmission echoed back to him in a loud feedback loop. He had so much more to say! He had to explain that the Emperor had not, in fact, received Leto's explanation.

From behind him in the corridor, he heard cruel laughter. He spun, ready to fight, when two large men entered the room, the Baron and his nephew, both dressed in garments highlighted with Harkonnen orange. Behind them came several armed Harkonnen guards.

The Baron clucked his tongue. "Look at this foolish man, Rabban— thinking someone friendly will hear his transmission! He has thrown his message into the void. Do you presume a local fur-whale ship might receive your signal? You can shout and scream, but no one will hear."

Beside him, Rabban held a bloody bone from his interrupted meal. Juices dripped onto his tunic. The Baron also had blood on his shirt.

Though his battered and tortured body ached, Gurney was ready to throw himself on his enemies. He had wanted to kill Beast Rabban for years, after the slave pits on Giedi Prime. . . .

"Come, join us for a meal before my nephew continues your interrogation session," the Baron said. "I must get back to Arrakis now, but I have given Rabban clear instructions. You are in good hands."

Gurney slammed his hand onto the comm controls, resetting the frequency so that his transmission could not be tracked. They did not know about the tiny spy-eyes. "Supper before torture? To prove you are fine hosts?"

"Excellent hosts," the Baron said. "And we want you to keep up your strength for your next session when my nephew plays with you a bit more. After that, I have a more imaginative questioner for you, Piter de Vries. He calls himself the 'Architect of Pain.'"

More Harkonnen guards hurried down the corridor, closing in. Gurney spat on the floor, not fearing any form of death they might inflict on him. "Then I accept your offer of lunch. To give me strength."

Rabban tossed the bloody bone on the floor in front of him. "There's lunch."

Like an enraged Salusan bull, Gurney charged toward Rabban, hoping to reach him, but Harkonnen guards seized his arms, threw him against the wall.

Rabban stalked forward, his face flushed, and slammed a bloody fist into Gurney's face, knocking him loose from the guards. Rabban shoved him down and kicked him hard in the ribs. Then, as if bored, he commanded the soldiers to drag him back to the torture chamber.

"We'll see what Piter decides to do to you. Then you'll wish you had me back!"

Whuen Malina Aru's private ship returned to Nossus, she was relieved to find Duke Leto Atreides still there. She had not intended to see the rebel headquarters again so soon, but the deep concern expressed by her Mentats had forced a change of plans. In her heart, she had already made her difficult decision to thwart Jaxson's chaotic schemes, but she wanted to take measure of this enigmatic Duke and his renowned code of honor.

She understood the best path forward for CHOAM, even if her radical son could not be a part of it. The eventual success of the real Noble Commonwealth vision would create a stable, evolved civilization, but for that to happen, she needed to deflect and extinguish Jaxson's extreme violence. Malina longed for a future that Frankos and Jalma—her good and respectable children—could administer, a thriving system of worlds and a more powerful CHOAM.

The other extremist players—the ones who followed her errant son—would have to be sacrificial lambs to provide cover for the Ur-Director's real plans. *They* would become the face of the despised rebel movement, and when those targets were crushed, Shaddam Corrino would never guess that the true revolution quietly carried on, under her guidance. Yes, the ends would justify the means.

But what was the involvement of the Duke of Caladan? Jaxson had been so pleased to recruit Leto Atreides, but Malina couldn't fathom the man's motivations. Was he really one of those secretly violent recruits? She needed to know, even if Jaxson had a blind spot toward his newfound friend. She realized with a sad twist in her heart that she, his own mother, was not Jaxson's friend either. . . .

Her pilot took her down to the isolated base that her son had built in the open rangeland, a homestead that would draw no attention on a planet that itself had minimal population—much like the old Aru family holdings on Otorio. Malina could see exactly why Jaxson had chosen this place.

Maintaining her act and demeanor, she emerged on the crushed-gravel landing area outside the main house. She wore the same comfortable business attire from her stopover at Giedi Prime, a suit marked with the CHOAM logo, but as a concession to her son's pride, she included a swatch of the family colors, crimson and black.

Har came out to follow alongside her, sniffing the air, as if still searching for his companion. Malina, too, felt the emptiness, and even with all the galactic machinations, she wanted to be back on Tanegaard so she could watch Kar's recovery . . . presuming the veterinary specialists were able to do their work properly. She swallowed hard, focused on the business here.

"Mother!" Jaxson seemed genuinely delighted, as if her return implied some kind of maternal acceptance. It was a psychological need that her son had likely never admitted to himself. He came forward to greet her, accompanied by a man she recognized as Duke Leto Atreides. The Nossus household staff, dressed as farmers, valets, and mechanics, remained alert, but none of them would make a move against the CHOAM Ur-Director.

The spinehound waved his prickly tail as he bounded toward Jaxson. Malina didn't stop him. Her son crouched down and opened his arms to welcome Har.

Leto remained stiff and wary before the hound, and Malina was impressed that he demonstrated caution, wisdom, and an understanding of predators.

Jaxson looked up at her, curious and concerned. "Where is Kar? You never travel without both of them."

She made a dismissive gesture, but her voice cracked with worry that she hated to show. "He is being tended. A digestive ailment. I had to leave him behind on Tanegaard."

Jaxson's heavy brows drew together. "What kind of digestive ailment?"

Malina sniffed, and she felt a flush of heat on her face. She didn't want to tell him, but the words came out quickly. "A stomach tumor. It sounds serious, but I found the best veterinary care."

Still scratching Har's ears, Jaxson lowered his voice. His altered face with maddeningly familiar features turned pale. "You sound worried."

"I am here on other business, then I will go directly back to Tanegaard to see to Kar. I can deal with many priorities at the same time."

Jaxson shouted for the household staff to set up guest quarters, prepare a meal, and do everything possible to make his mother welcome and comfortable. She warned, "I will not stay long. The business of CHOAM places demands on my time, and I must keep moving."

Jaxson quickly covered his expression of disappointment with a submissive nod. "I understand. And you should get back to Kar. The rest of my inner circle has already departed on their missions anyway. I'll be leaving Nossus soon for another rendezvous, and Duke Leto has an assignation of his own." He smiled.

Leto gave a formal nod. "I'm going to Cuarte to continue conversations with Lord Londine." He did not sound entirely pleased about it.

Malina made a quick gesture, and Har returned to her side as if spring-loaded. "I come with vital information for you. That's why it was so important for me to hurry here."

"You don't need a specific reason to come to Nossus, Mother," Jaxson said. "You've demonstrated your support for our cause. Once the true extent of our uprising is known, the rest of the Landsraad will fall in line. After all, we have Duke Leto Atreides on our side."

Seeming awkward and out of place, Leto asked, "Is your vital information something you wish to tell your son in private, or does it concern me as well?"

"Stay here. It concerns the rebellion overall," Malina said as thoughts turned in her head. She explained as if she were delivering a report to a board meeting. "Illicit spice operations have been discovered on Arrakis and destroyed. Baron Vladimir Harkonnen has reported rumors that the black-market operations were a front for the Noble Commonwealth, a way for the rebellion to earn significant undocumented funds." Of course, she knew the real explanation of the Orgiz refinery, but simply reporting the rumors to Jaxson could provide a worthy red herring.

Her son opened and closed his mouth. "I have several sources of untraceable funding, Mother, but I have not set up spice-harvesting operations." He glanced sidelong at Leto, then focused on her. "I have always raised my own money, without needing yours."

Malina nodded. "Yes, I publicly broke all ties with you and cut off any family financial assistance, so the Emperor's auditors will find no connection between us. But I know you are raising funds by some other means."

Leto muttered in a scoffing tone, "I would not trust anything Baron Harkonnen says. He is a corrupt and dangerous man, and his motivations are never straightforward." He narrowed his gray eyes. "Why would he reveal such a rumor to you, Ur-Director? To what purpose?"

"Because I am CHOAM. The Baron supplies melange throughout the Imperium, through legitimate channels. Of course he and I have commercial connections, but I am wise enough not to trust the man." She paused. "I trust very few."

Jaxson said, "If trust is balanced with skepticism, then you may be safe.

The Baron Harkonnen has great power and great potential." As Leto scowled, Jaxson beamed, changing the subject. "And we have more news, Mother! One of our newest and most dedicated allies, Viscount Giandro Tull, sent us a shipment of new prototypes!" He grinned mischievously. "A device that will change the rules of warfare!"

Malina was taken aback. She had not known about House Tull's involvement among the radicals, though she was aware the Viscount once had commercial connections with Duke Fausto Verdun, a man who had already been exposed, disgraced, and annihilated by the Emperor.

"Tull's devices temporarily render shields useless. Such a surprise would leave even Sardaukar vulnerable to projectile weapons." He clapped his hands. "Leto and I have tried them, and I will arrange a demonstration for you!" He whistled for the spinehound to follow, then glanced over his shoulder as he hurried off. "Leto, take her to the hangar and show her our new ship with the FTL engines installed."

Malina's expression tightened at hearing that, too. "I see you listened during those CHOAM meetings on Tanegaard."

"Of course, Mother—you gave me free access to everything. I took full advantage of the CHOAM knowledge you offered." He smiled wider. "It is tactically wise to have access to a ship that does not require the Guild or traditional foldspace shipping lanes."

The lone spinehound ran after him as he hurried to prepare a demonstration of the shield nullifiers. She followed Leto toward the adjacent hangar building, which left her alone with the Atreides nobleman—as she wished.

The Duke's expression remained careful. He walked along as if stepping on eggshells and made little conversation. She liked that he was cautious, which was a good thing in an ally, but also a possible indicator of a spy.

As they made their way to the large open structure, Malina spoke up. "My son is pleased that you joined his movement." *His* movement, not *our* movement. "He's wanted to recruit you for some time. I think he considered you a particular prize . . . which puzzled me because Atreides holdings aren't the greatest, nor is your military the strongest. Yet he considers you a special ally."

Leto turned to look at her with a troubled expression of his own. "What do you think it is, then? I was surprised by his interest as well." He seemed out of his depth. "Jaxson was quite insistent, even somewhat threatening at times. He holds damning information over the heads of some of his inner circle, but he used different methods on me. Initially, anyway—until he revealed that he has information against one of my Atreides predecessors as well."

Malina heard that information with great interest. "His true reason for recruiting you," she said, "is your popularity in the Landsraad and your well-known penchant for honor. You are a bauble for him to show off for those who accuse him of treason, if ever the movement becomes public." Her expression hardened. "But you seem a very unlikely candidate to want to overthrow the Imperium."

"That's exactly why Jaxson was so enthusiastic to have me," Leto said. "If an Atreides is in the Noble Commonwealth, then the cause must truly be righteous."

Malina gave a dry laugh. "And your people call you 'Duke Leto the Just.' I have done my research."

They stopped at the open hangar, where construction engineers and flight technicians were combing over the refurbished vessel. Malina ran her eyes along the hull, running calculations in her mind. "This is a standard, high-end vessel design. It was not originally fitted with that type of engine."

Leto also stared at the gleaming craft. "It was built as an Imperial treasury ship, loaded with millions of solari coins."

"Like the one Jaxson smashed into the Imperial Palace?" Disapproval oozed through her voice.

Leto surprised her. "This is exactly that vessel, thought to have been destroyed. Jaxson managed to divert the real treasure and crashed a decoy into the Promenade Wing."

Malina knitted her eyebrows. "How did he manage that?"

"I would not underestimate your son." He pressed his lips together.

"I never do. And he took all those solaris to fund his activities?" Now she understood at least part of his additional revenue.

"His core followers are . . . very dedicated."

Now that the noise of banging and welding drowned out their low voices, Malina became more serious, and she turned to the Duke. "Why exactly are you here, Leto Atreides? No matter what my son thinks, you are neither a radical nor a rebel."

He reacted with shock and indignation, as expected. "Jaxson's the one who pursued me, Urdir. I did not approach him."

"And you did not answer my question," she said.

He rocked back slightly. "You think you are a Truthsayer?"

"I have studied human personalities all my life, and Jaxson's other recruits make sense to me. I'm aware of their goals and personalities. Some have short-term aspirations, other simply have violent streaks. But you, Duke Leto Atreides . . . you're out of your element here. You are known to be altruistic, but you have gone out on a limb with my son. The question is why? I don't understand what you have to gain. Why would the Duke of Caladan risk everything to endorse a violent solution?"

Leto's expression became unreadable, perhaps a defense mechanism against fear or anxiety. "If you studied me, Urdir, then you know that I recently spent time at the Imperial Court. I tried to play by the political rules to strengthen my House, increase our holdings, and build a greater foundation for my heir. Instead, I witnessed appalling corruption, backstabbing. The Corrinos have ruled for ten thousand years. Jaxson made a compelling case that humanity would be better off if we were out from under that yoke."

Malina assessed the veracity of his words. "It is easy to become jaded, but less easy to embrace violence that wipes out an Imperial museum or countless bystanders near the palace. Such actions do not sound like Leto Atreides."

He shrugged. "I could list countless other moves made by Shaddam Corrino that do not sound like a benevolent Emperor either." A grimace crossed his face. "I want stability and peace—above all." His gray gaze bored into her. "And that is very much according to my own personality. Remember what I did with your son on Issimo III. He wanted to inflict pain and misery, but I convinced him to help instead. He has the drive to change the future. By allying with him, maybe I can guide him in a more humane direction. Then we all benefit."

She weighed the words, still not sure she believed them. "You might need help in doing so."

Leto was surprised. "Help from you? He respects you, Ur-Director—you know that full well. CHOAM's involvement changes the entire aspect of this rebellion."

"You are right, but I won't give up." She was cautious. Leto had chosen his words carefully, as had she. "These other radical nobles believe themselves to be catalysts, and they will cause great turmoil." She sighed. "But they are the soldiers we have. Perhaps they will succeed."

Leto drew a quick breath, as if he sensed something in her tone. "Do you disapprove of Jaxson's methods? You seem to support him."

Malina had run the calculus. Even before her Mentats delivered their assessment of the crippling damage her son would cause, she had made her plans. Jaxson, the black sheep, would have to be forfeit.

"Let me handle my son," she said. "Meanwhile, we will all work toward a stronger human civilization."

Every decision has the potential for honor and the potential for disgrace.
—Sardaukar teaching

Riding in the passenger seat of a small skimmer, Jessica glanced at Viscount Tull at the controls. One of Elegy's beautiful golden sunsets washed across the sky as he guided the craft over the rolling hills west of the estate lands. The engines were a quiet hum, and air whistled past them in their swift flight.

The unusual Tull aircraft had a partially transparent hull that let her see the internal workings, the retrograde clockwork machinery, with hydraulics to operate the struts and rudders.

"The visible machinery is not as complex as I would have expected," she mused aloud. "It is interesting, and looks antique."

"Our designers made it that way intentionally, but the components are modern. The craft looks disarmingly simple, even eccentric. My father once told me that old things are often best." He smiled wistfully. "Old things and old ways."

"There is wisdom in his words."

Giandro rapped his knuckles on the side wall. "This material is as strong as clearplaz, also manufactured from Elegy lichens, and we are expanding our exports around the Imperium."

She ran her fingers along the polished inner hull. "Marvelous. I knew the lichens were used to make exotic fabrics, but this structural material . . ."

His face was filled with pride. "Elegy has unparalleled soil and climate for versatile lichen species, and we have learned how to do remarkable things with them. House Tull exports recently expanded, thanks to our trade partnership with House Verdun." His expression quickly soured. "Shaddam Corrino and his paranoia ruined all that. And some of those poor refugees that just arrived . . ."

Jessica had her own opinion of Fausto Verdun. The surly Duke wasn't a particularly pleasant man, and had insulted House Atreides when he rebuffed Paul as a possible match for his eldest daughter. But Tull and Verdun did have many lucrative trade agreements . . . until the Emperor's Sardaukar leveled the Verdun holdings and massacred the Duke's entire family. Out of spite.

Leaving the sunset behind, they flew east into the deepening dusk. "I didn't bring you out here to talk Elegian technology. I'd like to show you something marvelous—and it'll make you understand many things."

He banked the aircraft up and over tree-covered hills, then swooped across open grasslands. Long shadows extended out in front of them. Jessica caught her breath as he quietly cruised above a scattered herd of animals. Horses—so many that she could not begin to count them, gracefully running beneath them. A pair of majestic stallions galloped in the lead, side by side.

Jessica leaned forward for a better view out the broad cockpit windowport. Giandro let out a long, appreciative sigh. The anger and hurt washed away from his expression. "These magnificent animals are the heart and soul of Elegy. For centuries, the precursors of our legendary thoroughbred bloodlines roamed these plains. My ancestors rode these wild animals, bred and raced them. They are unlike any other breed in the Imperium, the most precious prize of House Tull, and also my birthright. They belong here . . . not to be used as showpieces on some far-off planet."

"I've never seen more beautiful horses," Jessica said, and meant it. She remembered riding Tivvy out on the wooded path, though he had been somewhat intractable. These thundering animals, though, were wild, powerful, a force of nature.

Giandro appreciated the awe on her face. "Elegy does not have the depth or diversity of resources found on other noble worlds. For most of our history, this was an untamed planet, dotted with villages and rugged people who had the will to survive. Only in the past few centuries, with House Tull's increasing wealth from exports, have we risen in prominence as a Great House of the Landsraad. But we are still independent, and we value our prized horse bloodlines. They aren't just here for the taking."

She watched the herd of wild horses roll across the grassland, curving about as the aircraft hummed above them, as if in a silent dance. "Is that why you decided to support the rebellion? Because House Tull has an independent streak?" The question had troubled her, since he seemed quiet, not a vehement firebrand.

"I have my own reasons," he said.

She knew this was a recent development. The Sardaukar teams had scoured Elegy for any evidence of involvement, but had found none. She pressed, "Did the punishment of House Verdun provoke you?"

He looked at her with a bitter smile. "You mean the destruction of a strong business relationship? The loss of vast profits?" His eyes hardened. "The slaughter of my friend Duke Verdun, as well as his entire family? All innocents. Have you met any of the refugees yet?"

"I'm sorry," she whispered. "I understand how deep a wound that must have been."

Giandro circled above the magnificent horses that continued to run in the last glimmering of dusk. "But I am a member of the Landsraad in good standing. It takes an extraordinary catalyst to push a well-respected noble into actual rebellion against House Corrino."

"Then why did you do it?"

He let out a quick laugh as he changed course and headed back toward the hills. "Because I hate Emperor Shaddam."

His bluntness surprised her. "*Hate* is a very strong word."

"Indeed it is, but in this case, accurate." He looked wistfully through the transparent hull, toward the herd of horses in the gloaming. "It is a personal vendetta, and Shaddam doesn't even know—or care—the hurt he causes. Those horses, the perfect thoroughbred bloodline. House Tull has guarded the equine genetics for millennia. We are renowned throughout the Imperium, but we have never allowed them offworld, never run a race outside of Elegy. Everyone comes here. Those horses are . . . sacred to me and my family."

Jessica could not fathom what the thoroughbreds might have to do with the rebellion, or why the Viscount had so flagrantly turned against House Corrino.

"Emperor Shaddam fancied some Tull horses in his stables, for show, to impress others who might understand their value. He knows nothing about horses. And when my father refused to sell a stud, the Emperor found a way to take them for himself."

The nobleman's face was dark, burning with indignation. "I only learned about it recently. I don't know how—no doubt he sent poachers to capture them from the wild, just because he *wanted* them. Shaddam never rode the thoroughbreds, never showed them, just . . . kept them. Like a curio on a shelf. He intended to breed them, deliver Elegy mares and stallions—our horses!—as gifts to his noble cronies."

She remained silent for a long moment as he flew above the darkening landscape. "And that's what turned you against House Corrino?"

"That, and all those other things you pointed out." He let out a bitter chuckle. "I'm sure you expected some much more consequential political reasoning, but the provocation was sufficient in my mind. The Emperor took what was most precious to House Tull. I could not let that stand, and I could not let him give away our thoroughbreds on a whim, like handing candies to children."

Jessica felt a chill as she gripped a handrest on her passenger seat. "The horses in the Imperial stables. You said they were all poisoned."

"Swiftly, painlessly." He seemed disturbed to his core. "It was a tragic necessity to put them down, and for that, House Corrino must pay." He concentrated on flying, but continued to muse, "We used to race our stallions and mares in gala equestrian events watched around the galaxy. Our horses were undefeated against offworld breeds."

From what Jessica knew of Shaddam in his previous dealings with Leto, he was not a man who liked to be beaten. She was sickened by the Emperor's greed and what he had driven a gallant man like Giandro to do. "I know you must regret it."

By the control lights in the cockpit, she saw tears streaming down his face.

The aircraft outpaced the herd of horses beyond the plains to a large ranch complex. Guard towers surrounded a main house and outbuildings, along with military barracks, uniformed soldiers, and a landing field.

"We treat this as a game preserve," he explained. "And we must preserve the marvelous animals . . ."

He fell silent as he brought the flyer in to the landing field. She could tell he was haunted by what he'd been forced to do. The animals were, as he said, the heart and soul of Elegy.

All relationships contain an element of competition. Sometimes it is obvious, sometimes deeply buried.

—Bene Gesserit teaching

After departing from Castle Caladan on his excursion with Duncan, Paul worked the controls of an Atreides military flyer, taking them out over the long expanse of the great sea. Though this long-range craft was larger than the usual models he had trained on, he was comfortable in the pilot seat, soaring across clear, open skies. Though his outward demeanor was calm, he felt a rush of excitement for this training expedition, an adventure with Duncan Idaho.

The Swordmaster sat in the second seat, able to access and override with his own set of piloting controls, but he, too, was relaxed. They made excellent time heading south, flying over open water all day. This gave the young man an appreciation for the vast distances just on this one planet, which itself was merely a speck in the ocean of stars that formed the Imperium.

At first, he and Duncan talked at great length, discussing their upcoming jungle expedition, and when their casual conversation petered out, Paul mulled over the tedious but important business he had left behind in Thufir's hands. And he thought of his father out there on some other world, working among people who wanted to unravel the Emperor's rule. A chill went down his spine. . . .

By late afternoon, he spotted a blur on the horizon, which eventually resolved itself into a long, wave-washed shore and sandy beaches, with thick green jungles and high mountains beyond.

Duncan leaned back and pointed with his chin. "The Southern Continent, young Master. A great deal of wilderness here and not many inhabitants—it should be enough space to put you through rigorous training. We'll see if you can handle whatever I throw at you."

"I always have so far," Paul said. "And I'll throw it right back. Maybe you don't know what you're in for, Duncan Idaho."

The Swordmaster guffawed. "I accept the challenge. At least you didn't crash yet."

Paul cocked his eyebrows. "You know I'm a good pilot."

"True, but there's always a way for something to go wrong. Don't let your guard down." As if to reinforce the warning, a pocket of turbulence rocked the aircraft as Paul headed toward land.

"Prepare yourself, Duncan. I'll be hunting you, too."

The Swordmaster snorted good-naturedly. "Like a mouse hunting a lion."

"You would underestimate a mouse—that's what makes me dangerous."

Paul flew around the turbulence and banked west as the continent filled the horizon.

Duncan continued, "I'll give you a compliment, Paul. When I offered you this challenge, you didn't blink, didn't even take time to think about it. You just said yes."

Paul chuckled. The thrum of the articulated engines changed, louder and deeper as he shifted course and began to descend. "Did you expect me to ask questions like some ministry lawyer? Fine points and rules of a survival game? Did you want me to negotiate the terms of a primal hunt?"

"Oh, there are rules, young Master. Just run into the jungle and don't get caught—or killed. Unless you'd rather turn back now and climb into your safe, warm bed in the castle?"

"I'll rest after I complete your challenge." Paul scanned the uncharted lines of verdant hills that led to steeper mountains farther inland. He grew more serious. "I knew you were daring me, trying to push me to my limits. Asking questions would imply fear."

Duncan scratched his dark, wiry hair. "The good fighter, the good leader, is no stranger to fear. You need to manage it, and use it."

"Now you sound like my father!" The comment brought a moment of reserved silence.

The coastline below had white beaches scalloped with deep lagoons and dark, jagged reefs. This late in the afternoon, the lengthening shadows added a deeper green to the thick carpet of jungles inland. Silvery rivers wound through the trees, cutting deep gorges. Rising abruptly from the beaches, a ridge of tree-covered mountains was like a hunched green beast, and beyond that, another even higher mountain range with an enormous dominant peak.

He saw no roads, no large settlements, though he knew there were groups of Muadh followers who lived there. But he and Duncan would be far from civilization, relying on their own skills and resources. Paul wondered where they would land out here in this unmarked pristine wilderness.

"Cruise in gently," Duncan said. "I'll be glad to stretch my legs and use my muscles." He glanced at the young man beside him in the pilot seat. "And to hunt you down among the vines and bushes."

Paul laughed. "I'll use my mind as an exercise, too, and stay one step ahead of you." He tucked in the articulated wings and banked the engines. Along the coast, he saw dark reefs and lines of tide pools that looked like silvery mirrors reflecting the sky.

Something caught his eye. "What's that down there?" He cruised down just like when he had practiced flying over the fields in Caladan.

Clustered around the tide pools like herd beasts at a sunset watering hole, he saw dozens, maybe hundreds, of gray, fleshy shapes, smooth-winged creatures.

"Don't fly too low," Duncan warned. "Not with our wings retracted."

"We can switch on the suspensors if we need to," Paul said. "I just want to see what those creatures are. From one of Dr. Yueh's filmbooks, I recall seeing manta birds. They feed in the tide pools and are apparently common down here, but rarely studied."

"Never heard of manta birds," Duncan said.

Paul gave him a wry reaction. "Not surprising, because I don't think you've ever studied Caladan animal life."

"True enough."

As the ship flew low over the tide pools, the craft's shadow startled the numerous manta birds. In one unsettling wave, an entire flock of creatures burst up from the pools and rose into the air. They were similar to large manta rays he had seen when diving off the coast, but these creatures took to the air, their gray, rubbery wings like sails. They had long, thin tails like barbed stingers, and all along the smooth, wet surface of their wings, Paul saw a crackle of blue electricity.

The manta birds surged upward like a storm, and suddenly, they were all around the flyer. Paul grabbed the controls and pulled the aircraft higher, into a steep ascent, but the manta birds were almost as fast, and seemed terrified, swirling around.

One struck the hull, then three more, with fleshy, wet slaps. Another crashed across the cockpit windowport so that Paul couldn't see. He spun the aircraft in a corkscrew, heading inland and away from the waterline. The manta birds hammered the hull as the flyer careened through the entire flock.

Worse, his control panel sparked and flickered, then went dead. Tiny threads of blue lightning wrapped the aircraft like a cocoon, electrical discharges from the creatures. From his filmbook, he vaguely remembered the manta bird's defense mechanism. Now, linked together creature to creature, the sparks shorted out the vessel's systems.

Duncan was yelling, grabbing the secondary controls, but they were just as dead as Paul's. The Swordmaster flicked the comm, shouting, "This is Atreides flyer in distress, just inland on the Southern Continent! Our coordinates are—" Looking down in dismay, he saw that the entire board was dark and unresponsive.

Finally, like a wet rag blown off by the wind, the manta bird sloughed off the cockpit window and slid aside. Paul could suddenly see through a trail of milky slime that they were headed for the jungled ridge. He pulled the manual rudder controls and gained more altitude. The sputtering engines were barely responsive, but he did manage a burst of acceleration that carried them high enough to cross over the ridge. Then even those controls died, and Paul found himself flying inside an aerodynamic lump of metal.

Reaching the parabola of his unexpected jump, the aircraft began losing all the altitude they had gained. Duncan still worked the comm, but gave up. The two looked at each other for an instant, and the aircraft was an odd bubble of silence, just drifting . . . and falling toward the shadowy jungle below.

Below were steep valleys, thick jungles dotted by rock outcroppings. Ahead sprawled the slopes of the main mountain covered with jungles as well as a few intermittent clearings. Paul fixed on the open areas, places with a smattering of volcanic rocks, but at least without trees and vines.

Duncan became the teacher again, calm and reassuring. "This aircraft is now a glider, Paul, and we have to treat it as such. The retracted wings—you need to extend them so we can fly farther. Maybe with a manual rudder, we can maneuver enough to find a place to land."

"Crash, you mean," Paul said, not as a joke.

"Let's hope not." Duncan continued to try the secondary controls, with no luck.

Paul tried to use the wing-extension controls, but they were nonfunctional. Duncan operated the manual switch. "We'll have to crank them out ourselves." He briskly turned a lever, spinning it as fast as he could, and Paul did the same. He could feel the control being reasserted, at least a little.

The wings stretched out, and their aircraft glided onward, miraculously still aloft. He gazed forward, saw the slope, and openings in the tree cover. "There's got to be a place, Duncan," he said.

The Swordmaster nodded.

Paul held the rudder, turned the mechanical pulleys, and guided them so that they drifted down, still in eerie silence. He pulled up on the ailerons, but they were sluggish. The mountainside was right in front of them.

"Duncan, I—"

"Just land this thing, boy. Talk later."

Paul put his entire mind into each fraction of a second, and then the lower hull was grinding on the tall grasses, the scattered bushes. With a crunch and a grind, they scraped over a rough boulder, and then the aircraft was on the smooth meadow again, slewing left and right until they ground to a terrifying, exhausting halt.

Paul didn't move for several seconds after they had come to a rest. When he turned to look at his companion, both of them were wide-eyed, speechless. Paul broke the silence, but his voice was hoarse. "Well? Aren't you going to compliment me on such a good landing?"

The other man snorted. "Without that landing, Paul, I wouldn't be saying a word to anyone. We survived, and you showed some skill, but you flew too low in the first place, not heeding my warning."

The pair climbed out, battered and tense, then looked around as night began to fall. "Not exactly the way I wanted to start this adventure," Duncan said, "but we're intact and we have our supplies." He walked around the creaking, damaged flyer. "There are some spare components in the supply bin. I doubt it'll be enough to fix the entire aircraft, but maybe we can jump-start the comms, let Thufir Hawat know what happened so he can send in a rescue party."

Exhilarated after what they had just survived, Paul turned around and peered into the darkening jungle. "We planned to be here for a week. What's your hurry, Duncan? There's still a locator on the aircraft. Thufir worries enough that if he doesn't hear from us at the precise end of the time, he'll send in an entire force—you know it as well as I."

With an abashed smile, Duncan nodded.

"Then let's reassess what we have," Paul said. "We'll get some sleep, and in the morning, we have training to do."

Even our everyday activities are fraught with hidden consequences and political repercussions. No action is simply what it seems. We have become such political animals that we have forgotten how to be merely human.

—DUKE LETO ATREIDES, letters to his son

Even after he left the hidden base on Nossus, Leto did not feel safe. As far as he could tell, none of the other radicals suspected his true loyalties—certainly not Jaxson himself—but he continued to play a part that went fundamentally against his nature. Nevertheless, he was duty-bound to continue his charade.

Though he longed to go home, he made his way to another dangerous place—Cuarte and the holdings of Lord Rajiv Londine.

When he initially agreed to meet the rebel leader, Leto had known he was entering a pit of vipers. Lord Londine's planet was just another such trap. In his heart, he wanted only to rule the people of Caladan and mentor his son to become a leader. But Paul was already well-trained, with a solid moral core and a broad perspective. He would make a fine Duke someday.

But Leto had to make sure the Imperium existed for future generations of Atreides. He was committed to seeing this plan through, to bring down terrorists who had little care for the swath of bloodshed they left in the wake of their grand gestures. By now, having received the message from Gurney, Emperor Shaddam must be counting on him.

The CHOAM Ur-Director had remained on Nossus only briefly to exchange information and learn details of her son's plans. Leto still couldn't fathom the disturbing private conversation he had had with her. Was she trying to trap him? Or was she implying that their interests might be aligned, and not the same as her son's? That she had her own doubts about Jaxson? Not long after Malina Aru's departure, he and Jaxson had also left on separate routes, separate missions.

But his straightforward plan to put an end to this had now become vastly more complicated with the knowledge of Jaxson's secret cache of devastating data. Leto could no longer simply send a new communiqué to Kaitain and let Imperial justice run its course. He needed to find a different way. And for that, he was forced to continue his role at least for a little while longer.

After transferring twice at hub worlds, Leto at last reached the planet Cuarte. Because of the colorful fire gardens scattered around the capital area, Londine's pleasant homeworld received frequent visitors, including tourists, merchants, and trade representatives. Leto easily fit in, unnoticed among the others on the shuttle traveling to the surface. He had, however, informed Rajiv Londine of his imminent arrival.

For obvious reasons, this meeting would have to be discreet. Londine was an outspoken critic of the Corrino regime, and Leto could have no close public associations with the man. Now that he knew the nobleman's connection with the rebel movement—not just a critic and a malcontent, but willing to endorse actual bloodshed and destruction—Leto needed to be even more cautious.

On the other hand, until he could find a way to strip Jaxson of his dangerous memory stone and the data it contained, he had to pretend that he genuinely wanted an alliance, and might even be interested in Vikka Londine. This visit was supposedly for the purpose of courting her, and that would be the hardest part.

Even though Jessica was gone.

Under normal circumstances, with cold analysis, Vikka might have been an acceptable marriage candidate for the Duke of Caladan. He had spent a pleasant evening with her, arranged by Count Fenring himself. Did she even know about her father's violent tendencies?

But his heart was still wounded after so many years in a close relationship with a woman he thought loved him, and he could never forget how the Bene Gesserit had summarily annulled Jessica's contract as his bound concubine. The recorded image with her standing so close to Viscount Tull was burned into his brain. Clearly, Jessica had accepted a new assignment that had nothing to do with him, and she played her role just as well.

Except Leto now knew that Giandro Tull had also joined the movement to destroy the Imperium. If Leto exposed the identities of the radical rebels, would he be placing Jessica herself in terrible danger from Shaddam's wrath? He could not glibly brush it aside with the rationalization that she had made her own choices. . . .

Having withdrawn into himself on the hard seat of the passenger shuttle, he clenched his right hand into a fist, channeled his anger and confusion. He felt his muscles tighten, his fingers ache, and finally, he let the tension bleed off. He exhaled a long sigh and prepared himself as the shuttle landed.

Disembarking with the other travelers, he looked across the crowd at the reception area and recognized the gruff and long-faced Rodundi, who served as House Londine's chief administrator. Their eyes met, and Rodundi gave him a brisk nod. Together, they worked their way out of the spaceport crowds. It was midmorning, beneath a gray sky.

The chief administrator did not speak until they were well out of anyone else's earshot. "Lord Londine was expecting you, Leto Atreides." He sniffed. "Frankly, I am surprised you came."

Leto studied the chief administrator, trying to identify why the man always seemed a trifle distant. "I've learned to adapt to various possibilities." He tried to sound noncommittal. "I would be happy to see Vikka Londine again. I enjoyed her company."

Rodundi's face tightened. "We both know that you have other reasons to be here as well."

Leto remained aloof. "Yes, I have other reasons. As far as the public is concerned, I've long deflected the pressure to formally marry, but now, as you say, much has changed."

Rodundi accepted the explanation. "Follow me to the main house, sir."

The large estate covered a hill overlooking the main city. Rajiv Londine emerged from the open double doors and greeted Leto with arms spread magnanimously. At his side, his daughter smiled, genuinely happy to see Leto. Leading him into the foyer of the large manor house, Lord Londine sounded gracious. "I know you must miss Caladan, my good friend, but I am honored you came here to Cuarte, to mend fences and . . . pursue other matters." He glanced at Vikka.

"I'm glad to learn that I didn't offend you somehow, Leto." She arched her brow. "At first, I was confused and hurt by your abrupt departure from Kaitain and your silence. I thought we'd gotten along well."

The older nobleman said in a mollifying voice, "I explained to my daughter the horrible thing that Count Fenring requested of you. You should marry her just to spite that man." His tone was not entirely joking, and Vikka shot her father a quick glare.

Leto took a moment to consider his response. "That is never an appropriate reason to agree to a marriage. And Emperor Shaddam will no doubt cause difficulties. He wants you humiliated and ruined at all costs."

Londine raised his voice. "All the more reason to get rid of the corrupt fool."

Leto tensed, seeing many household staff members that had moved to within earshot. With Lord Londine's constant criticisms, Shaddam would certainly have planted spies on Cuarte. Nevertheless, the man's bluster did not fade. "I've written a fresh polemic, which I will deliver to the Landsraad assembly next time I speak. By now, I should have exhausted my criticisms of House Corrino, yet more and more failures and corruption come to light!"

Vikka let out an exasperated sigh. "Leto only just arrived, Father. Let's worry about business later. Rodundi can show him to his chambers, so he can freshen up."

The nobleman relented. "So long as you take Leto on a private tour of our fire gardens after dark. It would be a crime for him to visit Cuarte and not see our main attraction."

She turned her warm smile toward Leto and said teasingly, "I thought I was the main attraction."

For the next few hours, Leto rested and refreshed himself, but by afternoon, he decided to join Rajiv Londine for a planetary council meeting. He politely listened as representatives discussed local matters, during which the nobleman found ample opportunities to make barbed comments about the Corrinos. Although he wanted to keep a low profile, Leto was applauded when Londine insisted that the Duke of Caladan shared his opinions. Maintaining the charade, Leto accepted that portrayal, even though word of it would surely make its way back to the Imperial Court. Fortunately, Gurney's message would have explained everything to Shaddam. . . .

After the meeting, Chief Administrator Rodundi helped the lord edit the inflammatory speech he intended to give to the Landsraad. To Leto, the address seemed the same as all the prior invectives, but now that he knew the man truly meant to overthrow the throne, the words sounded different.

Following a fine evening meal, Vikka met him just after full darkness fell. She was dressed in intensely colorful skirts, a blouse, and a wrap over her shoulders. "You've come all this way. Follow me, and I'll show you something special." She offered him her arm and led him out of the manor house.

The night skies of Cuarte shone with two small moons and many stars. He and Vikka walked into the estate gardens, where walled-off areas enclosed small volcanic outlets. Steam whistled up through the openings, and Leto could smell sulfur in the air. All vegetation in the vicinity had died.

When he asked what to look for, Vikka said, "Just watch. It won't be long. The fire gardens make unpredictable showers and displays."

The nearest steam geyser suddenly sparkled and foamed with colorful glimmers like fireflies that sprayed upward. Vikka laughed in delight. "There are chemical powders underneath the ground and reactants in the air."

Four more colorful fountains spurted with spangles of green, orange, and pink. In a rhythm, one shower would die down as another shot even higher into the air.

Vikka continued, "Tourists come from across the Imperium. We locals have gotten used to the sight, but we never forget how lovely they are, never take them for granted."

Leto watched another colorful shower. The chemical tang in the air grew even more acrid. "I am impressed."

She gestured to the lights of the main city below, where a central park crowded with spectators hosted a much more spectacular display. "It's a great commercial boon for House Londine."

Huge colorful fireworks rocketed upward in the middle of the grand park. Even from the distance, Leto could hear the cheers of the milling crowds.

The Atreides Duke considered how quiet, bucolic Caladan would change if hordes of outside visitors arrived. In a way, he was glad that his homeworld didn't draw such attention.

Vikka continued, "Of course, Cuarte has many other commercial activities. My father was beginning to invest in your own moonfish industry. It's a shame that avenue has been ruined—for both of our Houses."

Anger burned inside him. "That was a treacherous attack by House Harkonnen, an unprovoked declaration of war between our families. But Emperor Shaddam refused to intercede. He simply laughed and called it a little squabble."

Vikka tightened her grip on his arm. "Imperial bastards. Together, our families will make a difference." She looked at him. "Together, Leto, *you and I* will make a difference."

But as beautiful Vikka Londine stood close to him, he couldn't stop thinking of Jessica with Viscount Tull. He had watched the recorded message twice, even kept a copy of it. Since leaving Caladan, Leto had tried to wall off his heart and his thoughts, but knew he was only pretending to himself. He was forced to accept that the situation had changed, though he did not understand why Jessica had done what she did.

Was he such a poor judge of human character? Even if Jessica had been coerced by the Bene Gesserit, even if they had assigned her as concubine to another House, she was still the mother of his son. Paul was the heir of Caladan, and Leto would never change that.

Vikka let out a sigh. "You are so unlike Clarton, my husband—I'm glad to be rid of him . . . though it took some doing."

Leto was instantly alert. "What do you mean?"

"I thought I'd told you about him during our dinner conversation at the palace? He was abusive, insulting." Her expression darkened with a frown. "He beat me with his words and dark moods, though he never left a mark on me that my father could see. Clarton was the oldest son of a powerful House Minor on Cuarte, and at first, we seemed a perfect match, but the marriage grew worse and worse over the years." She looked away. "And now Clarton's gone. Thanks to Jaxson Aru and his grand gesture on Otorio."

Leto felt a chill. "I know your husband died in the explosion there. I barely got away myself."

Vikka flushed. "Oh, Jaxson did not target you personally. At the time, we didn't know you might join our movement." She kept walking. "My father was aware of what Jaxson planned on Otorio. House Londine was invited to attend the gala, and so we sent my husband as our representative. And by sacrificing him there, we removed any suspicion that House Londine might be involved in the rebellion. It also conveniently took care of that cruel man."

She drew close to Leto again, touching his arm. Another gush of sparkling golden embers flew up into the air from a nearby vent. "Now I'm here with you."

Leto hid his reaction as he considered what this woman had done. Not only had she known about Jaxson's planned massacre in advance and done nothing to warn the people, she had used it to arrange her husband's death by sending him there to become yet another victim. Now she seemed pleased about it. He tried to imagine whether Jessica could ever employ such devious tactics to achieve her aim.

He would not have believed it of Jessica before. She'd always been so close to his heart, but after she abandoned him and their son, showing her true loyalty to the Sisterhood instead of him and quickly falling into the arms of another nobleman, Duke Leto Atreides no longer knew what to believe.

One must learn to discern the difference between an opportunity and a threat.

—BARON VLADIMIR HARKONNEN, Giedi Prime archives

B ack in the dry, heat-addled air, Baron Harkonnen settled into his Carthag headquarters, trying to distract himself with comforts. His recent visits to Giedi Prime and the more rustic Lankiveil only illuminated the starkness of this desert planet. But the power, wealth, and influence that melange brought to House Harkonnen mitigated all inconveniences.

At other times, a massage, a bath, or a skilled pleasure worker would be enough to set him at ease, but suspicious thoughts roiled in his mind. Now that he was back on Arrakis, the danger seemed sharper, clearer. That damnable Fenring and his eccentric Mentat kept digging into the wrecked Orgiz operations, still investigating, like a child worrying a loose tooth. Sooner or later, someone would yank it out—and draw blood.

Had he successfully thrown them off the scent by suggesting that rebel terrorists were behind the black-market spice? His ingenious ruse had intrigued the Count, but his investigations would reveal nothing. Then Grix Dardik's mental searchlight would swing back in the Baron's direction.

When he received a message smuggled in with a food shipment, the Baron didn't know whether to be intrigued or dubious. A little bit of both, he decided. "Dear Baron, I have confidential information about Noble Commonwealth smuggling operations on Arrakis. Meet me, alone and in person, and I will give you vital intelligence. You'll find it most valuable."

The unsigned message provided specific details on the meeting time and place. The Baron read the spice-paper note several times, considering possibilities, options. Then he summoned Rabban, who had also returned from Lankiveil, and gave him a special task.

Having come from his entertaining torture session with Gurney Halleck, and then turning that work over to Piter de Vries, Rabban was enthusiastic for another assignment. The Baron's nephew had been smug as well as obsequious ever since he'd wiped out the Orgiz site, but he overestimated how much confidence the Baron now placed in him.

Standing in the main office, Rabban read the covert message his uncle handed to him. The furrow lines in his brow resembled gullies between sand dunes. "I don't understand this. The Orgiz operations were never run by the rebels."

"I know that—so this spy is either bluffing or lying," the Baron said. "Or perhaps he does possess information that we need to know. Go to the rendezvous and seize him so we can conduct a thorough interrogation. You are good at that."

Rabban grinned. "Yes, Uncle."

"Don't seriously harm the man until we know what he's about. He may be a spy, or just a charlatan."

A flicker of disappointment rolled across the blunt features, but his nephew departed with a determined look on his face.

Two days later, after the appointed meeting time, the Baron sat in his office reviewing spice exports and productivity reports, but paying little attention to the numbers as he waited. Hearing a loud commotion in the hall, he sat up, ready. Grunting, Rabban pushed a dirty desert rat ahead of him through the door. Adjusting his suspensor belt, the Baron raised himself from behind his black ovoid desk.

The desert man's drab robes had seen better days, but they covered a well-maintained stillsuit. His face was lean and leathery from a lifetime of scant moisture, and his sparse beard was encrusted with dust. The man's dark eyes were deep blue from spice addiction.

Rabban shoved him forward like a puppet master guiding a toy. The captive blurted out, "Why have you seized me? You do not know who I am."

"That's what we intend to determine." The Baron tapped his pudgy fingertips together. "What is your involvement with the Noble Commonwealth? Tell us about the illicit spice operations." He couldn't begin to imagine what answer the prisoner might offer, since he already knew the answers.

The dusty man's expression contorted into a scowl. "I've heard of this silly rebellion against your foolish Imperium, but I am content with my desert. I am a Fremen."

Rabban pushed the man's head down just to demonstrate his superior strength. "Show the proper respect."

The Baron said, "You sent us the secret message, set up the rendezvous."

"I sent no message." The Fremen raised his chin. "I was paid to arrive at a certain time and place, where I should expect to see Harkonnens. I was warned you might capture me, and thus I have another message to pass along."

"What message?" the Baron asked. And he wondered, was this a trick, a trap? "Explain yourself."

The desert man's nostrils narrowed. "I was told to scold you for failing to follow instructions. You will have only one more chance. Next time, come in person, Baron Harkonnen. If you fail this second test, you will never hear from my employer again. Instead, he will sell his information to Emperor Shaddam."

The Baron felt a flush of heat in his cheeks at the thought of Shaddam learning what was happening here. "Very well, we will play by his rules. Rabban, hold this man in a Carthag isolation cell until our meeting is successful."

The Fremen struggled, expressing his outrage. The Baron decided he just might forget to release the man, no matter what happened. . . .

❧

ON THE APPOINTED day, the Baron's small convoy passed through the Carthag streets with no fanfare. Following the mysterious contact's instructions, he had chosen only Rabban and one deadly bodyguard to accompany him, a Burseg named Treyson. The two were armed with blades and cudgels, while the Baron carried hidden needle guns and poison pellets in case the stranger wore no personal shield, as few desert people did.

The winding route took their darkened groundcar through slums of ramshackle desert-hardened dwellings, and then a district of warehouses and mechanic shops. Spice-harvesting machinery was in constant need of repair, refurbishment, or decommissioning. The premature decommissioning of functional equipment, which was then repurposed for his secret operations, had been the core of the Baron's scheme to provide a back channel of melange to Malina Aru.

They arrived on time at the designated rendezvous, a parts warehouse crowded with machinery but few people. Earlier, the Baron's people had swept the building, finding it clean of traps or surveillance. He had considered stationing a contingent of spotters, snipers, and emergency security forces in the vicinity, but his curiosity outweighed caution. Perhaps the mysterious contact truly did hold valuable information that the Baron could use against Fenring. He decided to take the risk.

Emerging from the groundcar, he stood in a dark uniform and a purple-lined cape. He touched the dagger at his hip, checked his hidden weapons. Rabban and the bodyguard flanked him, gazing into the cavernous warehouse. Buoyed by the suspensor belt, the Baron's feet barely touched the ground as he moved forward. In an emergency, he could simply spring backward through the air and leave his two companions behind.

Inside the shadowy warehouse, the dry air smelled of oil and dust. As his eyes adjusted from the harsh glare outside, the Baron saw rows of shelves stacked many meters high with plasteel crates marked with serial numbers. Heavy machinery, engines, pumps, and centrifuges were wrapped in polymer film to keep out the desert dust.

The silence and dim, oppressive light weighed down on them. Rabban paced back and forth, grumbling. Burseg Treyson stood as if his feet were attached to the floor, swiveling slowly to scan for threats.

Impatient, the Baron called into the shadows, "I am here. Show yourself."

Three figures emerged from a row of enormous vehicle treads large enough to crush a building. Two were dusty, nondescript desert men with hoods, ragged cloaks, and nose filters fitted into their nostrils, while the third man wore clean and well-maintained robes. His stillsuit looked like an affectation. His hair was neat, his beard trimmed, and he wore a distinctive iron-gray earring in one lobe.

The Baron directed his gaze at the central man, obviously the leader. The other two desert men wore similar earrings.

"I'm pleased to meet you, Baron Harkonnen," the leader said. "And even more pleased that you followed instructions this time. Our discussion is the start of a profitable relationship."

The Baron did not move closer. "You know my name. What is yours?"

"Everyone knows your name." The leader's lips curved in a hard smile. "And very few know mine. We will keep it that way for the time being. First, however, we must check you for any signs of treachery." He glanced at Rabban and Treyson. "Separate these three and search them."

"You will not," Rabban growled. Treyson placed a hand on his weapon.

"Then you may search us, too, for mutual reassurance. You may wear your shields, and we have none. One person for one person. Are you not confident that your men are a match for me and my companions?" the leader added, tossing his clean desert cape over his shoulder. "Glossu Rabban, come with me over there, and you may personally search me." He gestured to his dusty bodyguards. "You, take the Burseg, and you," he said to the other desert rat, "check the Baron. Just a scan, no need to touch his physical person. We all want to have faith that we are safe."

Instead of arguing, the Baron was more curious to know this man's game, what knowledge he actually possessed about the spice smuggling. Was he just guessing? Or had he learned a dangerous detail? If he did know something, all three of these men would likely need to be eliminated. Either way, the Baron needed to know. Impatient, he said, "We will be close enough, Rabban. I can destroy this worm myself if he attempts anything." He had killed many men before.

On edge, he followed one of the dusty desert guards to a dim side passage where they would have privacy. The Baron glanced back at the offworld leader who'd moved away with Rabban. He hoped his nephew did nothing stupid—but that was always a possibility.

The Baron was ready to kill this man if he made an unexpected move, but when he looked at the desert guard, he finally noticed his face. Unlike the others, he was clean-shaven, his hair dark and curly like dense smoke. His cheeks were rounder and paler than most desert men's, softer. That was odd. Though the guard averted his gaze, he didn't have the solicitous demeanor of an underling. In fact, his eyes were intense, arrogant . . . and they were not the solid blue-within-blue of a lifetime resident on Arrakis.

"At last we have a chance to talk, Baron Harkonnen, my friend. I apologize for the convolutions in meeting you here, but you will understand the need for caution."

The Baron reached toward his hidden needle guns. His body shield was at full strength. "Who are you?"

The man laughed, spread his hands to emphasize his vulnerability. "Oh, you wouldn't recognize my features, not anymore, but the two of us have much in common, goals aligned."

"Who are you?" the Baron demanded again.

"Why, I am Jaxson Aru—I believe you've heard of me." It was not a question.

A cold wave swept through the Baron, and he instinctively backed away. Few names conjured such automatic hatred. He squinted, studied the features. Yes . . . it could be.

The man smiled. "Now that we have a chance for frank conversation, let me describe the aspirations of the Noble Commonwealth and how we can benefit House Harkonnen. Remember that every rebellion is perceived to be a violent, bloodthirsty movement—until they win, and then history views them as heroic freedom fighters."

The Baron sputtered. "Emperor Shaddam would have me eviscerated in public if he knew I had spoken with you."

A razor-sharp laugh. "Then don't let him find out. You're good at keeping secrets from the Emperor, Baron." He let the tantalizing comment hang in the air.

"I have no interest in your movement," the Baron said. "What do you want from me?" He was intrigued, though, and he played along. "You claim you were running the spice operations at the Orgiz refinery? A secret channel for producing and selling melange?" He snorted. "That's an ingenious way to fund terrorist activities."

Looking far more relaxed than he should have been, Jaxson made a dismissive gesture. "Oh, we had nothing to do with the Orgiz operations, as I suspect you know, but it is a charming and intriguing idea, one worth pursuing. Let me plant a seed, my friend. Most seeds in the desert never take root, but sometimes under the right circumstance and with an appropriate sprinkle of rain, they can bloom into something beautiful and strong."

"I have no patience for metaphors," the Baron said. "And we have no time for chitchat."

Jaxson agreed. "My followers are well-funded, with various sources of money to keep our operations going. But we can always use more—much more. You can offer us that opportunity, and it will give you a place in the upper echelon of a new independent commonwealth once we have overthrown the Corrino Imperium."

"Once all the stars burn out and the universe dies," the Baron scoffed.

Jaxson took no insult. "Oh, I believe we will succeed sooner than that. We've already made tremendous inroads. In spite of the recent rumors you have heard, the rebellion has no operations on Arrakis—yet." He raised his eyebrows, leaned closer. "Yet. However, that could change. What if I were to purchase and provide any additional equipment you need—off-books spice crews, harvesters, carryalls? At no cost to House Harkonnen. In exchange, Baron, you would provide me with significant supplies of spice, while you keep the rest for yourself." He smiled. "The Noble Commonwealth receives a valuable commodity, and you receive a large profit, of which the Emperor knows nothing. Keep your hands clean and your coffers full."

The Baron's thoughts spun. The opportunity was much like what he had already arranged with CHOAM, indeed a way for him to play both sides—and with the son of the Ur-Director. But he could not let himself look too eager. "And why should I be interested in your rebellion? My position is already powerful, overseeing one of the most valuable siridar-fiefs in the Imperium. House Harkonnen has run spice operations on Arrakis for eight decades. Why would I jeopardize that?"

Jaxson shrugged again. "In the short term, for immense wealth and profits! And in the long term, if the rebellion achieves its aim of creating a consortium of independent commercial worlds—planets that are not under the Corrino thumb—imagine how much more wealth House Harkonnen would have. You would be one of the most powerful men in the new commonwealth. You could even call yourself Emperor if you like."

Unaware of this private conversation, Rabban bellowed from the next row over, "Uncle, he is clean! Come and speak with us."

The Baron lowered his voice to the rebel leader. "I must consider this."

"Right now, I need spice, my friend—and a large shipment of it, as a gesture of your genuine interest. Otherwise, you are of no use to me after all. And please don't insult my intelligence by suggesting that you don't have your own hidden stockpiles. Through my private channels, I would sell it—I do still have CHOAM connections."

The Baron thrust out his lower lip as he considered. This possibility would not expose him as much as his direct black-market channel with Malina Aru. If caught, he could always blame the rebels, cite blackmail. He hardened his voice. "I will look at my . . . possible spice surplus and see what I can do. How do I contact you?"

Grinning, the man handed him a compact shigawire spool. "This contains instructions. I'll be glad to have you as a partner."

"Uncle!" Rabban sounded concerned now.

"I have agreed to nothing," the Baron warned.

"Of course not. We will simply test out this relationship." He spread his hands.

"Uncle!" Rabban shouted again.

The Baron no longer felt light on his feet, despite the suspensor belt. He shouted back to his nephew, "We are done here! Tell Burseg Treyson we are ready to go!"

When he turned, he saw that Jaxson Aru had disappeared somewhere among the alcoves of stored equipment.

I know I'm in a torture chamber, but it doesn't look like one.

This torture was on the inside, and no matter where his mind was, Gurney Halleck existed in a dark place on Lankiveil. That was part of the routine, but he refused to let it affect him.

The Orange Catholic Bible said what he needed to know. *Believe not the evidence of thy senses when thy soul knoweth otherwise.*

After Rabban and the Baron had departed for Arrakis, the new tormentor had arrived. The twisted Mentat gloated over him, using tricks far subtler than the Beast's brute force, playing with Gurney's mind to increase his suffering. Piter de Vries used drugs, sonics, and powerful methods of suggestion to make Gurney see something entirely different from the underlying reality.

Relishing the process, taking his time, the Mentat conducted a series of intense interrogation sessions, one after the other, trying to peel away layers and layers of intelligence about House Atreides. The loyal retainer resisted and endured, and in the back of his mind, it seemed to him that de Vries and his assistants were not really trying to get important information out of him. They had already found the Duke's message to Emperor Shaddam. Now, the twisted Mentat was just playing, indulging his perversions. . . .

Piter de Vries went about his pro forma duties, making his subject suffer for the sake of suffering. They forced him to relive the most terrible moments in his life, many of which Rabban himself had orchestrated—how the Beast had murdered Gurney's parents in front of him because he'd dared to sing songs that mocked Baron Harkonnen. What Rabban had done to Gurney's sister Bheth was far worse, abducting her, assigning her to brutal pleasure houses for Harkonnen troops. When Gurney had tried to rescue her, the Beast had forced him to watch in the slave pits as he raped and strangled her to death right in front of him.

In the many years he had served House Atreides after escaping from Giedi Prime, Gurney had not forgotten a moment of it, but he built up walls and buried that pain deep beneath scars. Rabban's recent torture sessions had resurrected those experiences, and now Piter de Vries flayed them raw.

But that still wasn't enough to break Gurney Halleck.

In a tempest of evil, we stand as firm as the tallest tree, he thought, quoting another of his favorite verses.

So the twisted Mentat resorted to hallucinations and nightmares, which were not worse than the real memories, but they could be manipulated to inflict confusion as well as pain.

Next, Gurney experienced the vivid horror of feeling his living brain being carved out of his own head, followed by the slow removal of his internal organs—intestines, liver, kidneys—and then the gouging out of his eyes. It seemed absolutely real, and when he tried to fall off the precipice into death . . . he woke from the drug slurry to find himself intact.

And Piter de Vries did it all over again.

Now the demented Mentat and his assistants were doing something to his hands and fingers, crushing his joints and making his knuckles swell. The pressure and pain were unbearable . . . yet Gurney refused to cry out, telling himself it was all in his mind.

Abruptly, the drugs and implanted suggestions splashed images of paradise across his vision, an escape to a calm oceanside, flower beds on the cliffs of Caladan . . . while at the same time inflicting terrible pain on his already-swollen fingers. But the only thing his mind was allowed to see was the beautiful Atreides world, while he physically experienced solely agony.

His fingers were broken and his hand crushed, yet his ears heard only pleasant baliset music, reinforcing the thought that he might never play his beloved instrument again. The excruciating pain!

His only relief lay in the paradise vision of Caladan, and now the image changed to a mountain meadow filled with flowers. His torturer wanted to weave, contort, and link the sensations, but Gurney clung to the serenity, drawing strength for its own sake without succumbing to the despair tied to it. He thought of the meadow as a place where he could strum his baliset, compose and sing a love song.

A lifetime ago, he had been in love with a beautiful young woman with dark brown hair and coppery skin. Both of them had been mere teenagers, and she'd said that she loved him, too. Her name drifted out of reach until it bloomed in his mind, like one of the meadow flowers.

Mimija.

How had it all ended? He could not recall, but since his songs were mostly ballads, he supposed that the story was a sad one. If Rabban had found her, he would have killed her. Did Mimija's life end in pain and misery, which the Harkonnens did so well?

Was she even real?

But a trickle of additional memories told him that Mimija had simply left the lovestruck Gurney, saying her feelings belonged to someone else and letting him suffer through his own heartbreak. So long ago . . . so trivial compared to all the other tortures, but agonizing in its own way.

The twisted Mentat had found the memory deep in his subconscious and rubbed salt into his wounds.

Now, in the mocking flower-filled meadow, Mimija strolled toward him, stirring up butterflies. The flowers rose up to her knees, but her skirts swished through them as she approached.

No! They are doing this to me!

Not willing to give his torturer the satisfaction, he struggled to escape what he was seeing, although his bruised and drugged heart wanted to be with her. Summoning all of his will, he erased the meadow and her image from his mind. But though she faded, she came back moments later with even sharper clarity and more intense colors. Mimija called out his name, but her mouth contorted cruelly, and she spoke in the familiar, menacing voice of de Vries. "I am killing you cell by cell, Gurney Halleck, melting you with each passing moment. You are dying."

Gurney couldn't close his inner eyes, but he slammed shut his mind, and the cruel voice began to fade, and moment by moment, so did the image of the beautiful young woman. Her mouth struggled with the vile words—as if she were possessed—until her voice became faint and incoherent. The meadow darkened in his mind, leaving only Mimija's image floating in the void, and then she also vanished.

He felt no relief, just the intensity of the physical pain in his smashed hand. His bones had been splintered, pulverized.

A mocking new image came to his mind, along with his own voice. He saw himself holding his baliset, trying to strum the strings with crushed, bleeding fingers. The only music that emerged was his scream of pain, no matter how hard he tried to suppress it. But he kept attempting to play the instrument, and each pass across the strings shot lances of pain through his entire body.

But the music in his memory, real music, gave him an anchor, and by humming desperately to himself, he could weaken the disturbing image. He no longer saw his damaged hand, only shadowy darkness that was empty and without hope. He kept moving his fingers, trying to play the baliset, but the sounds were all in his head.

Gradually, however, he was figuring out how to concentrate and block. He had pushed away the specter of Mimija, and he succeeded in drowning out the horrific bloody music. He made the imaginary vision dissipate, leaving him with dull, numbed darkness. He didn't see, feel, or hear anything.

Was he dead, then? He could not tell.

But Gurney still had his secret about his desperate message to the sparse spy-eyes scattered nearby on Lankiveil. No one knew about the tiny, passive devices he and Duncan had planted. If the spy-eyes functioned, they would have transmitted their data to other pickups, piggybacked on vessels leaving Lankiveil, onto Guild Heighliners, and then to other ships in the vast cargo holds . . . and those ships would transmit to other ships, and soon enough the word would trickle back to Caladan.

If Gurney managed to survive that long.

The answer to his salvation eluded him, like a fragment of data that Piter de Vries dangled enticingly on the edges of his awareness. But he clung to the slenderest thread of hope that he might get through this . . . and someday exact a terrible revenge on the Harkonnens.

Who is the hunter, and who the hunted? Even when the answer seems most obvious, sometimes it is not.

—Anonymous, from Old Earth

After a restless night surrounded by a cacophony of jungle birds and insects, Paul managed to get some sleep in the shelter of the damaged aircraft. With the first light of dawn, he rose, stretched, and found that Duncan was already inspecting the engines, the hull, the comm.

The Swordmaster leaned out of the cockpit, shaking his head. "The power surge from those manta birds wiped out our comm, and I don't see that we have the replacement boards to fix it."

"We can't contact Castle Caladan?" Paul frowned. "Isn't the locator beacon intact at least?"

"I think so. It's supposed to be autonomous. Hawat can find us when he decides to send a rescue crew, but we planned to be here a week. We wanted to be on our own." He moved around to the rear, then looked under the wing to one of the engine housings. "We do have some spare parts for the engines, and we might be able to patch it up enough to get airborne."

Paul nodded, but couldn't keep the disappointment from his face. "So we spend today making repairs?" On the slope, strong gusts of wind played around them, whipping his dark hair into wild tangles.

Duncan scoffed. "We have other things to do during the best of the day. I suggest we spend the evening working together to fix the engines, just in case. Meanwhile, though . . ." He gestured with his chin to the thick jungle on the mountainside, the outcroppings, the gorges with trickling streams. "We can spend our time hunting in the jungle . . . me hunting you."

"And me hunting you! That's why we came here."

Duncan reached into the cockpit behind the seat and grabbed a survival pack, which he tossed to Paul. The young man rummaged around inside and found a variety of clamps, grippers, cords, and other hardware. "Where are my weapons?"

"Just tools. You can improvise your own weapons from the jungle. No personal shields, no modern conveniences." On Paul's look of disbelief, the Swordmaster added, "Dig deeper. You'll find a perfectly serviceable knife."

At the bottom of the pack, Paul discovered a sturdy utility knife with a four-inch blade. Without complaining, he attached it to his belt.

Duncan, meanwhile, donned his own pack, then reached into the aircraft to pull out a light polymer-handled spear, then a sophisticated bow and a quiver of arrows, then an even larger knife, which he placed at his hip. He stared hard at the young man, as if he had transformed into a cold killer.

"This is a lopsided game," Paul said, "if you can call it that."

"If you think of it as a game, you will lose. In a primal sense, it is a hunt, and the hunter usually has the advantage over the hunted." He shrugged as he strapped on the quiver. "If the universe always followed fair rules, we would have no need for this training. But you'll find yourself often enough in lopsided situations. Learn how to survive this with me, and it will help you survive against a real enemy."

Paul was not surprised to find no food or water in the pack, but he would obtain what he needed from the land. He saw steep drop-offs around the landing clearing, swales and ravines filled with vines, trees, and thick under-brush. "So, I set off in any direction?" Though no path looked optimal, he had already selected the one he wanted to take.

"Go. I'll give you ten minutes' head start . . . or maybe less." His eyebrows arched. "Meet me back here at dark . . . unless I manage to catch and hog-tie you before then. Now, run for your life, boy!"

"I'm not a boy!" He bolted off, running sure-footedly into the thick vege-tation, which quickly swallowed him up. Paul told himself Duncan wouldn't really harm him—but the rugged wilderness certainly could.

❦

AFTER RUNNING DOWNSLOPE into the jungle, Paul crept and crashed through the trackless wilderness, trying to avoid deadfall and tangled vines. He would get as far away as he could in the time Duncan allowed him, but he had to prepare. He felt tense, but also exhilarated. The possibilities out here were endless, as were the dangers. He felt confident in his abilities, though. After all, Duncan had been his principal trainer.

The hunter usually has the advantage over the hunted.

The Swordmaster's words hung in his mind. Though Paul was running now, he could redefine his own role to become the hunter and turn the tables on his trainer. He smiled as he pushed thick vines aside and swung himself over a fallen tree covered with a carpet of moss and squishy mushrooms.

Eventually, he would circle back, try to mount his own ambush, and disarm his friend, declaring himself the winner of the game. Yet he knew it wouldn't be so simple.

Duncan would be setting his own trap, but Paul wouldn't fall into it. He didn't want an easy way out of this challenge, and he wasn't so eager to rush back to Castle Caladan. He and Duncan were determined to take these days for vigorous training, and Paul intended to get the most out of the experience.

After his eyes adjusted to the jungle gloom, he made his way along, letting the terrain itself guide him as he searched for a strategic location, a good defensive shelter, maybe a place to set up an ambush. He forded a stream in shallow water, climbed over a line of jumbled, lichen-covered rocks that would leave no mark of his passage, and when he reached the top of an outcropping, where he could see all around, he hunkered down and used his tools, along with thin vines and a long stick, to fashion a spear with a sharp tip—a weapon he could use against his opponent. To him, the challenge was real and extreme. This was going to be fun.

Now armed, Paul set out on a line heading upslope again, contouring around the flank of the mountain, then dipping down into another drainage, trying not to follow an obvious path that Duncan would anticipate. For the time being, his makeshift spear served as a walking stick. Gripping the crude weapon made him feel like a primitive hunter.

He remembered the natural studies Dr. Yueh had shown him. Before setting off with Duncan, he had reviewed filmbooks of the Southern Continent, so he knew something about the flora and fauna, including manta birds. He found and ate ruby berries on the way, as well as a dense edible fungus called volandi that attached itself to tree roots.

He came upon a game path, which enabled him to increase his pace, since he wasn't bushwhacking his way through underbrush. He heard chittering and squealing overhead and looked up to see five Dreis monkeys menacing him. He ignored their bluster and sprinted on, knowing that the boisterous animals rarely harmed humans.

He was more concerned to see hoofprints and scat, which clearly came from a Caladan boar. Encountering one of the beasts would be far more dangerous than facing Duncan. He held his spear more tightly and decided to leave the game trail again.

As he searched for a spot to slip into the dense foliage, he heard a whistle through the air, then a startling crack as an arrow smashed into a large fallen tree next to him. Shrieking, the Dries monkeys scrambled out of the branches, chittering in protest.

Paul sprang away, unable to guess how far away Duncan might be. A second arrow struck a mossy trunk to his left. He reacted instantly, trying to do the opposite of what his opponent expected. He bounded toward the first trunk, yanked the arrow loose, and took his prize with him as he swung himself over to the other side, using the hulk itself for shelter.

He thought of shouting out to taunt Duncan, but he kept quiet, creeping into a grove of tall, fanlike ferns and a clump of scarlet flowers abuzz with pollinating insects. As a hunter, Duncan was trying to flush him out. Although the Swordmaster's main skill was with bladed weapons, he was also an excellent shot.

Paul nudged a bush aside with the point of his spear. The arrow in his other hand could serve as a better weapon, but right now, he needed to gain more distance. He hadn't expected Duncan to track him so swiftly. If he complained, the Swordmaster would chastise him for expecting a fight for survival to be a fair contest.

Another arrow struck a tree much farther away, startling several shrieking birds, and Paul realized that Duncan didn't know where he was now. He smiled.

Working his way along a wooded hillside, he slipped down a slope to a gully that held a trickle of a stream. He ran along the rocks, careful to leave no footprints, then crossed to the opposite bank, where he found another game trail.

When he was confident he had eluded Duncan for now, he slowed his pace, keeping low and taking more care to look around. He heard a rustle of leaves to his left and swung his body, raising the spear.

On the opposite slope above the stream, he was startled to see an olive-skinned young woman moving along. He froze, watched her picking her way over the rough terrain, dodging tree roots on the trail. A lithe figure in khaki clothing, she had long black hair and wore a small bag on her back. If he encountered people here in the jungles, he had expected to see Muadh primitives in rudimentary clothing. Although she looked grimy and rumpled, she obviously came from a civilized settlement somewhere.

Startled, she spotted him, and their gazes met across the distance. It was as if time stopped. Then the girl abruptly slipped away, vanishing into the deep jungle and making no sounds he could hear.

If Paul shouted after her, he would shatter the stillness of the wilderness, and certainly draw Duncan. Although he knew she had nothing to do with their training game, he decided to follow her.

He worked his way down to the small stream, crossed on a fallen log, and then climbed back up the opposite slope. He made far too much noise, but he needed to get closer before she disappeared entirely. Stumbling upon the faint path she had taken, he sprinted along. Through openings in the vegetation, he caught glimpses of her, but she easily outpaced him.

Now he saw her ahead, scrambling up the side of a rock outcropping that protruded over a steep drop-off like a citadel. When she reached the top of the promontory, she glanced back at him, then spun about and seemed to leap off the opposite edge.

Paul gasped, but he guessed she must know a secret way down. With his heart pounding, he climbed with great care, slipping on the moss and loose rocks, and at last reached the top of the outcropping.

From that vantage, he looked down into a sheltered valley and a settlement, little more than a cluster of huts. A few dozen people moved about in their daily tasks, while others squatted around a central firepit, engaged in some kind of ritual, sharing dried brown objects. It reminded him of the barra fern ceremony he had witnessed far to the north—and he thought these must be Muadh primitives.

Below, the girl hurried into the settlement, speaking quickly to the first villagers she encountered. She must have known he was still watching her, but she turned her back on him and joined the gathered circle.

He didn't approach, but remained on the high promontory, watching them. These villagers were not part of his game with Duncan, and he didn't want them to get hurt. Surely his companion was now tracking him, but Paul wanted to lead the chase away from these people. Though he was very curious about the young woman as well as the Muadh villagers, this hunt was only between the two of them.

Working his way off the outcropping and into the jungle again, he spent the rest of the day exploring, dodging, playing cat and mouse. Occasionally, he spotted Duncan in the distance, heard the sounds of his passage, but no more than that.

Exhilarated, considering today's game a success, the young man took the last few hours of the afternoon to circle back to where he had landed the flyer. He wanted to get back so he could be there waiting when Duncan returned, perspiring, scratched, and flustered. The sun had nearly set by the time he crawled carefully around a boulder, peeped through thick shrubbery until he could see the aircraft in the clearing ahead.

Duncan was already there, sitting with his back to him, lounging in the shade beneath one of the variable-length wings. The Swordmaster drank from a beverage container, leaning against a landing strut.

Grinning, Paul crept forward, the spear in one hand, the arrow in the other. Without making a sound, he approached Duncan from behind. "I could kill you right now."

"Or maybe this is my trap, young Master." Duncan took another relaxed drink.

Paul called his bluff. "And maybe it isn't. We've met the challenge for the day." He stalked around to the other side and tossed his weapons on the ground.

The man laughed. "With that assortment, you might be able to defend yourself against a lizard sunning itself on a rock." He reached into a temperature-sealed case at his side and brought out another beverage container, which he extended.

Paul accepted it and drank happily. "Our game is not over, Duncan."

"No, it isn't. Not by a long measure."

Two viewpoints can either balance each other and create harmony, or clash and destroy each other.

—MOTHER SUPERIOR RAQUELLA BERTO-ANIRUL,
early days of the Sisterhood

Rolling the melange tablet over her tongue, Mother Superior Harishka let the cinnamon taste fill her mouth, sinuses, and throat. She swallowed, waiting for the soothing, regenerative effects of spice to kick in.

She had felt deep fatigue for a considerable time, more than just the weight of her significant years, but she dismissed it as a burden of the Bene Gesserit order. As she sat in her dressing cubicle and examined herself in the mirror, she noticed how haggard she looked. Nearly as aged and frail as the late Lethea, the former Kwisatz Mother, whose mind had withered into mad senility, Harishka looked so old that she wondered how she could possibly still be alive.

And yet, she was. There was still far too much Sisterhood business to do, far too much responsibility. For the time being, the peace of death would remain out of her reach.

In the mirror, her rheumy eyes brightened as she let a calm resolve wash over her, and she watched some of the wrinkles actually smooth out on her face. Simply by willing the change in her thoughts with the aid of melange, she could impart a transformation that shed decades from her appearance. But the stimulus of spice never lasted. For decades, frequent consumption had extended her life and vitality, though she didn't know how much longer she could continue along that path. As Mother Superior, she needed the energy to lead the entire order, and that required higher and higher dosages.

Before long, she would have to stop avoiding the mortal reality, though, and choose her successor.

As she turned her back on the mirror, she heard someone in her private reception area, recognized the voice of Reverend Mother Cordana, one of her closest advisers, talking to a servant.

Cordana and Ruthine had replaced her respected friend Reverend Mother Mohiam, who had become the Emperor's Truthsayer. At one time, Cordana and Ruthine had offered a balanced perspective, often fraught with disagreement. But rather than accepting the Mother Superior's decisions, Ruthine had gone behind her back, listening to conspiracies inspired by the dementia-addled Lethea. Defying Harishka's direct instructions, Ruthine and a handful of traitors set out to kill not only Jessica but her son, Paul Atreides, who'd been left vulnerable on Caladan. Once her crime was exposed, Ruthine had killed herself rather than face the consequences of what she had done.

Her counterpart Cordana, though, remained loyal and reliable, often advocating for Jessica, who now served as concubine for Viscount Tull. The Mother Superior relied on Cordana more and more. Though she was not equal to Mohiam in many respects, Cordana was a steady influence, a woman of both wisdom and compassion.

Granted access, the Reverend Mother slipped through the door with a crisp rustling of her black day-robe. Her gait was awkward yet somehow skittering, due to her twisted spine and bent shoulders, a physical failure that Sisterhood surgeries had not been able to correct. Despite her disarming handicap, she was a skilled fighter, with fast, deadly moves. Cordana had sharp, intelligent eyes and severe features.

"I bring excellent tidings from Elegy, Mother Superior," she said in her characteristic upbeat tone. "Sister Jessica convinced Viscount Tull to reinstate his stipend to the Sisterhood, exactly as she was instructed to do!"

Harishka felt a warm happiness to hear this news. "The full amount we received before?"

"Yes, he will reinstate the donation his father established, beginning immediately. I don't know how Jessica managed it."

The Mother Superior tried not to let her surprise show. "Your kindness paid off. You saw the true potential in Jessica, when Ruthine only wanted to destroy her."

"I am pleased at her progress, and I hope you are as well." Cordana lowered her gaze. "We have . . . not done right by Jessica. She has every reason to hate us."

"She is Bene Gesserit, raised and trained here on Wallach IX. We do not exist to make her happy. She exists for us."

The other woman frowned, obviously disagreeing, but she kept her words to herself.

Harishka also knew the complexities of Jessica, knew her vital part in the Bene Gesserit breeding plan, even if Jessica herself was unaware of her own parentage. Nodding, the Mother Superior continued, "Mohiam will be pleased to learn this as well. She has always had such high hopes for Jessica."

Looking happy, as if Jessica's success reflected on her own, Cordana took her leave and went to discuss financial specifics with the Mother School's comptrollers.

Enjoying the moment of satisfaction, Harishka left her quarters and walked alone into the central courtyard of the school complex, where she saw the brush-covered hills on the outskirts. The foliage had recently been a fiery orange of autumn, but was now a bleak brown.

Cordana had a notable weakness of personality—she could be too compassionate, too considerate of personal feelings. If Harishka were ever to consider her as the next Mother Superior, the other woman needed to keep a larger picture in mind and become tougher. The priorities of the Bene Gesserit extended far beyond any individual or noble house.

As Harishka walked past the tilled earth of harvested garden plots on school grounds, though, she had to admit that the opposite—a lack of compassion—was one of her own weaknesses. Though the major decisions of the Sisterhood were in her hands, wisdom required that she not operate in a vacuum and that she listen to advice, especially advice that she found difficult to accept.

Now, feeling the full effects of melange and energized by the good financial news, Harishka dispelled the aches and soreness that had plagued her. Following a stone pathway, she climbed steps set into a hillside south of the administration building. The steep staircase wound along the slope until it reached a viewpoint above the school.

Feeling the burn in her muscles as she climbed, the Mother Superior had a tendency to count steps. Even with the numerous buildings and hundreds of women and staff around the large school, she felt incredibly alone as she reached the summit.

Up there in the pavilion, a hooded figure paced back and forth, awaiting her.

It was the Kwisatz Mother, the masked and secret administrator of the intricate genetic plans of the Bene Gesserit. She served as the guardian of the infinite breeding lines leading toward the ultimate goal—a male Bene Gesserit who would bridge space and time and lead the human race to its full potential.

The Kwisatz Haderach.

The breezes whistled around the high lookout. Harishka strode across the pavers toward the other woman, looking at her masked face.

Since they were entirely isolated on this sentinel post, the Kwisatz Mother slid aside the veil to reveal her handsome features, an unremarkable face with a small mouth and intelligent hazel eyes. She offered an innocuous smile and a bland greeting. She was not a beautiful woman by any means, and even though many Sisters had seen her in normal garb across the school, no one paid particular attention to her. Nevertheless, the Kwisatz Mother could see far into the future along the helical chains of DNA in a way that even pre-science could not explain.

Harishka and the Kwisatz Mother had precisely aligned responsibilities, as if both were Navigators guiding the same great ship. The two met regularly and discreetly, and today's conversation would have great import, considering the repercussions of the choices they had to consider.

They sat side by side on a stone bench, which was cold and hard—just like the decisions they had to make. From this vantage, they could observe anyone approaching from the trail below. They had complete privacy, and the Kwisatz Mother left the veil off. Her expression remained serious.

"I studied the tapestry of breeding lines, the countless threads and tangles. I followed every possible path, every iteration in a way that exceeds even Mentat machinations. It is my life and my existence, and I draw conclusions, after so many of my predecessors brought us to this point." She pulled in a quick breath as if filled with anticipation. "We are close, Reverend Mother. So very, very close . . ."

Her voice had a husky undertone, a mixture of obsession and lust. "Jessica made a bold mistake, or a gamble, when she had a son by Leto Atreides instead of a daughter. We wanted a daughter with his bloodline . . . but the boy's existence is a paradox and an opportunity."

She leaned closer on the stone bench. Harishka remained silent, waiting, absorbing.

"The other likely possibility for a Kwisatz Haderach in this generation may be the boy Brom, the son of Xora and her Sardaukar lover. Another mistake, another paradox. Another hope. He is a little older than Paul Atreides and has been well trained here at the Mother School."

Harishka scowled at the actions of those two women. "After carefully building a genetic tree for thousands of years, each delicate branch is now disrupted by impulsive, disobedient Sisters. Jessica . . . Jessica has already been punished, and I believe she is under our control again. She is still young enough to produce the required daughter, if we ever allow her to return to the Duke. And Xora . . ." She felt a hot flush on her cheeks. "I expected so much more from that one, but she betrayed us, let herself fall under the sway of Ruthine's schemes, and now she's been murdered by an unknown perpetrator. It has all gone horribly awry."

Oddly, the Kwisatz Mother did not seem disturbed by the complications. "In such an extended breeding program, we must plan for the unexpected and consider rather than condemn these anomalies. Most of them will never show real promise to become a Kwisatz Haderach, but others . . . we only need one to succeed."

The Mother Superior was surprised. "Are you saying we should accept, even welcome these unwanted sons? Rogue children born of defiant mothers who refused to do as we instructed!"

The other woman responded with a dry chuckle. "We must test them, and only welcome and accept them if such is warranted."

"What do you propose? Now that Jessica has been reassigned to the Viscount Tull, it will be more difficult to bring Paul here."

The Kwisatz Mother nodded. "We can go to Caladan if we must. But first, I would like to consider Brom, the young man we already have in our possession, the one whom Sisters have been watching closely. We know much more about him than about Jessica's son."

Harishka recalled that Xora's son had befriended Jessica when she was held captive in the Mother School's isolation cell. Brom had saved her life, helped her to escape, until they were thwarted. She could see the irony in the connection between the two.

The other woman continued, "It does not matter that Xora was assassinated on Caladan. Only her offspring matters—and he will never know the identity of his mother. It is irrelevant information to him." She paused for a long moment. "We should consider when it will be time for Brom to face his destiny—and attempt the Agony."

Harishka absorbed the information. Perhaps she would have another victory soon, more good news that would help her shake off the weight of years. "Brom shows great promise. You are the Kwisatz Mother, so the ultimate decision is yours."

The secretive woman looked both eager and uncomfortable. "We are at a critical crossroads. You and I will decide together."

"You just want someone to share the blame if things go wrong."

The Kwisatz Mother reached up and reaffixed the veil across her face. "We are in control, Mother Superior. We stand on the shoulders of our predecessors, so blame does not apply to either of us. Like generations before us, we plan and plan, and breed and breed—" She paused. "And in that process, we are forced to take miscalculations into account."

"Fate," Harishka said solemnly, "is not a thing that can be calculated."

"It just intervenes. So now we proceed, to see which candidate excels."

"And which dies."

Whether one is savior or destroyer, hero or villain, depends largely upon perspective. And perspective can be altered with the careful filtering of information.

—MENTAT PITER DE VRIES,
notes on the disposition of House Harkonnen in the Imperium

Now that the terrorist leader had presented an unexpected opportunity, the Baron needed to determine how best to respond. Which alternative would most increase the wealth, power, and stature of House Harkonnen? Which would inflict the greatest harm upon his enemies? And which posed the greatest danger to him?

He had debriefed Rabban on Jaxson Aru's offer to help fund the Noble Commonwealth and reap great profits. His nephew was a bluster of emotions, short-term thinking, black-and-white decisions. The Baron let him express his opinion and fume, but this time, he devoted little attention to his views.

Instead, he met privately on Arrakis with his Mentat, Piter de Vries, whom he had withdrawn from Lankiveil, since there was little more he could do to the Atreides captive. Gurney Halleck was bruised and broken, still a prisoner, but worthless. The Baron needed his Mentat here.

Piter was a narrow-faced man with large eyes and fidgety movements. His long fingers and strong hands were good for knife work and strangulation. He was a brilliant man, sometimes annoying, but with the exceptional Mentat abilities that arose from his perverse, twisted training among the Tleilaxu. They had created him as a ghola from the previous Piter de Vries, who'd been killed fifteen years earlier.

He suspected the Mentat would be up to the machinations at hand.

Under pretext of conducting a melange inventory on behalf of Emperor Shaddam, the Harkonnen patriarch and de Vries went to one of the secure spice stockpiles in the city of Carthag. At the armored doors, the two dismissed offers of assistance from guards. "I trust few people but myself," the Baron rumbled to them. "My Mentat and I are perfectly capable of assessing this stockpile."

They entered the treasury of melange, and the heavy doors sealed behind them. The Baron felt silence and wealth weigh down on him. The air itself was filled with energy and life. Though the melange was packaged in airtight containers, the ubiquitous aroma made his skin tingle and his eyes burn. Supported by his suspensor belt to carry his great frame, the Baron walked lightly in a bouncing stride. He paused to spread his arms, lift his multiple chins, and close his eyes, absorbing it all in silence.

Melange extended life, clarified the mind, improved vitality—and much of the Imperium was addicted to it. Wealthy nobles and merchants were willing to pay any amount necessary to maintain their supply. That was the key to Harkonnen power.

Beside him, Piter de Vries remained wisely silent so that the Baron could have his moment. The Mentat withdrew a small, transparent vial of a cranberry-colored liquid from his pocket. He twisted off the cap and gulped down the sapho juice, then closed his eyes and uttered a quick Mentat mantra to focus his concentration. He wiped his lips with the back of his hand, smearing a few droplets of the juice and leaving stains.

After the sapho took effect, he blinked and said. "I am ready, my Baron."

Though jarred away from admiring the spice around him, this was what he wanted. He had brought the Mentat here for a reason. "I need your analysis, Piter. I've already explained Jaxson Aru's surprising proposal. From you I require projections and advice on what to do about him. Do we actually sell him the spice, off the record? Or should we refuse all further contact?"

The twisted Mentat tapped his fingertips together, humming as he considered, although the Baron knew full well that he had already been lining up projections. "My Baron, you yourself initiated the rumor that the Noble Commonwealth was responsible for the Orgiz operations. It was a safe diversion because we knew the rebels had nothing to do with it. Count Fenring and his frustrating Mentat could chase shadows all they wanted!" His gaze flicked away. "If we engage in a genuine alliance with Jaxson Aru, however, that would make our red herring true, after the fact."

"It is a convenient answer, and keeps our hands clean."

"Ah, unless we are caught, my Baron," Piter said.

"But we've done nothing yet, so how could we be caught?"

"Nothing about this new wrinkle, you mean. But this moment requires plans . . . careful plans," the Mentat muttered. "The profits would be substantial in such a scheme."

The Baron turned to the walls of spice, absorbing the wealth and power it already represented for him. This one warehouse held unimaginable riches, and the Baron had many such facilities. "I cannot spend profits if I am executed."

Together, they strolled down the high corridors, past crates of melange stacked to the ceiling. Every grain of spice was accounted for and reported to Imperial Observers. The Baron took great pains to make his legitimate operations transparent, the better to hide his other, more dispersed stockpiles. He ran more than one set of books.

"We could always string the man along," Piter suggested, "then throw him to the Imperial wolves at the appropriate time."

The Baron chuckled at the idea. "That would earn us significant clout with Emperor Shaddam, and undoubtedly a large reward. The safest alternative, although if the scheme fails, Jaxson Aru has a penchant for destruction on a grand scale."

The Mentat's eyes sparkled. "Do not forget we have an important secret weapon that neither the rebels nor the Emperor know about. We have the Atreides man on Lankiveil, and we intercepted Duke Leto's vital message. We're the only ones who know what Leto is really up to."

The Baron smiled. "I should have revealed that when I spoke to Jaxson in the warehouse, told him that he has a spy in his midst! Oh, then he would eviscerate my mortal enemy, the Duke of Caladan."

"It is like a hidden bomb, my Baron." The Mentat nodded to himself. "But we have much more to gain than that! If you expose Leto Atreides to the rebel leader, he would be killed, of course, but House Harkonnen would gain nothing by it monetarily, just the elimination of one of our enemies."

The Baron felt impatient. "Then what do you suggest?"

Piter smiled with his red-stained lips. "Much better if you could do the same thing that Duke Leto is attempting. *You* string Jaxson Aru along and set up a trap that would lead to his capture and put an end to the rebellion. Make yourself a great hero in the Emperor's eyes, and let Leto fall with all the other traitors, humiliating House Atreides all across the Imperium."

The Baron narrowed his black eyes, trying to understand what the other man was saying. "Continue, Mentat."

"As long as we entrap Jaxson Aru and his cronies *before* Duke Leto makes his move, then the Atreides will be considered one of the rebels to be snuffed out. No matter what Leto insists, no one will believe him." He tapped his fingertips together again. "Oh, he'll claim he sent his man Halleck as a courier, but how can he prove it? The man never arrived at Kaitain, never delivered any confidential message. We must simply eliminate him on Lankiveil. Thus, Leto Atreides will only be making limp excuses. He will be buried along with them."

Piter's smile widened as he gave the other man a moment to ponder. "You, my Baron, will be the one who brings down the violent rebellion—a hero!

And all the Landsraad will cheer your name. Kaitain will erect a statue in your honor. You will earn the Emperor's undying gratitude."

The Baron let out a low laugh, then drew in a deep breath. His enthusiasm energized him as much as the strong cinnamon smell did.

The Mentat held up a warning finger. "But, unless you act soon, the Atreides may take his own action and spring his own trap. Then the Duke of Caladan would receive the accolades, and you'd have nothing."

"We must not allow that! No time to lose." He still had the compact shigawire spool with instructions on how to contact the rebel leader. Yes, he would offer to sell the Noble Commonwealth a load of valuable spice, to prove himself as Jaxson requested—but he would need to plan better than Leto Atreides did. He would inform the Imperial Spice Observer of his scheme at the very beginning, so there could never be any doubt about the true loyalty of House Harkonnen.

"Excellent suggestion to make these plans within plans, to use one enemy against another, Mentat. I will allow you to live a while longer."

Piter showed no fear. "Of course, my Baron. I exist only to serve House Harkonnen."

The Baron inhaled the heady melange aroma again and led his Mentat out of the spice stockpile. Now he had to contact Count Hasimir Fenring as soon as possible.

When seeds are scattered, there is no way to predict when they will sprout,
or if they ever will. But when a plant finally grows, matures, and flowers,
it can provide the most wonderful feeling of joy and productivity.
—Filmbook excerpt, *Philosophical Wanderings*

In charge of basic Caladan affairs while Paul Atreides was off on his short training trip with Duncan, Thufir Hawat walked through the castle corridors, endlessly moving like a sentinel. Not wanting to miss anything, the old Mentat moved from the main reception and audience hall, through the dining chamber on the main level, then climbed to the Atreides living quarters in the central keep. The Duke's chamber had been empty for some time, and Lady Jessica's even longer than that, but Master Paul's rooms had the fresh lived-in clutter of a young man with many interests and distractions.

Castle Caladan felt alarmingly empty, not in a lonely sense, but in a sparse and skeletal way. Thufir was more alert than ever.

Continuing his patrol, he climbed up to the ramparts, where he moved from one viewpoint to the next so he could survey the grounds. His security forces also had redundant patrols, but he did not delegate all such work.

All appeared well. Caladan endured.

As a Mentat, he was able to control his outward expressions and moods, but right now, Thufir was filled with nervous energy. He paced around the ramparts, recalling how the Bene Gesserit had withdrawn Jessica for some scheme of their own, and he also knew what Duke Leto intended to do among the Noble Commonwealth rebels. Meanwhile, Paul was off in the southern jungles, running and sparring with Duncan Idaho. At least he wasn't worried about the young man, guarded by the Swordmaster.

His greatest nagging worry was the fact that Gurney Halleck had not yet returned from his mission to the Imperial Court, had sent no word at all. By now, he should have had ample time to deliver the Duke's message and return. In even the most conservative calculation, the man was five days overdue. Halleck was not one to be late.

Thufir completed his circuit of the high parapets above the sea cliffs and headed back toward the central keep. Before he left the rooftop level, he noted that the armory storage door was ajar, and that required special access. Warily, Thufir slipped a long knife out of his waist sheath as he stepped inside the stone-walled room. He saw the dim light of small glowglobes near the ceiling, but detected no movement, no unexpected shadows. He crept past racks of armory swords, dueling knives, personal shields.

Inside this chamber, the sword of Duke Paulus hung on display on the stone wall, the polished, nicked blade protected by a plaz case, alongside two of the Old Duke's personal daggers. On the racks nearby, Thufir noted some of Paulus's favorite weapons as well as those used in the young Master's training: lightweight swords, throwing stars, bolos, hooks, darters, and nets. Thufir himself had trained Paul with many of these.

Trying to understand how this display chamber had been disturbed, he didn't expect to hear a voice outside the room. The door swung open, and a short, thin servant in an Atreides household uniform entered. The servant jerked back, astonished to see the warrior Mentat crouched in full combat stance.

Recognizing the thin man, Thufir relaxed and straightened to face him.

The servant's demeanor shifted just as rapidly. "A secure transmission arrived, sir. A coded message cylinder imprinted for you." He extended a metallic tube, featureless and sealed on both ends. A dull red glow emanated from the caps. "My team was cleaning your quarters, sir, when the cylinder activated. We knew it was important, so I ran to find you."

Thufir reached out to take the cylinder, knowing what it was. Messages from star system to star system had to be carried on Guild Heighliners, delivered from place to place, and usually by hand from a delegated courier or service. But although transmissions could not cross the gulf of interstellar space in any reasonable time, once a Heighliner reached orbit, a coded signal could be automatically sent to a receiver on the surface. This cylinder had been set to receive such a transmission, a signal sent by hidden surveillance recorders, passive reconnaissance devices that he had set up.

He wasn't expecting this. "Thank you. Leave me to review what it contains."

The servant formally withdrew two steps, then skittered away. Thufir only paid attention to the warm object in his hands. What transmission was this? Which passive report from Atreides spies?

Thufir paid no attention to the fresh air and sunshine outside. The message had been sent from an innocuous merchant ship that traveled aboard a Heighliner, one that served as a confidential carrier of Atreides equipment.

He opened the cylinder, activated the message pickup, and skimmed a data upload from Lankiveil, reconnaissance recorded by the passive spy-eyes that Duncan and Gurney had scattered among Beast Rabban's holdings. Thufir had been waiting for this intelligence, which had to come back to Caladan by a roundabout way. Now, House Atreides would have a glimpse into Harkonnen daily activities, details that he could use for planning purposes. A Master of Assassins had to be aware of all enemies.

He did not expect to receive an urgent message from Gurney Halleck.

The transmission was brief and desperate. "Tell the Duke that I was captured by Harkonnens on Harmonthep! I am currently being held on Lankiveil. Couldn't make it back to Caladan!"

The words cut off there, with no further information. The Harkonnens had Gurney! Harmonthep . . . why would he have gone to that obscure planet? What was the delay? Thufir paused for a moment, digging into his Mentat data so he could review Heighliner routes and schedules. It was not likely, but one of the return routes from Kaitain did pass through the Harmonthep system. Possibly Gurney had taken a more convoluted path home after delivering Leto's message to the Emperor, where he was seized by Harkonnens.

But now he was held captive on Lankiveil, no doubt being tortured by Rabban.

The passive spy-eyes had gathered specific information on his location, a facility at the edge of one of the fjords on Lankiveil. Thufir's Mentat mind plunged into possible scenarios for a rescue operation. Was the man even still alive? Rabban would not rush through his sadistic pleasures.

He looked at the Old Duke's sword on display, the myriad training and defensive weapons stored in the armory chamber. Yes, he would have everything he needed. And he could not wait. With Paul gone and Duke Leto out of communication on his own quiet mission, Thufir Hawat knew that rescuing Gurney Halleck would be up to him.

A small Atreides military force would not be the best tool for success. Thufir Hawat would never launch an overt war against a rival noble house in the name of his Duke. It was not the place of a Mentat to do so. Leto, and then Paul, had left him to manage the routine business of Caladan, not authorizing a major strike.

He had to find a different way, and he had to move immediately. Gurney was being tortured at this moment, if he was even still alive. Thufir Hawat might be advanced in years, but he was still the Master of Assassins. He would do this on his own. He had completed similar missions for Duke Paulus in his younger years.

He would arrange swift passage to Lankiveil, and there he would do what must be done. Likely, it would be necessary for him to kill.

Their jungle survival exercise went back and forth over the next two days, tense pursuits through the rugged terrain, broken by laughter and challenges. Each evening, they would patch the other's minor injuries and debrief each other about the tactics they had employed, focusing on what Paul could learn from it.

In the meantime, Duncan had extracted the key burned-out components of the flyer's four engines and made a plan about how to combine the intact parts so he could get at least two of the four engines working again. Paul enjoyed being at the Swordmaster's side, optimistic that they could get the aircraft functioning again. Despite some concern about getting back to the castle before anyone began to worry, they tried to enjoy the training in whatever form it took.

The next misty morning, after each had sprung a clever trap on the other, Paul and Duncan sat on a huge, moss-covered tree trunk and sipped tepid pack water. Their conversation was laced with bravado and good-natured threats. Though the young man knew his friend would never let him come to harm, Duncan had not hesitated to give him a smarting bruise or two whenever he thought Paul was not performing up to his peak abilities. "Every game matters," he said. "Do not fool yourself into thinking that any test or challenge is merely for amusement."

In the humid tropical air, Paul wiped sweat from his brow. "And each time I push myself to extremes, I learn to become a better Duke of Caladan."

He had made up his mind to turn the tables on Duncan, to prove he was a worthy adversary. During their daily adventures, Paul had fashioned his own spears and crude clubs for throwing, as well as several nets woven together from green vines. He also had his knife and the arrow he'd kept as a trophy.

Duncan lounged back against a shelf fungus nearly as tall as he was.

"Enough rest, lad. This isn't a spa." He glanced at his chronometer. "I will grant you a half hour head start, and then you'd better watch out." The Swordmaster crossed his arms over his broad chest and leaned back, pretending to nap.

"This isn't a spa, Duncan," he teased, then calmly ate another piece of volandi fungus and washed it down with pack water. Finally, he rose to his feet, slung the pack over one shoulder, and strolled into the jungle. As soon as he was out of sight in the thick trees, Paul broke into a run, leaping over deadfall branches, keeping to rocks so he wouldn't leave footprints in the soft loam, taking a zigzag course.

Paul eluded his pursuer all through the heart of the day. He climbed trees and watched, seeing how he threw Duncan off the trail with broken twigs and scuffed soil, watching him circle around and come back to continue the hunt. But Paul thought of himself as the predator now. In the three days they'd been in the wild Southern Continent, the young man had gotten better at the game. It pleased and amused him to see how he could elude Duncan.

Now, the big Swordmaster walked directly under the broad branch from which Paul observed him. Without a sound, the boy dropped one of his vine nets, tangling the man in it. Duncan overreacted, stumbled, and twisted his ankle on a fallen branch. As he got back to his feet, his triumphant adversary swung down and jabbed him in the ribs with the blunt end of his spear, declaring it a mortal blow. Duncan thrashed himself free, still favoring one foot, but Paul had already scampered into the jungle again.

As the big man pursued him down a game trail, assuming his quarry would take the path of least resistance through the foliage, Paul circled around and crept after him, staying out of sight. Birds hooted in the whispering leaves overhead, and insects whined through the air.

Confident, the Swordmaster moved at a deliberate pace toward a fern-studded rock outcropping that rose above the tangled underbrush. It would be a steep climb, but a good vantage point. Close behind him, Paul thought he could trap him there and give him nowhere to go except over the sheer drop-off. Even though Duncan favored his twisted ankle, he still had his bow, making him a formidable adversary.

Paul crouched behind a thick clump of wild ferns, watching Duncan trudge up the steep slope of the outcropping, still limping. Reaching the summit, he looked over the brink and abruptly backed up a step, which made Paul guess that the cliff dropped off precipitously.

After surveying the view, Duncan found a spot where he could sit, setting his bow, spear, and pack to one side of the slanted rock. He rubbed his ankle, flexing his boot, then rummaged in the pack for a medkit. He carefully removed his boot, set it next to the bow, and unrolled a long strip of healing tape, with which he wrapped his ankle.

From his hiding place, Paul watched the sophisticated bow resting precariously on the sloped outcropping. It was a far better weapon than anything he had fashioned. He had one of the sharp modern arrows, but wanted to obtain the bow as well. If he tossed the throwing club, maybe he could knock the bow loose and send it tumbling back down the outcropping. Paul could retrieve it faster than Duncan could make his way down—especially with his boot removed and his sore ankle.

He inched closer, trying not to make a sound. Gripping his throwing club, Paul raised it, aimed, and flung it. The club made a whipping noise as it spun in the air. With instant reflexes, Duncan dropped the med-tape and lunged down for the bow—but too late. The club sent the bow skittering downslope.

Paul lurched to his feet, but to his dismay, the sliding weapon bounced on a protrusion and spilled the opposite direction over the edge. The bow fell off and disappeared from view down into the jungled gorge.

Even if he hadn't seized the weapon for himself, he had taken away Duncan's greatest advantage. And since the Swordmaster still had his boot off and couldn't run over the rough volcanic rock, Paul pressed his attack to score another victory. He was the hunter now, and his friend the wounded prey.

Duncan grinned for just a moment to see his student bounding toward him, then his expression became deadly serious. He snatched the long hunting knife out of a waist sheath, and Paul brought out his own knife to face him.

"Shall we call this a draw?" Duncan said. "Blades are my specialty."

Paul lifted his knife. "Maybe, but ask yourself how many of your techniques I have mastered." He approached with full wariness, although he tried to let Duncan believe he was cocky and overconfident. "I know you hurt your foot."

"Blade against blade, youth and speed against wisdom and skill." The Swordmaster lifted an eyebrow. "It might be a good duel."

Paul nodded to the precipice behind Duncan. "But the loser would go over the edge. Just like your bow."

Growing serious, though, Duncan yanked a thumb over his shoulder. "We should pause for now. Take a peek yourself, and tell me what you see down there."

Cautiously, keeping eyes on his opponent in case of a trick, Paul went to gaze across the gorge to the broad slopes. Instantly, he forgot about the hunt.

Beneath the outcropping, broad sections of the jungle had been cleared, and fields of green ferns grew in neat rows with paths between them. The patches of cultivated ferns formed rectangles, obviously different species. Haphazard camouflage netting covered some of the larger areas, but the security of this operation seemed more disorganized than what he and his father's party had discovered in the northern wilderness not long ago. Workers tended the plants, gathering them into large containers supported by suspensors. A larger complex was higher up the slope, facilities built into the mountain itself.

Paul felt a chill. Barra ferns. "This is an even larger operation than we saw in the north. And our comms are down, so we can't call Thufir."

Duncan stood beside him, nodded to the steep drop-off and the thick jungle below. "And thanks to you, now I don't even have my bow."

As the pair stood on the outcropping and contemplated solutions, one of the field workers pointed up toward where the two figures were exposed high above. Other workers also pointed, and soon, five burly guards came running on the field path. "Those are Chaen Marek's mercenaries," Duncan said as he and Paul ducked away.

The Swordmaster still hopped on his wrapped foot, struggling to keep his balance on the steep slope. Working together now, Paul scuttled forward and retrieved Duncan's boot and pack. "We'd better get back to the flyer. A few more hours of work and maybe we can get two engines functioning enough to take off."

Duncan checked the wrapping on his ankle, put his boot back on while wincing. Then the two worked their way along the steep and rugged mountainside, but the big man was much slower than usual. Both of them knew the mercenaries had seen them. They were now the prey in a more dangerous sort of hunt.

On his third morning on Cuarte, pretending to be a cooperative guest, Leto breakfasted with Rajiv and Vikka Londine. He continued to play his role while making note of disturbing details against Emperor Shaddam. They ate spiced eggs with fried noodles, a traditional Londine dish.

Londine twirled a forkful of the noodles and popped a bite into his mouth. "Vikka and I developed this special family recipe. We would cook together as a special father-daughter time."

"Clarton never liked the dish," Vikka said with a sour frown. "I should have taken that as a bad sign from the beginning."

Chief Administrator Rodundi joined them, looking businesslike. He carried a thin, rolled manuscript in his hand. "You asked me to make notes on your polemic, my Lord. I believe it is one of your most powerful editorials. I made only minor suggestions."

Rajiv Londine accepted the document with pride. "One must balance passion and precision to create a truly influential work of prose. I will publish this pro–Noble Commonwealth essay throughout the Landsraad." He chuckled. "You and I are aligned, Leto. In fact, if you intend to marry my daughter to ally our Houses, perhaps I should add your name as a coauthor? So we can stand together?"

"Agreeing with an opinion and shouting it out are two different things," Leto said, covering his alarm. "Shouldn't you be more careful now than ever? I prefer to keep my feelings and my involvement under wraps." He remained uneasy with all the knowledge Jaxson held against them in his small, black memory stone.

The nobleman's mood hardened, while Rodundi narrowed his eyes in suspicion. Leto added quickly, "For now at least. I can be more effective if my association with you remains behind the scenes."

"Even so . . ." Londine pushed the document over to him. "Read this and tell me what you think. I could use an objective opinion."

Vikka finished her noodles and eggs, then slid the plate aside. "Father, Leto and I plan to spend the morning out watching the breeze dancers."

"It's a quick read," Rajiv insisted.

Seeing no way to avoid it, Leto took the document. "Of course, sir. Give me an hour." He excused himself and left the dining hall for his private room, so he could close the door and be alone. He took a moment to catch his breath.

He sat at the writing desk and paged through Lord Londine's newest screed. The provocative statements would certainly enrage Shaddam. Having read some of the previous speeches, Leto knew that other Landsraad nobles snickered behind the Emperor's back, relishing the acerbic criticisms, although they would never admit it openly. This one, though, crossed the edge of genuine sedition. In the end, however, Leto only jotted down general compliments, knowing Rajiv Londine would never change a word.

He met Vikka at the appropriate time at the rear of the manor house for their morning outing. She wore comfortable trousers and a dark jacket, appropriate for a walk in the woods, rather than a courtly function. She slipped her arm through his and led him along a winding trail into the hills, which climbed a stony hogback.

Previously, her demeanor had been the perfection of etiquette, but now on the rugged terrain, there was nothing demure whatsoever. Her sturdy shoes made easy work of climbing the boulders, and she seemed to be challenging Leto to keep up with her.

Reaching the ridge of the hogback, they had a vista of Cuarte's open skies, as well as the main city, the estate grounds, and distant agricultural fields. In the city park below, Leto saw sparkles of light where fire fountains sprayed glittering spangles.

Vikka found a comfortable rock, and Leto sat beside her. They drank from flasks of cool sparkling water, enjoying the quiet moment, but Vikka kept scanning the skies as if waiting for something. When she saw a cluster of pearlescent nodules drifting toward them, she pointed. "There they are—breeze dancers! Mindless things, but beautiful. The wind currents usually bring them around the knoll in late morning."

He shaded his eyes, looking into the bright sun. The creatures were like a cluster of soap bubbles trailing ribbons and tendrils, tossed about by the vagaries of the wind. Each pearlescent sphere was about the size of a groundcar wheel. "They look like Caladan jellyfish."

"Really? Can your jellyfish fly?" she teased. "I shall have to visit your planet—very soon."

The breeze dancers bobbed and jostled as they drew closer to the top of the hogback. Vikka's eyes sparkled as she took Leto's hand. "Come, we should duck in the shelter of these rocks."

He was suddenly wary and protective. "Is there danger?"

"They won't attack, but the tendrils can burn your skin if they touch you."

Leto had been stung by a jellyfish more than once, and he had no interest in repeating the experience. He and Vikka huddled shoulder to shoulder in the lee of a large rock and looked up at the silent breeze dancers floating by. Eventually, the cluster wandered off into the sky.

By the time they returned to the manor house, Leto felt more relaxed than he had expected. Walking down the halls, he and Vikka were comfortable in each other's company.

She paused at the door to her own quarters. "I enjoy being with you, Leto Atreides. Come, I can make the day even more special for us." She gestured him inside.

The invitation was clear, but he was instantly cautious, uncertain of his position here among the insidious rebels, and also unwilling to expose himself to the vulnerabilities of romance. He could never forget Jessica, yet he could not risk making Vikka suspicious. "I'm not sure this is wise, although I—"

Vikka took his hand. "You are involved with my father and Jaxson Aru. Surely you know we must take risks for the greater glory."

Marshaling his arguments, hoping he wouldn't have to be hurtful and blunt, he followed Vikka inside the large room, but she led him to a long, narrow table instead of her bed. The polished wooden surface was covered with ornaments and paraphernalia.

"This will be an exquisite experience," she said, opening a narrow drawer beneath the table. "Look, a fresh supply, newly delivered from Caladan. You should be pleased. We'll both be so calm and warm together. So intimate, even without touching." Her face was flushed with anticipation.

She withdrew two dried remnants, tight brown curls lovingly displayed on a silver tray. They looked like bent mummified fingers.

Barra ferns.

Leto recoiled, taking two steps back. He needed a moment to find words after his indrawn gasp. "That's ailar."

She laughed. "Of course it is, the Caladan drug. My father pulls a small amount for private use out of his larger shipments, although this is the first new supply in some time." She clucked her tongue, oblivious to how pale Leto had become. "My father wouldn't let me take the risk when there were so many unexpected deaths from the previous strain. He was quite shaken when Lord Atikk's son died of an overdose."

"Atikk's son . . ." Leto's voice trailed off into a whisper. "Atikk blamed me, challenged me to a blood duel!"

"And you handled it masterfully." Vikka smiled as she picked up the brown curl of fern and twirled it between her fingers. "When I learned how your enemy was secretly poisoned in his quarters, I realized there was much more to the Duke of Caladan than I'd expected."

"I had nothing to do with that, nor with the death of his son. Ailar is an abomination—and your father traffics in it?"

"This new variation of the ferns is perfectly safe. It's from new growing fields and has been fully tested." She let out a harsh burst of laughter. "Of course you know all this already, Leto! You must be aware of my father's distribution network. I assumed you were involved."

Leto took another step away from the table. "I burned all of the barra fields, destroyed the operations."

Vikka was confused. "Yet new shipments are arriving. The Noble Commonwealth makes substantial profit from selling ailar. It funds many good works."

Leto's voice was like a battle hatchet. "That drug has tarnished my reputation, caused the deaths of hundreds, if not thousands of Caladan citizens—not to mention all the others in the Imperium." He withdrew from her quarters.

Surprised, she called after him. "Wait! I thought my father made you a business proposal—this is vital for the future of the Noble Commonwealth. Why are you even here?"

Standing out in the corridor, he punctuated each word with a hard snap. "I will not be a part of this."

Feeling like a fool and blind to the obvious, Leto stalked back to his quarters. He gathered his traveling kit and left the manor house without saying farewell, then made his own way to the Cuarte spaceport.

Vikka would tell her father what had happened, and Leto was in no mood to have Rajiv Londine come rushing after him in an attempt to make amends. He needed to get away and get back to Caladan, at least to catch his breath . . . to see Paul and discuss his next steps with his closest advisers—his *trusted* advisers.

The Caladan drug had returned, despite all their efforts! Thufir Hawat had already unraveled some of the distribution and captured a local drug seller up near the moonfish operations. Obviously, the resurrected ailar market was far more extensive than he could have ever imagined.

And it was being used to fund Jaxson Aru's terrorist acts!

Now, more than ever, Duke Leto was determined to bring down the rebellion and everyone associated . . . even if it meant the end of Rajiv and Vikka Londine.

Justice *is achieved by inflicting a severe and appropriate punishment upon a criminal. Fairness is achieved by properly defining and identifying such criminals.*

—EMPEROR FONDIL III, annals of Imperial law

The Baron didn't like the old city of Arrakeen, with its ancient buildings and outdated infrastructure, the dust and decrepitude that was so unlike the more modern Carthag. Nevertheless, Arrakeen was where Count Hasimir Fenring kept his Residency, a massive and ostentatious pile of frivolous architecture. Fenring was a man of Kaitain who thrived in the Imperial Court, and he was very out of place in this dust hole.

Nevertheless, the Baron traveled to the older city so he could speak face-to-face with Fenring. He dressed himself in expensive garments, a chain around his thick neck, and several rings, as if he were appearing in the Imperial Palace. Maintaining appearances was a minor concession to achieving his larger aim, and it would keep the Count in the proper mindset.

Other than his driver and simple security escort, the Baron traveled alone, choosing not to invite either Piter de Vries, who often rubbed people the wrong way, or Rabban, who was sure to plant his foot in the wrong place. He might have trusted Feyd-Rautha in the conversation, but his younger nephew was still back at Giedi Prime.

Fenring's household staff and security guards ushered him through the water-sealed doors. Lady Margot met him in the receiving foyer, smiling as if she were the hostess for an exclusive banquet. "My husband and I are pleased to receive you, Baron Harkonnen. We always enjoy your pleasant company." How smoothly she lied!

Margot Fenring had been raised, groomed, and indoctrinated by the Bene Gesserit: blond hair, blue eyes, an example of physical perfection that met high societal standards of feminine beauty. Her long-standing marriage and clear emotional bond to the shifty Fenring had always been a mystery. If those two didn't actually love each other, they certainly played their parts well.

"Why yes, Lady Fenring, we should do this more often," the Baron said.

"But I'm afraid it's not a social call. I have vital and fascinating information for your husband. He and I should talk in private."

"Privacy is a subjective thing, my dear Baron—hmm?" Count Fenring appeared from a side alcove, dressed in a flowing purple cape, a loose shirt with ruffled sleeves, an ornate golden belt, and baggy pantaloons—inappropriate attire for a desert climate, but the Count could adjust the climate within the sealed Arrakeen Residency to whatever he decided it should be. Fenring's dark, close-set eyes flashed as he waited for his guest to explain himself.

Then the frustrating Mentat bustled into the room. Grix Dardik bobbed his overlarge head and squinted one eye, as if it helped him focus better. His Adam's apple stood out like an angular protrusion on his thin neck. "The man has vital and fascinating information." Dardik leaned closer, just above Fenring's shoulder. "We must hear it, my Count."

Dardik wore a motley assortment of expensive, gaudy clothes, none of which matched—wide cuffs, an extended collar, buttons in inappropriate places. He bobbed his head again and whispered too loudly, "What does he have to say? What does the Baron know?"

The Count frowned at his Mentat. "We will find out more quickly if you stop being annoying. Simply observe and remain unobtrusive." Fenring gave the Baron a curious look. "Come, I have a silence-shielded room. We can talk there."

"Silence room," Dardik said. "Solid walls, four chairs. One. Two. Three. Four! One for each of us. Vital and fascinating information." The Mentat squinted his other eye.

The Baron was uneasy with the strange man's presence. "I'd hoped this would remain a private matter between us, Count. We don't need an audience."

Fenring brushed aside the idea. "Come now, I require my Mentat for proper analysis." He shot another sidelong glance at Dardik. "Although he grows more problematic and less useful day by day."

The Baron sensed he couldn't push the matter further. "Yes, I have a Mentat of my own. I haven't done away with him quite yet."

Dardik's voice had a whining tone. "I simply serve you, my Count. You should listen to my intuitions and projections."

"I would listen more often if you spoke less frequently." Fenring strolled off with a prowling gait, expecting the Baron to follow. Margot and the Mentat were close on either side.

The silence room was a small rectangular chamber like a vault. The walls were thick sandstone blocks that looked as if they had been there since some medieval time. The joints between blocks were fused solid, and a film of vibration-dampening polymer had been applied to the floor, walls, and ceiling. Oddly, a small alcove in the sandstone held a vase with three fresh-cut orange flowers. Fresh blooms on Arrakis?

Margot Fenring smiled at them as she entered the room. The Baron realized that much of Fenring's eccentric behavior could be explained by a desire to keep his lovely wife happy. Perhaps that was why he remained in the stately Arrakeen Residency rather than in more modern quarters in Carthag.

The Baron was disappointed to see the room's plain central table and four small chairs, none of which would support his massive weight. Rather than showing embarrassment, he adjusted his suspensor belt and remained standing. The stark chamber was designed for absolute privacy, but without amenities. He already wanted to be away from here and back to Harkonnen headquarters.

Fenring took one of the seats. "Now then, ahhh, my dear Baron—explain this vital and fascinating information, hmm?"

The Baron spoke with conspiratorial seriousness. "I have a way to trap those spice thieves who ran the Orgiz refinery. I know who they are now."

Fenring's attention snapped toward him. "And how have you come by this information? My Mentat and my investigators found nothing."

Beside him, slumped in a chair like a broken marionette, Grix Dardik hummed a strange tune to himself and seemed half-asleep.

The Baron ran a fingertip over the amethyst gem in one of his rings. "I wish I could claim superior prowess, Count, but the truth of the matter is that the answer came to me. You will recall that I already voiced my suspicions that Noble Commonwealth rebels were involved with the spice smuggling."

"A claim with no proof," Dardik said.

"And now I have proof—and a confession," the Baron snapped. "Jaxson Aru himself tried to recruit me into their rebellion. He suggested that House Harkonnen could become one of his most powerful allies, if only I provided him with more melange."

Anger flared crimson across Fenring's face. "The man is a butcher! You remember, ahhh, what he did on Otorio and at the Imperial Palace."

"I do, Count Fenring, but don't sound so indignant. We all have plenty of blood on our hands. I do not make decisions while fainting with emotions." He glanced at Margot Fenring, but she appeared to be more composed than anyone there.

Fenring leaned back in his seat, looking up at the Baron. "Explain yourself."

"The Orgiz refinery was secretly installed and administered by the rebels, but internal rivals swept in and destroyed the operations. Now the Noble Commonwealth is left without their lucrative black-market spice channel."

The Baron paused, hardened his expression. "Jaxson Aru wants me to fill that void, in secret."

"Preposterous!" Fenring muttered.

"Unwise," agreed the Mentat.

"It also presents us with the opportunity for a vital gambit." The Baron drew out the words. "Emperor Shaddam has wanted to eradicate these radicals for a long time. They are like weeds that keep cropping up. He is desperate to stop Jaxson Aru. And we can do it, Count Fenring—you and I."

Fenring let out a nasal hum as he considered. "I told the Emperor we already took care of the spice thieves and executed the perpetrators, so this new information would be rather, ahhh, embarrassing. However, perhaps if we explained that the rebellion made more extensive inroads than we suspected, his anger will not be turned toward us."

"My thoughts exactly," the Baron said. "And if we play this right, we can unravel the Noble Commonwealth movement itself, rather than just dispense with a few spice pirates. Think what a great victory that would be—for you and me. We could reveal all of the secret traitors who work to undermine Corrino rule." He lowered his voice. "I already have strong evidence that Leto Atreides of Caladan is among them. They must all face justice."

Lady Margot raised her delicate eyebrows. "Leto Atreides?"

The Baron made a dismissive gesture. "The Duke of Caladan presents a façade that is too good to be believable. Now we know why—it is all camouflage. Everything will be exposed once we bring down Jaxson Aru."

"Hmm," Fenring said. "But what is your plan? How will you respond to that man's overture?"

"Such is my question for you, Count. You are the Imperial Spice Observer. I wish to be completely aboveboard so that you know my plans, lest I be caught up and branded a traitor as well." Still refusing to sit, the Baron moved lightly around the confined room. "Jaxson Aru demands that I deliver a large shipment of spice to him, an off-books cargo that will finance his rebel activities and also demonstrate my dedication to the movement. It is my . . . initiation."

His gaze bored into Fenring's. "To consummate this deal, I will need the spice for such a shipment. Because I have no illegal stockpiles of my own, this must be Imperially sanctioned melange, a supply from a Carthag warehouse. I will use it like cheese in a rat trap. Inform Shaddam of what we are doing. Once I set up the rendezvous with Jaxson Aru, then we can spring the trap, capture him, and expose his conspirators."

"Hmm." Fenring tapped his fingers on the table as he pondered, then he nodded slowly. "Ahhh."

"But proof!" Dardik interrupted. "We must have evidence. We must have proof. How do we know this isn't a trick set by the Baron Vladimir Harkonnen?"

"Your Mentat skills are faulty," the Baron growled.

"Dardik is unorthodox, I agree," Fenring said, "as well as frustrating. But often brilliant. Unfortunately, he has failed me quite often, of late." He stroked his narrow chin and nodded. "I am reluctant to risk so much spice, but the potential reward makes the risk worthwhile. Jaxson Aru has always enjoyed grandstanding, placing himself where he can flaunt his invulnerability, but that will catch up with him soon enough. Yes, take the necessary melange from an Imperial stockpile here on Arrakis. Then spring your trap."

"I will have my hands around Jaxson Aru's throat." The Baron chuckled. "But we need to inform Shaddam. I may require the use of his Sardaukar."

Fenring seemed satisfied, although his odd Mentat remained barely able to control himself.

The Baron turned to the sealed door of the silent room, beginning to feel claustrophobic. "I'll respond to Jaxson Aru and set the wheels in motion for a rendezvous. Then we will go hunting."

A MOST PECULIAR man without boundaries or common sense, Grix Dardik barged into the private Arrakeen offices just as Fenring was about to retire to a luxurious dinner with his Lady Margot. "I studied the evidence, Count, and there is none! Nothing to study." He clenched his jaw, hardened his lips, then spat out the rest. "This is not correct!"

"Whatever do you mean?" Fenring rose from his desk, pushing aside the spice-paper documents and the carefully forged export manifests. He had easily diverted a significant portion of melange for the Baron's plan. Such transactions could be disguised, and in the worst case, he could always wash his hands of the matter and use House Harkonnen as a convenient scapegoat.

Dardik flurried his fingers in the air as if trying to catch unseen gnats. "No Noble Commonwealth involved with Orgiz! No rebels on Arrakis. I would know. The records would show."

"Records can be modified."

"Not to me," the Mentat insisted. "Orgiz wreckage—no evidence of rebel involvement. No hint of Noble Commonwealth. This is something else."

"No hint of anything, ahhh," Fenring said. "The rebels were careful."

"Easy to be careful if they do not exist!" Dardik said. "Something fishy. Yes, yes, my Count. Fishy—fish. Even here on Arrakis!"

"There are fools on Arrakis, too," Fenring said, impatient. He was hungry for dinner with his wife. "You always annoy me, and you continue to do so more than ever."

"This scheme is false. The Noble Commonwealth was not at the Orgiz refinery. There's another explanation. The Baron is hiding it!"

"Why would the Baron conceal rebel activities? He is the one who came to us, hmm."

"The Baron is not hiding rebel activities!"

Fenring was exasperated. "Then what are you saying?"

"The trap he described is in reality a different sort of trap. This deception is a deceit." Dardik cocked his head from side to side like a metronome.

Angry, Fenring strode up to the odd man, bunching his muscles. "I have made up my mind. You will accept it."

"This scheme is unwise, Count Fenring. Report Baron Harkonnen to the Imperial throne." The Mentat's brow furrowed as a distracted thought rattled through his head. "Though why speak to a throne? A throne cannot hear. No, no, we should talk to Shaddam himself."

"You will do no such thing," Fenring said. "This is a carefully orchestrated plan to quash the rebellion, and I am engineering it with the cooperation of Baron Harkonnen. You will assist."

"It is not within my Mentat projection. Too much margin for error. Large margin. Very marginal. Shaddam needs to know."

"I instructed you to leave it alone," Fenring said. "We have a plan, and if we capture Jaxson Aru, then all other priorities pale in comparison."

"You are pale, and I am pale," Dardik said. "And yet we live in the desert." He shook his head. "No, no, no! Too many questions and dangerous answers. I must—"

Fenring's tolerance had limits, and he had reached them. He raised one hand to grasp the Mentat's scrawny neck, while he placed the other against the side of the large head, pushing with great force in the opposite direction. In an instant, the vertebrae snapped and twisted. Dardik's head lolled to one side, and Fenring shoved him to the ground. The odd man smashed his temple on the side of the desk as he fell dead to the floor. His remarkable brain, so useful at times, was gone.

"I warned you numerous times," Fenring said to the corpse. "I said I would tolerate you only so long as you are useful—and you've ceased to be useful."

Leaving the body to cool while hoping his dinner was still warm, Fenring looked back at his spice-paper documents, stacked them neatly, and went off to enjoy a pleasant evening with Lady Margot.

For some, profits and power are a way of life. For others, violence is a way
of life. None of those paths lead to peace.

      —JAXSON ARU, Noble Commonwealth manifesto, revised

With the intricate web of routes provided by the Spacing Guild, coded communiqués could easily be piggybacked on other packages and rerouted to their undocumented recipients with no one the wiser. The Noble Commonwealth sent most of their secure messages this way.

Jaxson received Baron Harkonnen's response as he waited aboard the orbital-transfer station above Elegy. Thanks to the facial cloning, no one would recognize him. The rebel leader had not informed his new ally Viscount Tull that he was here, so close, but he enjoyed the view of Tull's verdant world. He considered how well this planet would succeed once it was part of the free commonwealth. It made him long to be back at the Nossus base, which Jaxson saw as a reflection of Otorio.

A tiny shigawire knot, almost too small to hold between his thumb and forefinger, was delivered to him as he sat at a polished plasteel table in a café. The server presented a cup of spice coffee, which Jaxson had ordered, and the communication knot, which he had not. The worker departed without a word.

As Jaxson picked up the small tangle of data-infused threads, he stroked his new etched-metal earring, feeling the tenderness on his lobe. With rising anticipation, he removed a tiny player and fed the tendrils of shigawire into its access port. As the message loaded and began to play, the device connected to a tiny Ixian speaker inside his ear canal.

The Baron's answer was just what he had hoped. "I've considered your offer and weighed the potential gain against the risks. Provided we can be discreet, I will offer a cargo of melange, enough spice to finance your movement for a year. Consider it my investment to the cause. No record of this melange exists. No one will know you have it, and no one will know that I have given it to you."

Jaxson sipped his spice coffee, stared through the windowport at the cloud-swirled skies of Elegy far below. The words continued playing in his ear.

"Smuggling you the spice will be a complex and dangerous operation, and you must follow my lead," the Baron continued. "It will take me several weeks to arrange, but I have contacts in CHOAM who can provide appropriate transit documentation. Once it is arranged, I will send you final instructions, which you must follow or all this will be for naught."

The tiny thumb reader destroyed the shigawire filament as it played the message. For extra security, Jaxson snapped the player in half and disposed of the pieces in different incinerator receptacles.

When he heard the boarding announcement for his passenger vessel, he got in the queue with other travelers. Jaxson knew that Baron Harkonnen was treacherous and self-serving, but he was also confident that the wealth dangled in front of him would tempt the ambitious man. Jaxson had his own fallback plan, security, and a clever escape route. Besides, he also had sufficient information against the Baron in his black archives, stored in the memory stone. Once he had a chance to give the Baron a taste of the devastatingly poisonous data he held, the nobleman wouldn't dare turn against him.

Jaxson smiled as he remembered what his mother had said. "There are security systems—firewalls and vaults, classification levels, double-and triple-chain access blocks."

Malina Aru had looked at him, making sure he was listening, and Jaxson drank it all in, even more so than she realized.

"But one less quantifiable factor," she had continued, "is the security provided by bloodlines. Family ties. The Aru line has either run or been instrumental in the highest levels of CHOAM administration for centuries. That is why it's so vital for you, along with your brother and sister, to achieve your full potential for the Company."

After the tragic death of his father, Jaxson had been swept away from his quiet grieving at the sacred family estate on Otorio. A stern parent, Malina had simply assumed he would devote himself to more important things now.

And Jaxson did—although his definition was different from his mother's. "Yes, I know all about the responsibilities of the Aru bloodline, Mother," Jaxson had said, and she assumed that meant he was in full agreement with her. "I know my obligations."

But the Aru bloodline came straight down to him through his father, not his mother, and CHOAM had quietly voted Brondon Aru out of all positions of responsibility, handing the reins over to his far more ambitious wife. Then they had sent Brondon into quiet, embarrassing exile to putter away his days with the useless amusements of the very wealthy.

Once she brought her youngest child to Tanegaard, Malina threw him full force into everything she believed he needed to know, giving Jaxson access. She sent him into the deepest levels of security so that he could be immersed in everything that was CHOAM. Malina had been so pleased with his brother's obvious earnestness, how he pored over the information, learning as fast as he could.

She'd never guessed what he was really doing.

Learning even more, on Kaitain, he sat through interminable meetings in the Silver Needle building, listening to his brother drone on with administrative priorities, using so much tact, care, and diplomacy that even the simplest things took ten times longer than necessary. Frankos was impatient with his obvious boredom, which he misinterpreted as a lack of interest rather than a disagreement on tactics.

During Jaxson's internship on Tanegaard, Malina had sent him to work for some time in the heart of the fortress vault, the large, armored chamber that was the size of a small double-walled warehouse in the middle of the mammoth shielded administrative buildings. This, he learned, was where all of CHOAM's deepest secrets were held.

Slavishly loyal clerks, who had known nothing else in their entire lives, worked inside the fortress vault, arranging hard copy evidence and physical artifacts. The fortress vault contained a warren of storage lockers stacked high, two stories of cubicles and work areas, chambers and sub-vaults, silent and introspective Mentat accountants.

Jaxson worked there, and he impressed his mother. The Ur-Director mentioned to her aide-de-camp Holton Tassé that she was satisfied, even impressed with his change of heart.

But Jaxson had used the opportunity to make his own copies, smuggling in an Ixian memory stone after he had learned about the insidious treasure trove of information CHOAM had maintained over the years. One of the bland, emotionless Mentats had explained offhandedly to Jaxson that CHOAM held on to all of that damning blackmail information as an arsenal of doomsday information to be released only under the most critical circumstances.

This was another instance where Jaxson's definition of a thing differed from his mother's.

Now, after listening to the Baron's response, Jaxson smiled to himself as he got in line with other passengers in the transfer station above Elegy. He slipped his finger inside his pocket and ran his thumb over the smooth, cool surface of the memory stone.

He had used some of this terrible information as a way to ensure the absolute loyalty of his fanatical inner circle. In fact, most noble families were just as vulnerable, if he should ever decide to use this single last resort. His mother and CHOAM had kept the black archives as insurance, which they never intended to use.

Jaxson, though, was somewhat bolder in his approach. It was the only way to succeed.

With rising confidence, he boarded the shuttle and politely offered his first-class seat to a frail old woman who smiled at him. He worked his way to the crowded section in back. In general, Jaxson didn't like being close to so many people, but it was a necessary sacrifice.

He looked at everyone sitting shoulder to shoulder, patiently waiting to be carried across the gulfs of space, and he reminded himself that these were the people he was fighting for, not just the noble families. Everyone would benefit from a commercial commonwealth instead of the despotic Corrino regime. All the Landsraad would thrive, and they would celebrate him, as would his mother, his siblings. Together, they'd entirely reshape the Imperium. House Harkonnen would be among the strongest beneficiaries, as would House Atreides and his friend Duke Leto.

Jaxson sat back in his seat and closed his eyes, listening to the buzz of conversation, the excitement, the anxiety. Many travelers had never gone off-planet before, while others were veteran businesspeople on their way to Kaitain or other trading centers.

Knowing of the deadly rivalry between the families, he had not told Leto about recruiting the Baron. Leto would have balked at the idea, insisting that Jaxson could not trust any Harkonnen. But the Duke of Caladan was not objective, and the Baron would likely say the same thing about Leto.

Rivalries and disputes were what kept a political system vibrant and energized, and competition made commerce more profitable. Leto would have to accept reality, fulfill his part of the plan, and reap the long-term benefits along with all of them. And the Baron would do the same. Hurt feelings and petty emotions had no place in the future of human civilization.

Once the Noble Commonwealth ripped apart the Corrino Imperium, then everyone could be happy and satisfied.

Most people claim to understand honor and to adhere to its principles, but
they can prove it only by facing a supreme moral challenge or crisis.

—DUKE LETO ATREIDES

They scrambled through the jungle, in and out of mottled patches of
afternoon sun and forest gloom. Paul and Duncan were running together now, working in tandem, no longer training or playing a game. Chaen
Marek's mercenary guards at the barra fields had seen them, so they had to get
back to their damaged aircraft, complete the repairs, and get back to Castle
Caladan as swiftly as possible. Paul hoped their landing site had not been
discovered.

He helped the limping Swordmaster over rough, rocky areas, with no time
to scout ahead for the easiest path. The jungle was thick along the slopes,
and the ravines were steep. Speaking little, the two concentrated their energy
on breathing and moving forward through underbrush, trying to stay out of
view of any pursuers. Duncan refused to acknowledge the pain in his ankle,
insisting that the healing tape had taken care of the sprain, but Paul could
read his companion's drawn expression.

The young man had already planned what he would tell Thufir Hawat,
how Atreides forces would mount a swift response to obliterate the fern
plantings—again. Part of him wanted to wait until his father returned to
lead the raid, since the initial strike against Chaen Marek's operations had
cost so many lives. A nagging voice in Paul's head told him he was too young
to make such significant decisions. But these were the mature actions required of a Duke, and his father had placed him in that position. Besides,
Leto Atreides himself had been barely more than fifteen when he'd become
the ruler of Caladan, not much older than Paul was now. . . .

They worked their way through the jungle, thrashing against a veritable
siege line of vines and branches. At other times, the volcanic soil was so poor
that they had to cross barren areas that left them exposed. Paul led the way,
while Duncan watched out for any scout overflight.

"We can't be sure if they'll send pursuit," Paul said. "Can't even be certain they saw us."

"Oh, they saw us, lad. We can hope they think we are members of another primitive Muadh tribe." Duncan pushed dark, sweaty hair out of his eyes. "But we should assume the worst."

After traversing a rolling area devoid of vegetation, Paul glanced behind them to the edge of the jungle and spotted several figures scrambling over rocks in and out of the dense foliage. "The worst is following us," he said.

Shouts came from the pursuers as the pair reached the edge of the trees again. Duncan put on a burst of speed, but Paul could see how much it was hurting him. At least the hunters behind them didn't fire, but they spread out along the slope in an obvious flanking move.

The Swordmaster muttered a curse as he climbed over a fallen log, swinging himself to the other side. "We can run faster now. My ankle is better."

Paul increased his pace, though he could see that Duncan was by no means up to his normal abilities. Now he regretted dropping the vine net on him from above, which had resulted in him twisting his ankle, but the injury seemed to be responding to healing subdermal drugs in the med-wrap. As if sensing his thoughts, the Swordmaster said, "Don't blame yourself. It was part of the hunt." He plowed ahead, pushing foliage away.

Paul said, "Now this is a different hunt, an even more dangerous game, if you want to call it that."

Duncan's tone changed. "This is my failure. I have placed you at grave risk, young Master." Leaning down, he adjusted the med-wrap around his ankle, then moved along the slope more nimbly, defying any pain. "Though I do wish I still had my bow."

A puff of smoke and sparks erupted from a swollen tree. From behind them, the mercenaries shot blasts of red light, blindly mowing down swaths of the jungle. Branches crashed around them, and Duncan ducked, pushing Paul down and covering him with his own larger body. More indiscriminate lasbeams sliced through the foliage. Chunks of rock broke away on the steep slope, tumbling and crashing into the underbrush.

"Fools," Duncan hissed. "They can't be sure we're not wearing shields!"

Paul remembered the Atreides scout flyers that had found Marek's hidden drug operations in the north. The mercenaries had fired lasguns, knowing the interaction with shields on the scout craft would result in a devastating pseudo-atomic explosion. They had been reckless, and fanatical.

These were likely the same.

Now a blast of more intense white light struck a hummock of volcanic rock poised on a steep slope. The big boulders broke apart and began sliding and thundering downhill. Dark birds scattered in all directions, shrieking. Monkeys dashed away as the avalanche gained momentum, sliding back toward the handful of pursuers.

Several hapless men shouted as they tried to scramble out of the way, but the crashing rocks and broken trees slid down to inundate the party. Paul did not feel sorry for them.

Duncan's face was grim as he pressed Paul to keep climbing out of the deep ravine. "The mountain took care of them, and that gives us a head start. But there will be more." Still limping, he defiantly bounded ahead, gaining distance on Paul as he pulled himself uphill through the trees by grabbing vines and knobs of rock.

Paul caught up with him, and they worked their way between two massive slabs of stone before sliding back down the other side. This wasn't the Arondi Cliffs, by any means, and Paul had climbed steeper slopes than this, but his legs were burning from the pace of this exertion. The slippery, moss-covered ground was still dangerous. Loose rocks slipped out of the soft soil and broke, making his balance precarious. Duncan hovered protectively close, where he could grab Paul if he lost his footing and started to fall.

A level ledge allowed them to keep moving without the constant fear of falling. Sweat dripped into Paul's eyes, and he wiped his vision clear. He needed both hands, but he kept gripping the lone arrow as a weapon. He had dropped the makeshift spear during their headlong flight.

He pressed ahead, leading the way across the rock shelf beneath another outcropping, when something clattered at their feet. A sophisticated hunting bow, the one Duncan had been carrying. Its string had been severed.

They both froze. Paul looked around the jungle, expecting to see more of Chaen Marek's pursuers poised to attack. Earlier, some had split off from the main party and made flanking maneuvers.

On the ledge above, a small, pinch-faced man came into view. His skin had a sickly pallor, and his face bore the distinctive rodent features of many Tleilaxu. Imperious, he glowered at the pair. Half a dozen armed men, clearly offworld mercenaries, emerged to stand with him. They held lasrifles.

High overhead, Paul saw a small and silent suspensor-borne flyer cruising just above the thick treetops.

Neither he nor Duncan spoke. Both assessed the situation, glancing downhill into the jungle ravine, a narrow path back down along the churned area that had been ruined by the avalanche. It was a thin and risky line of escape, but Duncan would never be able to descend with his injured foot, especially with mercenaries in pursuit.

The Swordmaster noted the route at the same time. "You go that way," he said in a low voice, but with the command of a training master that Paul knew so well. "It's imperative that you escape, get to the flyer."

"No, I'll fight at your side."

Duncan seized the single arrow out of Paul's hand. "No arguments. I will deal with Marek myself. At the very least, I'll give you a fighting chance. Go—you can only win the game if you survive."

The drug lord gestured, and his mercenaries began to pick their way down toward their quarry.

Conflicting responsibilities and emotions churned through Paul's mind. He couldn't leave Duncan to die, but he also understood the best option, the path to a possible strategic victory. Duncan Idaho would sacrifice anything necessary to protect the heir of House Atreides.

"There are no options, Paul," Duncan called. "We must make our own."

Before he could argue, the Swordmaster lunged up the rock face, grabbing a vine and a tree trunk to pull himself toward the Tleilaxu drug lord. Brandishing the arrow as his only weapon, he did not doubt that Paul would do as he was commanded.

The young man bounded downhill and across the ravaged hillside. The ground was loose and unstable after the rockfall, but he chose his footing carefully to maintain his balance and plunged into the verdant jungle, knowing it would swallow him up.

Behind him, Marek's mercenaries fired streaks of hot light toward him. He heard Duncan's defiant roar, surely meant to buy him more time.

Paul dodged, scrambled, and vanished into the jungle.

Even if an old fighter's physical skills are waning or apparently lost, he can surprise himself in a time of great need, moving with the skill, agility, and speed of a much younger man.

—JOHIN'O, *The Art of the Warrior*

The unmarked craft dropped out of the hold of the Heighliner orbiting Lankiveil. Thufir Hawat had contracted the fast ship from a mercenary service, and it bore no Atreides markings. The craft sped down toward the misty, northern latitudes, transmitting no ID beacon, requesting no landing instructions. Its hull had been enhanced with stealth materials to blur any signal from normal monitors. To Lankiveil's relatively primitive surveillance and security systems, the lone craft would appear to be a smuggler, drawing little attention, not worth the bother.

Thufir had to maintain the deception for only a few minutes, and then he would be on his own.

The warrior Mentat was past his prime as a combat commando, and knew it, but he also knew that no one else was better suited for this particular urgent mission. He could not entangle Duke Leto further because that might have significant repercussions in the Landsraad. If the extraction was successful, Gurney Halleck could testify in Imperial Court what the Harkonnens had done to him, but there was a very strong possibility that Rabban had already killed Gurney and eradicated the body down to the last cells.

Thufir would find out for himself.

Piloting the enhanced mercenary ship, the Mentat was prepared for this operation by the images Duncan and Gurney had taken during their previous surprise raid here. The scattered spy-eyes left behind for passive data-gathering also included real-time images of the facilities and the situation on the ground. Those devices had allowed Gurney to send his desperate message, which had been delivered to Caladan only by roundabout means.

Thufir Hawat had all the information he needed, and he came with a plan, developed using all his tactical skills as a Mentat.

Rabban's holdings were on the night side of the chill world, and Thufir flew the unmarked vessel down in darkness, without running lights. He sat bathed in the stealth-glow of instruments, locating the torture facility on the rough outskirts of one of the main villages. Thufir hoped Count Glossu Rabban would be here in person.

So I can kill him.

With Mentat clarity, he envisioned Rabban's beefy face, his small, dark eyes, full lips, and cruel smile. This man had harmed House Atreides in many ways, but eliminating Beast Rabban was not the priority. He needed to rescue Gurney, or die in the attempt. Success or death. There was no middle ground.

Cold gray clouds locked in the night, and snow covered the headlands around the fjords. Rabban's complex was its own set of structures north of the harbor. Thufir had assessed the best approach, the vulnerable points, and he landed the nondescript ship on a field of dirty ice and snow just above the buildings. The interrogation facilities were separate from the rest of the rustic village, where people lived calm, chilly lives fishing, hunting fur whales, or farming in the rocky soil. But Thufir had no grudge against the people of Lankiveil. He knew his real target.

After he landed in silence, he saw no lights flashing, heard no alarms. Before he swung out of the landed craft, he swallowed a vial of sapho juice to make certain his thoughts were swift and sharp. His aged body felt energetic, all aches and soreness dismissed. He was ready, infused with adrenaline and the sense of extreme urgency that the situation demanded.

From studying reconnaissance, Thufir understood the likely interior layout of the secure buildings, and he had already identified a vulnerable point. The Lankiveil guards would not be expecting such an assault, not even a one-man rescue, because they remained confident that no one knew about the captive.

Wearing dark camouflage garments, he sprinted toward a rear entry point. He remembered a nighttime operation he had conducted when he was much younger, a rescue mission for the Old Duke in a last flareup of the Ecazi Revolt. Back then, he'd had ten commandos, six of whom had survived. Now he was a force of one, only Thufir Hawat, the Atreides Master of Assassins.

His pack contained weapons and special equipment. Film lenses applied to his eyes enhanced his ability to see into the shadows. His belt held a short sword and various knives, as well as his personal shield, which was not yet activated. He inhaled a deep breath of the moist, chill air, feeling the cocktail of prophylactics, stimulants, and other necessary chemicals in his system. He was ready.

During his intricate planning, Thufir had pulled together all available information on Rabban's Lankiveil holdings. The new monolithic building had been built on the site of a much older structure, from when Rabban's parents had been the nominal rulers of the cold planet. Now, as he had expected, Thufir discovered an old drainage system tunneled into the rocks, and he knew the conduits would provide access into the new building. Though the cold air was intense, Thufir used Mentat skills to block out most of the discomfort. He bent over, using cutters and pry bars to break into the drainage access using the old network of pipes.

Through his light-enhancing film lenses, he could see his way without resorting to bright hand lights, which would have been seen. The cold and wet was miserable, but he worked his way underground in the direction of the new complex, reaching the point where the old tunnel connected to the new drainage system. From there, he had a straight shot into a lower level of Rabban's fortress.

He moved quickly and smoothly, trying not to think of his age. He had been an expert fighter during his early years serving Duke Paulus Atreides. Those had been halcyon days of steadfast service and camaraderie, and even though he now spent most of his effort in training, strategy, and tactics, and counsel for his Duke, he was still a formidable fighter. He had his Mentat mind, his plans, and a good deal of his strength. He alone would be more than sufficient for this operation.

Ducking low, seeing through the shadows of the cold, empty tunnels, he focused on the present. He needed to find Gurney Halleck.

At the end of the frigid tunnel, he dismantled the fasteners that held a wall grate in place and emerged into a sub-basement chamber illuminated with low light. He flexed his muscles, stretched, mentally drove back the cold, and moved on.

Just outside the subbasement chamber, he smelled a terrible odor growing stronger—the unmistakable stench of death. At the base of a set of stone stairs leading upward, he came upon three corpses heaped in disarray, arms and legs akimbo. Obviously, these victims had been thrown down the stairs, tossed away like garbage. On a closer glance, he saw the bodies were bruised and torn. Obviously, the victims had been tortured before being killed.

Breathing through his mouth and ignoring the smell, he checked their smashed faces, saw enough to be sure that Gurney was not among them. One had his eyes gouged out, and another his hand severed, and the third his skull smashed open to expose brain tissue. The blood had darkened and dried, and the cadavers—undoubtedly here for days—had begun to bloat and rot, even in the cold temperatures.

On occasion, as the head of security for House Atreides, Thufir had been forced to use extreme methods to extract vital knowledge from a spy or saboteur.

But he had never treated anyone like this. His stomach sank. What were they doing to Gurney now?

He paused in place, listened, gazed around as he gathered data, assessing what he saw and comparing it with what he knew from the intelligence briefings. He listened into the frozen silence, made sure no one was approaching.

He stepped over the bodies and assembled data from what he saw of his surroundings, running Mentat calculations and determining the odds of anyone discovering him. With a whisper of metal and leather, he slid his short sword from its scabbard and held it in one hand, with a long dagger in the other. Both weapons bore the hawk sigil of House Atreides, excellent weapons that Thufir had used for years. On full alert and with mounting rage, he crept up the shadowy steps.

On an upper landing, he found a severed hand, no doubt the appendage missing from the body below. Then he saw a bloody arm sawed off from a different corpse he had not yet seen. And it was much fresher.

At the top of the stairs to the main level, a plasteel door blocked his way. Before trying to open the barrier, he went almost motionless, placing his ear against the metal, while also touching the surface with his fingertips. He knew the construction of such doors, a plasteel exterior with layers of filler. The surface was cold, but not frozen, suggesting that the other side might be heated. He assumed guards or Rabban's troops must be waiting there.

He concentrated, slowed his breathing so that only wisps of white steam drifted up. He had made himself go into a partial hibernation, and then he warmed himself again, preparing. His mind was fully aware, calculating at hyper speed.

If torture victims were discarded here in the cold lower levels, they must eventually be taken away, incinerated, buried, or dumped into the cold waters of the fjord. But if the human wreckage was tossed here initially, it implied a certain amount of laziness as well as a harsh intent to instill fear. In all likelihood, the torture chambers were nearby.

Applying every bit of concentration to his senses, he heard activity on the other side of the barrier, a distant hum of voices. He gradually built a picture of the ebb and flow of movement, and his body was loaded like a spring, ready to move fast—

Suddenly, the door swung open with a metallic thump, casting bright light from the outer corridor. Thufir's film lenses instantly filtered the illumination to the proper level. A pair of Rabban's guards stood there, carrying a bloody body with the missing arm.

They did not expect to see a stranger on the other side of the door. Thufir was already moving even before they registered that anything was wrong. Holding the victim's bloody body in their hands, they could not move to defend themselves. The old warrior darted forward, a blade in each hand, stabbed one man in the heart and the other in the throat. The guards were dead before they could gurgle a sound, before they could even realize what had happened.

As both men collapsed, Thufir grabbed them and used gravity to shove them back through the doorway, along with their grisly burden. All three corpses tumbled down the stone steps, and Thufir was through into the main section of the facility. He closed the plasteel door behind him and began sprinting through the corridor, constantly glancing from side to side and over his shoulder.

He heard voices ahead, saw a closed door with blue light under it. The rest of the corridor was empty, and he sensed his target in the sealed chamber, thought he heard a snippet of his friend's voice, in pain. Pausing outside the room, he removed another device from his pack, adjusted a needle gun, preparing it to fire. The torturers, and their subject, would not be wearing personal shields. When he was ready, his pack back in place, he strode up to the door and pulled it open, just as if he were one of the guards returning to his post.

His film lenses could not block out what he saw inside the chamber, though he made a lightning assessment before the Harkonnen techs could respond to him. A man and a woman dressed in black worked an appalling mechanism comprised of stretching and stabbing components. They operated intricate controls, adjusting the various settings of the monstrous equipment.

Gurney Halleck was strapped to the device, making small sounds of anguish but obviously trying to suppress any expression of pain.

But he was alive, and all of his limbs were intact, though he was blood-splattered.

The stretching, stabbing device dragged the subject to extremes, making him twitch, jerk, and spasm. Intense blue lights flashed and strobed around the machine. Gurney's eyes were closed. He was probably barely conscious, his bruised face racked with agony.

Thufir's mind locked on the important point. Gurney was alive!

He immediately shifted his plan. Already moving into the chamber, each moment fragmented into smaller and smaller instants, he swung up his dart pistol and fired a needle directly at Gurney. The dart plunged into the battered man's shoulder.

Then the Mentat triggered the gas canister in his pack. He could hear the hiss emitting from the nozzle, but the fumes were invisible. He lunged toward the two startled torturers as they looked up from their work and tried to with-draw from the torture machine. The male tech spun toward a table covered with knives and pointed rods, but halfway there, he faltered, suddenly disori-ented. The woman's blood-spattered face paled, and she looked sick.

Thufir strode in calmly, a blade in each hand. He did not fear these vile people. The male torturer pawed at a knife on the table, but could barely make his fingers move. The razor edge of his intended weapon slashed the side of his own hand, but the man didn't seem to feel it.

"Allow me to introduce myself," Thufir said with a cruel smile. "I am the Atreides Master of Assassins, and I am on duty." He could still hear the last whispers of gas sputtering from the pressurized container. He slapped the knife out of the torturer's reach. The man seemed astonished that his arm would not work. He wheezed in a deep breath.

Thufir explained, even as the pair of torturers were obviously fading, "I flooded this room with a deadly nerve toxin. You already inhaled it."

The woman collapsed to her knees. Thufir stepped up to her, then shoved her away from Gurney on the complex rack. "I, of course, took the antidote as a precautionary measure, and I administered it to my comrade as well." He plucked the needle out of Gurney's skin. "We are both immune."

The male torturer grasped at the implements on the table and slumped to the floor, bringing the tools down with a clatter.

"You, however, are not," Thufir said.

As the torturers died gasping like Caladan fish left out in the sun, Thufir hurried to the mechanism and deactivated the controls. The searing blue lights sparked, then went dark. He swiftly worked the release catches on Gur-ney's form hanging in the rack and harness. One of the bruised arms flopped loose, then the other. Thufir caught his comrade protectively, then propped him up so that he could loosen the other bindings.

With a shout, a Harkonnen guard ran into the torture room. He pulled out a blade of his own, snarling at the Mentat. "Stop! You are—"

Then he staggered, gasped several times, and lurched forward.

Thufir paid no attention to him. "I have you, Gurney—you're free. The nerve gas will take care of anyone else here who might try to stop us. I'll get you out of here and back to Caladan. You have already sacrificed enough."

The dying guard sprawled on the ground, wheezing, retching, and finally fell still.

Gurney groaned, and Thufir supported him, smearing his own uniform with the other man's blood. He looked closely at Gurney's face, saw the old inkvine scar on a bruised, purplish jaw. His eyes were badly bruised, swollen shut. But Gurney recognized the old Mentat's voice. "No . . . not enough. I failed."

"You didn't fail. I am taking you out of here."

The battered man could barely retain his hold on consciousness, but Thufir had prepared for this. The last heavy items in his pack were two small suspensors, which he attached to Gurney's garments. When he activated them, they hummed and raised the man gently into the air, keeping him hanging there, adrift.

Gurney tried to struggle, but the suspensors kept him inert. Thufir placed a reassuring hand on his face, then moved the weak man along beside him, guiding him like a floating package out into the corridor. He held his short sword in his right hand, using the other to maneuver Gurney.

Leaving the torture chamber and the three bodies on the floor, Thufir went about covering his tracks. He activated a pair of time-delayed explosive charges and tossed them into the chamber, after calculating how much time he had and how far he had to go. Gurney fought to regain his strength, but Thufir relied only on himself.

Pulling his comrade behind him now, the warrior Mentat rushed down the corridor, following his planned escape route. He moved silently, his senses alert.

From behind them, he heard approaching footsteps, and five uniformed guards came around a corridor at a fast clip. Seeing him, they drew their blades and bounded forward.

Thufir looked ahead, knowing he had to get to the plasteel door and the subbasement, and from there to the drainage systems outside. Even with the aid of the suspensors, Gurney slowed him. Thufir had to stall the oncoming guards.

In another part of his Mentat mind, he calmly counted down the seconds remaining.

He pulled open the plasteel door, swung it wide out into the corridor so that it blocked two-thirds of the passage.

One of the rushing guards paused to duck inside the torture chamber, where he, too, inhaled the nerve gas. And did not emerge.

Thufir maneuvered Gurney—still on suspensors—through the doorway and down the stone steps. Gurney was twitching more now, lifting his bruised hands. As Thufir ducked into the stairwell right behind Gurney, he seized the fresh corpse on top of the stairs and dragged the body back into the corridor, wedging the door open and blocking most of the corridor as the guards came running.

Only a few seconds more.

While Gurney drifted down to the lower level, like an autumn leaf falling slowly to the ground, Thufir turned back to glance at Rabban's thugs. A Mentat could study the slightest movements of an opponent and project how each one would attack, and utilize that data to counter each strike.

The four remaining guards worked together to push the plasteel door against the mangled corpse, partly closing it so they could get past more easily. As they saw only the old Mentat facing them, they paused in momentary confusion.

Now that Gurney was far enough down the stairs and Thufir had both hands free again, he drew his knife as well as his short sword. Seeming to slow and freeze time, he studied the four Harkonnens, assessed which one filled the role of leader, calculated the odds, made four projections, and then combined them into one—a vision into the future through firm probabilities. He swam in among the men in the corridor, swirling and striking, each moment clear in his mind.

Thufir lashed out with the knife and caught the point man, made a quarter turn to thrust the short sword into his torso. His first blow ripped open the side of the leader's chest, and the follow-through hit the man's heart from the side, and he fell.

With their leader down, the other three guards reeled, tried to regroup, and one man lunged forward—exactly as the Mentat had projected. Thufir's knife was already rising, placing the deadly point in the inevitable position, and the attacking guard impaled himself. Thufir gutted him with a precise upward slice of his short sword from the groin to the chest.

He leaped over the man's body to confront the other two. So far, he had anticipated all of this, every move. Just as he'd expected, the remaining guards fought as a pair, coming at him together from opposite angles.

With a neat slice of his sword, Thufir decapitated them both. Their heads and bodies tumbled to the floor, blood spurting.

He didn't bother to shove the body parts down the stairs. No time. Instead, he ducked behind the plasteel door and nudged a corpse out of the way, so that the door slowly swung closed again. At the bottom of the stone stairs, Gurney was struggling to free himself from the suspensors.

Thufir bounded to the lower level as the countdown in his mind reached its end.

Right on schedule, the explosives went off in the torture room on the level above. The boom rocked the floor and walls. Plates shook loose from the ceiling, and part of the upper corridor caved in.

Thufir snagged the rescued Atreides fighter, pulling him toward the drainage pipe and the escape access. "Very well, Gurney Halleck, the fun part is over. We still have to get out of here and back to Caladan."

Loyalty is a primal thing, a blood-deep instinct to serve and protect the pack. Unfortunately, as our species evolves, loyalty becomes less of a natural response and more artificial.

—MALINA ARU, Ur-Director of CHOAM

U pon her return from the undocumented side trip to Jaxson's base of operations on Nossus, Malina Aru knew that a crushing weight of CHOAM business would loom before her. Holton Tassé and other senior aides were unsettled by the Urdir's capricious schedule when they could normally account for every hour like clockwork. She had departed for Giedi Prime to meet with Baron Harkonnen to discuss his failure to maintain the profitable black-market spice-export channel—which neither Tassé nor any of her underlings knew about. Then she had gone off to Nossus, an even more dangerous secret to be kept from the Company at all costs.

When her vessel settled onto the rooftop landing zone of the gigantic citadel administration building, Malina emerged, bracing for a rush of bureaucrats and administrators, committee chairs and division heads, each one clutching at matters they considered vitally important.

But she could not give them priority. Not yet.

As Holton Tassé strode forward like an advancing warrior, with eleven other CHOAM uniformed functionaries directly behind him, Malina held up her hand, which was like a blast door slamming in their faces.

"Not now," she said. "Not yet."

Behind her, Har trotted down the ramp, sniffing the air and glancing around. His silvery fur bristled. She reached down to pat his head, feeling a surge of warmth as well as urgency. "Take me to the infirmary. Once I know about Kar, then I can see to your other concerns."

The aide-de-camp's demeanor shifted abruptly. He straightened, then turned. "Follow me, Ur-Director."

The Tanegaard citadel city had sophisticated medical facilities, which were used by the countless human hive workers to maintain the health of CHOAM employees; it was considered an investment to maintain their assets and workflow. Tanegaard had numerous Suk doctors under lifetime contracts for the upper-echelon executives and countless others on retainer as needed for the rest of the planet's population.

While she was gone on the recent brief but mandatory mission, one entire medical suite had been converted into a veterinary center for Kar. Malina pushed forward with Har as always at her heels. When she reached the doorway and the sealed transparent walls, an attendant tried to prevent her from letting the spinehound enter with her. The attendant failed.

A surgical bed designed for humans had been moved off to one side of the sterilized room. A large holding chamber like a transparent cage contained her other spinehound, and Malina spotted him immediately.

Seeing her enter, Kar pricked up his ears and raised his head. She was alarmed to see her pet so droopy and wrung out, as if much of the life force had been drained out of him. Kar's abdomen had been shaved and the bare area crisscrossed with strips of woundplaz. Two Suk doctors turned to face the Ur-Director, and they nodded solemnly as she pushed forward. "Ur-Director, we have reason for optimism."

"Then you have reason to live," Malina said. Har growled at the two doctors as if sensing that they had inflicted pain on his brother spinehound. As she approached the plaz walls, Kar seemed to swell with more energy, rising to his feet. His molten-copper eyes brightened. "You harmed him. Weakened him." It came out as an accusation.

"We cured him using extraordinary measures," countered one of the Suk doctors.

The other added, "The tumor had grown rapidly, spreading tendrils throughout the stomach and intestines and into the liver. It was a terminal condition."

Cold and clammy with fear for the well-being of the beloved animal, Malina bent down to place her palm against the side of the plaz kennel. "But Kar is alive."

"The spinehounds were grown in Tleilaxu vats," said the first Suk with an expression of distaste on his face. "Their lab techs and executives understood the problem far better than we could, Ur-Director—no doubt through tests and experiments on thousands of other spinehound subjects. They provided us with new tissue, replacement internal organs."

The other doctor interjected, "At considerable price."

"I am the Ur-Director of CHOAM!" Malina snapped. "There is no price I will not pay. The Tleilaxu know better than that." But she realized there would be a price from those people . . . and she would take care of it.

Without asking permission, she opened the plaz door, and Kar made his best effort at bounding out. Malina caught the spinehound, careful with the sharp daggers of his fur, and pulled him close. Har came forward to lick his brother's muzzle.

Despite the impossible political pressures weighing on her and the terrible decision she had made about her renegade son, for the moment, her love and care went to these two animals. They would never turn against her, never question her, and always be faithful. Jaxson could have learned a great deal from these spinehounds.

"We will feed Kar properly—energy supplements, antibiotics," she said to the Suk doctors. "His recovery will go faster if he is back with Har—and me."

The doctors bowed, knowing from the tone of her voice that their opinion would not be entertained.

She felt lighthearted, relieved, and satisfied. She had been *so* concerned about her ailing hound, even with all the other matters hammering her.

But when she saw Holton Tassé standing at the doorway to the medical unit, the heaviness returned. He said, "Urdir, I have an important report for you." He glanced at the Suk doctors, the medical infirmary personnel.

She nodded and walked with him, maintaining a slow pace. Kar limped slightly and moved with an awkward, halting gait because of the surgery and woundplaz bandages, but he dutifully kept up.

Tassé led her into a small room with rounded interior walls that looked as if they'd climbed inside the shell of an egg. When the door was sealed and the neutralizing fields thrummed along the inner surfaces, the aide-de-camp closed his eyes, reciting precise details from memory. "Urdir, we have continued our investigation into the potential leak of data from the black archives. None of the originals or physical backups are missing. The documents and tangible artifacts have not been disturbed."

"Then what gives you cause for concern?" she asked. She wasn't flippant or impatient; such was the man's defined job, and he had never been unnecessarily paranoid before.

"I found indications that the highly secret data was reviewed by a person or persons, although to my knowledge no one was authorized to do so."

"Who did that?"

"Unknown, but the fact remains that if the data was accessed, then all or portions of it could have been copied."

"Copied . . ." Malina took a seat, and the spinehounds eased down to the floor on either side of her. Kar moved quite gingerly. "How could anyone copy such an enormous amount of data?"

"There are technologies, Urdir—mostly forbidden and highly uncommon, but not impossible." At last, he opened his eyes. "An Ixian memory stone, for instance, or a Richesian data coil, though the capacity of a coil would be much smaller."

Malina's thoughts spun. That archive was CHOAM's deadliest information—an insurance policy that was their absolute last line of defense. To use it, or threaten to use it, would be so far beyond the pale that—

A cold thought rippled through her so deep that it made her gasp. She *knew* who had done it. Kar began to whimper, and Har pricked up his ears. Holton Tassé remained motionless, implacable.

Malina considered Jaxson's radical inner circle, the rebels who were willing to burn down the Imperium to rebuild as they liked, rather than the careful transformation into a free Noble Commonwealth. Jaxson could use the poisonous information in the black archives as a cudgel, and she didn't doubt the others would as well.

After her conversation with Duke Leto Atreides on Nossus, she still hadn't decided on his true motivations. As her Mentats had warned her, the man's participation was anomalous, unsuited to his character. But she could not concern herself with one minor nobleman. She had to move now, in a preemptive act that would place them all in front of the massive hammer of Imperial justice.

Enough was enough. She needed to take drastic action to save CHOAM.

In all things, I have sought the just and honorable course, but it is arrogant to think that my personality and force of will are all that shape House Atreides. Rather, it is the long historical legacy of our Great House and our remarkable Caladan that have shaped me, as well as my son, so that we are able to leave the proper traditions for generations to come.

—DUKE LETO ATREIDES, planetary archives

As the Duke returned home at last, he felt heartsore, shaken, and on edge. He needed to be with the wide-open skies and expansive oceans, where he could hear the whisper of Caladan seas and feel his world and his heritage. There, his bruised heart and soul could recharge, though he knew his great battles were not yet over.

When Leto arrived at the Cala City Spaceport early one afternoon, Thufir Hawat was not there to meet him, and when he made his way back to the castle, he was surprised to find the ancient stone edifice relatively empty except for a disarray of small crises. The planet of Caladan was calm and stable, but its headquarters seemed abandoned.

He had left Paul to serve as steward here in the role of Duke with his cadre of regents and advisers, but the young man and Duncan had been gone for several days on a training exercise to the south. Though he was disappointed at not seeing his son right away, Leto found nothing untoward about such an expedition, knowing the Swordmaster would keep Paul from harm. Thufir Hawat was thoroughly capable of managing the administrative work and daily business—but apparently Hawat, too, had rushed away from Caladan on some mysterious errand.

At least his beloved homeworld was at peace and untroubled. The work of overseeing the holdings of House Atreides continued through numerous deputies and ministers, but Leto remained unsettled. While he had not required the fanfare of a loud homecoming, he wanted to see Paul, if only to talk with him about what he had done.

Being among the dangerous rebels had left him frayed, and the discovery of Lord Londine's involvement in the abhorrent "Caladan drug" infuriated him. Leto wanted to wash the foul taste out of his mouth. But he could not cleanse himself of the radical movement until he disarmed Jaxson Aru and stripped him of the dangerous, explosive information contained on his memory stone. Leto had to tread carefully, thinking he alone held the fate of the Imperium in his hands.

Leto stalked through the castle, changed clothes in his quarters, and then emerged to find the household staff making arrangements to welcome him. They were glad to have their Duke back, but he was anxious for answers. He spoke to several primary retainers, finally extracting the broad strokes of the situation.

Worse, Leto learned that Gurney Halleck had not yet returned from his mission to Kaitain. Had something gone wrong with delivering the message to Shaddam?

Now he sat at a small desk on a covered private balcony, sipping a cup of bitter local tea as he reviewed a stack of summary documents the ministers had gathered for him. He just wanted the comfort of small, local matters. It was cooler than expected out here, but he had an efficient outdoor heater overhead, and a heated deck beneath his feet.

His quarters—his empty quarters—had the large and lavish bed that seemed far too vacant now that Jessica was forever gone.

He listened to the rumble of the surf against the rocks. It was high tide, and all the pools below the castle were submerged, turning the beach and rocky walkway down there into an angry swirl of water. High on the cliff, Leto was caught in another kind of undertow, swept up in the tides of history, and he had to swim or be smashed against the reefs.

Sensing movement, he looked behind him to see the Suk doctor standing patiently at the door of his balcony. The servants had let Dr. Yueh in, but the quiet medical man waited to attract Leto's attention. The Duke smiled in relief. "Yueh, please join me. At least I can count on you. Tell me what's happened since I was gone."

The sallow man entered. He wore clean, professional Suk robes, and his long hair was combed silky smooth and bound with a silver ring in a ponytail behind his back. The diamond tattoo on his forehead was a constant reminder of Yueh's supreme training, conditioning, and unbreakable loyalty. "My Lord Duke, we did not know when you would return. We had no way of contacting you."

Leto gestured for him to sit. "That was my intent." He refilled his tea and held the pot for a moment, looking around awkwardly without seeing a second cup to offer the doctor.

Yueh stroked his long mustaches. "I'm happy to give you a report, my Lord—the state of Castle Caladan, from my perspective."

"Indeed, Yueh. I would like some answers. I feel as if my household has scattered to the four winds. First Jessica and now Thufir, Gurney, even Paul and Duncan, all gone . . ."

"Your son and Duncan Idaho are merely on a training exercise and not expected back for several days." Yueh frowned. "I cannot give you details about Lady Jessica, I'm afraid. Yes, my wife is a Bene Gesserit, but I've not spoken with her in some time." Though he sounded deeply sad, his demeanor became professional again. "Caladan is such a safe and quiet place, a pocket of peace in the Imperium. Yet there is much that troubles me."

Leto drank more tea, deep in thought. "I couldn't agree more, Yueh. Though we may think we are peacefully isolated, Caladan is still a vital cog in the Imperium. That is why Jaxson Aru wanted to recruit me, to help disrupt the machinery of House Corrino." He clenched his hands, feeling the hard metal of the ducal signet ring on one. "Do you know why Gurney has not yet returned? He should have been back from Kaitain some time ago."

Yueh looked away. "We received alarming information, Sire. Gurney Halleck is being held prisoner by Glossu Rabban on Lankiveil."

Leto shot to his feet. "Gurney captured by Rabban? How did that happen? The Baron's nephew hates him. Gurney will not survive long. We must call the Atreides forces, launch a full military assault to rescue him."

"That is why Hawat is away, Sire. We had no way to contact you, and he made his own decision. He departed on a solo mission to rescue Halleck, so as not to embroil House Atreides formally in an overt military attack."

"Hawat alone? But he is . . ."

"Old?" the Suk doctor asked. "He is still a warrior Mentat, and he has fought countless battles for House Atreides. This is one more in a long résumé."

Leto nodded. "Aye, and a wise man he is. Any direct attack would bring Landsraad censure down upon us." He ground his teeth, angry and dissatisfied, then slowly sat back down. "I don't like this, but if anyone can do it, Thufir can."

"We must have faith that God will reward the righteous," Yueh said.

"Now you sound like Gurney," Leto muttered. "We must also have faith in the abilities of our men." A chill ran down his back. "Do we know whether Gurney was seized before or after he delivered my message to the Emperor? Is it possible that Shaddam doesn't realize my actions with the rebels are a deep-cover ruse?"

The Suk doctor shrugged, and Leto felt heat rise in his cheeks. The doctor said, "As a worst case, we must assume he did not." Yueh took the offered seat next to the desk. "And what about you, my Lord? Will you remain here now? Are you finished with your mission? The people of Caladan need their Duke."

"They do." Leto looked down at his signet ring, rubbing it with his thumb.

"But the Imperium also needs this rebellion to end and its perpetrators brought to justice. The radical movement is far worse than I'd expected. The destructive tentacles extend throughout the Landsraad, a poison creeping like gangrene in our political system."

Briefly, he explained to Yueh what he had learned about Lord Londine and the continuing distribution of ailar. "The fern-growing operations are based right here on Caladan, under our noses again, but we don't know where. Damn! After we obliterated the operations in the north, I assumed Chaen Marek would be more careful in the future." His hand tightened into a fist. "I can't deal with this until I bring down Jaxson Aru."

He went out on the balcony, with Yueh following. The clouds out over the water turned gray as the wind ruffled his dark hair. Leto turned toward the other man. "I need to make plans, Yueh. Caladan will have to take care of itself a little while longer, and we know Paul and Duncan will return soon. But I cannot stay."

The Suk doctor looked alarmed. "Where are you going, Sire?"

"To intercept Jaxson Aru." He thought of the rebel leader and his memory stone. "This is a more delicate and dangerous time than ever, and I may be the only one who can defuse his ticking bomb."

As sea breezes picked up, the two men gathered up the summary documents and retreated into Leto's quarters from the balcony, and Yueh closed the double doors against the wind.

Leto was focused on solving yet another problem, though, mitigating the risk. "If the Emperor never received my explanation, then he will think that I have joined the rebellion—and we know the reprisals Shaddam can inflict. Remember what the Sardaukar did to Duke Verdun's world."

He placed a firm hand on Yueh's narrow shoulder and his voice grew grave. "You are the only one here I can trust completely. You know all of my plans. Let me make a recording, a full explanation that you will hold for safekeeping, just in case . . ."

The Suk doctor's eyes flicked back and forth. "A wise decision, my Lord. I will be happy to assist. Let me bring a portable imager."

Alone in the large, empty chamber, the Duke composed himself and strengthened his resolve. This needed to be done.

When Yueh had set up the recording device inside the private chamber, Leto delivered a thorough explanation in a calm, professional voice. He talked about how he had accepted Jaxson's invitation to join the rebellion, but only with the purpose of slipping inside the movement. He described how he meant to work toward preventing further violent actions as a rogue infiltrator. He detailed what he had done on Issimo III, how he had prevented a horrific tragedy there. With rising anger, he spoke of Gurney Halleck's mission that should already have revealed everything to Shaddam, and how his man had been captured. Rabban, almost certainly with the knowledge and support of Baron Harkonnen, had subverted vital information, preventing the Emperor from receiving it.

The Suk doctor flinched at the mention of the Baron, and Leto didn't blame him. The thought of the fat, vengeful nobleman made him sick as well.

Being thorough, Leto also listed names of the other conspirators he had met on Nossus, those who planned to spread the violence. He wanted such radicals to face Imperial justice, and he hardened his thoughts toward Rajiv Londine.

After completing the recording, he pressed the tight shigawire spool into Yueh's delicate hands. "Hold this for me, and use it if necessary. Paul already has my last testament to him, but this is more detailed and unequivocal. It should be proof of my intentions. You are the only one who knows it exists."

The doctor's mustaches drooped as he frowned. "Shaddam and his cronies can still find a way to disbelieve you, Sire. They will say that you recorded this just to cover yourself."

"Then I'll rely on you to convince them. Three others—Thufir, Gurney, and even Paul—can vouch for my actions if they are here to speak on my behalf. But let us not consider that—it won't come to such an end." He squared his shoulders. "I intend to stop Jaxon Aru myself."

Knowing he could not tarry, he prepared for travel again back to Nossus, not sure when the rebel leader would expect him, but Leto felt an increasing anxiety. He had no time to lose. He regretted that he wouldn't have a chance to see Paul before departing.

But Duke Leto would reconnect with his son when he returned, triumphant, to Caladan. For now, he had to plunge back into the rebel snake pit.

How do you know when you have met the love of your life? If you need to ask this question, you have not yet met that person.

—The journals of Lady Jessica

Paul careened into the primal tangle of the jungle, using the survival skills Duncan had taught him, as well as his mother's sophisticated Bene Gesserit observational techniques, and the cautious wisdom of Thufir Hawat. Even as he disappeared into the morass of foliage, Paul took note of his surroundings, the slanted trees, the cluster of orange flowers, an odd outcropping like a broken tooth. He ran pell-mell, and he heard Chaen Marek's hunters crashing after him, but he memorized his random path, always keeping track of where he was . . . and how he could get back to the flyer.

Thanks to Duncan's quick turnabout against the mercenaries, the young man had a head start, and once he had gotten out of sight, ducking and dodging through the deepest underbrush, he forced himself to use cleverness rather than panic. This was no longer a game, and it was deadly. He knew how ruthless Chaen Marek was, but when the men had surrounded him and Duncan, they obviously wanted to capture them, not kill them. If the Tleilaxu drug lord were to learn who Paul really was, that would dramatically alter the situation—with the heir of Caladan as a hostage. Paul vowed not to give Marek such leverage over his father.

It was up to him, his wits, and his skills.

The jungle was even thicker in the deep valleys farther down the mountain. Paul plunged into the leafy gloom, scratched by branches and thorns, squelching soft mushrooms under his feet. He wanted to circle around, ambush the captors and free Duncan—but he had only his knife, not even the lone arrow anymore. The Swordmaster would be angry if he took such a foolhardy risk.

Paul needed to get to the flyer and spend hours there making the last of the crude repairs, in hopes that he could limp back to Castle Caladan, where he could rally a full military response. No other priorities were comparable.

Driving back his wild instincts, he determined where to go, instinctively heading toward where he had brought the flyer down for its hard landing.

The jumbled terrain did not let him travel in a straight line, but he set his bearings. If all went well, he might be able to reach the aircraft by nightfall. How long would Chaen Marek keep Duncan alive? He was sure he could count on the Swordmaster.

Now he moved with slower steps in the dappled sunlight, scanning with his eyes and ears. He prowled through thickets, tried to leave no mark for trackers, sometimes moving along game trails, other times pushing thick leaves out of his way or ducking around massive fallen trees. The steep, uneven slope gave him a proper sense of the undulating mountainside, and occasional glimpses of the ocean helped him align where he should find the aircraft.

Steep rilles and deep valleys pushed him off course, and he had to work his way around to where he could make more headway toward the isolated clearing. He remembered seeing a wider path on an adjacent slope, not quite a road, but a trampled route no doubt used by the primitive villagers hidden out here.

As the sun lowered in the west, he concluded that if he could get on that path, he would at least have a landmark, and he could keep moving even after dark. By now, he thought he had outpaced any pursuit, but he remained wary.

He crossed a streambed with water trickling down from the slopes. He drank the cool liquid, then filled a water bottle from his pack, thinking of immediate survival as well as longer-term plans. As he crouched next to the brook, behind the whispering water, he heard buzzing from the opposite bank. It reminded him of insects like large cicadas, growing louder.

Cautiously, he moved downhill, but the sounds followed him. Paul hopped over a pair of protruding rocks and crossed to the opposite bank to see if he could get a better vantage. But thick vines in the underbrush twitched and writhed, then moved, rising from the underbrush—not vines, he realized to his shock, but swollen, snakelike creatures that came up from the soft ground, through the jungle duff and mulch. They writhed and quested, lifting on all sides, towering above him.

He froze, fearing they would respond to motion, but saw no avenue of escape.

The serpent creatures had no apparent eyes, just smooth, throbbing scales on their undulating bodies. Sparkles of static danced around their blunt heads, and crackling electrical charges jolted between the multiple snake heads, reminding Paul of deadly elecrans out on the Caladan seas. But these were land-bound, clearly physical creatures, not braided energy like the ocean elemental beings.

Aware of his presence, the rising serpents swayed, and began to close the circle around him. Three of the blunt-headed snakes lunged toward him, then snapped back in surprise when Paul slashed at them with his knife and a stick he grabbed as a makeshift spear. With these insignificant weapons, he doubted he could last long.

As the serpents sparked small discharges of internal electricity, they hovered in the air, as if assessing him. Paul bounded toward one of the snakes with his pointed stick outstretched. The serpents seemed to be blind, but perhaps they had highly developed hearing. He shouted a loud battle cry, drawing the attention of the electrical creatures.

But before he threw himself against the monster, a young woman's voice shouted out. "Not like that, fool! Drop to the ground!"

Paul knew how to react to barked training orders in a dangerous combat situation, and he responded instantly. The nearest crackling snake lunged as the teenager dropped to the dirt. The blunt-headed serpent shot past him violently, then snapped back like a whip. The other snakes rose, sending bright discharges between their heads.

Paul rolled, still ready to dodge an attack, but as he looked up, he heard rough voices in the underbrush, men and women speaking in heavy accents. A series of spiked cords twirled around the heads of the snake creatures, barbed lines that squeezed in around each long, scaly body. When the barbed loops tightened, the fleshy serpent heads bulged, warm membranes that emitted more crackles of electricity. As the spiked bolos continued to tighten, the serpentine bodies writhed and finally collapsed.

When the dying snake things slumped back to the thick jungle floor, the soil itself roiled as if coming alive, and the wormlike creatures softened, immersing partly into the loose duff and disassociating, as if their body mass had been composed of jungle debris . . . just as elecrans drew upon water. As his strange rescuers kept pulling and tightening the spiked cables, the multiple serpent creatures perished.

One of the blunt, blind heads dropped heavily onto the ground next to Paul, still sizzling and cracking with static electricity. He sprang to his feet, dodging out of the way, and found himself surrounded by strangers, who were as curious as they were threatening.

He looked at the young woman whose voice he had heard first, the same olive-skinned girl he'd seen earlier. Now his eyes locked with her brown-eyed gaze, and he saw that she was close to his age, maybe a year or two older. And while the other people with her were obviously Muadh natives, in skins and rough woven garments, the girl had lighter skin and wore a rugged khaki jumpsuit that was stained, rumpled, and torn from hard use.

While Paul struggled to find the right words, the girl blurted out, "You are out of your element here." She spoke perfect Imperial Galach, not some rough dialect.

Paul brushed leaves and dirt from his clothes. "So it seems, but I don't usually need to be rescued."

She laughed, as if the large snakes had been nothing to worry about. "Before coming here, you should have learned more about the dangers of the Caladan jungle."

"You're right, I should have been better prepared." He felt embarrassed, thinking also of the manta birds that had shorted out his flyer. He was filled with questions, but what he said first was, "Thank you."

A loose sack over her shoulder held more of the thorny ropes. She tossed one to him. "The Muadh here are very proficient with these spiked bolos. They're easy to use, and you can take care of yourself now."

"Wait!" Paul said, willing to learn but also remembering his urgent obligations. "I need help. My friend has been captured. We need to stop the people growing the barra ferns. The drug has killed many on Caladan and offworld."

While her Muadh companions stood silent and suspicious, she motioned for him to accompany her. "We know all about the ailar and barra ferns . . . and how those people take innocent captives." She hesitated, and a troubled look crossed her face. "Come, allow me to introduce you to the people I live with. They've taken care of me." Almost as an afterthought, she said, "My name is Sinsei Vim."

Captivated by her brown eyes, he replied, "I am Paul." He didn't tell her more of who he was. He glanced at the other eight natives, five men and three women. "You are not Muadh? You seem different, have a different appearance."

She looked impatient with the assumption. "The village is Muadh, but I am not."

Sinsei set off, moving at a brisk pace through the jungle, and Paul had to hurry to keep up. The other Muadh accompanied them, spreading out, while the young woman seemed focused on a destination. She moved ahead, lithe and athletic, her movements almost feral.

"I have spent some time in the Caladan wilderness before." He tried not to sound defensive. "But there is still much for me to learn."

She glanced over her shoulder. "Chaen Marek and his mercenaries are the most dangerous parts of this jungle. They take advantage of the Muadh, and they . . . they have my father. Your friend is not their only captive." She looked worried for a moment, but brushed it aside. "You shall be my pupil, then. We'll help keep you alive, even though Marek's hunters are trying to find you."

The Muadh moved through the jungles along routes that only they could see. Sinsei explained that she and her father were botanical researchers, contractors hired by CHOAM to investigate these jungles for possible commercial viability, but her father was more interested in pure research. In his solo explorations of the jungle, he had been captured after stumbling upon the barra fern operations.

Paul frowned. "We can work together to free them, both Duncan and your father. The Muadh should help."

She gave him an appraising look. "The Muadh are reluctant to fight. They are at peace with the jungle and the mountain. They helped me get away and made sure I survived. They are gentle, generous people. And Marek's experiments have done terrible things to them." Sinsei pushed a leafy branch aside, as if to deflect her annoyance. "They are too content in believing that a solution will present itself."

Thinking of the Archvicar and the calm, peaceful Muadh workers in the pundi rice fields to the north, Paul was incensed at the further damage Marek had done. "I am not willing to leave it to that."

She cocked an appraising eyebrow. "Perhaps you and I can do what needs to be done."

They traveled unmarked jungle paths and quickly they came upon a sheltered settlement, a cluster of small homes and open shelters. The Muadh came forward to greet the stranger. One of the burly warriors who accompanied them, a man named Yar Zell, explained who he was, and that Chaen Marek's mercenaries had another captive.

Paul stepped forward, assessing these people as allies. "Duncan Idaho meant to put me through rigorous survival training. Not exactly like this."

Sinsei caught the name and turned quickly. "Duncan Idaho, the Atreides Swordmaster? That would make you Paul Atreides, then, son of the Duke."

Paul nodded reluctantly. His life was already in the hands of these people. A village elder came to stand before him, a deeply wrinkled woman with beautiful silver-white hair who was called only Old Mother. "What are you doing on our sacred mountain? The rocks of the great mountain are imbued with the spirits of our ancestors." The ancient woman regarded him closely. "We consider the mountain itself to be a living thing, far more alive than we are."

Zell, the warrior, scowled. "We should never have allowed those people to cultivate their crops on the other side of the mountain. They capture and kill anyone who wanders too close to their sacred ferns."

Old Mother's nostrils flared. "*Our* sacred ferns."

Sinsei introduced the others as more Muadh villagers joined them. She explained, "All Muadh tribes perform rituals involving the benign species of barra ferns. These villagers know how to find the ferns in the wild, and they also explore and revere their mountain. My father and I were studying the ferns before he was captured by Chaen Marek."

Full night had fallen now, and the villagers brought out a lumpy porridge of some kind. Paul made up his mind to do what he could to fix the damaged flyer, and rescue Duncan as well as Sinsei's father. Even if he had to go by himself.

He fought his restless anxiety as he talked with the young woman, learning about her scientific education on Kaitain, her work assisting her father. He noticed her smiling at him, and even under these miserable circumstances, he found himself attracted to her.

A wash of stars filled the dark sky overhead, and Paul realized how exhausted he was. He wanted to raid the drug camp now, find some way to break Duncan loose, but he was incapable of doing it, not now, not by himself. He couldn't let his emotions drive him. Tomorrow, rested, he would make his move.

The Muadh villagers provided him with a simple mattress on comfortable reeds, along with a thin blanket woven from jungle grasses. That night, as he lay in this unfamiliar place worrying about his father and Duncan, he drifted off into a surprising and pleasant dream about Sinsei Vim, even a sweet kiss. When he awoke in deep darkness to the sound of night insects, he realized that he had dreamed of her instead of the mysterious desert girl who haunted so many of his recent dreams.

Paul silently scolded himself for worrying about moody dreams. He had to focus on rescuing Duncan, without distractions.

Our perceptions tell a compelling, convincing story, often irrespective of the facts.

—Mentat exercise

The fact that Fenring agreed to travel with him to Kaitain convinced the Baron that they might actually sway the Emperor to believe in their scheme. The plans and deceptions were falling into place, and they might actually trap the terrorist leader. Such knowledge filled him with warm satisfaction, like a spice-rich banquet.

The two men rode together in an ornate diplomatic frigate, which rested comfortably inside the Heighliner hold. "Do not fear, my dear Baron," Fenring mused. "Yes, Shaddam will be upset when we reveal the true spice thieves, but he will quickly be distracted by our plans to capture his nemesis."

The Baron had dealt with Shaddam IV frequently in the three and a half decades of the Emperor's reign. The Padishah Emperor was a hard man who accepted no failures and tolerated no incompetence. The Baron and Fenring just had to make sure his ire was directed at Jaxson Aru rather than at them. Even though he and the Count were often at odds, in this matter, the two men were aligned.

Relaxing in the lavish diplomatic ship now, he made himself comfortable for the journey. He sipped fine Kirana brandy—at Imperial expense, of course—and ate a full seafood meal just because it was such a novelty after his time on the desert planet.

Fenring sat at a writing desk in the ship's parlor, humming and muttering to himself. "Ahhh, my own investigations have expanded beyond the Orgiz refinery, Baron. We uncovered connecting threads among some of the perpetrators, some of which may surprise you."

"I don't like surprises," the Baron said.

"They will, ahhh, benefit you, have no fear."

Count Fenring was distracting, but he was much better company than his annoying aide. "You chose not to bring your Mentat along? You insist that he is brilliant and insightful, but I've always found him to be problematic."

"Ahhh, Grix Dardik no longer serves me in the same capacity." He stroked his chin. "His behavior was disruptive, and I kept him in my service only so long as he was useful." He paused. "Alas, he no longer proved useful."

The Baron chuckled. "I have the same attitude toward my own Mentat. In what capacity does Dardik now serve you?"

"He, ahhh, serves as fertilizer in my wife's private greenhouse chamber. The flowers seem to be blooming quite nicely over him."

The Baron did not request further details.

When they arrived at the Kaitain spaceport, an official transport whisked them away in an unmarked motorcade through the crowded streets. The vehicles took them into an ambassadorial receiving level deep beneath the monolithic palace.

Count Fenring sat back and smiled. "As soon as I explained that we have a scheme to capture Jaxson Aru, the Emperor cut short his court duties to meet with us. Chamberlain Ridondo has prepared a private room where we can present our plan."

The Baron nodded. "Let us hope the room is more elegant than your silence chamber in Arrakeen."

Fenring puckered his lips. "It serves its purpose."

Imperial guards took the pair from the darkened groundcar along vaulted passageways, through connecting service lifts.

Chamberlain Ridondo met them halfway. The ponderous lantern-jawed man seemed to be suffocating under his own self-importance. He raised a spatulate hand and gestured them forward. "Come, Shaddam is waiting for you. He is most anxious to hear your report."

The Emperor waited for them in a large conference room with walls as thick as a bunker. He sat at the head of the table, as if holding court. The walls were covered with paintings of previous Emperors, all of whom looked down on the proceedings with disapproval.

Pastries, fruits, and sliced meats had been arrayed as an afterthought, rushed there by servants. Napkins and empty plates had been placed at three of the chairs. One of the seats was of an expanded construction to accommodate the Baron's girth.

Shaddam stared at the new arrivals and ignored the food. He had not touched a morsel. Fenring pushed aside the empty serving plate in front of his chair so he could erect a holo-player. The Baron's stomach growled as he went to his seat, but seeing that neither of the other men ate, he refrained from serving himself.

The Count cleared his throat, a far more extensive noise than was necessary. "We have news for you, Sire—information that demonstrates the extent of the Noble Commonwealth treachery against you."

Shaddam's expression twisted as if someone had turned a screw in the back of his head. "What is it now? I already know the traitors are widespread."

"The rebels have, ahhh, worked their tendrils into the spice operations on Arrakis," Fenring said.

The Emperor turned his glare toward the Baron.

"Not yet, not yet—but I've been contacted by their leader," the Baron said. "They made an attempt to recruit me. I have learned that . . ." He hesitated, then decided to let Fenring fend for himself. "Even though Count Fenring caught and punished a small group of smugglers, the true perpetrators were organized by Jaxson Aru himself. A large hidden refinery was found in the deep desert, but as my military swooped in to capture the thieves, a rival group destroyed them. No honor among thieves."

He tapped his thick fingertips on the table, while Fenring glared at him with his darting eyes.

The Baron continued without looking at the other man. "By removing this channel for melange sales, we forced the rebels to take desperate measures. Jaxson Aru thinks I may wish to join his movement, and so the Count and I are dangling bait in front of him. Soon he'll be like a fish on a hook."

Shaddam pinched the bridge of his nose. "That is interesting news."

Before the Baron could reveal their plan to trap the Noble Commonwealth leader, Count Fenring spoke up. "But there is much more, Sire. As you are aware, Jaxson Aru surprised us all when he made himself into a hero on Issimo III. Rather than harming the desperate colonists, he, ahhh, aided them! He arranged a massive humanitarian rescue operation that dwarfed your own efforts."

Shaddam spoke in a low, rumbling voice. "That gesture caused as much damage to my Imperial name as an outright attack. I should have been the one to provide so much food and equipment!"

And yet you did not, the Baron thought, but chose not to speak the words aloud.

Fenring activated the holo-player. "Sire, these are images I obtained from Issimo III, some of them taken by the Imperial corps of engineers." He displayed the chaos of supply ships landing together, taking over the Issimo spaceport. Cargo vessel after cargo vessel disgorged enough sealed crates to fill a dozen warehouses—agricultural machinery, construction equipment, metal plating, polymer sheets, radiation shielding.

Shaddam watched the activity with a deeply furrowed brow, saw the flurry of people, even noted the incensed Imperial engineers who were surprised by the relief effort.

Fenring said, "After full interrogation, it was clear the cargo ship captains were not aware who had hired them to perform the operation. They simply played the message clip in which an arrogant Jaxson Aru took credit for the good deed and opened his arms to the welcoming cheers."

"I know all this, " Shaddam said. "I hate it."

"But do you know *this part,* hmm?" Fenring paused the flurry of images and focused on two figures moving among the workers. He expanded and enhanced to display a pair of men wearing Imperial colors, uniforms of the Corps of Engineers. "These are not members of any Imperial work crew. Their identities were falsified."

The first man looked vaguely like Jaxson Aru, but his features were different. An unknown brother perhaps? The Baron leaned closer, intrigued.

The second man was unmistakable.

Duke Leto Atreides.

He sucked in a quick breath. "Leto Atreides was there? With them?" From Gurney Halleck's implanted message, he knew Leto's plans to infiltrate the rebellion. But here he had damning evidence, and the Emperor could see it as well.

"The Duke of Caladan is a traitor," the Baron said, stating the obvious—and turning the tables on his enemy.

"Indeed he is," Shaddam growled.

"Ahhh, hmm, I found it astonishing myself," Fenring said. "One can never know what is in a man's true heart—even someone who clings to honor for all to see." Next, he called up other documents, turned them toward the Emperor. "On these records of the food supplies delivered to the colonists, note that one of the primary shipments consists of pundi rice, Caladan's main export."

"Benevolence instead of bloodshed." The Emperor pursed his lips. "That does sound more like Leto Atreides than Jaxson Aru."

"The Atreides is still a traitor," the Baron insisted. He fought to control his smile. All these clues were building an uncontestable case against the hated Duke.

"Also, many of the shipments, particularly the expensive construction equipment, were purchased through a blind corporation, which I have traced to Viscount Giandro Tull of Elegy," Fenring added. "Another piece of the puzzle."

The Emperor seemed confused. "My Sardaukar already investigated Tull. They found nothing."

"Hmm," Fenring said. "Perhaps they should look deeper."

The Baron interjected, drawing attention to himself again. "Once we spring my trap and capture Jaxson Aru, we can interrogate him and learn all of the information. We can wrap up the underlings after we destroy the ringleader. But we need your help, Sire." He explained how the terrorist leader had solicited his help in Carthag, and how the Baron had promised to deliver a shipment of melange. "It is the bait in a trap. Once he agrees to the rendezvous, we will have him."

Fenring added, "We need a contingent of Sardaukar and possibly the quiet cooperation of the Spacing Guild. This must operate under the flag of House Corrino."

"And so it will!" Now, with his mood changed, the Emperor filled a plate with favorite dishes. The Baron hesitated only a moment, then served himself as well. The meeting had turned into a celebratory feast.

"I shall put myself at great risk to achieve this goal, Sire," the Baron said, "but I count on your efficient security forces to wrap up the loose ends."

Our Mother Superiors never understood love, yet they have preached against it for millennia. They fear an emotion they have never known, and because I have fallen in love, the Bene Gesserit are wary of me.

—LADY JESSICA

Jessica walked past the guarded Tull stables, smelling the primal aroma of the thoroughbreds. Each time she saw the animals now, she understood much more about what they meant to House Tull, how they had been a trigger for the Viscount to turn against the Corrinos. Could Emperor Shaddam even imagine such a cause and effect?

This morning, she had another destination in mind. Jessica looked toward the color-strewn lichen forests in the nearby hills—a place for her to feel calm, where she could organize her thoughts. The stable master offered to saddle a horse for her, but she insisted she would rather walk.

Jessica took a trail into the woods, careful not to step in the intermittent manure piles from previous equine activity. She paused to look at an unusual blue shrub with star patterns on the leaves, then moved aside some of the dry mulch to see the elaborate roots wrapped like pretzels and protruding aboveground. With a sigh of nostalgia, Jessica remembered how she had liked gardening as a young Acolyte back in the Bene Gesserit Mother School.

Continuing her walk, Jessica made her way to the serene little lake she had seen before. The lake was accessible via a rocky trail, and from above, she could see an old wooden dock among the boulders on the shore with four small open boats tied up to it. Drawn to the shimmering water that reflected the cloud-laced sky of Elegy, she picked her way down the slope.

Before she reached the lake, though, she heard approaching hooves coming at a slow pace above. Thinking that Giandro had followed her again, she turned but saw only one of the Tull household guards hurrying along on foot, leading a saddled horse.

Jessica waved to him, knowing the animal could not make its way down the steep path to the lake.

The guard paused above. "Apologies, my Lady. I've been dispatched to ensure that you are comfortable and safe. Let me know if you need anything."

"Thank you. I'm going out on the lake. It reminds me of Caladan." Her voice grew quieter. "Don't worry, I'm still familiar with boats."

The guard tied the horse to a tree and hurried down the uneven path to catch up to her. "I can help you, my Lady. I'll even row, if you prefer."

She realized that the Viscount might have been too earnest in his instructions. Jessica knew that Giandro's attitude toward her was indeed warm, though at times he seemed so eager, like a puppy seeking approval.

When they reached the dock, the guard wanted to do all the work and take her out on the boat, but she politely declined. "I know that you, and the Viscount, have admirable intentions, but I am perfectly capable of taking care of myself." Seeing the man's hurt and worried expression, as if wondering how he would explain her refusal to the nobleman, she softened her words. "I know you mean to serve, and I will ask for help when I need it."

He flushed and bowed as she walked down the dock to the last boat tied up at the end. The guard stopped by one of the other boats. "I'll row a distance behind you, to give you privacy, but also to make sure you are safe."

Exasperated, Jessica said, "If you must."

He steadied the boat for her as she climbed in, raised the oars, and inserted them into the oarlocks. She rowed away from the dock out onto the still water, enjoying the calm, as the guard hurried to prepare the second boat. As promised, he rowed after her, keeping what he thought was a discreet distance, although out here in the wild solitude, any other human presence was a distraction.

When she reached the middle of the lake, Jessica shipped the oars and just let the vessel drift. She closed her eyes and imagined another lake, inland and surrounded by trees on her beloved Caladan. The boat bobbed gently in the water, and she felt the wind on her face, the warmth of sunlight filtering its way through tall trees. For a moment, she felt at peace.

It had been at least a year since she and Leto had gone out together on a boat for a lovely, romantic day. She remembered a picnic lunch on a small island just offshore. Even with his responsibilities as Duke of Caladan and a member of the Landsraad, Leto had found time to be her partner. Such memories reminded her of how much she missed him, and now it took all her Bene Gesserit skills to block off her emotions. The Sisterhood had intentionally created her current situation, caused the problems that she now had to endure.

Her quiet moment was broken by a faint shout from the shore, and she turned to see another rider on the high path waving a bright blue banner, a signal of some kind. In the other rowboat nearby, the guard shaded his eyes, watched the movements of the flag. He called across the water to her, "My Lady, it says you have an important visitor. Please return to shore immediately."

Her heart skipped a beat. A visitor? For her?

"Who?" Jessica called, but the guard obviously didn't know. On the path above the lake, the messenger turned his horse about and galloped off.

With a flash of hope, she wondered if Leto had come for her, if he'd found some way to make the Sisterhood retract their orders. Jessica had indeed done everything they'd demanded. She had met the terms they'd imposed, even restored the generous stipend from House Tull. Was Mother Superior Harishka true to her word?

She was already working the oars, rowing back to the dock. The guard followed, still calling out with his offer to help, but she pulled with all her strength. Reaching the dock, Jessica sprang out of the boat and called back to the red-faced guard, "If you want to help, please tie up my boat. I am taking the horse."

She hurried up the steep trail to where the saddled horse was tied to the tree on the main path. She intended to gallop back to the manor house to see this important visitor.

But the visitor had already come to her. Before Jessica could mount up, she was surprised to see a dark-robed woman making her way along the forest trail—a Reverend Mother who moved with an uneven gait, her spine out of alignment, yet her speed was fluid and strong.

Now Jessica's pulse raced even more. She knew this woman—an ally. Reverend Mother Cordana had fought on Jessica's behalf against Ruthine's murderous plans. Behind Cordana came three other Sisters, trying to keep up with her remarkable pace.

Jessica stood firm on the path, although her mind was a clamor of questions and concerns. "I was told I had an important visitor. I did not expect it to be a representative from the Mother School."

Cordana scuttled up to her, flushed with the effort, but smiling. She shrugged back her dark hood and brushed a lock of mouse-brown hair from her forehead. "Dear Jessica, when I learned that you were out here, I thought it would be a nice place for us to talk. Isolated." She looked at Jessica with dark, piercing eyes, and then past her toward the lake, where the guard was still busy tying up the boats.

Leaving the horse tied to the tree, the two women went off to an old fallen log in dappled shade. A good place to talk. The other three Sisters remained apart from them, ever watchful, much like the Viscount's persistent guards.

Jessica could no longer contain her questions. "You came from the Mother

School. Are you here with a new assignment for me?" She hesitated only a second. "I did as I was instructed. I passed the Sisterhood's test. The Viscount publicly acknowledged me as his concubine, and I even convinced him to reestablish his stipend. Am I being sent back to Caladan? To Paul?"

And to Leto?

Cordana clucked her tongue. "Patience, child. You must learn patience and obedience."

Jessica was having none of it. "I have learned both, but I've also learned not to be passive and to ask for what I've earned because . . . because the Sisterhood does not always act of its own accord."

The Reverend Mother laughed, as if delighted by her intractable response. Jessica had always admired Cordana because of her strength of character. This woman had overcome difficulties to become one of Harishka's most valued advisers, and she had shown great strength in championing Jessica even when the venomous and demented Lethea advocated that Jessica and her son be killed.

"The Sisterhood sent me to you now, perhaps not with the entire reward you seek, but to see how you are doing."

Jessica's thoughts seesawed. "I used the skills I learned at the Mother School. I've accomplished much already here with Viscount Tull. But if you go back and report that I am happy and contented here, then I will never be sent home to Caladan! And if you claim that I am miserable and resistant, they will refuse to send me back. What is the answer that will serve me?"

"There is always hope for you, Jessica. Harishka admires you, even if she does not always show it."

Jessica shifted her position on the hard log. "I'm glad the Mother Superior admires me, but I have another goal. Is there any hope for me to be sent back to my family?"

"The Sisterhood is your true family." Cordana looked over at her. "You don't accept that?"

"I have more than one family. Why do you make me choose among them?"

Cordana looked up at the lichen trees and smiled. "Elegy is pleasant enough. Why don't you just resolve to remain here and settle down with Viscount Tull?"

"He is a fine man, and a gentleman." She dropped her voice to a whisper. "But he is not . . ."

The horse rubbed its side against the tree. Down by the lake, the guard finished tying up the boats at the wooden dock.

Cordana clucked her tongue again. "You know it would be best if you forgot about Duke Leto Atreides. Let him raise his son to be his heir, the next Duke."

"I will never forget him." Jessica struggled with her anger, even if Cordana was still the most sympathetic ear among the Bene Gesserit. She changed tactics. "Reverend Mother, you have never been sent off as a breeding mistress, as a concubine. It is dangerous for me to say, but perhaps love is not something you can understand."

"There are many kinds of love. Perhaps my lack of experience in one area strengthens my understanding in another. I can love and respect others, like you. I can understand and empathize, but I cannot ignore the order's admonition against weak emotions." Cordana reached back, pressed a hand against her bent spine. "In some ways, perhaps my handicap is a blessing because it enables me to focus on my work."

Jessica decided to be bold. "I know what Mother Superior Raquella commanded long ago, but I also see the strength in love. I admit that I dearly love Duke Leto Atreides, and the son I bore for him. My love strengthens them, and all of us."

Cordana's eyes shone bright. "Truth is also an important virtue."

The Reverend Mother's hand remained on her wrist, and Jessica placed her own hand over it. "I know you convinced Harishka to give me another chance. You sent me the warning that let me save my son, when Ruthine and her treacherous allies wanted to murder him. I am forever indebted to you for that."

Cordana squeezed Jessica's hand. "We all have roles to serve."

Jessica shook her head, feeling angry now. "I am far more suited to serving the Sisterhood beside Duke Leto as he rises through the ranks of the Imperium. Think of what I could accomplish at his side. He is a much-admired man in the Landsraad."

At last, the guard had trudged up the rocky path and stood by the horse, but the three Bene Gesserit Sisters blocked him from getting closer to the pair seated on the fallen log.

Cordana lowered her voice. "This will not go into my report, but maybe I can convince Harishka to restore you to Caladan and your beloved Duke."

"You would do that for me?" Jessica's heart pounded.

The other woman shrugged her uneven shoulders. "We do better work for the Sisterhood if we are happy. I will do what I can." With surprising agility, Cordana rose to her feet from the uneven log. "I have every confidence in you."

Saying a thing and proving a thing are entirely different.
—CHIEF MAGISTRATE LUPE ALAAN,
Kaitain Imperial Court

A prisoner, Duncan Idaho was stretched downward over a chasm, his arms and legs secured by cords. His captors had found a convenient natural opening in the rock for this bizarre, cruel demonstration. If the cords were cut, he would plunge down into the treetops and rocks, far below. Duncan refused to show fear, but maintained a passive expression, keeping his eyes open.

His senses drifted, and his head spun because of the drugs skirling through his brain. The odd, disconnected sensation made the threat more surreal and also more terrifying. After the mercenaries captured him, they'd brutally forced him to ingest raw barra ferns, variant specimens that looked like shriveled spider legs. His mouth burned, and his throat clenched.

And the drug worked on him.

Muadh natives voluntarily consumed the natural barra ferns, using ailar for their peaceful rituals. Chaen Marek's men, though, had crammed the foul-tasting material into his mouth.

Now the Tleilaxu man leaned forward closer to Duncan's face and touched the cord as if it were the taut string on a musical instrument. "A simple adjustment of the rocks holding the cords, and you will plummet to your death."

"But what a thrill on the way down," Duncan mocked. "Falling straight into thin air! It would be a glorious drop all the way."

The drug lord's face pinched even more. "Until the end."

"I have had a rich and full life serving my Duke." Duncan's head throbbed from the drug. Perhaps it was emboldening him, or just making him not care. From the evidence around him, it seemed that Paul had indeed gotten away, and that was all that mattered. "In contrast to your pitiful little existence, Chaen Marek. You see, I remember our last confrontation in the fields to the north."

Marek did not look insulted. "And I remember you, Atreides swordsman.

You and your Duke caused enormous harm to my barra fields, but I have more than recovered here." His expression darkened. "Now you found me again, and sacrificed yourself to let the Duke's son escape." His lips twisted in a frown. "But we will find the boy, or the jungle itself will kill him. You failed in your charge to defend him."

Duncan seemed to be drifting, flying above the jungle on a stream of ailar, but confidence anchored him. "I trained him. We'll see whether or not I failed."

"Brave words for a man dangling over a precipice."

Duncan chuckled. "The danger makes me feel more alive." He thought of how Paul insisted on pushing his own abilities to the limit and living life to the edge, whether scaling the sheer cliffs below Castle Caladan or flying into an elecran-infested storm on the sea.

Marek appeared disappointed and confused by his reaction. "Then why don't you plead for your life?"

Duncan laughed, longer and harder because of the drug coursing through him. With amplified senses, he heard the cachinnation echo across the rocks, with hollow counterpoints from lava tubes and caves in the mountainside. "Face me yourself. I will fight you bare-handed against any weapon you have. You've drugged and disoriented me, yet you are still afraid."

The Tleilaxu stepped back, obviously intimidated even though Duncan was bound and suspended. "Why would I take such a foolish chance, when I could just kick one of these anchor rocks loose and watch you fall? That would be just as exhilarating—for me. You have seen our operations, so you know you can never leave."

Even as he dangled, Duncan lifted his head to look around the mountainside, saw the outbuildings and processing barracks hidden by thick jungle foliage, the extensive barra fields, operational caves on the eastern rim of the volcano blocked by a wall of large boulders.

"Perhaps you are the arrogant and overconfident one, Swordmaster," Marek said. The odd little man danced along the edge of the cliff, then performed a smooth backflip in the air and landed on the edge next to Duncan. "My combat skills might surprise you."

Duncan looked at him sideways. "Do you seek to torture me with talk?"

"Or the delicious edge of false hope, watching your resolve soften, and then I will drop you anyway."

The blood was rushing to his head, and the yawning chasm below seemed to mock him. Jungle birds flew in the open air far, far down, which made the disorientation even greater. "I don't care what your motives are. I am resolute."

"We will make you useful to us, Duncan Idaho. With so many new strains of barra ferns, we need to test the ailar. You are a more viable human subject than the Muadh primitives we capture, who are often less than articulate. We want to witness the effects."

Marek motioned to four mercenaries, who drew Duncan back from the precipice like a dangling cargo load. One of the anchor rocks tumbled over the edge, and he watched it plunge out into the open air before crashing and breaking apart on rocks below. But the deadening drug had made him numb to threats and false hopes.

Standing aloof as others performed the work, the Tleilaxu gave orders to one of his men who carried a broadsword and a dagger. Duncan stood on shaky legs, flexing his arms and feeling the thunderous rush of blood roaring back into his limbs. The guard extended the longer sword to Marek and the knife to Duncan, as if taunting, but Duncan refused to take it. Instead, he just glared at the drug lord. "Even that longer blade won't protect you from me."

To his surprise, Chaen Marek offered the sword as well. "Then take this, swordsman. I need no weapons against you."

"I am a Swordmaster, not a mere swordsman."

"Prove it."

Suspecting a trick, Duncan refused to take either blade. He moved away from the cliff face to stabler ground. The disorienting drugs made him stumble, but he maintained his footing. The taste in his mouth was still awful. He eyed Marek warily.

The drug lord smirked at him. "At least you didn't hurl yourself over the edge. That new strain previously engendered madness and paranoia. We had quite a time with our other subject, Dr. Vim." He placed the tip of the long sword on the ground. "I will make a note of that."

"Experiment on yourself, Chaen Marek, and you will get even better data."

The Tleilaxu stood fearlessly on the brink, as if taunting his prisoner. Unconcerned, he looked down over the edge.

Duncan could have thrown himself upon Marek and might have gotten to him before the guards could stop him. But even as debilitated as he was, he knew what the drug lord wanted him to do. Was this a test? Some provocation to make him kill himself? With a quick lunge, he thought he could knock this vile man over the edge.

But then he could never save Paul, and his primary duty was to guard the heir of Caladan. He was not afraid of his own death, but his mandate was to survive.

What was this Tleilaxu up to? Was it a trap within a trap? Duncan's thrumming mind whirled with the possible consequences. Marek had said the strain of ailar could instigate paranoia, or was that just to make the prisoner second-guess his every move?

The small, gray man placed the sword on the ground next to the dagger,
pushed both of them closer to Duncan. "In combat, you are undoubtedly my
superior, but I am nimble enough that I might escape your blade, for a time.
Ultimately, you would catch me, though."

Scowling, Duncan glanced around. Both weapons were at his feet and
within reach, but he did not accept them. What if some form of contact poison had been painted on the handles?

Duncan found himself paralyzed by doubts. It had to be the effects of ailar.
He spat on the ground, trying to get rid of the awful taste. None of Marek's
guards made any move toward him. The sword and dagger were right there at
his feet, and he could have grabbed them, lunged in an attack.

With a shrug, the drug lord indicated the tempting blades on the ground.
"I don't need those against you because you and I are allies."

Duncan's stomach twisted. "Impossible."

Fearless, Marek stepped closer to him. "*Allies*, yes. Many of my drug sales
go directly to Lord Rajiv Londine, and your Duke is courting his daughter.
Soon, we will officially be partners, you and I."

Duncan's mind reeled. "You're lying."

"It is more extensive than that," the Tleilaxu continued. "I also know that
Duke Leto Atreides, the man who obliterated all of my ailar operations in the
north because the Caladan drug besmirched his reputation, has joined the cause
of Jaxson Aru and his rebellion."

Ice went down Duncan's back, and he shuddered. No outsider should have
known that! Only a very close inner circle of Leto's advisers had been told
the real plans.

"Jaxson informed me himself. The sale of ailar across the Imperium has
been profitable, and that money supports the activities of the Noble Commonwealth."

A hot flush of anger rose to his cheeks, but Duncan could not find words
to deny Chaen Marek's appalling revelations.

Defiant, he kicked the weapons away. "I want nothing to do with you
or your activities. You forced me to eat the barra ferns. Maybe all of this is
a paranoid hallucination." He crossed his arms over his broad chest. "I gave
Paul the opportunity to escape. That is enough for me. If my life is forfeit, I
gladly pay the price."

Marek seemed intrigued by his response, and he silently measured the
words. Duncan was still sure this was all some sort of deception, and he didn't

intend to do anything the drug lord expected. "Until you learn the truth of what I say, I will trust you as much as you trust me." He nodded toward his companions. "And that is not at all."

The guards seized Duncan by the arms, and he did not struggle as they led him away.

A lesson must be learned, and extreme lessons are often learned only by the peripheral survivors.

    —PADISHAH EMPEROR SHADDAM IV, annals of Imperial law

The Empress was going to be a problem. Shaddam could see that.

The insidious rebellion had spread like a cancer, afflicting the gullible and eroding the strength of his rule. Now that he had an opportunity to eradicate the terrorist Jaxson Aru—and all his coconspirators—Shaddam intended to take decisive action. He set the wheels in motion.

But Aricatha continued to press him with questions, never-ending questions.

Shaddam spent the day in his private war room, where he felt at home and in control. After delivering his report, the Baron had already begun to make arrangements for the rendezvous trap, willing to risk a large cargo of spice as bait. The melange would be deducted from personal Harkonnen accounts, should he fail.

Count Fenring joined him in the war room as a sounding board and adviser, and occasionally he served as a frustrating check on Shaddam's more audacious ideas. His Truthsayer, Reverend Mother Mohiam, also attended, along with numerous strategists and well-seasoned military commanders (most of whom were political generals rather than combat commanders because it had been a long time since outright war shook the Imperium). He had summoned Colonel Bashar Jopati Kolona of the Sardaukar, who would lead his elite troops in the real punitive work, although the officer had not yet arrived.

Empress Aricatha was there, too, smiling sweetly but not afraid to express her concerns. Though Shaddam enjoyed his new wife's company in social situations, he had not invited her to participate in the attack planning. Nevertheless, she had not been denied entry, and she sat at the Emperor's side. Her dark eyes were often adoring when they looked at him, yet now they seemed hard and skeptical as he laid out his new plans.

She leaned close and insisted, "But you know Leto Atreides well enough, my dear. This must be some kind of trick. False information."

"Hmm," said Fenring, fidgeting in his seat. "Ahhh, the data speaks for itself. The images from Issimo are impossible to deny. The Duke of Caladan was there along with Jaxson Aru, trying to create sympathizers for the rebel movement."

Aricatha countered, "The images are blurry. Other people could look like Leto Atreides. Or if that is Leto, we don't know that he was cooperating, necessarily. He may have been forced to participate."

"Or he may have been a Tleilaxu Face Dancer—if those shape-shifters even exist!" said Shaddam in a sarcastic tone. He snorted at the ridiculous suggestion. "Why hunt for outlandish explanations when the simplest answer is plainly obvious? Will you make the same excuses for Viscount Tull, Tuarna Vok, Remy Myer—or even that gadfly Rajiv Londine, who makes no secret of how much he hates the Imperial crown? We have just received the full list. The other radicals are simply less obvious, but just as guilty. As is Leto Atreides."

Reverend Mother Mohiam listened intently, but offered no useful conclusion.

Aricatha's disapproving frown, though, was as powerful as a shout. He could see that the Empress was stung by his rebuke in front of the others, although he had not intended to hurt her. "I am sorry, my dear. Your heart is just too large and your disposition too gentle to see the ugliness of human nature." He patted her hand condescendingly. "But I assure you that it does happen. Jaxson Aru is a poisonous, charismatic man. Even if he somehow tricked Leto Atreides, or Viscount Tull, or any of the others, that does not absolve the conspirators of guilt. They must pay the price for their treason."

She tossed her rich, dark hair. "You should investigate further, make absolutely sure before you repeat what you did to House Verdun." She glanced at the Truthsayer, who seemed embarrassed. "The repercussions will resound throughout the Landsraad. If you make a mistake, the nobles will turn on you like a pack of wolves."

"There is, ahhh, no mistake," Fenring said. "We will not allow it. Even if other evidence comes to light after the fact, we shall handle it appropriately."

Shaddam nodded. He had been frustrated with Fenring about the spice pirates on Arrakis, and had never been convinced that the matter was as cleanly resolved as his friend assured him. But now with this sudden turn of events, he was pleased with the Count, and he would be even more pleased with Baron Harkonnen if the man's scheme resulted in the capture of the elusive Jaxson Aru. But that was only one piece of his sweeping retribution against the traitors.

Shaddam had his own secret source, who had provided him with the names of the corrupt and radical nobles, Jaxson's inner circle—many of them seemingly upstanding members of the Landsraad! He would wipe them all out.

But Aricatha simply wouldn't let the matter die.

"Duke Leto was just here on Kaitain," she said, and her edgy tone began to remind him of some of his previous wives. "He spent weeks trying to work within the Imperial system, courting Landsraad positions. I met with him myself, looked him in the eye. It is clear he had no sympathies for the rebellion."

Shaddam grimaced. "I won't argue about this anymore, my dear. The decision is made."

"Decisions can be changed," she retorted. "Won't you even consider the possibility that I am right about him?"

Exasperated, Shaddam glanced at Fenring and was relieved when the Count responded for him. "Leto Atreides, ahhh, made his ambitions plain not only to every noble in the Landsraad, but to me as well. We offered him a perfectly acceptable way to expand his holdings and increase the influence of House Atreides, if that was what he truly wanted. Why, the Emperor and I tried to broker a marriage with him and Vikka Londine, as you well know. He refused to pay the price, turned down our most generous offer."

"And what was that price?" Aricatha asked. "Vikka Londine is a friend of mine, despite her opinionated father."

"You should choose your friends more wisely, my dear," Shaddam said with an undertone of warning. "And that includes the Atreides Duke."

Fenring continued, "We asked Leto to control her outspoken father, oust him from his role in the noble house, but he refused to do so. Rajiv Londine has insulted the Padishah Emperor's authority with his constant criticism. Now with our new list of verified traitors, we know, ahhh, that Londine is not only an outspoken critic, but is also actively trying to destroy ten thousand years of Imperial history and stability. He is a rebel, a member of the Noble Commonwealth. There is no question."

"And what proof do you have?" Aricatha persisted.

Despite his love for the new Empress, Shaddam just wanted her to leave. "We have a complete accounting that identifies the primary traitors, those who cooperated with Jaxson Aru. The Atreides Duke is one of them, and so is Rajiv Londine."

"But where did you get this list? Anyone can write down the names of your alleged political enemies. That does not make them terrorists."

Shaddam rose to his feet. "Enough!"

Inside the sealed war room, the political generals and military strategists had been watching the exchange with growing uneasiness. Shaddam flushed, immediately regretted raising his voice, but he had no choice. He continued in a calmer tone, "I welcomed Duke Leto Atreides here on Kaitain and offered him legitimate ways to expand his power. He turned them all down and went back home. I thought he would be satisfied with a quiet life, but now we learn that it was all a deception, that he instead chose to harm me! Leto may be my cousin, but that does not earn him my forgiveness."

When Aricatha opened her mouth, he raised his hand like an executioner lifting his ax. "Please leave, dearest, before we regret this conversation."

An Imperial guard stepped close to escort her away. She looked outraged, but cooperated and kept any further comments to herself.

Fortunately, at that moment the Sardaukar colonel bashar arrived at the door, bowing with respect. "I am responding to your summons, Sire."

Jopati Kolona was clean-cut, well trained, and perfectly loyal. The Sardaukar officer had conducted several harsh reprisal missions, including the obliteration of Verdun holdings, and he had never refused an order. Occasionally, Kolona let a flicker of his feelings show when he disagreed with Shaddam's decisions, but he always conceded to the Emperor's authority. This demonstrated that Kolona was a thinking man and able to reach his own conclusions, but also that he was loyal.

"Ahhh, Colonel Bashar—just in time." Fenring rose to his feet, smiling. "The Empress is just leaving."

Aricatha stalked past the Sardaukar without meeting his gaze or speaking a word. Unsettled after her abrupt departure, Shaddam was already thinking of baubles he could give her as recompense. Unlike his succession of previous wives, Aricatha truly understood him. She loved him, and he loved her—an odd feeling for a man like Shaddam Corrino, who had spent his entire life entangled in Imperial politics and intrigues, whose best friend could scheme and kill better than anyone else in the Imperium.

Kolona presented himself inside the war room, bowing again. He acknowledged the generals before turning back to face Shaddam as if he were the only person in the room. "Your message said that you have an important mission for me and my Sardaukar, Sire."

"It is a vital mission that will save the Imperium," Shaddam said.

He hoped to see the man glow with appreciation, but the officer gave only a businesslike nod. "We attempt to fulfill every mission to your satisfaction, Sire. Shall I prepare a squad of Sardaukar?"

"Not enough. We need all the Sardaukar."

Now Kolona's eyes widened. "*All* of them, Sire?"

Fenring interjected, "Multiple teams with separate targets for concurrent strikes. The shock, ahhh, and the lesson will reverberate through the Landsraad."

Kolona squared his shoulders, though his expression became unreadable. "Like our strike on Dross."

"Yes, like the House Verdun strike," Shaddam agreed, "but an order of magnitude greater, with multiple targets. We now know the compatriots of Jaxson Aru, and they must all be eradicated. No mercy. Nothing of their holdings is to remain."

"No chance for forgiveness, even with the benevolence of Shaddam Corrino?" Kolona asked. "How, if they are dead, would they learn your lesson?"

With no patience for this today, the Emperor felt his face grow warm. "The survivors in the Landsraad will learn the lesson. These traitors are already lost to me. After the bloody devastation on Otorio and the attack on my Imperial Palace, there can be no tolerance or mercy for such monstrous treachery."

Fenring extended a sheet with the names of noble families. "We, ahhh, have these specific targets, known traitors. Their guilt has been confirmed."

The Sardaukar officer scanned the document, then glanced at the Truthsayer, who remained silent. "Confirmed? By what means?" He was starting to sound as annoying as Aricatha.

"By means that I find sufficient," Shaddam replied.

The colonel bashar looked at the list and tried to hide his disbelief. "Elegy . . . Viscount Tull? I inspected that world myself and found nothing."

"Which is why you won't be sent there on this punitive mission. Other Sardaukar will take care of that target."

Kolona's expression hardened further. "Then what is my objective, Sire?"

"Because of your past achievements, I've chosen you to eradicate the loudest of these troublemakers. Take a legion of troops to Cuarte and eradicate Rajiv Londine and all his holdings. When that is finished, I want you to go to Caladan and do the same to Duke Leto and all of House Atreides."

I do not need to know the underlying points behind a decision. I only need to know the mission. I only need the names.

—Sardaukar oath of service

Per the terms of long-standing treaties, the Padishah Emperor could commandeer any Heighliner for the transport of Imperial military forces. The Spacing Guild was required to comply because the suppression of insurrection or widespread civil war benefited the Guild and CHOAM as much as it helped the Imperial throne.

Now, on Shaddam's orders, multiple Sardaukar strike forces were organized for various targets. Colonel Bashar Jopati Kolona was concerned only with his own personnel, his fighter craft, and his weaponry. He did not fool himself into thinking that this was a "combat" engagement. It was a mission of destruction, plain and simple, a massive surprise attack.

Still, it weighed on his heart, like his previous orders to obliterate the holdings on Dross and kill the entire Verdun family, not only the guilty Duke, but his innocent wife and daughters, all tainted by association. Kolona had felt no Sardaukar honor when he'd done that, but he had followed orders.

He remembered his years of ruthless training, thrown as an orphaned child onto Salusa Secundus, the Imperial prison planet. And when he survived that test, young Jopati had been released from the ruthless prison into a different kind of punishment—or, as the Sardaukar learned to consider it, a reward—when he was recruited to become one of the elite Imperial soldiers.

He never forgot the reason his own noble family had been overthrown. A treacherous surprise strike in the middle of the night from Duke Paulus Atreides had crushed House Kolona, turned the few survivors into renegades.

During his training years, Kolona had held a deep vendetta against House Atreides. Many years later, though, he'd been amazed when young Leto Atreides voluntarily and incomprehensibly relinquished the Kolona holdings his own father had seized. Leto claimed that Duke Paulus had been coerced into the scheme by Emperor Elrood. Back then, serving as an Imperial guard inside Shaddam's throne room, Jopati Kolona had stood in silence, showing no reaction. He had never fully understood, although his opinion of Leto Atreides had changed.

Now, Caladan was one of several targets on his list after his Sardaukar squad left Londine's planet a smoking ruin.

The Heighliner entered orbit over Cuarte, and military ships dropped out like a swarm of angry hornets, armored vessels crowded with troops and carrying full loads of shock wave explosives Inside the flagship transport, Colonel Bashar Kolona sat shoulder to shoulder with dozens of grim Sardaukar, all ready for blood. The dropship held seventy soldiers, while other attack vessels held even more. Lord Londine's small standing army could not hope to resist a Sardaukar assault.

As the troop carrier rumbled through the air, a soldier—whose name Kolona did not know—muttered, "It would have been easier to just wipe them out from above, drop bombs through the atmosphere, turn the city into fire and glass."

Disapproval was plain in Kolona's voice. "Are you not willing to put in a little effort?"

"We lost too many good Sardaukar on Otorio," said the soldier. "The Noble Commonwealth doesn't deserve any kindness from us." He smiled stiffly. "Not that we're known for that anyway."

"We are slaughtering them down to the last man, woman, and child. To complete this mission, we must go in ourselves, not remain high overhead, dropping bombs. This one is very personal to our Emperor."

The other man started to reply, then faced ahead, falling back into his own thoughts. "Yes, Colonel Bashar."

All those years ago, when Atreides forces had struck House Kolona's ancestral planet, they had offered no warning, simply swooped in over the manor house and dropped their bombs, killing his mother and oldest brother as they stood on a balcony to watch the stars. That time, Duke Paulus and Emperor Elrood had meant to seize House Kolona assets and occupy the world.

That was not the Sardaukar mission today.

"Our honor is not a measure of theirs," Kolona grumbled, partly to himself, partly to the armored man beside him. "We will read aloud the Emperor's sentence and carry out our orders in person, hand to hand."

The soldier's gauntleted hand strayed toward the hilt of his short sword. "Yes, Colonel Bashar, I could use the physical exercise."

Half of the one hundred Sardaukar ships landed around the manor house. According to his briefing, Kolona knew that the capital city held several hundred thousand inhabitants with another fifteen thousand or so offworlder tourists who came to see the legendary fire fountains of Cuarte. Kolona re-gretted the loss of those innocent visitors who were not even citizens serving under the traitorous nobleman. Still, the solaris they spent went into the coffers of Rajiv Londine . . . which then went to finance terrorist activities. Shaddam allowed no exceptions. They all needed to be punished.

Warships landed in the connected courtyards of the manor house. Mem-bers of Londine's household staff milled about, staring in disbelief while oth-ers were wise enough to flee for cover, which would do them no good once the mansion was leveled to the ground.

As he was the officer in command of the operation, Kolona's dropship landed first, right at the front doorway of the manor house. He emerged in full dress uniform; no camouflage or desert uniform configurations would be used on this strike. Even without his rank insignia, his demeanor identified him as the person in charge.

Near the dropship, a majestic gush of sparkling embers spewed out from a fire fountain display. Two of his tense vanguard fighters spun with their las-rifles and blasted the geyser plume, thinking they were under fire. Sulfurous steam and more sparks boiled upward.

"Stop!" Kolona shouted.

Thrumming bombers circled overhead, ready to unleash their final dev-astation of the city, but Kolona had his initial operations to complete first.

The tall doors of the manor house burst open, and the indignant noble-man emerged. Rajiv Londine wore a loose scarlet shirt and tight trousers. His steel-gray hair had been brushed back, leaving his face clear to show his infuriated scowl. "You are trespassers! Imperial troops require a permit to—"

The lord's daughter stepped up beside him, looking angry but more in con-trol. "They have the weapons and the personnel to do whatever they wish, Father." At least Vikka Londine understood the magnitude of their danger.

From the rear, the nobleman's chief administrator, a man named Rodundi, showed clear alarm. As soon as Rajiv Londine stepped forward to take charge of the situation, Rodundi ducked back into the manor house.

Kolona shouted for all to hear, "By order of Padishah Emperor Shaddam Corrino IV, Rajiv Londine has been branded a traitor to the Imperium!" He did not pause to wait for a reaction. "As punishment for consorting with the violent terrorist Jaxson Aru and the Noble Commonwealth movement, Londine's holdings and his population are forfeit. I, a colonel bashar of the Sardaukar, have been sent to carry out these orders."

Londine spluttered. "I protest! I will file a formal appeal in the Landsraad Hall. I will—"

"You will be dead," said Kolona, not as an angry threat, merely a statement. "You have no recourse, and no opportunity for appeal." He turned to his soldiers and shouted, in his voice of command, "Blades!"

With a whispering musical ring of metal, the Sardaukar drew their swords.

"Carry out your orders," Kolona said. He stalked forward, raising his own weapon. Since he was commander, he took it upon himself to strike down the treacherous nobleman. A single hard blow severed Londine's head from his shoulders, spouting blood just as bright as the color of his shirt. The man collapsed.

His daughter screamed until another Sardaukar thrust his sword through her heart.

Kolona lifted his bloody blade and advanced into the manor house as the other Sardaukar fell to their task with enthusiasm. The colonel bashar knew it would be a long, grim day.

THE FACE DANCER, wearing his long-standing disguise as Chief Administrator Rodundi, saw grave peril as soon as the first Sardaukar ship landed. He had anticipated such a punitive reaction when Lord Londine's invective grew more extreme. Shaddam IV had never been a patient or tolerant man, and although the Landsraad clung to their supposed freedoms of expression, those freedoms were not absolute. As a shape-shifter created by the Bene Tleilax, he was familiar with Imperial intolerance, and knew the vulnerabilities that a man like Rajiv Londine faced.

But even the Face Dancer had not expected such an overwhelming retaliation. He was aware of scorched-earth tactics the Sardaukar had used on Dross, and these soldiers would surely do the same here. Now it would take all of his skills and flesh-morphing abilities to slip away.

Just as he had ducked into the large main foyer, with the doomed Londine blustering out in the courtyard, the slaughter had begun. Running, the Face Dancer came upon a terrified middle-aged woman, a low-ranking household servant. "Chief Administrator, what are we to do? Should we surrender or hide?"

The Rodundi simulacrum ran his eyes up and down her shape, her drab and loose garments, and immediately made up his mind. "Come with me into the side alcove for a few moments."

The servant didn't ask why, simply trailed after him. As soon as they were inside the shadowed shelter, he struck her on the back of the neck, a blow hard enough to snap her vertebrae. Her head lolled to one side, and she crumpled.

Concentrating hard, the Face Dancer shifted his own facial bone structure, muscles and skin, compacted his spine, became shorter, and soon assumed her precise appearance. He shucked off the now too-baggy clothes of Chief Administrator Rodundi and stripped the servant of her uniform. A servant would still be a target in the Sardaukar massacre, but he would be less noticeable than the easily recognized Rodundi.

Outside, the screaming reached a crescendo with the sounds of blades and hacking meat and bones as a counterpoint along with a series of shouted gruff orders. Before the Face Dancer reached the far end of the receiving hall, the doors burst open, and soldiers surged inside. They caught a glimpse of the "drab serving woman," and he ducked down a side hall toward the kitchens. Several Sardaukar bounded after her.

More household servants rushed out to see what was happening, and they were cut down. When one soldier charged after the supposed household servant, the shape-shifter led his opponent along, thinking about the next stage of his plan. He found a small storage room that would serve his purposes.

Running on the servant's shorter legs, he ducked inside, leaving the door ajar so the pursuer would know exactly where to go. The Sardaukar strode into the room, easily spotted his quarry in the shadows. "No!" the servant cried. "Please spare my life. I have children."

"And I have orders." The soldier's blade dripped with blood, and the Face Dancer wondered how many he had already killed out in the courtyard. Hidden in her drab dress, she held a knife of her own—Rodundi's blade—and knew how to use it.

The Sardaukar stalked forward, showing no glee or malice. He raised the bloody sword. "I'll make this quick. Lots of killing to do today."

"We think alike," the Face Dancer muttered. The thin, middle-aged woman darted under the Sardaukar's blade, moving with the lightning-fast skills of a trained assassin. His own blade dipped upward, slowed to just the right speed, and passed through the body shield, then thrust the tip beneath the Sardaukar's jaw. With a quick, hard push, he drove the thin knife through the roof of the soldier's mouth and into his brain. The expression was one of disbelief rather than pain.

He did not need to worry about the blood that splashed all over his victim. That was part of the disguise, too. The shape-shifter stripped off the man's uniform and body armor, touched the dead soldier, and within moments adjusted his own body and features to look identical. He donned the gore-stained garments, gathered the Sardaukar weapons, and took a moment to assume the role. Then he emerged into the mayhem of the manor house, where the Imperial soldiers ran rampant, killing every person they found.

The Face Dancer—one of the Sardaukar now—took part, pretending to enjoy the bloodshed as much as any other soldier. He worked among them, safe in his new identity.

Whenever it became possible, perhaps after the Sardaukar ships returned to the Heighliner, he would slip out from their regimented and scrutinized lives to assume a different identity. He knew all of Rajiv Londine's hidden accounts and access codes. Not only was he the chief administrator, he would also *become* Lord Londine by the time he made it back to Nossus and Jaxson Aru.

The sacred Tleilaxu mission depended on the success of the powindah rebellion—the rebellion of the unclean outsiders—and the laboratory-bred Face Dancer would use his wiles to maintain the charade, so long as there was a chance of winning.

❧

FOR THE REST of the day, Colonel Bashar Jopati Kolona continued to supervise and participate in the massacre. By the time the day waned into sunset, tens of thousands of people had been butchered by hand. Because some of the desperate citizens found ways to fight back, Kolona lost twenty men, which he considered a disgrace to Sardaukar abilities and tradition.

As night fell, he'd had enough, and he declared an end to the mission, calling for a return to the dropships for the final bombardment. He withdrew all personnel, not out of surrender, but as a tactical move so they could embark on the second phase of utter annihilation. From now on, Kolona decided to opt for efficiency. They had collected enough images of the massacre to make the Landsraad tremble, and the Emperor would be pleased. No doubt Sardaukar teams would be just as successful on other known rebel planets.

And this was only Kolona's first assignment in this long, grand operation.

When the hundred armed ships withdrew, bombers closed in. Wave after wave of deadly explosives leveled the manor house and grounds, then the city and the Cuarte spaceport. The detonations cracked open numerous thermal areas, producing plumes of sparkling lights, eruptions of steam and incandescent minerals. It was a beautiful show, Kolona thought, but no tourists would ever see it.

He and his Sardaukar had accomplished their mission. Once they regrouped and reloaded, he would drill his elite teams, and upbraid them for losing twenty fighters to civilian rabble. He had to be off to impose similar Imperial retribution on other rebel worlds, finally ending with Caladan and House Atreides. Once, he might have relished that, but this time, he did not.

Even the greatest of heroes cannot always act in a heroic fashion.
—SWORDMASTER RIVVY DINARI of the Ginaz School

While the aftereffects of the explosions still rumbled back in Rabban's torture facility, Thufir crawled inside the dry drain pipe, seeing the way with his light-enhancing film lenses. Groaning and barely conscious, Gurney Halleck drifted behind him, buoyed up by the suspensors, which filled the dank, confined passage with a soft hum.

Thufir heard another rumble behind him, braced himself for a muffled shock wave as other incendiary items detonated inside the torture facility. By now, the entire interior of the building would be on fire.

Finally breaking through to the cold, snow-strewn landscape outside, Thufir exited the pipe and dragged Gurney after him. His battered companion was mostly awake now, struggling to move, despite his obvious injuries. "I'm going to keep the suspensors on you, Gurney, but now I want you to use them to assist you in running. We have to hurry—my ship isn't far."

"Run . . . for our lives," Gurney said.

Thufir set out over the uneven ground, and the other man tried to assist where he could. Behind them, fires danced inside the blocky building where Gurney had been held and tortured. Alarms were sounding, and security forces rushed in from the nearby town.

"I don't know if Rabban himself was inside the facility, but he would never let us escape," Thufir said. "This is our only chance."

The noise from Gurney's throat reflected disgust rather than pain. "Rabban . . . not here. On Arrakis."

Thufir grunted. "Good."

"Why are you here?" Gurney asked, in a croaking voice.

"I am rescuing you." The warrior Mentat hurried him along. "A solo mission, so as not to entangle our Duke."

Gurney's face twisted in alarm and pain. "The Duke! Did he go to Jaxson Aru?"

Thufir put the man's arm over his shoulder, helping to guide him at greater speed. "Yes, you know he pretends to support the rebel cause, to stop them from doing more terrible things. Emperor Shaddam needs to be ready, as soon as the Duke exposes the traitors."

The waiting ship lay shrouded in darkness, but Thufir could see it through his enhancement lenses.

Gurney groaned and forced them to stop. "I failed! The Emperor does not know—damned Harkonnens captured me before I could even reach Kaitain. They found the message in my arm!"

Thufir turned to face the blood-smeared man. "The Emperor never received our message? We thought you were captured on your way back to Caladan." He had made an invalid assumption, based on Guild ship schedules, the capture on Harmonthep. Mentat computations spun through his mind now, a cascade of new implications, new disasters. "Then Shaddam will think Leto Atreides is one of the traitors!"

Gurney tried to detach the suspensor mechanism from his shoulder. "Can't move with these."

Thufir stayed his hand. "Come, the ship is just over there. I'll get you medical attention once we're out of here."

The other man made a sick sound and lurched forward with a bouncing movement enhanced by the mechanism. "Out of here."

Thufir guided him across the cold, rough terrain to where the darkened ship rested. Far behind them now, the burning torture facility was swarming with guards and emergency responders. No aircraft in sight yet, but soon the Harkonnens would spread out and search for the infiltrators. Fortunately, every person who had actually seen them was now dead.

When he activated the ship's code-locked hatch, low sensor-lights came on, illuminating the interior. Gurney saw the way ahead, and he insisted on stumbling aboard as best he could.

Taking both men by surprise, dark-uniformed sentries came running across the shadowy field, shouting, "There! Spies!" Thufir saw four of them, all with drawn blades, but he was disoriented by the shifting light from the ship, his enhanced lenses, and the surrounding darkness. The Mentat raised his own sword, placing himself protectively in front of Gurney. In silence, rather than with an animal howl, he waded in with his weapon. The old warrior would have to dispatch all of them.

Without bravado or challenge, he lunged forward and ran his sword through the first man's belly. The man choked out a scream and dropped to the cold ground. Thufir didn't give him a second glance as he hacked at the next man. The sentries shouted for more help, and Thufir knew he didn't have much time.

Behind him, Gurney struggled to disconnect the portable suspensor that held him upright, but before Thufir could call out to him, he found himself in a furious battle with a third guard. This Harkonnen soldier had time to prepare himself and gauge his opponent, and he fought with more caution and calculation. Thufir couldn't kill him as quickly as he needed to.

A fourth guard approached from the side, distracting him, and the Mentat saw he would have to slay them both as swiftly as possible.

Then the guard coughed blood and looked down at the tip of the sword protruding from his chest.

Gurney grabbed the sword and shoved harder, ran him the rest of the way through. The effort seemed to take his remaining scraps of energy, and as the dead guard dropped to his knees, Gurney collapsed beside him, holding a long knife he had taken from the first man Thufir had killed.

The Mentat faced the final opponent. He had no time for finesse and threw himself at the man, thrusting and parrying, driving the Harkonnen back. "For noble House Atreides!" The name caused a flicker of hesitation on the enemy's face, and Thufir struck him down. "And for what you did to Gurney."

Knowing that more sentries would be running in response, and attack flyers might be sent from the nearby airfield, he went to where Gurney had collapsed. Though the Atreides fighting man was clearly spent and in great pain, he wore a grin on his scarred face. "Couldn't let you have them all to yourself."

Thufir applied one of the suspensors again, lifted his companion, and threw him over his shoulder, refusing to hear any further argument. Moving on legs that ached with exertion and age, he made his way aboard the waiting ship and sealed the hatch.

He took only enough time to spread Gurney onto the nearest passenger bench, then sprinted to the cockpit. He activated the sensor-blurring systems, raised the vessel from the cold ground, and soared into the air, a completely dark vessel.

Even when the shadowed fjords were far below, he could still see the burning torture facility—and the outlines of heli-craft in the illuminated sky, swooping toward his ship. Thufir dodged, trying to go beyond their sensor sweeps. The heli-ships were too late, and not capable of reaching higher altitudes. They dropped back and returned to the burning base below.

On the passenger bench, Gurney cursed as he tried to get comfortable under the heavy acceleration. The dim light of the ship's interior still seemed too intense for him, although his eyes were nearly swollen shut.

Glancing back, Thufir said, "I will tend to you with a medkit as soon as we reach orbit. We still have to evade sensors until we get locked aboard the Heighliner."

"I'll be fine, thanks to you—though that was damned foolhardy."

"And successful. I accept your gratitude," said the Mentat. "Your nightmare is over, my good friend."

Another groan came from the man's throat as he looked around. "Seven hells! Did you leave my baliset behind? I don't suppose you'd consider going back for it?"

Both men roared with laughter as they sped off in the night, heading toward orbit, where the giant Guild ship still had not finished loading all the outbound craft and cargo from Lankiveil.

Despite his sense of victory, the warrior Mentat continued another set of calculations. Duke Leto was still among the dangerous rebels, pretending to be one of them. The Padishah Emperor would surely take his revenge.

Occasionally we are able to decipher our dreams and connect the real and subconscious worlds. But not often enough.

—PAUL ATREIDES, private journal

At the first glimmer of dawn in the Muadh village, Paul awoke and emerged into the jungle, anxious to assess his surroundings, to repair the damaged aircraft, and find a way to rescue Duncan.

The people were already stirring, some cooking a breakfast porridge laced with protein-rich ants, others moving into the thick forests to hunt. Paul turned as the village matriarch strode up to him, a businesslike expression on her aged face. "You learn quickly, boy. You want to go fight those evil people who have taken your friend, but before you learn about our weapons, come and experience more about the special place in which we live."

Sinsei joined them, her face freshly scrubbed, her hair tied back. Her durable jumpsuit looked out of place, but she seemed to fit right in among the Muadh. The villagers glanced at the three of them as they went into the heavy forest, then turned back to their work as if Paul's urgency had nothing to do with them.

"I need to fix my flyer, so I can get back home and bring help, if we need it," Paul said, hurrying to keep up with the crone. "Quite a bit of work remains to be done."

"We know nothing of aircraft," said Old Mother, lifting a thorny branch out of the way.

"I can help," Sinsei suggested. "Though I'm not an expert in mechanics."

Paul was surprised but glad to hear the offer. "I need to rescue my friend."

"And my father," the young woman insisted. "But the Muadh don't fight." She sighed. "I have tried."

Paul followed Old Mother through jungle thickets, past an explosion of yellow flowers around which buzzed iridescent beetles. Sinsei kept up, smiling at him while deftly dodging the branches, leaves, and dew-wet vines.

The old woman was amazingly spry, flitting like an invisible wind through the undergrowth. Though the foliage was too thick for Paul to see very far around them, the tribal leader found a clear path on the base of the mountainside until the trail leveled out to a view of the forest below.

Sinsei stood beside him, catching her breath from the exertion. He could smell her perspiration, the sunshine on her skin. She gave him a nice smile, and her blue-green eyes sparkled in a way that warmed Paul inside. He felt close to her in the short time since she had rescued him in the deep jungle. She possessed a quiet dignity and tenderness.

Duncan had often encouraged him to meet young women, to enjoy his youth. He had even taken Paul into the back streets of Cala City, trying to find a girl who matched the one who so frequently haunted his dreams. Paul had described her, sketched her, and he'd even been sure he had seen the dream girl out of the corner of his eye. . . .

Looking at Sinsei now, he suddenly realized that last night he hadn't experienced the persistent dream of the desert and the dusky young woman. Not since he'd come into these jungles to train with Duncan.

Angry, Old Mother gestured across the valley toward the larger fields where Chaen Marek had ripped up the jungle and planted acreage. The camouflage screens blurred the extent of all the fields, but they were still obvious to this ancient woman.

"Those are wrong," she said. "This . . ." Pausing, she pointed down through green moss next to a rotted fallen tree. Thick, fleshy ferns grew up, some already with fully extended fronds, others just curled nubs.

Paul recognized them. "This is what should be."

"Barra ferns," Sinsei said. "The Muadh call them sacred plants." Her face tightened as she glanced toward the large, camouflaged drug fields.

"Not like those poisonous operations . . . Not like those people who have Sinsei's father, and Duncan," Paul said.

"We find the ferns when we need them," said the matriarch. "The mountain gives them to us when they are required. Those other plantings . . . they are not required." Her face became a bitter sneer.

"Then we should go and fight the intruders," Paul said. He knew that the Swordmaster could take on several mercenaries by himself, and Paul could fight as well. So could Sinsei. They could get free.

"That man makes an abomination of our barra ferns, our rituals." Old Mother turned her glittering eyes toward Paul. "The ferns are not sacred to him. They are drugs. He threatened us. If we had not agreed to leave his plantings alone, he would have burned our village." When she sighed, a rattling noise came from her throat. "One day, the intruders will be gone, and then the Muadh can return to normal."

Sinsei looked angry in a different way. "The outsiders will not go away willingly, Old Mother. They reap great profits from the barra ferns."

The crone's face was filled with deep sadness. "We are not warriors. We cannot mount an army to defeat these evil outsiders."

Sinsei squared her shoulders. "My father and I came with our instruments, our records, and our curiosity. We were prepared for rugged wilderness, to take care of ourselves out in the jungle—but not for treachery and outright war."

Paul glanced down at the spiny bolo she wore at her side. "Sometimes we need to learn new skills," he said.

◆

AFTER THE OLD woman returned to the village, Paul asked Sinsei to help him find his way back to the Atreides flyer on the rocky side of the mountain. He glanced along the mountain slope, knowing where Chaen Marek's base was, where Duncan was being held.

When Paul and Sinsei reached the edge of the clearing, he saw the battered aircraft, its engines partly disassembled, but some of the repairs had been made already. Seeing the damaged hull, Paul remembered the thrill of fear when he had brought it in for such a hard landing.

He strode forward now for another look at the flyer's engines. Inside, the locator beacon was automated and no doubt still functioning. But Thufir Hawat would not expect them back at Castle Caladan for at least another two days, so no one would be looking for them yet. Earlier, Duncan and Paul had changed some of the damaged components, and they had expected to work together replacing the burned-out engine parts and patching the aircraft enough to limp away. At the time, Duncan had felt no urgency about completing the repairs. The two had thought of it as another learning experience, making off-the-cuff fixes with whatever spare parts were available.

Paul sighed now. He wasn't supposed to do it alone. . . .

Sinsei offered to help, although she was abashed. The self-confident young woman had studied botany and alien zoology at the Imperial academy, and she understood the jungle environment; she could speak at length about ecology, just like her father, but she had no experience as an aircraft mechanic.

"And I am the son of a Duke," Paul said as he crawled on the ground beneath the hull, extending a tool into the starboard engine compartment. "But Leto Atreides is not a foppish nobleman, and he raised me to get my hands dirty as well."

Duncan had already set out the viable components, pieces, and modules from the repair kit. Paul could not rebuild the engines completely, but by cannibalizing components from the four tandem engines, he might have enough to get two of them functioning, just enough for them to fly. He had already checked the comm array, and it was hopeless. The interconnected electronics could not be repaired through brute force. Two of the engines, though . . . It would have to be enough.

Determined, he looked up at Sinsei. "We'll get this working again, but I'm not leaving without Duncan." He drew a breath and modified his statement. "We need to rescue him—and your father."

⟢⟤

PAUL AND SINSEI stood on a grassy practice range on the outskirts of the Muadh village, where she demonstrated how to use the spiked bolo. "It's a skill you might be able to use," she said.

He watched her hurl the weapon at a practice target made with tied clumps of grasses and branches, forming the torso, crude arms and legs, and head. Even though the young woman was a civilized researcher who had gone into the wilderness with her father, Sinsei was quite proficient with the bolo. Paul needed every advantage to rescue the two prisoners. She showed him how to make different angles of attack, while standing, kneeling, lying on her stomach, or running.

The young man was determined to learn, since he had no modern weapons with him. He and the Swordmaster had expected a challenging exercise. Now, it was a matter of survival for all of them. Training for real life, to extremes.

Though the Muadh would not fight, their jungle scouts had learned that Duncan was still alive, and they'd even found where Sinsei's father was being held. The burly warrior Yar Zell had developed a detailed sketch of the mountain caves and outpost where the ailar was processed. If Paul could find his way through, then he might have a chance of freeing Duncan, slipping him and the researcher away.

As Sinsei demonstrated the use of the bolos, Paul tried the flexible, spiked weapons. The young woman handed him a short bolo with glistening metallic teeth on the weighted sections and smaller thorns on the cord connecting them. Pointing at one of the targets, she said, "Now you try it."

He grasped the bolo in both hands and drew his arm back, imitating her movements. Keeping his wrist and hand below his shoulder, he let the bolo fly. It made a whipping, whistling noise as it snaked through the air, just as it had done for her, but the bolo flew past the target.

Sinsei handed him another one. "Try again."

Several native spectators had gathered, including Old Mother and Yar Zell. The pressure made Paul focus harder, and he tried to relax. This time the spiny bolo wrapped around the lower part of the human-shaped target, tightened, and the spines dug deep into the clumpy "thigh." If it had been a real man, the weapon would have amputated the leg.

One of the onlookers chuckled, but Old Mother silenced him.

"With a gentler wrist action, you can simply tie the person up," Sinsei said. "When thrown in that manner, the spike bolo will make them bleed, without maiming them." She tossed deftly, and this time the bolo wrapped around the target's legs without causing damage. "Still, it has quite a shock value on the victim."

Looking at the crude target, he imagined it was Chaen Marek, with the bolo wrapping around the gray Tleilaxu neck. "Sometimes I may want to cut all the way through."

She arched her eyebrows. "Sometimes that is the only way."

⤝

THAT AFTERNOON, MAKING plans while awaiting more details about Chaen Marek's camp, Sinsei led Paul to a rocky creek bed. Together, they sat on mossy rocks and watched the cool, fresh water tumbling down the mountainside. She gestured along the stream. "In the dell below, there are diversion channels to send the water to our crops. The jungle may look natural and undisturbed, but it has been nurtured to help our people."

Paul picked up on a detail. "You talk as if you are a villager. You said *our* crops, *our* people."

She smiled. "The Muadh saved me, and they will help us now. My father and I learned much from them. They are an easy people to like." After a shy pause, she glanced at him. "You are easy to like as well, Paul Atreides."

Emboldened, but more terrified than facing any sword duel, he took the cue and bent toward her for a quick kiss, then pulled back, startled with himself. They sat there for a time, listening to the flowing stream as they talked more. Here in the deep jungle, in the most primitive of settings, she told him about her elite education on Kaitain, how she had been a talented botany student, and how she had joined her father's research staff. Paul was reminded of his own father off on a mission pretending to be a terrorist, and his mother who had been pulled away by the Bene Gesserit.

The young man also remembered his own responsibility, his place on

Caladan—and the danger they were all in. "Under other circumstances, I would enjoy this moment much more," he said to her. "But I can't let personal feelings distract me from rescuing my friend and your father."

~~~

THAT NIGHT AFTER the jungle darkness closed in on his sheltered hut and the thrum of insects surrounded him, Paul lay on his bedding, thinking of the mission they would have to mount the next day. But he also thought of Sinsei, her smile and her bright eyes, her voice.

In a complex trap, it is sometimes difficult to determine who is the hunter
and who is the prey.

—JAXSON ARU, Noble Commonwealth manifesto, revised

Baron Harkonnen did not like to be bait. As the head of a powerful House, he manipulated people, pulled strings, and sacrificed the weak when necessary. He watched it all from a position of power and safety, while others did the incriminating work.

Now, by his own design, he found himself at the center of a spiderweb. The question was whether he, or Jaxson Aru, was the more poisonous spider.

While Count Fenring continued to scheme with Emperor Shaddam about a broad-based crackdown on the other traitorous nobles, the Baron had dangled this opportunity that the terrorist leader could not resist.

Under normal commercial circumstances, he would never have accompanied a shipment of melange, certainly not a contraband load like this one. He had Harkonnen spice crews, even Rabban, to perform such tasks. But this was by no means a normal circumstance. The risks were too great and the rebel leader far too cautious. The Baron needed to do it himself, with sufficient security, of course.

Now he waited inside the Harkonnen spice transport that a Guild Heighliner carried to the rendezvous he had arranged, a Guild transfer depot world named Bellaris. The spice transport's hold was packed with sealed containers of melange. Although the vessel's registration number remained unaltered, the Harkonnen griffins on the sides of the hull had been scoured off. The ship looked battered, rumpled, and a bit disreputable—an unobtrusive trader's craft.

The Baron and a small agreed-upon contingent of security forces were aboard the transport. The radical leader would take possession of the ship and the spice, and the Baron had arranged his own transportation back to Giedi Prime once the deal was done.

Once the terrorist's fate was sealed.

Jaxson Aru was satisfied with the precautions, but he had no idea about the surprise Emperor Shaddam had arranged. The rebel leader was understandably eager to count the head of House Harkonnen among his secret allies.

The unmarked Harkonnen spice ship was docked inside the Heighliner hold among hundreds of vessels: loaded cargo ships, large frigates, small diplomatic yachts, scout vessels, pleasure craft. The varied ships were stacked in docking clamps like tightly packed grapes in a cluster.

The Emperor's Sardaukar knew exactly where the Harkonnen ship was in the cavernous hold, and they lay in wait.

Most occupants of the traveling vessels remained aboard their own ships, waiting for the Navigator to fold space and carry them to the next star system. For those on longer journeys, impatient with the myriad stops and multiple delays of loading and unloading at each world, the Guild allowed travelers to pass through connecting walkways and airlocks into the multileveled outer skin of the Heighliner. Deck after deck was filled with Spacing Guild personnel, crew members, engineers, maintenance workers, as well as support staff who worked the numerous restaurants, shopping plazas, and drinking establishments.

Now that the Heighliner had arrived over the transfer depot, the Baron received a coded acknowledgment from the quietly waiting Sardaukar, then left the spice transport for his private rendezvous. He had relayed a description of Jaxson's altered appearance to the Imperial commandos.

The Baron had chosen this specific Heighliner and arranged the schedule for their secret exchange, but Jaxson was the one who had specified where they would meet in person—a crowded, boisterous bar on the outer deck that advertised intoxicating beverages from a thousand worlds. Followed by his best bodyguards, the Baron entered the establishment, alert and wary. Drug-infused smoke filled the air, as well as the wailing atonal notes of semuta music.

With the Heighliner's low gravity, the Baron did not need his suspensor belt, although his size made him easily recognizable. An unfamiliar man in the crowd met his gaze as soon as he and his companions entered, and he noted other glances, whispered voices, and quick hand signals. Looking around, he spotted Jaxson Aru standing by one of the side doors. The rebel leader wore voluminous brown and black robes that made his body a shapeless mass, as if he were some kind of pilgrim, but he had made no overt attempt at disguising his features. His new etched-metal ring dangled from one earlobe.

Jaxson was surrounded by five bodyguards, also in baggy robes, and no doubt others were dispersed throughout the bar for security. Jaxson's immediate companions each carried a cubical case, sealed and unmarked, about the size of a human head. They did not volunteer any details as to what they contained.

The Baron made his way toward Jaxson, trying to conceal the anxiety he felt. This man had unleashed bloody destruction just to make a point, and he would surely kill the Baron without flinching if he suspected a double cross. But Baron Harkonnen had his guards, too, and they were the best of the best.

We are all friends and allies here, he thought. Outwardly, he smiled.

The Baron held up his hands as he approached Jaxson Aru, to demonstrate that he carried no secret weapons, though either man could easily have fooled scanners or other security protocols. Ironically, it was the trust and mutual fear that gave them the most protection—and Jaxson's greed.

"I brought what you asked. Everything has gone smoothly," the Baron said.

"Smooth as a knife in the back." The terrorist leader led the way to a corner table, where the two of them sat. Jaxson looked around the bar, then placed his hands on the table surface next to colorful vials of some potent blue beverage. He slid one of the sapphire-colored vials toward the Baron, while Jaxson's security guards stood behind the visitor, alert.

The Baron looked down at the drink, tempted and curious, but pushed it away. "Business first, to prove intent."

Jaxson scoffed. "You think I would drug you and take advantage of you?"

"I would consider doing it to you," the Baron admitted. "Let us not give you that temptation."

Jaxson chuckled. "I shall be glad to have you as a partner in our cause, Baron Harkonnen. In our free commonwealth, you could be a formidable trading partner . . . or become a commercial enemy." He sipped from one of the blue vials himself, tried to cover his grimace at the potent taste. "I think we should stay friends."

The Baron reached into a pocket of his voluminous garments and withdrew a package wrapped in brittle, coated paper, which he unwrapped to reveal a cake of rust-colored spice redolent of cinnamon. "A sample, in case you need verification."

Jaxson smelled the melange, closed his eyes.

"I have one-point-three metric tons of the product hidden aboard the spice transport inside the hold. It is yours, as our first major business transaction."

Jaxson smiled. "One-point-three metric tons. Let me see, the value in the open market would be . . ."

The Baron waggled a thick finger. "Ah, but you will not sell it on the open market, and you can charge whatever price you like. The value will be significant."

Jaxson said, "And acceptable." He slipped the sample to one of his men, who tucked it away.

The Baron glanced at the blue elixir again and decided against it. "Let us complete our transaction." He didn't want his demeanor to crack. "Come with me to my ship. I will show you the cargo, transfer the controls and authorization, and then you may take the spice to use however you wish."

Jaxson leaned back, self-consciously touching his earring. "What is your hurry, Baron? The Heighliner will be loading and off-loading cargo for another five hours."

"I have other business," the Baron said. "And I wish to be finished with ours."

Cocking an eyebrow, Jaxson rose from his seat. "Very well, I understand impatience." With a spring in his step, he followed the Baron out of the drinking establishment, moving faster than the big man wished to move. The security guards came close behind Jaxson, and as the group departed from the noisy bar, other nondescript companions joined them. The casual but ominous group outnumbered the Baron's escorts. But he had his own defenses and was not worried.

They went through the inner decks of the Heighliner hull and worked their way inward to the giant hold where the unmarked spice transport hung in its docking clamp. Jaxson's own hidden vessel must have been among those hundreds of ships in the cavernous space, no doubt camouflaged with a false identification number and registration.

The group crossed the docking bridge to the spice transport's access hatch. At the armored doorway, Jaxson hung back with the Baron and sent his disguised rebel guards in ahead, carrying their odd boxes under their arms. "Just a quick inspection, Baron. One can't be too cautious."

"Never too cautious," the Baron agreed. He allowed the other rebels aboard while he remained outside, letting them look wherever they liked. "Send my own crew back out, and we will turn over the ship to you. We've arranged our own transportation home."

Once inside the Harkonnen cargo ship, Jaxson's henchmen fanned out, descending into the hold, while the Baron waited outside, maintaining his calm silence. The rebel guards wouldn't find anything to arouse suspicions.

His own people exited the ship and crowded on the transfer bridge. Though they were dressed as scruffy crew, each one was a talented fighter, sworn to the Harkonnens, willing to give their lives. But that would not be necessary. The trap was set, and the rest would take care of itself.

After twenty minutes, Jaxson's security men returned to report. "It's all clear. A cargo load of spice and nothing else, as far as we can see."

The rebel leader moved toward the hatch, eager to be aboard. "Now, Baron, show me your wonderful commodity. This is the start of our productive business relationship."

They entered the spice transport through the pilot deck and rode a lift down to the large main hold, which was filled with crates. The smell of cinnamon hung in the air. The Baron wore his personal body shield but was reluctant to switch the unit on because that would raise Jaxson's suspicions. His hand fidgeted; he had to be ready.

The terrorist leader stared at the spice containers, his eyes flicking back and forth. "The melange income will assist us in great ways! We have already reaped significant profits by infiltrating the ailar drug trade. I never use the stuff myself, but that money financed our operations."

"Ailar?" The Baron's throat rumbled. "Yes, the Caladan drug. I'm surprised Leto Atreides doesn't keep all the profits for himself."

"Leto Atreides has different priorities." Jaxson kept smiling. "But this load of spice will be as profitable as many months of ailar sales."

"Naturally," the Baron said. He wanted to reveal Leto's secret plan, his treachery and his continued allegiance to Emperor Shaddam . . . but he could not make the Atreides Duke out to be a heroic infiltrator! The Baron wanted House Atreides disgraced and crushed. "This is a very important day for us."

Then the Sardaukar struck.

In addition to the larger cargo doors, the spice hauler had four external airlocks, two on the upper deck, one in the pilot compartment, and the last down in the cargo hold. Now, the mechanisms hummed as the interior doors unsealed.

Jaxson's security troops spun about as the airlocks opened, and Sardaukar fighters boiled through, all of them carrying bladed weapons. They activated their body shields while commanding the rebels to surrender or be executed.

Jaxson reacted as if he had always expected treachery and kept an alternative plan ready. He reached into the pockets of his baggy, drab robes and drew weapons of his own. "You made a bad decision, Baron."

The Baron activated his personal shield just in time as Jaxson hurled a throwing knife at him. The sharp blade struck the shimmering shield, failed to penetrate, and dropped harmlessly to the deck.

One of the bodyguards yelled, "Protect Jaxson! Get him out of here!" As a group, they folded around the rebel leader as the Sardaukar charged forward.

Retreating from the heat of the battle, the Baron headed toward the lift that would take him back to the pilot deck.

Another squad of Sardaukar clambered down the deck ladders, sliding into the main cargo hold. A stray blast breached one of the melange containers, spraying strong spice powder into the air.

Three of Jaxson's fanatical bodyguards threw themselves upon the approaching Imperials, raising their weapons with confidence, as if they could match the skills of the Sardaukar. They were not correct. The Imperial troops killed the three of them in moments.

The Baron retreated to the safety of the lift and activated the controls to raise him away from the melee. He would leave the ship and take shelter in the transfer corridor, where his own men could protect him. Fortunately, the rebel guards were too busy being slaughtered to worry about petty vengeance.

Jaxson yelled, "Helmets! Emergency mode!"

His security men cracked open their mysterious cases and pulled out armored atmosphere helmets with transparent face shields. Jaxson tore away his bulky brown robes to reveal a fully-fitted environment suit. "This cargo is forfeit, and our trust is gone."

He caught the helmet tossed to him, popped it over his head, and sealed the collar lock to pressurize his suit. Three of his bodyguards drove back the Sardaukar long enough for two others to don helmets.

One of the men was stabbed, a kindjal thrust through the protective fabric of the suit and deep into his ribs before he could put the helmet in place. Jaxson and the second suited man retreated to the wall. As the open lift whisked the Baron higher, he watched the rebel leader working the wall controls for the cargo door and realized what the man was trying to do.

Sardaukar bounded into the battle. Although they had breached the spice transport from the outside, most had already removed their enclosed helmets for fighting.

Jaxson called a farewell to his wounded and dying men. Only two, besides himself, had managed to affix their helmets and activate their suits. He overrode the bay door release, and the gap split open. Atmosphere vomited out into the vacuum of the Heighliner's hold, and the Sardaukar were swept away along with tumbling barrels and cases of melange.

Jaxson and his two suited companions dove out into the emptiness, not pell-mell, but controlled. Like flying commandos, they rode the wash of outpouring air and shot out into the cavernous Heighliner. The Baron felt the roar of wind, and his ears popped, but he held on until the lift reached the upper deck and locked in place, where the pressurization was still intact.

Alarms thrummed inside the spice transport. Several Sardaukar fighters on the pilot deck growled in dismay as they scanned the screens. The wide bay doors had dumped everything out into the vast Heighliner hold.

A Sardaukar captain lurched up in front of the Baron and demanded, "Where is Jaxson Aru?"

"He's loose inside the Heighliner hold," the Baron said. "But he's wearing an environment suit. He planned for this."

The Sardaukar captain touched his comm, contacting Guild authorities.

Jaxson Aru and his two surviving companions would be tiny specks inside the immense hold, and the Baron was sure they had their own escape ship in a docking clamp somewhere. With the flurry of vessels coming and going at Bellaris, the rebel could certainly slip in among them and escape to the planet.

The Baron felt angry and crestfallen. This was supposed to be his triumph! He turned to the Sardaukar. "You failed, Captain! I set up this trap, and I played my role, yet you let him slip through your fingers."

He quailed just for a moment as the officer turned toward him with murder in his eyes, then the Sardaukar became stony again. "We will track him down," he said, and a faint smile twitched his lips. "I just received word, and we can continue the trap. We know the location of the Noble Commonwealth headquarters planet. Nossus. We shall crush him there."

Bad things often occur in the middle of the night.

—Tleilaxu warning

Extending their stay on Elegy, Reverend Mother Cordana and her entourage received accommodations in the guest wing of the Tull manor house. Though Jessica resented the stern obligations the Sisterhood had imposed on her, Cordana was one of her allies. She was indebted to this one Bene Gesserit, at least.

Upon seeing the luxurious accommodations, Cordana was reluctant to accept them, saying she needed only austere quarters such as those at the Mother School. Jessica could tell the older woman was sincere in her embarrassment, not speaking out of false modesty.

The overdressed, prissy house manager seemed upset to hear the complaint. "You are important visitors, and we must be hospitable. House Tull has always been grateful and generous to the Bene Gesserit order, especially the old Viscount, and now his son has come around, too."

Cordana wrinkled her brow. "And to be hospitable, you should respect our wishes. Do you not have servants' quarters or something of the like? Truly, we will be more comfortable there." She glanced at her entourage. The other Sisters bowed their heads and nodded.

The house manager chuckled that she could not continue the conversation. "I will check back with you in the morning!"

The woman turned to leave, but Jessica intercepted her. "I assure you that Reverend Mother Cordana means what she says. She really doesn't want to stay in the finest quarters."

The house manager scoffed. "We do have horse stables available, though I'm not sure when the straw was last changed."

Jessica gave her a withering stare, which took the other woman aback. The Reverend Mother hobbled out of the room to join the discussion. With exaggerated movements, Cordana seemed to be emphasizing her deformity to appear self-effacing. "Very well, my Sisters and I appreciate Viscount Tull's generosity. I do not wish to cause undue hardship for you." She paused, then added in a lower voice, "But when the door is closed, I shall sleep on the floor."

The house manager's expression became pinched, and she whispered to Jessica out of Cordana's earshot, "That is a most unusual woman."

"Sometimes that is a good thing," Jessica said in a low voice.

The house manager wrinkled her face in obvious disagreement but departed without saying more.

After making certain the visiting Sisters were settled in their rooms for the night, Jessica stayed behind to talk at Cordana's request. The Reverend Mother said, "It's about time we got to know one another, since our lives seem to be intertwined."

"I do owe you a great debt," Jessica admitted. "A sincere one, for what you did to help me and my son. That is different from the impositions the Sisterhood made."

The two of them found comfortable chairs in the room's sitting area. "I understand your heart, Jessica," Cordana said. "I know that you have served us, and you have suffered. I want only what is for the best."

Jessica hung her head low. "But it has already been several months. The more time passes, the wider my rift with the Duke. I fear that is the Sisterhood's plan after all."

The Reverend Mother shifted in the extravagant chair, trying to find a comfortable position. "The Sisterhood has many plans."

During her time as an Acolyte at the Mother School, Jessica remembered how severe Mohiam had been, such a stern teacher. "The Bene Gesserit would say that hardships strengthen me. When will I be strong enough to satisfy them?"

Cordana shifted, pressed a hand against her twisted spine. "Fighting the physical battle every day of my life has made me stronger and more resilient, but also more compassionate to others who face challenges, whether physical, mental, emotional . . . or political. I admit that I have never been in love and do not regret it, but I do sympathize with your plight. Human emotions . . ." Her voice trailed off, then she chuckled and said, "Such a lot of trouble, aren't they?"

"It's hard to go against personal feelings," Jessica said.

Though they sat in a relaxed environment, Jessica still felt a tension. Reverend Mother Cordana might be her ally, but she was still a Bene Gesserit to the core, and Jessica understood the Sisterhood in ways she had never wanted to know.

Finally, the Reverend Mother leaned back into her chair with a fluid movement that belied the awkward discomfort she normally displayed. "I will return to Wallach IX and report to the Mother Superior that I find the situation here on Elegy satisfactory to the Sisterhood. Even exemplary on your part."

Jessica felt a weight lift from her. "So this was not just a cordial conversation."

"Oh, it was that—and a bit more. I could have departed already, hurrying back to the waiting Heighliner, but I chose to remain because you intrigue me, Jessica. You made decisions that caused great turmoil among the Bene Gesserit when you bore a son instead of a daughter. And yet you seem strong, despite your regrets."

"Oh, I have plenty of regrets," Jessica said. "The Sisterhood resents me because of Paul—that is no secret. But that doesn't mean I can never have an Atreides daughter . . . unless they continue to keep me away from Leto!"

Cordana gave her a sharp, hard look. "What you say cannot be denied."

It was well past midnight when Jessica returned to her own quarters in the Viscount's wing. She had a grand suite adjacent to Giandro's for the sake of appearances, since she was officially his concubine, and Jessica had enjoyed many late-night discussions with him.

She knew Viscount Tull cared for her and respected her, and although she did see a glimmer of genuine romantic interest beyond the gallant façade he maintained, he had never tried to force her. Despite what the Sisterhood demanded, he realized that her heart still belonged to Leto.

Though she was tired, her thoughts churned with both relief and confusion. After speaking with Cordana, she knew she had passed some kind of test, and the Reverend Mother—a close confidante of Mother Superior Harishka—might even help arrange for her to return to Caladan. Her joy at that idea was tempered by sadness, knowing the hurt that Giandro would experience if she were to leave Elegy.

She was about to open the door to her chambers when alarm bells sounded through the manor house. Turning to the hall windows that looked out on the estate grounds, she saw flashes of orange in the distance, followed a few seconds later by the rumble of explosions. Before she could see more details, armored shutters slammed shut over the plaz, blocking the view.

She heard yells of panic, then brusque orders. Giandro Tull rushed down the corridor toward her, clipping on a weapons belt as he ran. "Jessica, come with me to the underground shelter. I need to keep you safe."

"What's happening?"

He didn't answer as he bounded ahead. As she raced after him, the Viscount's guards charged along the corridor, shouting to one another. Jessica felt another wave of alarm, and she insisted, "What about Reverend Mother Cordana and the other Sisters? We have to keep them safe."

That caught his attention. He glanced over his shoulder. "We are under attack by an unknown force. We're activating all defensive measures now, but don't worry, I have no interest in facing Bene Gesserit wrath, too. My guards are escorting them to the same shelter."

A lev-major ran up, flushed and out of breath. "We've identified them, Sire. It is a Sardaukar attack! They descended without warning or explanation."

Giandro's running steps faltered. "Sardaukar? Why Sardaukar? Have they issued an ultimatum?"

The officer had no answer to the question. "Ground troops emerged from personnel carriers. Thousands of shielded fighters with blades, slaughtering civilians as they make their way here from the spaceport."

"Sardaukar!" Jessica cried.

The Viscount's face darkened. "They already came here. They searched everywhere and found nothing!" He looked at Jessica, his eyes bright with both fear and indignation. "If they have accusations to make, then they should bring me before an Imperial magistrate. This . . ." He could barely control his fury. "*This* is why we must destroy the Corrino Imperium."

Jessica wondered if Shaddam had somehow discovered that Giandro Tull was the one who had euthanized his stolen thoroughbred horses, or if he'd learned that Giandro had sent weapons and supplies to support the rebellion. Either way, she was sure House Tull must be doomed, just like House Verdun.

Giandro reached a decision. "We will use our new shield nullifiers—we have dozens of prototypes here. Set them off as the Sardaukar arrive on the grounds, and then they will be vulnerable to our projectile weapons. They'll never expect it. We might . . . we *will* have a chance!" He turned to Jessica. "But I need to ensure your safety."

Tull household security forces did as they were commanded, bringing out the ornate, boxy devices that would emit a scrambling pulse to neutralize all personal shields in the vicinity. The manor's defenses included antique projectile weapons, even large-bore projectile launchers.

The invading Sardaukar left a swath of fire and blood behind them, citizens of the city, the corpses of the Viscount's household staff. But after the nullifiers were triggered and the stifling wave washed over them, the Imperial soldiers suddenly found themselves vulnerable to weapons long thought to be obsolete.

On the lower level of the manor house, Jessica ran past a window where the shutter system had jammed partway down. Through the crack, she saw an eerie yellow light outside, rising flames as well as projectile fire, even explosives. She still couldn't believe the Emperor's elite troops were attacking here. A flushed and perspiring guard hurried her past the window, so that she no longer had even a glimpse of what was going on outside.

As Giandro's escort led Jessica to the secure vault under the main level of the manor house, another soldier issued a rushed report. "We're slaughtering them, Sire. They can't believe they're no longer invincible! We are mowing them down." His grin faltered. "But they keep coming, more and more, climbing over the bodies of their comrades."

As they reached the door of the sheltered underground chamber, two more guards arrived, hurrying the Bene Gesserit entourage. Cordana and her companion Sisters were in disarray, looking like hunted animals. The Reverend Mother covered her anxiety with indignation. "Why are Sardaukar attacking here? They've put a Bene Gesserit envoy and staff at risk. We will file a complaint directly through the Emperor's Truthsayer!"

Beside her, one of the Sisters muttered the Litany Against Fear.

Jessica felt deep dismay. "I doubt anything the Sisterhood says, even from his Truthsayer, can sway the Emperor's action now."

As the Bene Gesserit entered the armored chamber, Giandro took Jessica aside. Leaning close so she could feel his warm breath on her face, he whispered to her, "I'm sorry I got you into this, Jessica. I remember what the Emperor did to my friend Fausto Verdun." He shook his head, harried and shaken.

"I am here to serve you, not to question you," Jessica said. "I know you are a good man."

"Our shield nullifiers give us a brief advantage, and we can hold them off for a time, but the effect diminishes, and we cannot use the nullifier devices again. Soon enough, their personal shields will reset, and the Sardaukar will overwhelm the manor house. I meant to keep you safe, but I'm afraid that even this chamber won't be sufficient." As they stood just inside the armored protective chamber, the Viscount looked at the Bene Gesserit, then back at Jessica. "You'll be bottled up here, and I would expect the Sardaukar to leave no witnesses. After all those casualties, they could never admit it . . ."

Reaching a decision, Giandro gathered Cordana and the small group of Sisters. "There is a small chance, and very dangerous, but you might be able to get to the spaceport." He drew a deep breath. "You could survive this, but the Sardaukar will never let me leave. My sentence has been set in stone."

"We will declare diplomatic immunity," Cordana said. "Even the Emperor's soldiers have no right to harm the Bene Gesserit. They wouldn't dare!"

Giandro gave her a sad, fatalistic smile. "I wouldn't test that. Your argument may work with spaceport officials, but here in the manor house . . ." He shook his head.

Jessica followed him as he urged the group to a set of stairs. "What do you mean? How do you expect us to get away if the Sardaukar are surrounding the manor house?"

He opened a hatch to a tunnel barely tall enough for a person. Widely separated small glowglobes added enough light down a long passageway. "This leads to my stables on the perimeter of the estate. Can all of you ride?"

Surprised, the Sisters looked at one another before nodding uncertainly. Reverend Mother Cordana sagged. "I cannot."

Jessica straightened. "Then I'll help you. If Stable Master Darci is there, he can saddle the horses for us. If not . . . we will manage."

Giandro looked at them with a grim expression. "Be safe. Get away. If you reach the spaceport, board a shuttle that will take you to the orbital transfer station and make your own way from there. Just get away. Use my accounts, Jessica. I . . . I won't need the funds anymore."

She began to argue with him, reassure him over the rumble of explosions outside. The Sardaukar continued to the estate, even though the Viscount's army was massacring them without their personal shields. But the shield nullifier had a time limit, and their shields would return. And they were Sardaukar. "Don't stay here," she urged Giandro. "Come with us."

He shook his head. "I could try to escape with you, Jessica. I could flee like a coward, and the Sardaukar would hunt me for the rest of my days—which would be few." He embraced her with awkward, stiff formality, then stepped away. "I have a different plan here, and these attackers will suffer more than they realize." He kissed her hand in the way of a gentleman. "Stay safe, my Lady."

She didn't ask about his plan, just met his steady gaze, feeling so much unspoken there, and then he hurried off to his own defenses.

Leading the group of Bene Gesserit, Jessica ran through the low underground tunnel to the stables.

A GLOW OF orange fires gave the night a hellish illumination, and the smell of smoke and human carnage was stifling.

At the top level of the manor house, Giandro Tull and his officers crossed a short bridge to a defensive wall. From above, he watched Sardaukar charging across the grounds, fighting hand-to-hand even though their personal shields had failed. Hundreds of the Imperial soldiers had already been cut down by Tull projectile weapons, but even so, the elite troops overwhelmed Giandro's best defenders.

As the Sardaukar pressed ahead to the barricaded doors of the manor house, Giandro could see the flicker of shields reappear around some of them. The barrage of deadly projectiles simply sparkled as the bullets were deflected again.

"My Lord, the nullifier effect has worn off," one of his captains reported. "We have only one prototype device left, our last line of defense. Should we deploy it? Gain ourselves a little time? It would let us kill a few more of them."

"No, Captain. We might kill dozens more that way, but we are facing thousands."

As he stood above the furious battle, Giandro felt immensely weary, knowing the bloodshed would reach him within moments. Longingly, he glanced to the east, where the large stables loomed, dark in the heart of the late night. Several miles beyond, the glow of the spaceport seemed mockingly close, but offered no hope—not for him.

"I would rather kill them all," he said.

An hour had passed since he'd sent Jessica away with the Bene Gesserit, and by now, they should have mounted their horses and galloped across the open fields toward the spaceport. Enough time had elapsed.

It would have to be.

On the ground level, the Sardaukar crashed through the front doors and flooded into the manor house, their body shields back to full strength. Hundreds of others spread out inside the building and across the estate grounds, hunting. Giandro wondered if the Emperor intended to steal his thoroughbreds again. Surely the Sardaukar would slaughter the stable master and anyone working there—especially if they discovered that Jessica and the others had gotten away.

As he looked down at the countless Imperial troops and all of their flickering shields, he withdrew another weapon he had retrieved from the armory. A lasgun.

"This will take care of all of them at once," he said.

THE EERIE YELLOW light of the continuing battle shone behind them as Jessica hunched over the galloping thoroughbred, holding Reverend Mother Cordana steady on the saddle in front of her. She headed toward the main Elegy spaceport, knowing what Giandro had done for them, and though her heart was torn, she understood that he had seen no alternative.

Back at the stables, Darci had already saddled several horses when the women arrived, and they'd mounted up within moments. Jessica had urged the panicked stable master to ride off with them, knowing he would surely be killed by Sardaukar, but the loyal man refused, saying he would stay with the horses.

Now the fires, smoke, and explosions of fighting resounded behind Jessica, spooking the thoroughbreds—but the animals were happy enough to run in the opposite direction. She and her companions rode off into the night, with the lights of fires in the sky behind them.

Reaching the spaceport perimeter, they dismounted and let the horses run free. As the thoroughbreds galloped away, Cordana hustled into the terminal building and toward the shuttle loading platform, with the others behind her.

The Reverend Mother stepped up to the uneasy spaceport employees and declared that she and her group were under diplomatic protection as envoys of the Bene Gesserit. Her demeanor of command was indisputable, tinged with an undertone of Voice.

It was enough to clear the way, and the women boarded the delayed shuttle. Cordana issued commands for the ship to depart and take them up to the new transfer hub that had drawn so much additional space traffic to Elegy.

Jessica sat crowded together with the other Sisters, pressed against a windowport. Her stomach was twisted in knots, and she looked out as her craft launched, rising high and fast on suspensor engines. Below, she could see the fires around the manor house, the extensive lichen gardens burning, and knew that Giandro Tull—a good and decent man—was surely besieged, captured, possibly executed. She felt a terrible sensation of sadness.

Then a blinding flare blossomed out, sweeping in concentric ripples from the heart of the estate. Jessica shielded her eyes, turned away from the windowport. The glare flooded the shuttle's interior, and moments later, a shock wave buffeted the craft, but the pilot stabilized them.

A pseudo-atomic explosion. She knew what Giandro had done, what he'd felt he had to do.

Beside her, one of the other Sisters had not been so quick to shield her eyes. She cried out that she couldn't see. "It is only temporary," another Sister consoled her.

"We have all been blind," Cordana said in a grim voice. "In another way." She looked over at Jessica. "Again, we will take you back to the Mother School on Wallach IX, Jessica of Caladan."

Even serious pressures in life become insignificant when a trapdoor unexpectedly opens beneath your feet.
—DUKE PAULUS ATREIDES, strategy lessons for his son, Leto

G rowing more determined the longer he considered his plans, Leto used the connections and codes Jaxson Aru had given him so he could travel without being noticed. He arranged undocumented passage from Caladan and transferred twice, using a separate identity that the rebels had provided for him.

Finally, he made his way back to Nossus.

Jaxson was still gone, however, and the fortified main house remained nearly empty. The skeleton staff knew that the rebel leader trusted Leto, but he wondered if Rajiv Londine had sent a warning about their dispute over the ailar drug. Leto's outrage over the other nobleman's betrayal was real, not part of his quiet infiltration plan.

How much had Jaxson himself known about the illicit market for the "Caladan drug"? About Chaen Marek's hidden operations growing the barra ferns? Did the rebel leader know that Rajiv Londine was one of the primary dealers of the deadly substance? Or that ailar itself was funding Noble Commonwealth activities? Jaxson certainly knew of Leto's disgust over the drug, how it had hurt his people and tainted his own reputation. Was Jaxson also aware that the drug—sold by Londine—had killed Lord Atikk's son and exposed Leto to a kanly blood duel?

More importantly, did he care?

At the main house, Jaxson's security staff was like a small army. Some had been volunteer "targets" when they'd tested Tull's shield nullifier devices. The building had its own defenses, powerful perimeter shields as well as a network of tunnels like an underground warren. But the Noble Commonwealth's greatest defense lay in obscurity. No one would look on Nossus if they barely knew the world existed.

Leto's original plan had been to expose the base and send the coordinates to Kaitain. But now that he knew about Jaxson's dangerous black archives of damning information about House Corrino and so many noble families, he couldn't simply call down the Imperial hammer. Jaxson would activate the memory stone if he felt he had no choice . . . or the data would automatically be broadcast if he were killed.

Leto's personal goal now—a mission only he could do—would be to somehow deceive or overpower the man and steal the memory stone, find a way to destroy the ticking time bomb before it unleashed its total chaos on the Imperium. Leto was sure he could get close to Jaxson, but so many things could still go wrong.

Inside the isolated headquarters, he tracked down the house manager, a doorman who was clearly trained for far different activities. "Do you have any word on when Jaxson might return?"

The house manager looked long and hard at Leto, as if analyzing the reason for his question. "I cannot tell you, sir, for security reasons. And I do not know the answer myself—also for security reasons."

Leto had expected nothing else. Jaxson's movements were secretive and capricious. He traveled frequently and without plans, just to stay one step ahead of pursuit, but Leto resolved to wait here on Nossus as long as necessary. The rebel leader would certainly return to his base soon, no doubt in preparation for making another bloody, violent "statement."

Leto wanted to be back home on Caladan where he belonged, far from the morass of Imperial politics. He longed for his old life with Jessica and Paul, but he had no chance of restoring that until after the rebellion was defeated. Perhaps then he could claim any reward from the Emperor, maybe even coerce the Bene Gesserit into sending Jessica back as his bound concubine.

But she had so readily accepted her assignment to Viscount Giandro Tull. . . .

He still had the message that Tull had sent, where Jessica stood at his side, smiling and showing her support. He had called up the recording again, intending to watch it, but could only endure a few seconds before switching it off again. He had seen all that he needed to see.

Even if he could force the issue with the witches, Leto doubted if that was the favor he should request. The very thought of Jessica, and the grayness that his life had become because of their dispute, made his heart heavy.

He sat alone on the open veranda of the main house, trying to feel the calm of bucolic Nossus. He looked at the rolling hills, the herd beasts wandering through the grasslands, the nearby hill with its fledgling olive grove. Jaxson drew peace from a place like this, but Duke Leto needed to hear the whisper of the ocean, smell the damp, salty air. . . .

When an unexpected ship hurtled down through the atmosphere, the household staff went on high alert and rushed about gathering weapons from the armory, preparing the shields around the property. They were grim, professional, and not prone to panic.

Leto asked five people before someone finally provided an answer. "Lord Rajiv Londine is declaring an emergency. He requests sanctuary, says he must land immediately."

Leto scowled at the thought of the duplicitous nobleman. "What happened?"

"He gave few details." The house guard ran off.

The small vessel landed in the outer fields beyond the hangar that held Jaxson's refurbished faster-than-light ship. The newly arrived shuttle bore no insignia, but Londine had transmitted the proper identification codes, which allowed him through the Nossus defenses.

Leto and five armed house guards bounded to the edge of the cleared landing area just as the vessel's hatch opened. The dapper nobleman emerged wearing the jumpsuit of a trader, far more subdued than his usual garish Cuarte colors. His steel-gray hair was mussed, his expression harried. Leto barely recognized him.

Londine swayed and caught his balance, as if he had a hard time adjusting to the gravity of Nossus. He scanned the stony guards, and when his gaze fell upon Leto, his expression lit up with surprise and relief. "Leto Atreides— you're here, too! I have been through a terrible ordeal."

Leto remained cool and suspicious. "We did not part under the best of circumstances, sir. I have no desire to be your ally, and I intend to inform Jaxson about your ailar operations as soon as he returns."

Distracted, Londine fluttered a hand and looked up into the open skies as if afraid bombers might arrive at any moment. "Those are insignificant matters now—so much has happened! The Sardaukar overwhelmed my planet! They attacked Cuarte, murdered Vikka!" His expression fell, and tears sprang into his eyes. "Right in front of me. They thrust a sword through her. I only got away because Rodundi threw himself to my defense."

Leto reeled. "Sardaukar went to Cuarte? But why? Because of your inflammatory article?"

"They somehow know we are allied with the rebellion!" Londine said. "The Imperials swept in, massacred everyone. No mercy."

The house guards listened with sharp intensity.

Leto asked, "Then how did you escape from the Sardaukar?"

"I had made alternative plans for this extreme circumstance." He hung his head, shook it from side to side. "I hated Shaddam Corrino, but even I believed he would abide by some shred of Imperial law." Londine swayed, on the verge of collapse. "Please, let's go inside the main house. I need to rest."

The guards encircled him, and Leto followed. The consequences thundered around him, as well as the personal shock of Vikka's death. "But how did Shaddam know about your secret activities? Your connection with the Noble Commonwealth?" He remembered, though, how bold and lax the nobleman had been. Even so, he pressed, "What evidence did Shaddam provide?"

Londine glared up at him. "At first, I thought that *you* might have exposed us because you were upset with me over the ailar sales."

Leto hardened his expression. He had intended to do exactly that in the early stages of his plan, but once he learned of Jaxson's insurance policy, he had never sent such a message. "It wasn't me. I revealed nothing."

"Somehow, they knew about the Noble Commonwealth inner circle. All of us! As I escaped, going from place to place to lose any pursuit, I just learned that Elegy has been attacked as well! Viscount Tull is murdered and much of his city destroyed, wiped out in a pseudo-atomic explosion."

Now Leto felt even more thunderstruck, and his heart felt suddenly hollow. "Elegy?" Jessica had been there at Tull's side! And if the Sardaukar had assassinated the Viscount along with a purge that wiped out everyone else . . . was Jessica still alive? It didn't seem possible.

Rajiv Londine was grim, shaken. "I suspect many of the other planets are also targets. Somehow, they know all of our names, Leto!"

The Duke's throat went dry. Among the clamor of emotions and terror over what had happened to Jessica, he suddenly realized that Caladan, too, might be in danger.

Londine looked around, panicked again. "Where is Jaxson? Is he safe?"

"He hasn't returned from his own mission yet," Leto said. "He said he had a prime recruit for the cause. No one knows where he is."

"But we must act, dispatch a warning to our allies, though it's probably already too late! The Noble Commonwealth is being torn apart, crushed. Jaxson will know what to do. If there was ever a time for him to make a last desperate gesture, it is now." Londine seemed frantic, shattered, as if all his rebellious talk and deadly criticisms had been mere posings, but now they had become much too real. "Maybe we can exterminate the Corrinos. One final attack on the Imperial throne would change everything."

Despite all the horrific news, Leto still did not trust Rajiv Londine. He would keep his distance from the man, filled with questions and his own dread.

JAXSON ARU ARRIVED back on Nossus the following day, also in a desperate mood. He flew a battered escape ship dispatched from a Heighliner that he had somehow diverted from its scheduled route. The rebel leader had only two of his dedicated guards with him, declaring that the rest had been slaughtered by Sardaukar in a trap. Jaxson himself had barely escaped.

"I had a rendezvous with Baron Harkonnen to acquire a large load of spice," he explained, his face flushed and angry. "The Baron betrayed us, brought the Sardaukar down upon our meeting."

"Harkonnens will always betray you," Leto said.

Thanks to his recent, brief visit to Caladan, the Duke knew that Gurney Halleck was being held prisoner among them, unless Thufir Hawat's rescue mission had succeeded. Had the Emperor in fact received Gurney's vital message, or had the Harkonnens disrupted that, too? How he hated them!

Leto was in so deep he was drowning. He had reached the endgame, and he alone needed to bring this to a satisfactory conclusion. But the Sardaukar were rigid, ruthless, and asked no questions. This crisis required subtlety and finesse, or the repercussions would resound for generations. Likely, they meant to punish Caladan and every other connected world, unless he could stop it.

When Leto stared at Jaxson, he saw a frightened and angry man. The rebel leader fidgeted with his new etched-iron earring as if it were a worry stone. "We have to make our final plans. The Baron betrayed me at our rendezvous, but he never knew about Londine's or Tull's involvement in the rebellion. He does not know about Nossus. If Shaddam is dispatching these punitive strikes across our worlds, then we must have a traitor in our midst. Someone told the Emperor about my closest allies." He looked at Leto, Londine, then his own household guards. "We are all exposed."

As a Swordmaster, Egan Saar had many victories, vanquished opponents, and blood spilled—all in the service of his masters who employed him, or for his own self-gratification.

Rarely, though, had he endured humiliation, the embarrassment of failure.

Presenting himself to Feyd-Rautha after his return from the mission on Caladan, Saar had been smug and overconfident. He remembered dispatching the victim, the fight and the blood . . . the satisfying wet sensation of his razor-edged blade striking the soft flesh and hard bone as he severed the head of the concubine of Duke Leto Atreides. His target. That woman, a Bene Gesserit bitch named Xora, was certainly dead.

But she was not the right one.

Egan Saar had been made a fool. When the Baron's cocky young nephew revealed the information to him, he'd been gloating as much as he was dissatisfied. The twisted Swordmaster had absorbed the information, fighting back disbelief. But looking at the images Feyd-Rautha had compiled, he could see it was true. Saar had killed the wrong target, struck down the wrong woman. He did not care about her or her innocence, only that the real target had eluded him. It made him seem inept. He was one of the elite Swordmasters who had trained on the rigorous islands of Ginaz, and he had completed his deadly instruction, twisted under Tleilaxu assassins.

Now he had failed.

As Feyd-Rautha had looked at him with a sneer, rebuffing him, dismissing him, Saar had said, "Then I shall return and finish the job properly."

And so the twisted Swordmaster had melted back into the shadows and garish lights of the massive Harkonnen headquarters.

His instincts and anger made him want to rush onto the first Guild Heighliner and make his way back to Caladan to strike down any likely opponents.

He would leave a string of bodies until he had inflicted the pain so desired upon House Atreides.

But he had been brash and sloppy before. This time, he would be careful, a slow blade instead of a flailing cudgel.

Without asking permission, Saar withdrew into the undercity, breaking into Harkonnen databases, studying information compiled by surveillance efforts, reports delivered from passive spies on Caladan.

He researched House Atreides, memorizing thick files on Duke Leto and his household, his weapons master Gurney Halleck, his Mentat assassin Thufir Hawat . . . and his own Swordmaster, also trained on Ginaz—Duncan Idaho.

There were entire shigawire spools of covertly obtained images of young Master Paul. The boy seemed weak and vulnerable, an easy target if Saar could manage to get inside Castle Caladan. He pocketed the spools for future reference.

But because his original target had been the Duke's beloved concubine, Saar was more interested in killing her—first.

His specific mission was to cause devastating pain to Leto Atreides, to break the man's heart and tear his soul to shreds, and that became a personal goal for the Swordmaster, too. Previously, he had accomplished his missions through swift, efficient kills. This time, though, the pain would be more drawn out—a challenge, but a satisfying one. After he killed the Lady Jessica, then he could find a way to murder Paul, too. After all, he was just a boy.

The twisted Swordmaster wouldn't even charge Feyd-Rautha an additional fee. In fact, Saar decided he was no longer doing this for the money at all. After his shame and humiliation, he might never even return to Giedi Prime. That was not the object.

As silent as a shadow, Saar crept into part of the Harkonnen intelligence archives to search for any new reports of Lady Jessica. Upon first embarking on the mission, he had not thought to check since she had been the bound concubine of House Atreides for nearly twenty years. Why had she gone away? And where? Did she leave the Duke's service?

Egan Saar was adept with a blade and swift with the killing stroke, but his mind was also sharp, filled with tactics and nuances, able to see connections like a brilliant strategist. Now, alone in a secure archives room, he studied the disconnected records, looking for a thread that no one else had spotted. He strung thoughts together, an offhand reference here, a footnote there.

He learned that Jessica had indeed been withdrawn by the Sisterhood, her contract with Duke Leto canceled—apparently against his wishes, and hers. Disappointed, he learned that she had been recalled to Wallach IX and the

Bene Gesserit Mother School, a fortress and closely monitored by the secretive order. It would be impossible for him to infiltrate there and make his kill. He would not be able to complete the mission as he wished.

One last seemingly unrelated report caught his eye, and he loaded the spool into the reader, spinning up the wires. He raced through the succession of images until he found one of Jessica again, surely the same person—yes, there was a slightly out-of-focus image, and it was her face. She had been reassigned to another noble house, the Viscount Tull on Elegy.

He leaned back and smiled, then reviewed the images again. Elegy, with a new transfer station in orbit. It would be easy for him to get there. He had no doubt that he could bypass Viscount Tull's security.

Saar rose, gathering all of the intelligence he had compiled, and turned to find a gray-uniformed, pale-faced Harkonnen administrator glowering at him. "Who are you? What are you doing here?"

Saar strode toward the door. "I'm leaving. I have what I need."

"You will stop!" The administrator raised his voice. "Security breach!" Saar winced at the shrill call, grinding his teeth, annoyed at the inconvenience. In a smooth, rolling movement, he approached the frightened administrator, drew his killing knife, and plunged it into the base of the man's throat. He danced out of the way so that the spouting blood would not soil him.

A second clerk came running in, eyes wide, just in time to see the other man fall. Saar turned to him and closed in without a sound, striking him down as well.

He could have declared that he had access to comb through Harkonnen records, could have called Feyd-Rautha, but that would be no fun. Egan Saar drew his sword along with the killing knife and turned to meet the Harkonnen guards that rushed in response to the alarm.

Feyd's orders, echoing his uncle's command, were to inflict anguish and suffering on House Atreides. Because Feyd had witnessed the twisted Swordmaster's embarrassment, Saar felt like inflicting some pain of his own. Feyd-Rautha certainly didn't care about these underlings, but even so, Saar enjoyed himself as he plowed through them and left a line of bloody corpses, fourteen in all.

Before he departed from the data archives and slipped into the dark alleys and shadowy underworld businesses, he reaffirmed his decision not to come back here ever again. Finishing the mission was its own reward.

AS PART OF his earlier mission, Feyd had provided falsified papers and a new identity for Saar, but the twisted Swordmaster decided to use his own false documents to keep the trail clean.

After stowing aboard a Harkonnen transport ship to orbit, then making his way onto the Guild Heighliner, he tracked down the most convenient route that would take him to the Elegy Transfer Station. He spent the entire time making, and relishing, plans to murder Jessica.

When he finally arrived and disembarked at the Elegy hub, he was surprised to learn that the planet itself was interdicted. Viscount Tull's holdings had recently been the focus of an overwhelming Sardaukar assault. The spaceport had been ruined, the entire estate obliterated. A posted notice stated that the action had been a demonstration of Padishah Emperor Shaddam IV's intolerance for traitors.

That only made the next step more difficult for the twisted Swordmaster, because then he had to steal a small shuttle from the transfer platform, which involved killing a few more people and leaving a cluttered trail behind him. But he had learned from his failure with Feyd-Rautha not to make assumptions, no matter how sure they might seem. He had to go down there himself to verify that Lady Jessica no longer existed as a possible target. If she was indeed dead, her loss might cause the anguish in Duke Leto's heart, as his employer desired, but it was not of Egan Saar's doing. Therefore, it didn't count.

His stolen shuttle landed on the outskirts of what had been the main Elegy spaceport. The landscape was still smoking, uplifted and jumbled rocks, buildings collapsed and turned to melted lumps of metal. The site of the manor house was a clean, bowl-shaped crater. Saar couldn't believe that a Sardaukar aerial bombardment would have caused such a thing. It looked like a pseudo-atomic explosion. Then he decided that it was exactly that.

People still survived in the aftermath, those who had lived in the outlying farmlands or peripheral villages. Now they moved about listlessly, moving bodies and body parts, looking for what remained of their lives, but the task seemed beyond them. Saar stared at the people, then assessed the devastation, the ground-zero point where Viscount Tull—and no doubt his new concubine—would have been.

There was nothing for him here. If Egan Saar was to finish the true mission, he had to change the goal. The next destination was clear.

He would make his way to Caladan and kill Paul Atreides.

The distinctive barra fern grows nowhere else in the Imperium, although
many have attempted to transplant it. Only on Caladan does it thrive.

—Imperial botanical survey

The experimental strain of ailar made Duncan sick, light-headed, and disoriented. He experienced no hint of exhilaration that a thrill-seeker might desire.

While holding him captive and treating him as an experimental subject, Chaen Marek's men had administered the drug in different oral dosages, forcing him to ingest the fern nubs. He tried to spit it out, but the potent chemicals filled his mouth with a bitter taste. Then, as the ailar began to affect him so that he lowered his defenses, they forced him to consume more.

Although his thoughts shuttled around his mind in uneven circles, like an aircraft caught in a tailspin, Duncan understood that he was sprawled out on a hard floor inside a guarded cave. Even with the looping confusion of the ailar, part of his mind remained remarkably sharp—a disconnected, objective part. Though he couldn't move his body much, he appreciated the mental clarity he retained.

So he could still ponder, and plan.

Thinking back on how the drug lord had provoked him, taunted him by offering weapons to use—and no doubt die—he reconsidered his decision. Duncan had thought the price was too high, that it was some kind of trick . . . or was it a way to emphasize his drug-induced paranoia by letting his doubts paralyze him?

Exactly as the drug lord planned.

By now, Paul should have been able to escape. He had faith in his young ward, knew how clever and skilled he was. Duncan had allowed himself to be captured so Paul could get away. The young man would find the downed aircraft, and the Swordmaster was confident he could complete the repairs on his own. Logically, at that point, Paul should simply fly back to Castle Caladan, where he could rally Atreides troops for a military mission.

But Duncan also knew that Paul wouldn't so easily abandon his trainer, even though that was exactly what a potential Duke should do. Paul was sure to be up to something, and Duncan could not prevent it. He had to be ready. He had to survive.

Over the past day, he had endured one numbingly heavy ailar dose after another, and the Tleilaxu man had studied his reactions, made notes, and continued his experiments. Marek taunted him, made Duncan believe he would not survive.

In the low light, he could see the pocked igneous rock, gray with dark streaks. He was inside a hollow lava tube that wormed into the mountain. Though the ailar experiments kept him disoriented, he knew he was not the only prisoner held in the drug-processing camp. One other man was also held in the mountainside enclave, though he was usually unconscious.

That fellow prisoner—a wan botanical researcher from Kaitain who had stumbled upon the barra fern plantings—spoke little even when he was awake. Dr. Xard Vim was morose in his confinement, as if he had given up all hope. Now, saturated with an experimental strain of ailar, Vim lay trembling on the cave floor. He stared in Duncan's direction, his eyes blinking too often. Blood ran from one of his ears onto the stone floor. Duncan tried to reach out and offer aid, but he was unable to help the man.

"Sinsei . . . ," Vim said in a rattling voice. "She is gone." Then his eyes shone brighter. "She got away!"

Duncan knew that the man had a daughter, a research companion, who had escaped into the jungles when he was captured. But then Dr. Vim slumped and seemed to take no hope from the knowledge. Although Paul was skilled in survival, Duncan had no idea of Sinsei Vim's abilities.

"If I can break free . . . ," he whispered, intending to sound reassuring, but his limbs seemed to mock him. He couldn't even twitch. His fellow prisoner did not respond.

A few hours earlier, both captives had been forced to consume a potent experimental strain of the ferns. Now, Vim shuddered and retched, fighting off the toxin coursing through his body. Duncan had plunged into his own dark and twisted unconsciousness, but he was recovering more quickly than his companion. Still, his muscles felt like jelly.

Occasionally, Marek or one of his henchmen observed the two men, took notes, then departed. The captive scientist clearly needed medical attention, but Duncan had no medkit, no first aid at all. He didn't think the Tleilaxu drug lord was particularly interested in the data from the experiments. He just liked to torment his prisoners.

Lying helpless on the rough stone floor, Duncan stared past Dr. Vim to the mysterious lava tube behind him, a passage that wound into the mountain. He blinked his eyes and focused his thoughts, wondering where it led. He wanted to crawl into the passage, explore it, and escape. With difficulty, he moved a hand, scratched the side of his face, but that was the extent of what he could accomplish.

Beside him, spasming, the other captive hoarsely called out his daughter's name. Vim was still bleeding from one of his ears. With his heightened acuity, Duncan saw every red drop. Rolling over, the doctor whispered in a shaky voice, "They've done a terrible thing to us."

"But we have to survive," Duncan managed to croak. "We can help each other."

He broke off, hearing footsteps, the rustle of clothing, and the faint ticking of equipment behind him in the main laboratory chamber, where Marek tested his sample ferns. The lights in the holding cave brightened, and a shadow fell over him. Two human figures came into view.

"Such a touching scene," Marek said with a sneer, addressing his companion, some kind of an assistant. "They look like they're about to embrace each other."

Duncan worked his mouth, wanting to spit again, but he could not manage it.

"Note the different reactions from the samples you gave them," the assistant said. "But neither of the strains killed them. Therefore, we can release the product."

Marek nodded. "And we can continue to modify the fern variants so that it gives the maximum addictive pleasure, without killing our customers."

The other man bent over Dr. Vim. "This one is experiencing a more severe reaction. He is bleeding from the ears. It could be a brain hemorrhage."

Chaen Marek gave the captive a sharp kick in the middle of his back, and Dr. Vim groaned as he tried to squirm away. "His reflexes are slower than with the previous sample, but he will live. Add that to your notes. Flag this particular ailar strain for secondary consideration."

Muttering a curse, Marek kicked Duncan in the back as well, but the Swordmaster refused to cry out, not even when his tormentor kicked him two more times. "I will find ways to hurt you, Atreides sword-fighter," the Tleilaxu said, then stalked out of view.

❧

WHEN DUNCAN RETURNED to consciousness, he found himself alone. A smear of blood stained the cave floor where Dr. Vim had been, but the other prisoner had been dragged away.

His senses were less fuzzy now. He had passed through the coursing of the ailar, and most of the drug had been flushed out of his system. Lying in an awkward position, he tested his arms and legs, found that he could move. With difficulty and considerable pain, Duncan rose to all fours and stood up, wavering from side to side. His entire body ached. Looking around, he saw no sign of Dr. Vim.

The Swordmaster took a tentative step, wobbled, and took another. Judging from the minimal light at the cave entrance, he thought it was either early morning or late afternoon. Farther down in another chamber, a small crew of workers packaged dried ferns. Any other time, the Swordmaster could easily have eliminated these opponents before they even realized they were under attack. But he could barely walk, much less fight.

Steadying himself, he stumbled in the other direction, into the twisted lava tube. With each step, his blood flowed and his muscles loosened, and finally Duncan was able to regain some of his coordination.

He pulled himself into a widening passage that turned deeper into the mountain, then began a shuffling run. The light dimmed as he followed the rough tunnel, but he felt his way along the lava rock walls. He struck his head against a protrusion, but ignored the pain and kept going.

Though disoriented, he felt he was heading along the slope of the mountain, perhaps back toward the surface. If he could find another opening, some exit into the jungles, he might lose himself in the wilderness. Eventually, the ailar would wear off.

He wished he could make sure that Paul had gotten to safety.

Weary, his head pounding, Duncan regretted that he couldn't bring Dr. Vim with him. His breathing echoed loud in the confined passageway.

After what seemed like hours, he began to see dim light ahead—enough to give him the strength to hurry. A crack appeared in the volcanic rock, and sunlight filtered through thick ferns, mosses, tangled vines. He grasped the side of the cave opening, thrust his head out into the open air to see the jungle sprawled out before him.

Then an icy laugh burst out of a thicket nearby. Chaen Marek emerged with two armed guards next to him. On the other side of the opening, two more mercenaries came into view.

"The great Atreides Swordmaster is not so great after all," Marek said. "We embedded a tracker in you. We can follow wherever you try to run."

The guards lunged forward, and even though Duncan tried to fight them off, he remained weak, disoriented. They pummeled him back into unconsciousness.

*The answer to a difficult choice can be drawn from many directions—
logic, self-interest, retribution, or directly from the heart and soul. But
after the choice is made, one must live with it.*

—ARCHDUKE ARMAND ECAZ,
conversations with the Duke of Caladan

As the Suk doctor who had served House Atreides for many years, Wellington Yueh was a trusted member of the household. That trust, not only from young Master Paul and the Lady Jessica, but from the Duke himself, was what hurt him the most now. It made Yueh's decision all the more agonizing.

The Caladan ministers, proxies, and administrators still conducted planetary business even with Duke Leto gone and Paul still training in the southern jungles. Fortunately, the young man and Duncan Idaho would be back before long.

Here in the castle, though, no one else watched Yueh closely, and that gave him the freedom to work without too many questions asked. This was the opportunity he was supposed to look for, and he could not ignore the threat being held over his dear Wanna. Yueh had never asked to be placed in such an untenable situation, and his conditioning precluded breaking his vows.

But Baron Vladimir Harkonnen knew all about Suk Imperial conditioning, and Yueh dreaded what sort of pressure the evil man would bring to bear on him . . . and what price Yueh, or his Bene Gesserit wife, would have to pay. The Baron was a ruthless man with tremendous resources and a focus as sharp as a laser.

Yueh was not a target, but a tool.

During the day, people moved through Castle Caladan in an orderly bustle of paperwork, household duties, and business matters. Documents were delivered to the administrative wing or couriered down to Cala City. As Yueh went about his activities, looking busy, no one disturbed him or even noted his passage. Fortunately, no medical emergencies occurred, so his services were not needed.

The mood among the staff was dark and heavy, however. The people of Caladan had been in turmoil ever since Lady Jessica's unexpected departure, not to mention the headstrong woman claiming to be the new concubine— who had been murdered in her bed in a Cala City inn. That crime remained unsolved, and the bloody assassin might still be out there, which kept the townspeople on edge.

Though Duke Leto tried to hide his emotions with a brave façade, his sadness sent ripples through the populace. He had returned to Caladan only briefly, and then rushed off-planet again, without explanations. Although Yueh knew the Duke's plans to thwart the violent movement, the rest of the populace had no idea whatsoever. They felt their own Duke had turned his back on them. Their concern and confusion was palpable, and Yueh could say nothing to allay their fears.

The people loved Paul, too, but not with the same intensity—not yet. It was unfortunate serendipity that he and Duncan had not been here for Leto's brief visit. By design, they had made it impossible for anyone to contact them down in the jungles. Yueh thought it was audacity, or foolish optimism, that they believed nothing bad could happen to them.

Yueh felt the responsibilities weigh on him. He himself had implanted the message crystal in Gurney's arm. If the man had been captured by Harkonnens—especially Rabban—then he didn't have a chance. He also had grave doubts that Thufir Hawat would be able to rescue him.

Had the Harkonnens prevented Gurney Halleck from delivering his message to Kaitain? Everything depended on that.

Just in case, as evidence to be used in extreme circumstances, Leto had recorded his newest explanatory message, full details about his covert scheme to infiltrate the rebel movement and bring them to the Emperor's justice. Even if Leto's recording was not sufficient to prevent an Imperial retaliation, it would provide strong rationale for reconsideration. But no one else knew about the recording—only Yueh.

He was aware that Paul himself had an earlier code-locked message from his father, a final testament should he be killed on this dangerous mission. Yueh knew where that was held, but such a message would not be proof, merely an emotional apology to his heir.

Worse, Yueh was aware of the Baron's other insidious plans. He felt helpless, like a small, terrified animal pinned to a vivisection board, just waiting for the first scalpel cut.

The Suk doctor was even more sickened to discover a threat just smuggled to him by a secret Harkonnen operative. The Baron was unorthodox and resourceful.

For his scientific research, Yueh had received a library of invasive mites, similar to the ones that had killed off most of the moonfish to the north. He already had specimens of the Lankiveil parasite that Rabban had unleashed on Caladan, but he wanted to continue his research.

Somehow, the Baron had managed to insert a micro-message inside the specimens. The doctor had found it while scanning the ferocious-looking mites under a heavy magnifier. The small pernicious creatures had crablike claws, long fangs, beady eyes, and an oversize egg sac—but the message engraved in the thin plaz film next to the specimen was even more horrendous.

A wave of cold went as deep as his marrow. The Baron could get to him even here, and he had Wanna in his clutches. His instructions to the Suk doctor were vague and damning nevertheless, the foulest sort of blackmail. The threat was blindingly clear.

As an unwitting pawn of the Harkonnens, Yueh had been ordered to help bring about the downfall of House Atreides, either to destroy Duke Leto's reputation, or better yet, to take his life.

Sweating profusely, the Suk doctor stood inside his laboratory room. Over the years, he had collected a library of flora and fauna, natural specimens because the life-forms of Caladan were not well catalogued. He had collected many of them during his expedition to the northern forests with Leto, Gurney, and Paul.

Now, as if he were approaching an unstable explosive, he placed the mite specimen under the magnifier and studied the Baron's message again. Afterward, jittery and nauseated, he sealed himself in his private quarters, sat on his narrow bed, and reviewed another message, one that had come from the Bene Gesserit—a letter explaining that Yueh's wife, Wanna, had vanished and that the Sisterhood was looking for her.

It all fit, providing more impossible proof than Baron Harkonnen could ever show.

Yueh had had no contact with his wife in such a long time, but he still loved her. It was a bond that fused their hearts and minds, even if public displays of affection had never been part of their relationship.

Wanna was missing, and the Baron kept invoking her in his threats. The Harkonnens did indeed have her, and were holding her against her will.

Yueh did not doubt that the Harkonnens would inflict appalling tortures on his wife. Physical pain, psychological rape, explicit mutilation. And they would draw it out, not to accomplish anything specific, but just because they reveled in it.

Yueh's Imperial conditioning as a Suk doctor was supposedly unbreakable. If he had been forced to stand in front of Wanna and watch Rabban flay the skin from her body, he might be able to endure it, but he did not *know*. He had no details and no hope. The uncertainty gnawed at him with fangs sharper than any predator.

Defeated already, he went back to his biological samples, the recent shipment for his research. He separated the hideous mite specimen and destroyed it in a sterilization furnace. He could destroy Leto's confession and testament just as easily, removing any claim that the Duke had merely been undercover to serve the Emperor. No one would know, so long as Leto was apprehended out there and brought to trial with the rest of the rebels.

No one would know.

It would be so easy to do what the Baron commanded. This way Yueh could free Wanna, pay his ransom to the Harkonnens.

But Yueh himself would know.

He retrieved Leto's recorded message, the confession and explanation, and ran his fingertip along the tight shigawire. He remembered every word the Duke had said, how earnest he had been, how trusting of Yueh. Leto would never imagine that his own Suk doctor might break his Imperial conditioning and betray him like this.

Yes, he could so easily erase and then disintegrate the recording.

Yueh held the message in the palm of his hand and struggled with his decision, thinking of Wanna and of his Duke, and of the intense loyalty he owed to each of them.

Crisis leads to opportunity, and opportunities can easily lead to disaster. Recognize both and learn to adapt.

—Landsraad Political Strategy Manual,
edition tailored to the Great Houses

An unscheduled Guild ship arrived over Nossus, shrouded in communication silence, and Leto instantly realized what it must be.

Down in the isolated headquarters, Jaxson Aru consolidated his household army, raising defenses and locking down his compound. "Somehow the Emperor knew about our fellow inner-circle members. He has surely found out about Nossus. The hammer of judgment is at hand." He looked serious rather than cocky as he regarded Duke Leto and Rajiv Londine. "And we need to deflect that hammer blow."

"Your main defense was in the fact that no one bothered to notice this obscure planet," Leto pointed out. "You expected to slip away before the noose closed, but now Imperial forces are overhead."

Pale and sick, Rajiv Londine stroked his cheek as if to keep his face in place, unconsciously mimicking Jaxson's habit after his facial-cloning surgery. "When the Sardaukar come down here, they will overwhelm us—just like on Cuarte. They will annihilate everything, kill all of us. We know they did the same thing on Elegy, too." He looked around the main house and gazed into the empty sky, knowing the gigantic Heighliner was up there. "We have nothing that can stop them."

"I can stop them." Jaxson withdrew the small, dark memory stone from his pocket. "They will be sorry if they push me into a corner."

Leto felt a deep chill as he imagined the consequences if the rebel leader triggered that last desperate measure. Leto, Londine, Jaxson, and everyone here might well be wiped out in the Sardaukar purge, but the repercussions would shake the Imperium for generations.

Jaxson tucked the stone safely away, then turned back to the main house.

Leto's heart was heavy, not just for himself, but for all the other losses that swirled like a storm around him. He still struggled with the dread that Jessica must be already dead along with Viscount Tull. And what if Sardaukar troops were already storming Caladan? How could Paul ever survive?

He cursed Baron Harkonnen and Beast Rabban under his breath because they had intercepted Gurney Halleck. If Leto's message had gone through, Emperor Shaddam would know the Atreides loyalty, and at least Caladan would be safe.

In the little time they had remaining, a frightened Londine suggested that they could simply flee, scatter away from the main house and hide in the vast unpopulated areas of the planet. The Sardaukar could spend years hunting them down.

"We don't have years," Jaxson said. "And we don't want our last act to be one of sheer cowardice."

"Then what about the tunnels beneath the main house?" Londine suggested.

The rebel leader just frowned at him. "We will not hide—we'll prepare."

Even once the Heighliner reached orbit, the Sardaukar forces needed time to mount a large-scale military operation, loading personnel into troop carriers and deploying hundreds of attack ships.

Independent of the military operations, a drone projectile from the Heighliner streaked like a bullet toward Jaxson's hidden base. Landing hard, the shielded cannister plowed into the grassy pasture not far from the main house, spraying up showers of dirt.

With Leto close at his side, Jaxson bounded forward to see what it was. A seam opened in the projectile's hull to reveal inner workings. "That's a courier drone," Leto said, having seen such devices dispatch news and notices to Caladan.

"It must be the Sardaukar demanding our surrender," Londine said, coming up behind them. "It will be their ultimatum. We have no choice." He swallowed. "On Cuarte, they didn't even bother to send such a warning."

Still puzzled, Jaxson stroked the metal ring in his ear. "I recognize this cylinder design. It's a commercial communiqué used by CHOAM—not military." He bent down, ignoring the hot metal of the shell. Reaching in, he found the activator and projected an image—a solido-hologram of Ur-Director Malina Aru.

"Jaxson, my son, events have coalesced around you like a shigawire garrote. Emperor Shaddam knows the location of Nossus as well as the identities of your coconspirators. He launched multiple strikes on his chosen targets, and several planets are already in ruin. He will crush your rebellion—and he knows where you are."

Her image flickered, as if she struggled with obligations and difficult decisions. "I loaded this courier drone aboard the Sardaukar transport, and it will be triggered to launch as soon as the Heighliner enters stable orbit. I know my words will reach you before all the troops descend, so I can offer you a slender chance, a last hope. All is not lost, if you can make it to me."

The lines in the Ur-Director's face deepened. "Even knowing what is to come, I will not underestimate you, Jaxson. If you slip free and get safely off of Nossus, then make your way to Tanegaard, I can offer you sanctuary in the CHOAM citadel. Our defenses there surpass anything the Imperial forces could breach—and Shaddam Corrino would never dare an outright confrontation with CHOAM."

Malina seemed about to say something else, but reconsidered. She ended the recording. Her image faded, and the message cylinder melted into a frothing pool of silvery denatured metal.

Jaxson grinned at his two companions. "I knew my mother would come through. She is on our side."

"But how do we get away from here?" Londine asked.

Leto shaded his eyes and gazed into the bleak sky, where he saw dark ripples and vapor trails. The Sardaukar ships were descending already. "We have to dig in. How long can we last?"

"As long as we need to." Leaving the smoldering grass fires from the landed message cylinder, Jaxson sprinted back to the main house, shouting for his guards. Dedicated to the Noble Commonwealth cause, they were willing to die for Jaxson Aru; Leto had seen that in their eyes. Their expressions showed no fear, only stony determination with a glint of fanaticism.

For Leto, the dread inevitability became crushing, and he saw only blind ends rather than possibilities. He had successfully infiltrated Jaxson's deadly movement, gathered the names of the other conspirators and even the location of Nossus. But he'd had no chance to divulge that information to Kaitain because he knew about Jaxson's memory stone.

How then had the Sardaukar known so quickly? Who had told the Emperor about Londine, and Tull . . . and him? Jaxson had suggested there might be an infiltrator inside the movement—could there be two?

The Sardaukar ships dropped down in a full-fledged invasion. Emperor Shaddam clearly meant to make another bloody statement on Nossus.

Once Leto and his companions reached the fortified main house, Jaxson turned on the house pentashields, forming an unbreachable secure barrier. Even so, Leto didn't feel safe. Behind those shields, they were bottled up and trapped.

After the military dropships disgorged a full division of Sardaukar, the attackers reached the edge of the powerful house shields, thwarted by the defenses. Watching through the window, Leto knew the Imperial troops could bombard the area from above, perhaps damage or overstress the pentashields enough to make them fail. For now, though, the Sardaukar simply laid siege.

Flanked by fifty armed fighters, a commanding officer strode up to the perimeter shields, haughty and cold. His voice boomed through an amplifier. "Jaxson Aru, the Padishah Emperor commands that you be captured alive and brought to justice. Surrender now, and we can limit the pain and duration of your execution. There may also be leniency for your coconspirators."

Jaxson flashed a smug smile to Leto. "It was a mistake for him to admit that he wants me alive. It means the Sardaukar will not just obliterate us outright. That offers an opportunity."

"The end is still inevitable." Londine wiped sweat from his brow. The nobleman no longer sounded like the firebrand critic of Imperial corruption.

"It's Shaddam's pride," Leto said. "He wants to execute you himself."

Jaxson caressed his memory stone. "Oh, I have one last card to play. Whatever pain and torture Shaddam imagines he can inflict upon me, this data will cause a thousandfold more repercussions as soon as I trigger it. His reign will never recover, and it will be the end of the Corrinos for all time."

"Nor will the rest of the Landsraad recover," Leto warned. "It cannot be undone. But the Ur-Director gave us a chance."

The Duke had to stay close to the terrorist leader, find some way to seize or destroy the device. If Jaxson tried to release the black archives, Leto would have no choice but to fight him, try to smash the stone—and hope that worked.

"I can at least threaten them." Jaxson let out a dry, cold chuckle. "I deserve some enjoyment out of this scenario!"

From the manor house, the rebel leader opened a channel, and his amplified voice boomed out. "I would not be so sanguine of your position, Commander. I have in my possession a bombshell that Emperor Shaddam and all the members of the Landsraad would not want to see unleashed. I have records of illicit business dealings, noble alliances, commercial treacheries, and secret agreements from the annals of CHOAM. Decades' worth! Unless you withdraw, I shall release the data far and wide for everyone to see."

The Sardaukar milled about in ragged ranks beyond the perimeter. Other officers rushed to speak to the commander in intense, whispered conversations, and the man finally stepped forward to address the shielded manor house. "Even if you were to take such outrageous action, your transmission would go nowhere. Nossus is interdicted. We can block any signal. This alleged blackmail data would never be dispersed to the Imperium at large."

Jaxson retorted mockingly, "Cling to your confidence if you like, but I have thousands of hidden recorders and repeaters aboard every Guild Heighliner. You may think you can stop my transmission, but it will be held on delay like a ticking explosive. It will be released sooner or later. There would be nothing you can do to stop it."

The Sardaukar formed additional defensive lines around the shielded perimeter. The commander fell back to wait, in deep discussions with his experts.

"Is that true, Jaxson?" Londine said, eyes wide. "You really have such a cache of dangerous data?"

The rebel leader pretended to be aloof, but his tension plainly showed. "I have enough redundancy. Once I choose to release the black archives, the information *will* get out. It'll be like a plague of data."

Leto stepped closer, cautioning, "Then that would truly be the end of our civilization, and we would face generations of inter-House warfare. I did not know Jaxson Aru was so fatalistic and so eager to give up. Our immediate efforts should be directed to finding a way off-planet, accept your mother's offer of sanctuary. We will be safe on Tanegaard." He didn't believe it for a minute, still uncertain about the Urdir's motives, but he knew that Jaxson accepted the possibility.

The rebel leader's eyes held a malicious glint. "I have a hundred fighters in my household army. They will defend me to the death."

"Even if they are the best fighters, a hundred of them against Sardaukar is still nothing!" Londine whined. "We need a better plan."

Jaxson smiled. "The Sardaukar fight so well only because they are shielded. Thanks to Viscount Tull's nullifiers, we can strip them of that advantage. They have only blades, and we have an armory filled with unexpected explosives and projectile weapons. If we neutralize their body shields, we can surely defeat hundreds of them."

"Surely? I would not be so confident when speaking of Sardaukar," Leto muttered. "And there are thousands of Imperial fighters aboard those troop carriers."

By now, night had fallen, and the ranks of Sardaukar dug in around the main house. Inside the pentashield, half of Jaxson's household guards remained on patrol glaring out at the implacable enemy that stood against them.

Leto knew of the underground passages, the escape tunnels and bolt-holes that Jaxson had constructed beneath his base. Some passages led to the outbuildings beyond the barrier of the shield, and Jaxson had proudly shown him one exit cleverly hidden in a large rock in the new olive grove.

Leto knew he had to take his own last chance.

After Jaxson and Londine retreated to their private quarters, exhausted from the events and dreading the following day's conflicts, Leto crept to one of the tunnel access points inside a supply closet. Sealing the door behind him, he ducked into the shadowy passage, making his way around curves and corners, then up a slope, until he slid aside the faux rock covering. Surrounded by full darkness, he emerged in the gloomy olive grove.

In shadows, he looked across at the extraordinary force of armed Sardaukar facing the main house. Behind the blur of shields, the bright windows of Jaxson's fortress shone in defiance against the invaders. Leto had a desperate plan, and thought that if he could get a message directly to the Sardaukar commander, explain his purpose as an infiltrator, perhaps he could control this situation. Tonight might be his only chance because the main house would certainly fall soon.

And then Jaxson would trigger his final option.

After marking the hidden opening so he could slip back to the manor house and finish dealing with Jaxson and his memory stone, he began to creep toward the perimeter of troops. His next step would depend on how the Sardaukar commander responded.

Seeing the ferocious troops spread out ahead, he made his way closer, ducking low. He didn't want to openly surrender because that would unravel all his deceptions. He had to deliver his message about the situation, then slip back to Jaxson until he found a way to neutralize the devastating memory stone. Although he remained alert, he was startled when an oily shadow loomed up beside him—a burly and menacing Sardaukar foot soldier in night-camouflage armor.

"You are my prisoner. All terrorist lives are forfeit."

Leto raised his hands, made no threatening move. He wore no body shield, though he carried a defensive dagger as always. "I have information for your commander. I am Leto Atreides, the Duke of Caladan. Emperor Shaddam has already been informed of my plans by private message via secret courier to Kaitain." He hoped that much was true. "I need your cooperation."

The Sardaukar drew his blade. "I have no information of such an arrangement."

"You are not the commander, are you?" Leto had to continue his bluff until he could speak to the officer in charge. "If you don't accept my words now, then this entire operation will unravel. Jaxson Aru's threat is real—he does indeed have a copy of the black archives, and he will trigger his fail-safe. You must not let it come to that. Bring me to your commanding officer."

The Sardaukar growled, "Our orders are to defeat the rebel leader, not to participate in secret spy operations." He raised the blade, forcing Leto to draw his own weapon.

"Don't do this," Leto said. "We must handle this carefully."

"We have orders to take Jaxson Aru alive, but not the others. It would send a useful message if we strung up your dead body, head down in front of the manor house." He swung the blade, as if intending to dispatch his captive without any fuss.

Leto countered with his dagger, surprising the Sardaukar with his audacity and quickness. His blade struck the soldier's body shield, but at the incorrect angle and speed. The humming field deflected the edge.

Angry, the Imperial warrior advanced in deadly silence, ready to strike him down, but Leto retreated into the shadows, intending to lose himself in the olive grove. He'd expected a chance to explain himself, considering the opportunity he offered, but this soldier was not hearing him. The Sardaukar's blade crashed hard against Leto's dagger, numbing his arm, but by force of will, he maintained his grip on the weapon.

"I'll toy with you for practice. Haven't had a chance to kill a rebel yet."

Leto faced the Imperial soldier, cold and determined. Despite his training with the best weapons masters on Caladan, he doubted he was a match for this opponent.

An unexpected voice called in the night, not far away. "Hold on, Leto!"

The Imperial soldier looked up just as a ripple of silvery light washed over them, followed by a cascade of similar energy bursts that appeared all around the Sardaukar encampment. The big fighter in front of Leto grunted in surprise as his personal shield flickered and failed.

Laughing, Jaxson Aru triggered a second ornate cube cradled in his hands—Tull's shield nullifier.

An uproar rushed through the Sardaukar ranks. The soldier in front of Leto jerked backward as red craters erupted in his chest, now that his body shield was gone. Projectile weapons from Jaxson's armory cut him down like a headland deer in a meadow.

Jaxson sprinted over to Leto. "Trying to fight them yourself? I see I'm not the only one who wanted to do a little nighttime hunting!" He grinned, as if he knew why Leto had gone beyond the perimeter. "But we have a plan. This is our diversion."

Staccato gunfire stuttered from around the manor house, tearing into the flanks of the massed Sardaukar. Jaxson's guards had triggered dozens of shield nullifiers among the ranks, leaving the Imperial soldiers suddenly and completely vulnerable.

Before the Sardaukar could comprehend their peril, the fusillade of bullets and explosive projectiles mowed them down in scores, then in the hundreds. Sardaukar were feared for their blades and shields, as well as their ruthless fighting skills, but Jaxson's new gambit had just changed the rules of engagement.

Leto ran beside the man. "Remember our tests—we only have twenty minutes or so before the personal shields recover."

Jaxson grabbed him by the arm. "That's why we have to move. Londine is already making his way to the hangar. The house pentashields have been dropped so my guards could make a full assault." His expression turned grim. "Twenty of my private soldiers will accompany us aboard the escape ship, and the rest will stay here to kill as many Sardaukar as they can. They only need to delay the enemy long enough for us to take off. And then we'll go to Tanegaard."

Leto quickly grasped the new situation. "We're . . . going in the FTL ship?"

Jaxson bounded toward the hangar, forcing Leto to follow. The explosions and gunfire reached a crescendo. Using countless antique weapons, the guards unleashed a storm of deadly bullets, and bellows of pain came from the throats of the Sardaukar as projectiles tore them apart.

Even with the setback, though, the Imperial soldiers rallied, formed ranks, and raced headlong toward the main house. Jaxson's guards continued blasting away with high-powered rifles and launchers that would have been useless against shields. Bodies piled up, and yet the Sardaukar kept coming.

Leto could see they would overwhelm Jaxson's defenders soon, even without body shields.

He raced to catch up with Jaxson, clinging to threads of hope. "If we make it to the hangar, we can get away. There's no need for you to trigger your memory stone."

Jaxson's lips twisted in a sneer. "We'll save that threat for another time. Right now, let's get aboard the ship."

Five rebel guards stood outside of the open hangar, rifles raised. They shot any approaching Sardaukar, just to give Jaxson time to get inside. The crew and personal guards were already aboard the ship, powering up the suspensor engines and priming the FTL drive. Since this vessel did not need to be carried aboard a Guild Heighliner, they could simply fly it themselves. And go to the CHOAM stronghold.

Rajiv Londine was already inside the passenger compartment, strapped into a seat. "Isn't this too dangerous? I've heard that faster-than-light ships are slow and unreliable."

"Would you rather stay here?" Jaxson asked, and the nobleman quailed.

The Sardaukar charged toward the main house in a frontal assault. Now that the pentashields were down, they had launched their own incendiary projectiles, and one wing was already engulfed in flames. The rebel guards inside kept firing.

"Our base will fall soon." Jaxson shook his head. "First I lost Otorio, and now Nossus." He drew an angry breath as he threw himself into one of the primary seats. "I hate everything about the Corrinos."

The escape ship vibrated and roared as the pilot ignited the engines. He used standard suspensors to lift its bulk off the ground, pushing it out of the hangar, smashing the doorframe on the way.

Outside, Jaxson's remaining defenders did not back down, but continued to fire their projectile weapons. They massacred countless Sardaukar, but the Imperial ranks seemed inexhaustible. The FTL engines increased power, and the refitted Imperial treasury ship rose from the collapsing hangar in its hurry to burst into the sky.

Hanging on to his seat, Leto looked down to see the main house overwhelmed by troops and engulfed in flames.

The escape ship ascended steeply toward orbit, heading away from the looming Heighliner overhead. Jaxson's pilots set course for Tanegaard.

Leto felt clammy with sweat, breathing hard. The Sardaukar were limited to crossing space on Heighliners, so he and Jaxson had gotten away, and Leto had prevented the terrorist leader from triggering his memory stone, so far. He felt as if he had gotten a reprieve. Now he had to find another opportunity to destroy the data once they reached the CHOAM stronghold.

He still meant to bring down the violent rebel movement, but he could not tear the Imperium apart in the process.

When a dangerous rescue is attempted, it will either be a great adventure or a great tragedy.

— *Mark of the Warrior*, an anonymous publication

Paul had learned tactics and strategy from his father, as well as from Swordmaster Duncan Idaho, Weapons Master Gurney Halleck, and the Master of Assassins Thufir Hawat. Just as important, his mother had taught him complex thinking and the nuances of human nature, as well as bodily control and hand-to-hand combat. In addition, Sinsei and the Muadh had shown him how to use the effective bolo weapons.

He could not wait any longer. Duncan had already been held captive for two days, and the young man could only imagine what sort of tortures the Tleilaxu drug lord was inflicting on him—and on Sinsei's father. The damaged aircraft had been repaired to the best of his abilities, though the comm was still nonfunctional, but Paul refused to leave until he had his friend with him. He was ready to make a rescue attempt.

Though the Muadh supported him, and hated the secret ailar operations, the natives would not throw themselves into a violent attack. Still, Yar Zell and other skilled hunters had provided useful reconnaissance, slipping through the jungle and climbing alongside the packed roadways that the drug operations used for moving and shipping ailar. They had drawn diagrams, describing in detail what to expect beyond the storage overhang and the barracks in the volcanic caves. The Muadh had identified a secret way up the steep, nearly inaccessible mountainside to the rear of the drug operations. Paul would have to climb, and he was up for it.

Sinsei insisted on joining him, and he was glad to have her beside him for the challenging venture. He had no doubt of her abilities.

Old Mother gave them a blessing just before they set out, accompanied by half a dozen Muadh guides. The party moved at a brisk pace along hidden paths, through natural fern forests and mossy glades. The Muadh flowed along as if they were part of the terrain, avoiding pitfalls, finding a clear route through the jungle. Sinsei walked beside Paul, both armed with the flexible, spiny bolos, as well as sturdy ropes they might need for climbing.

They reached the outer slopes below the mountain complex. Concealed in the thick foliage, Paul scanned the caves and structures above, beyond a rugged headwall. Sinsei stood close, gestured toward the rough, sheer cliff that led up toward the rim. "That's the way? It looks pretty difficult."

Paul stared at the rock outcroppings, the pockmarked volcanic lumps that broke through the jungle and provided a challenging ascent. "I've faced tougher climbs in the sea cliffs near Castle Caladan, and I haven't fallen yet."

The other Muadh in the group nodded as if they had complete faith in his abilities, and in Sinsei's. Paul had a gleam in his eye as he smiled at Sinsei. "And I've always meant to climb the Arondi Cliffs near the pundi rice paddies in the north." In front of them, the wall looked like a cluster of rotted teeth embedded into the steep mountainside. "This should be no problem at all."

Sinsei squared her shoulders and adjusted the rope wrapped around her. He had seen her scramble up trees, dance from branch to branch as she grabbed vines and pulled herself over. He knew how nimble and balanced she was. "No problem at all," she repeated. "And my father is up there." She wiped sweat from her forehead. "Let's get started."

Looking up at the cliff and studying the dark protrusions, the angled cracks, Paul shouldered his coil of rope. A rock overhang blocked the main route, but a narrow cut to the left might let them get around and above the obstacle.

He pulled himself onto the first fallen boulder and reached out to the nearest wide ledge covered with moss and weeds. He scrambled quickly, with Sinsei following his lead, but he had to slow when the ascent became more complicated.

Behind them, the Muadh watched.

Using upper-body strength, he heaved himself onto the next ledge, then helped Sinsei up. They made good time along a sloped trail to the larger outcropping and found their way around a section of loose talus. Finally up and around the overhang, they rested on the high vantage, looking down to see the others hidden by trees and leaves.

Now Paul unraveled the climbing rope and worked his way higher, pressing hands and feet against the sturdy walls of a crack, and when he reached the next high point, he anchored the rope, which Sinsei used to scramble up after him. Exhausted and sweating in the humid jungle air, they anchored the other rope above the outcropping as they neared the top, so they could more easily make their way back down. Paul couldn't guess what condition Duncan and Dr. Vim would be in, even if they managed to free them.

He and Sinsei reached the top of the cliff with an abruptness that surprised him, and he pulled himself onto a flatter area overgrown with flowering bushes that offered some shelter. Loose stones spilled out from under their feet, pattering and crashing into the plants, but the natural jungle sounds drowned out any noise they made.

Crouching, Paul looked ahead to the thick foliage near the dark openings of caves near the rim. Chaen Marek's base was in there. He held his breath, watched and listened. "We made it this far," he whispered. "The Muadh think they're being held in there, through that main grotto entrance."

The young woman responded with a hard smile, "We can trust what they told us. Let's continue with our plan." She moved ahead of him, and Paul strengthened his resolve, although their "plan" was little more than relying on instincts and fighting skills to slip inside and release the prisoners.

By the time they reached the front of the complex, it was late afternoon, and the skies were studded with clouds. The jungle shadows had turned into gloom, but not yet dark enough to activate the blazing security lights installed around the ailar-processing complex. They timed their climb for this, when he and Sinsei would be the most invisible, and they had to take advantage of it.

From behind a thick bush, they watched a loaded suspensor wagon roll out onto the steep dirt road accompanied by two of Marek's mercenaries. The vehicle trundled away from the entry grotto to a cleared landing zone where a pickup vessel would take the drugs away.

As soon as the vehicle was away from the complex, Sinsei tugged Paul's arm. "This is our chance. We can get inside the main passage, head straight, and then turn right to a set of chambers where the prisoners will be."

Without waiting for his reply, she rushed forward. Paul did not try to talk her into greater caution. Duncan would have approved, he thought. At the edge of the cave opening, Sinsei paused to hide behind a thorny flower-tree as she peered into the well-lit cave. When she saw no one moving, she whispered to Paul, "The receiving area is empty. We can get past it into the main tunnel."

Loosing her spiny bolo, she darted ahead like a liquid shadow, and Paul followed her, clinging to any scrap of cover. They entered the front grotto, which had been hollowed out in the dark volcanic rock. The first chamber was just large enough to accommodate the processing equipment and piled storage containers ready for shipment. The two of them took shelter beside a stack of crate modules, waited, listened, and saw brighter lights ahead.

Paul moved out first this time. "Straight down the corridor," he said. He held the bolo in one hand and his knife in the other. Sinsei did the same.

They passed through the front grotto, down a passage, then into a brightly lit side room—a laboratory facility. At the threshold, Paul came to a halt when he saw a Tleilaxu man standing at a table covered with samples. The laboratory complex looked jarringly sophisticated in the primitive rock-walled cave. Racks of fern samples stood adjacent to a bank of chemical-analysis equipment, while dried ferns were displayed next to documentation for the various samples. The Tleilaxu man was preoccupied, performing the work alone as if he trusted no one else.

Sinsei caught her breath, poised next to Paul. The man—Chaen Marek himself, no doubt—heard the rustle, turned.

Like a spring-loaded projectile, Sinsei threw herself forward, already spinning the bolo in the air. She hurled it at Marek, aiming low, and the flexible weapon struck the Tleilaxu's lower legs. The cord wrapped around him, and the spines dug in.

Two seconds behind her, Paul also threw his bolo, and his weapon struck higher and looped around Marek's chest, catching his arms. Together, Paul and Sinsei tackled the drug lord to the stone floor of the laboratory chamber.

Marek's mouth opened, and he sucked in a breath of pain preparatory to a shout, but Paul slapped his own palm over the drug lord's face. He pulled out his knife and held it close to the Tleilaxu's throat. "I have other weapons besides the bolo, and this one will kill," he hissed. "Where is Duncan Idaho?"

The Tleilaxu's eyes flicked in a combination of fear and anger. Sinsei was more aggressive. She placed the point of her dagger directly in front of Marek's left eye. "I can blind you by half, or I can take both eyes—your choice," she said. "Where are the prisoners? Where is my father?"

He grunted and squirmed. Paul said, "He doesn't believe you're serious."

Sinsei's expression darkened, and she moved the dagger closer. Another millimeter, and it would burst his eye. Finally, Marek grunted. "Back chamber. Damn you, powindah woman!"

"I was hoping you'd resist a little more," she said.

As the drug lord squirmed, the spiny bolos dug deeper into his skin, and he winced in pain. Sinsei held him down, while Paul quickly searched the laboratory shelves, finding cloth and tape. They wrapped the drug lord's hands and legs and forced him into a fetal ball with more wrapping, then gagged him and dragged him behind another stack of crates.

"He'll be secure here long enough for us to release Duncan and your father," Paul said. Sinsei was already moving into the next chamber.

Following her ordeal and narrow escape, Jessica arrived at the Mother School again, but she had not expected to return under such terrible circumstances. After serving on Elegy, she had hoped to be restored to her normal life with Leto and Paul, but now Elegy had been attacked by the Emperor's vindictive Sardaukar, and her nobleman was killed. If not for Giandro's gallant sacrifice and a bit of desperate luck, she and the visiting Sisters could have vanished along with him in the pseudo-atomic flash.

The skies of Wallach IX were gray and gloomy, and the perpetual chill gnawed at her bones. Jessica knew tricks to keep herself warm, but at the moment, she didn't have the energy or the will. Feeling dismal, she accompanied Cordana across the plaza, after they stepped off the landed shuttle. The familiar school buildings, the pale walls and red tile roofs, seemed to close in around her. This place had once been her home, but now she felt trapped. She was sheltered among the Bene Gesserit again, but not safe.

She wondered if she would ever be allowed to leave.

In the late evening, only a few lights were on in the dormitories and instructional buildings. The central fountain in the plaza, rimed with frost, was illuminated by a soft glow, and the cascade filled the air with cold mist. The droplets were like ice on Jessica's face, but she did not find it refreshing.

She wondered what would change now that she was back. Reverend Mother Cordana had promised to be her advocate, to explain that Jessica had done all that was asked of her.

Cordana turned to gesture upward to the fourth floor of the administration building. "The lights are on in the Mother Superior's office. Harishka needs to hear our news immediately—from both of us."

Still shaken and exhausted from the frantic evacuation, Jessica would have preferred to withdraw to her quarters for much-needed sleep. Using her Bene Gesserit credentials on the Elegy transfer platform, Cordana had booked direct passage to Wallach IX, but during the uncomfortable flight, Jessica had remained in shock. Privately, she had allowed herself to cry for Giandro Tull. The Bene Gesserit entourage had been in transit for three days, but she was still processing her emotions, not just her fear, but also her deep sense of personal loss.

As soon as their Heighliner reached Wallach IX orbit, Cordana had already dispatched a detailed summary of all the events on Elegy. The Mother Superior had time to consider the grave turn of events.

Jessica had played her role with House Tull. Though she had never loved Giandro as she did Leto, she had respected him as a friend. The Viscount had cared for her, bent rules for her. He had been a true nobleman up to the last moments of his life, but Imperial history would remember him only as a rebel and a traitor. At least in his final flash of glory he had made the Sardaukar invaders pay a heavy price.

She would not underestimate how strongly a person might defend against a stain on his honor. And that made her think of Leto again. . . .

Jessica set her jaw and followed Cordana into the main building. The Bene Gesserit would no doubt sanitize her involvement on Elegy, erase her presence from the records, perhaps keep her hidden here at the Mother School for the rest of her life, as they had done with Xora. . . .

Walling off her emotions as the Bene Gesserit expected, Jessica entered the Mother Superior's office, where she had been previously dressed down. The ancient woman sat behind her large desk, as if it were a bulwark against a military assault. Harishka did not look pleased, and her voice held clear accusation. "Jessica, did you know that Viscount Tull had thrown in with the violent rebel movement? Is this the reason he withdrew funding from the Mother School, so he could divert money to the Noble Commonwealth?"

"Yes, it was the reason, Mother Superior, but I convinced him to restore his regular stipend to us. As I was ordered to do."

Harishka's face darkened. "But now that he has been branded one of the terrorists, we've lost that source of funding. Reverend Mother Cordana was nearly killed herself, along with her entourage. You are all lucky to be alive. What if the Emperor decides you yourself were guilty of collusion? Then the shadow will fall across the entire Sisterhood! What if the Sardaukar attack our Mother School because of you?"

Jessica remained firm. "I was a mere concubine in the manor house, Mother Superior. Any Imperial spies would have paid me no heed." She hardened her voice, took a half step closer. "I was the Viscount's concubine, *as you ordered*. I was accepted into the Tull household. I convinced the Viscount to restore the funds you so desperately wanted. I proved myself. *As you ordered!*" She crossed her arms over her chest. "And I obeyed."

The bold words stunned Harishka, and Cordana looked unsettled. "Jessica speaks the truth," the Reverend Mother said. "She did exactly as we asked. That would have been my report to you, Mother Superior, if the circumstances had not changed so dramatically."

The room fell silent for what seemed like a very long time. Harishka's face remained a blank mask, but it could not completely hide her inner turmoil. Finally, she said, "You performed . . . acceptably, Jessica, even if the outcome is not what we would have wished." The admission seemed to come with great effort. "House Tull is gone."

Realizing she had nothing to lose, after having lost so much already, Jessica dared to suggest, "Mother Superior, please send me back to my old life and duties, to . . . my son. I did my duty on Elegy, and I do not deserve reassignment to any place except Caladan. I proved myself."

Cordana intervened, as her promised advocate, "Jessica is bound to her Duke Leto, and we know that her son has tremendous potential." Her dark eyes seemed to hold many layers of meaning. "Perhaps she can serve us best on Caladan?"

Harishka glared directly at Jessica. "It seems we live in the midst of chaos. You have not heard about Duke Leto Atreides?"

Jessica's heart sank. "What is it, Mother Superior?"

Harishka drew the silence to agonizing lengths. "We received detailed information from the Emperor's Truthsayer. We know what Shaddam knows . . . about Leto."

"Mohiam . . ." Jessica felt cold.

"Leto Atreides has apparently joined the rebel movement himself, just like Viscount Tull. He has been seen in the company of Jaxson Aru himself, participating in rebel activities." Harishka sniffed. "It is likely that House Atreides will face the same Imperial punishment, and Caladan may suffer the fate of Elegy." She spread her hands. "Therefore, we cannot let you go there under any circumstances. You must stay here with the Bene Gesserit."

She was shocked to the core. "No, that can't be!"

Cordana tried to comfort her, and Mother Superior Harishka began to explain the logical repercussions, but Jessica broke away and left the office, plunging outside into the night.

A mother's love is the most misunderstood obligation, as well as a trap, that is wired into our genetic programming.

—Bene Gesserit manual

The duty of CHOAM's Ur-Director was to manage crises and solve problems in such a way that each party emerged equally dissatisfied. Profits were to be distributed fairly among the worthy, while CHOAM continued to gain power and wealth.

For the time being, though, Malina Aru set everything else aside, even the security breach investigation with Holton Tassé and his team of CHOAM Mentat accountants. Jaxson was the most vital problem, a rampaging bull among the fragile alliances and history of the Imperium. With their gradual undermining of Corrino political power, the broader Noble Commonwealth movement had worked to guide human civilization. Victory under Malina's terms would let CHOAM achieve a vaster potential than the straitjacket of Imperial autocracy.

But Jaxson's approach would simply cause pain and suffering, not to mention excruciating financial loss. Malina hadn't really needed her Mentat accountants to tell her that. If Jaxson's wrecking ball succeeded, the time required for CHOAM to rebuild a stable commercial system was inestimably long. But her radical son would not see reason. He was caught up with shining eyes and erratic thoughts, refusing to consider alternatives and unwilling to surrender. And if he really did have a copy of some of the black archives of destructive data, matters would be far worse.

If she could lure him here to Tanegaard, then she could resolve the situation in the only possible way.

Now she waited for word in the enormous administrative stronghold. As Imperial pursuit closed in, would Jaxson rush here and throw himself under his mother's protection? Malina didn't want to admit to hoping that the Sardaukar would wipe him out on Nossus. That would be a neat solution, but she would not gamble on that outcome. Sardaukar commanders were trained not to underestimate an enemy, but she doubted the Imperial troops or even Shaddam gave Jaxson the credit he deserved.

He was the most dangerous man in the galaxy.

It was Malina's greatest disappointment that he could not be salvaged. She had sent Jaxson off to Otorio in his early years so he could live with his inadequate father, while Malina had groomed Frankos and Jalma for important positions. If only Jaxson could have turned out like his siblings.

If Malina had only expended the effort, taken him under her wing at the right time, maybe she could have forged him into a different sort of person. She had thought his mindset was changed when he came to be trained after the death of his father. She had opened the doors and all the resources of CHOAM to him because he was family. Instead, Jaxson was a feral pet prone to turning on its owner. Malina had tried to rehabilitate him, but now that dangerous pet had to be put down.

The Ur-Director walked along the towering corridors filled with countless offices, gleaming lights of cubicle windows and data-storage closets. As she approached the large fortress vault, both of her spinehounds trotted close. Kar's woundplaz bandages had been absorbed, leaving discolored swaths of fur on his belly, but he kept up with Har. A faint growl came from Kar's throat as he picked up on Malina's unsettled mood. She reached down to soothe him, then did the same for Har. She knew how to handle and control dangerous things.

But not Jaxson.

In these desperate times, she had again summoned her other two children to Tanegaard. Frankos arrived that afternoon on a direct diplomatic craft from the Silver Needle on Kaitain. Jalma came by way of a hederwood delivery from Pliesse. With furrowed brow and hard gaze, Jalma looked much like her mother.

Frankos looked grim beside his sister. He sighed. "What has Jaxson done now?"

"Far too many things. Your brother will be coming here if he can escape the Sardaukar." The two looked suddenly wary, and Malina continued, "That's why I called you—so we can be a united front. Jaxson's secret base is being overrun by Imperial troops."

"Will he be able to escape?" Jalma asked.

"Knowing him, he might just find a way, and I promised him sanctuary if he could get to Tanegaard."

Frankos looked scandalized. "Why would you do that? It exposes CHOAM and puts us in great danger."

"I did it to set a trap," Malina said. "I already gave Shaddam the names of Jaxson's inner circle. We cannot allow such people to represent the Noble Commonwealth and our long-term goals." She pressed her lips together. Har and Kar sat down on their haunches, as if fascinated by the political conversation. "The Emperor was outraged. He has already dispatched his Sardaukar to eradicate those radicals."

"So, you're sacrificing them?" Jalma asked. "Londine, Tull, Ellison, Vok, Myer? I don't know them all, but I thought they were our allies. Even Leto Atreides?"

"They chose the wrong side and are paying the price—and that price will gain us cover so our real work can continue . . . quietly and effectively. It is the only way."

Jalma's expression looked pinched. She nodded. "It is the only way."

"Jaxson is our family." Frankos slowly drew in a deep breath. "But he has always frightened me."

Malina continued, "Since I, the Ur-Director, was the one who provided this vital information to Shaddam about all those nobles, any suspicions against CHOAM have been erased. The Emperor will feel beholden to me and will reward us with lucrative new contracts. We can pick up the pieces after all the damage those terrorists have done. But there is another concern."

For the first time, she told them about the security breach, the possibility that Jaxson had copied part of the black archives, which CHOAM reserved for only the direst circumstances. "Those records contain dangerous information on every powerful family in the Imperium," Malina said, "including House Corrino. And us."

Jalma primly took a seat at the conference room table and reached down to scratch the spinehounds. "I would prefer not to be around when he gets here. *If* he gets here."

"I would prefer none of this myself," said Malina. "But that is the painful responsibility of people at our level of power."

"I want to look him in the eyes," Frankos said, reddening. "Jaxson brought great harm and disappointment down upon our family. If he must be a sacrificial lamb, then we'll just have to put up with our guilt." He glanced at his sister.

Jalma agreed with a slow nod.

Malina sat back and closed her eyes, simply listening to the clamor of her thoughts, then she opened them, drew a calming breath. "Once it is all over with him—one way or another—you two will rebuild with me." She tapped her fingers on the tabletop. "And now we wait for Jaxson."

We are all prisoners to some degree, and we are all free. Our true identity is decided by our hearts.

—DUKE MINOS ATREIDES, epitaph

Paul and Sinsei did indeed find Duncan Idaho in the next chamber, a squalid, austere cave that didn't even have bars or a secure door. The big Swordmaster sat slumped against the wall next to a gaunt man whose large eyes were hollowed with shadows. Sinsei's father! Stubble covered Dr. Vim's chin, and his brown hair was clumpy and ragged, as if it had not been washed in weeks.

"Duncan, we're here to free you," Paul said. The Swordmaster's bindings were minimal, his wrists lashed together with only a single cord. The muscular man looked as if he could have snapped the ropes if he'd tried, if he were not so sick and groggy.

Duncan lifted his shaggy head. "Paul . . . young pup, young . . . Master Pup." He tried to smile, but in his pain and discomfort, it did not come easily.

Sinsei dropped to her knees in front of her father and shook his bony shoulders. His glazed eyes finally managed to focus on her. "Daughter . . ." Then Dr. Vim winced and shook his head. "No! Another hallucination. Not real!"

She wrapped her arms around him. "I'm real, Father, and we're here to get you out."

Paul saw the dull reflection in Duncan's eyes. "Both of them are drugged."

"Ailar . . . ," Duncan said. "Marek kept feeding us those damned ferns."

Paul cut his bindings, and the big man flexed his arms, stretched and swayed, then tried to struggle to his feet. Paul had hoped he would be a juggernaut against Marek's mercenaries if they needed to fight their way out of here. But judging by the Swordmaster's condition, they would have to find another way.

Sinsei had also gotten her father to stand, and he opened his eyes, trying to focus on her. He stretched out his arms like a scarecrow and wrapped them around her. "Sinsei!"

Paul raced through alternatives as if it were one of Thufir Hawat's mind exercises. Since they couldn't fight outright against the mercenary force, they would have to slip out with their weak companions. But they had a hostage, Chaen Marek. "The guards are ruthless and loyal, but we have their leader. We can get out of here."

"A hostage," Sinsei said, then she looked at her father. "Maybe it will work."

Duncan lumbered after them, regaining some of his balance as they made their way into the laboratory chamber. The drug lord was where they had left him, bound with tape and gagged, though he had struggled so much against the spiny bolos that he bled profusely from numerous wounds.

"We need him to walk—we can't carry him," Paul said, glancing at Duncan and Dr. Vim. "And we also have to help these two."

The young woman removed most of the tape binding, leaving his hands secured behind his back, and disentangled her bolo from Marek's legs. The man's grayish face grimaced, but the tape and cloth covering his mouth prevented him from making a sound. Paul dragged the Tleilaxu to his feet. "Your comfort is not my concern. We're getting out of here." He looked up at Duncan. "We *are* getting out of here."

The Swordmaster ground his teeth and nodded.

Sinsei darted ahead to scout the open receiving area, verifying that it was still empty. They hurried forward, taking advantage of any cover they could find.

When at last the group emerged into the jungled mountainside, the dusk was no more than a burning glow on the western horizon. Forest insects set up a louder hum, a prelude to the symphony they would unleash later. The increasing night sounds covered the rustle of their own movement as the group left the path and worked their way around the slope.

Though Chaen Marek resisted and struggled, Paul and Sinsei forced him along while Duncan and Dr. Vim worked their way one step at a time, still recovering. They remained in the trees, holding on to mossy trunks on the steep slope. Some of the loose earth and volcanic pebbles tumbled out from beneath them. It was a painstaking flight, and the jungle was getting darker every moment.

Behind them the bright security lights of the complex flared on, and they all froze in the jungle shadows. Chaen Marek squirmed, made a muffled sound from behind his gag, but there was no response—no shouts, no alarms—from the complex.

Paul ducked. "They haven't discovered that Marek is missing yet. We have to use every minute." He pushed the bound Tleilaxu forward, but the drug lord resisted, tripping himself up against fallen branches and tangled shrubs.

As they went farther from the complex, Sinsei gave up on caution, hurrying her father to the top of the rugged volcanic cliff, where they had left their ropes. Duncan Idaho pushed his way forward, shaking his head and still trying to snap out of the fog of ailar.

Dr. Vim was delirious, jittery, and Duncan managed to explain that the other man had been given a different strain of the drug, test after test. Sinsei's father paused and hunched over to vomit on the ground. The young woman held his shoulders, offering her support and love.

Standing at the top of the outcropping, Paul looked down in discouragement, but he forced himself to focus on the problem at hand. "We have ropes. We'll have to rappel down."

"I can take my father," Sinsei said. It seemed an audacious suggestion, but the man was gaunt and thin, and Paul knew how strong she was.

"We can loop the rope. Make it into a sort of harness," Paul said.

Duncan made a grumble deep in his chest. "I can climb."

"You can fall, too," Paul replied.

The Swordmaster just let out a laugh. "I won't."

"And what about him?" Sinsei looked at Marek.

"Tie him up and lower him with the rope. That's what we have to do."

The young woman's face became a vengeful grimace. "We could attach the rope to his neck." She approached the drug lord.

Though his hands were bound and the spiny bolo wrapped around his upper arms, he squirmed and thrashed. Marek contorted his body like a corkscrew and threw himself into Sinsei.

In the jungle shadows Paul saw a flick of silver, the gleam of a razor-edged blade pop out from the fabric in the Tleilaxu robe—a secret retracted weapon in the fold of the cloth. As he writhed, Marek slashed a shallow cut into Sinsei's arm.

She gasped more in surprise than pain and pulled back. It was a thin line like an incision, but she still looked down at it in horror. Though Marek could not speak through his gag, his eyes looked triumphant.

Dr. Vim yowled, "Tleilaxu poison!" The gaunt scientist threw himself on Marek. "Butcher!"

Before anyone could stop him, he rammed the bound Tleilaxu, and they both plunged over the rock outcropping. Sinsei screamed, but the two men tumbled, crashing through the underbrush and striking the boulders far below.

Sinsei slumped to the ground in grief and sudden dizziness, and Paul rushed to her. She stared at the cut on her arm, which was already red and inflamed. She poked at it. "What's . . . Tleilaxu poison?"

Forcing clear awareness through his ailar fog, Duncan moved quicker, took the rope. "Got to get her out of here, Paul." Then he swayed, shook his head again. "Get all of us out of here."

With a heavy heart, Paul fastened the ropes to the trees, dropped the lines down, and tried to think of how he would best manage this. Sinsei was reacting badly to the poison, in addition to the anguish, and Duncan still did not have his balance or strength.

As he looked over the edge of the steep cliff, he saw figures moving down there, people climbing up out of the jungle shadows. For a moment, he thought the mercenary guards had mounted an attack.

But they were the Muadh—Yar Zell climbing first. Pulling on the ropes, they scrambled up.

"We need your help," Paul said when they were near, his voice hoarse. He felt ready to collapse, too.

*People think the home is the place of greatest safety, which is why it can be
such an effective trap.*

—Fremen saying

Three of Jaxson's ten remaining household guards had been trained to
pilot the refitted FTL ship. They had already plotted a course for the
CHOAM stronghold planet. After breaking free of the Sardaukar gauntlet
and leaving Nossus behind them in flames, the ship plunged across open
space. They flew entirely off the grid, following no Spacing Guild route, using
no Navigator. They could not be tracked.

Even so, Leto did not feel any relief, but rather a sense of spiraling further
out of control. He was bottled up on this ship with desperate people—who
believed he was one of them. If the rebels had any inkling otherwise, they
would surely kill him.

During the tense flight, Rajiv Londine repeatedly described how the
Sardaukar had overrun Cuarte, how they had murdered his daughter right
before his eyes, and how only Chief Administrator Rodundi had saved him.

Leto was sickened by the thought that the same thing might happen to
Caladan, to Paul. Jessica might already be dead on Elegy, another target of
Shaddam's wrath.

Though he listened with a heavy heart as Londine recounted the terrible
day in grim detail, Leto felt that the man's emotions were off-kilter. His misery about certain aspects of the debacle seemed unbalanced. The nobleman
had always been angry and indignant, but on a theoretical basis, like a parlor
game. Perhaps he simply didn't know how to handle a real tragedy, or how to
face the consequences of advocating a bloody revolution.

Though the escape ship was small and crowded, Leto avoided Londine as
much as possible. He stifled the angry words he wanted to say, blaming the
man—among other things—for the pain and suffering caused by distributing
the "Caladan drug." Jaxson Aru had benefited from those profits, too, using
them to fund the work of his rebellion. Did Jaxson even know what a painful

twist of the knife that was—to prey upon the people of Caladan to promote his own aims?

The voyage to Tanegaard lasted more than a week, during which time Leto sought every opportunity to seize the memory stone so he could destroy its volatile contents. But the rebel leader never allowed the object away from his person. This crew was ruthlessly loyal to the man, and Leto would never get away if he directly tried to harm him. Even if he somehow managed to steal the stone, taking it more than a few meters from Jaxson's body field—he claimed—would trigger the dead-man switch and transmit the entire data dump into deep space, where some relay station would eventually pick up the signal, and then the information would proliferate . . . just as Jaxson wanted.

Leto didn't expect his chances would get better after they reached Tanegaard, but still he had to keep his eyes open. He himself remained the only chance for a proper resolution.

When the FTL ship reached the stronghold planet without forewarning, CHOAM security forces immediately went on high alert: orbital blockades rushed into position, and pentashields shimmered above the administrative fortress buildings. High-priority messages, then demands, were transmitted from the administrative citadel, but Jaxson ignored all of them.

He took the time to change his clothes, checking his physical appearance and masking the weary shadows under his eyes. When he finally sent a request to speak to the Urdir herself, he looked proud and confident, although Leto knew how desperate he truly was. Tanegaard would be his final sanctuary.

Jaxson flashed an unconvincing smile into the comm screen. "I have not been to Tanegaard for years, Mother. Thank you for welcoming us with open arms." He grinned. "We had a setback on Nossus, an unfortunate invasion by Sardaukar forces, and therefore, we accept your offer of CHOAM protection." He lounged back, aloof again. He touched his exotic new earring, as if to show it off. "You and I have much to catch up on."

On the screen, Malina Aru's face appeared stern and worried. "I am glad you got away alive. Our CHOAM protective measures are superior even to those at the Imperial Palace, as you will remember from your time here. As Urdir, I grant you safe passage. Follow these coordinates to the central administrative fortress and land on the designated platform. I'll meet you personally." She turned away, paused, and added, "Your brother and sister are also here."

"Ah, so we will stand together as a family." Jaxson beamed. "Against the corrupt Corrinos."

Watching the Ur-Director from out of the frame of view, Leto didn't know how to read her expression. The CHOAM leader was a cold and impenetrable woman—intelligent, competent, and always focused on business rather than emotions. Jaxson, though, seemed not to notice her wariness when she faced him. The simple fact that his mother had joined his cause—had she really done so?—gave Jaxson the affirmation he needed.

Londine fidgeted constantly, but kept his words to himself, as did Leto. They didn't have alternatives other than surrendering to Imperial forces or going completely renegade. Leto would never leave Caladan and Paul behind, even if he had been painted into a corner. He had to find out if they were all right. And the Tull holdings. . . .

Jessica.

Tanegaard's orbital defenses parted, and the city shields dropped to let the vessel fly in to the designated landing area. Jaxson's ten remaining guards and crew were silent, professionally guiding the ship to the main data fortress. Looking out the side windowport, Leto observed the stacked buildings and towering office complexes that filled the landscape to the horizon. The yellow flags of CHOAM flew from the tallest structures.

Tanegaard City was clean and efficient, on a world of high-level finance, administration, and transactional records. Even so, the CHOAM planet looked cold and unwelcoming to Leto, like a continent-size version of the Guild Bank he had once visited on Kaitain.

As they landed on a huge rooftop where CHOAM security personnel had lined up to receive them, Lord Londine marveled, "I have never been to such a place."

"Few have," Jaxson said. "I spent more than a year here being trained and indoctrinated. My mother led me through the intricacies of business operations, and granted me access to learn whatever I wanted to learn. I know this secure place very, very well, its records, its byways, its impregnable fortress vault. My mother hoped that working here would convince me to become a CHOAM acolyte, but through my father, I developed a more important political awareness."

When the suspensor engines brought the ship to rest on the pad, Jaxson's pilot and crew emerged first, fanning out on the rooftop. They acknowledged the CHOAM security but formed their own protective cordon around the rebel leader and his two guests.

The CHOAM guards parted, and Malina Aru stepped forward in her trim business suit, flanked by her spinehounds. The beasts trembled with excitement, and when she released them, they bounded forward. Their fangs were long and sharp, but their tails were wagging.

Jaxson bent down to pet them, smiling with joy. "Kar, you're all better now!" He inspected scars on the spinehound's stomach, the shaved patches of fur.

The rebel leader rose to his feet and greeted his mother with a broad smile. Malina's expression showed little warmth, but Leto doubted she had ever demonstrated much maternal love. "I am sorry it has come to this, my son," she said. "It is best that you stay inside our main citadel under CHOAM protection. Everything will turn out for the best."

She gave an offhanded nod of acknowledgment to Leto and Londine. The spinehounds regarded the other two men, feral eyes burning. Malina turned briskly about. "Come into a controlled environment and settle down in your sanctuary. We will have time to talk."

She vanished into the shadows of the rooftop opening where the air was cool, dry, and smelled of metal and polymers.

Jaxson's security detail followed, keeping the rebel leader in sight. Leto glanced from side to side, gathering information in the hope that he could use it. He was still trying to understand Malina Aru's priorities and motivations.

Inside the enormous citadel, the other two Aru children were waiting, though they did not appear happy to be there. Crowding into a large cargo lift, they all descended countless floors to the main level of the administrative building. The spinehounds sat beside Malina Aru and kept watching Jaxson.

The rebel leader mused as he watched the lights of the floors flash by. "I remember this building, and its great fortress vault . . . where I spent a lot of time at work." His eyes had an unreadable glint, and Malina's brow furrowed with concern.

He was the first to emerge from the lift, walking with a light step as he looked up at the high, open spaces of the giant structure. Clerks and administrators in CHOAM uniforms moved about like ants intent on their business, not bothering to acknowledge the important visitors.

Jaxson nodded toward the immense, thick-walled fortress vault ahead of them. It was larger than the hangar building on Nossus, but here it was dwarfed by the sheer size of the surrounding citadel. "When you showed me the ultra-secure core chambers, Mother, you promised me that even atomics couldn't blast down the walls." He chuckled. "Hyperbole, I think."

"Per design, though it has never been tested," Malina responded. Her expression was sour. "Let us hope we won't need to defend against that."

Jaxson's ten private guards followed, not speaking a word. Each man carried a defensive blade at his side as well as a flechette pistol that could fire a deadly rain of silver needles against an unshielded target. They kept the projectile weapons from Nossus, assuming that very few people in the CHOAM citadel would wear personal shields during their daily business.

Frankos stalked along, disturbed and preoccupied. The CHOAM President was taller than his brother, and quieter. "We need to resolve this unpleasant matter soon, so we can get back to Company business."

"Conduct all the business you want, brother, but remember where you are," Jaxson quipped, and then added a sigh. "Frankos, you always placed unnecessary import on meetings and documents. Our concern now is the overthrow of the entire Imperium."

"Leaving it in chaos," his sister countered. "I don't think you understand what you're doing."

Jaxson frowned. "Jalma, I thought you were on my side!"

"I may agree with your conceptual endgame, but I am not convinced about your tactics. Even in the long run, you may cause more harm than good."

Quickening her pace, Malina ushered them down the long, high corridor. "Your actions cut off our options, and we are being placed in an untenable position by the Emperor's need for revenge."

"Then we will do what we have to do." Jaxson sounded confident, glancing at Leto and Londine.

"We have holding rooms for you all, secure facilities with reasonable comforts," Malina said, seemingly aloof as she led them down a long corridor adjacent to the central fortress vault. "Stay here until we resolve the situation."

Jaxson gave a sly grin. "Even when placed in an untenable position, I still have a weapon of last resort. I doubt you will approve, Mother, but it is what it is. I may hold our only leverage if the situation goes terribly wrong."

Malina paused in her tracks, narrowed her eyes. "What exactly do you mean?"

Jaxson withdrew the memory stone, his insurance policy, and she looked at him with fatalistic resolve rather than the shock he seemed to expect. "You left traces of your intrusion behind, Jaxson. My aide-de-camp detected it. I suspected it was you—after I had granted you unwise access." She extended her hand, palm up. "Give it to me."

The rebel leader curled his fingers around it. Leto tensed, ready to rip it out of his hand and trust the CHOAM security to protect him . . . but Jaxson's guards also twitched, subtly turning their flechette pistols to point toward the Ur-Director.

Jaxson said, "Once released, the destructive information can never be stopped. I'll just keep it for now. Let's not allow this to get out. Just imagine the embarrassment it would cause the poor Empress. . . ." He gave her a hard, meaningful look.

Turning pale, the Ur-Director imperiously extended her hand again, and with parental firmness, she said, "Give me the memory stone now. The black archives must never be used."

He chuckled nervously and slipped it back into his pocket. "You did offer me sanctuary here, Mother, but I don't think I want to surrender my most valuable card."

Frankos's jaw dropped open, but he struggled to force his words out. "The heart of CHOAM business is predicated on complete confidentiality. Even after all you've done, you are still a member of the Aru family. Exposing those transactions would be worse than detonating a stockpile of atomics on a populated world."

"Then let us make sure that's unnecessary." Jaxson's face hardened, as if he had lost all respect for his brother. "By design, any ultimatum must be a doomsday threat, or Shaddam Corrino will not fear us enough." He looked at the fortress vault rising in the middle of the citadel's interior.

One of his guards abruptly touched a comm in his ear. His eyes flicked back and forth as he listened to a data stream, then he spun to Jaxson. "Sir, our ship's sensors just detected the arrival of a powerful military force— hundreds of attack ships entering orbit over Tanegaard. Configuration and transmission frequency suggests they are Sardaukar."

Jaxson coiled like a snake ready to strike as he looked around for a target. "The Sardaukar followed us here! Mother, we must mount all CHOAM defenses."

Malina and her daughter both bristled.

Frankos glared balefully at his younger brother. "It's what you deserve, Jaxson. It is what needs to happen."

The rebel leader's expression fell into disbelief as his mother said, "The Imperial forces are here at my invitation. A Heighliner delivered them several days ago, and they were waiting in system, running dark. I knew you would come here." Her mouth was a grim line, all business. "Now we are allowing them through our planetary shields, and they will take you into custody, Jaxson." She glanced at Leto and Londine. "As well as your fellow conspirators. We will tie up the details and be done with the entire terrorist movement here and now."

Jaxson swayed. "But you promised sanctuary! You're my mother."

"Yes, I am your mother, but I'm also the CHOAM Ur-Director, and that takes priority."

Frankos and Jalma tensed, but did not contradict her.

Malina's words were damning. "In the event that the raid I arranged on Nossus was not successful, I lured you to Tanegaard, where I could put a neat and peaceful end to the conflict. It's over, Jaxson. Now it is time for me to salvage as much as I can."

"The raid . . . *you* arranged?" Jaxson could barely speak.

Even Leto was astonished. He had wondered about the Urdir's loyalties, and now he knew.

Rajiv Londine wailed, "The Sardaukar knew to come to Cuarte! Were *you* the one who called them?"

"I provided Emperor Shaddam with a list of the terrorists I saw on Nossus." She crossed her arms over her chest. "I am not proud of what I did, but the Imperial throne now owes CHOAM an enormous debt of gratitude. The future of the Company depends on you being taken out of the picture, Jaxson. Tanegaard may be impregnable, but our defenses will not be used to save you."

In a flash, Jaxson pulled out his own flechette pistol and sprang to Frankos, who stood closest to him. He nudged the pistol against his brother's ribs while pressing the sharp point of his dagger under his chin. A storm of anger filled his face. "Then I will use the Tanegaard defenses for myself."

His ten guards responded in a swift, simultaneous motion as they aimed their flechette pistols at the unshielded members of the party. Leto and Londine were caught up in a whirlwind, and Jaxson pushed his brother toward the monumental vault behind them. "To me!" he called to his guards. "Leto, Rajiv, stand together. We will take dear Frankos hostage."

"You have nowhere to go," Malina said, not impressed with his threat. "Surrender now. It is your only choice."

"Do not underestimate a desperate man, Mother." Jaxson jammed the sharp knife harder against his brother's jaw. Frankos twitched, and his eyes were fiery with indignation, but he didn't move. Jaxson looked down the long, cyclopean corridor to the towering meters-thick doors. "We'll make our last stand in the fortress vault."

Leto tried to stop him. "Jaxson! Work with your family, not against them!"

Ignoring Leto's entreaty, Jaxson nudged his uncooperative brother forward. "Instead, I'll do something audacious." His guards brandished their weapons, pushed back the Ur-Director and Jalma, who glared at him. As the group hurried toward the enormous vault, Leto wanted to break away, but he didn't dare leave Jaxson now. He still had to get the memory stone, and this would be the most dangerous time to attempt it.

A guard touched the comm in his ear again. "The Sardaukar are coming."

"Into the vault!" Jaxson barked.

As they rushed ahead, Leto thought the imposing chamber looked like a tomb.

Public opinion can shift like a slender willow in an erratic breeze. That is why I prefer to be made of iron.

—CROWN PRINCE RAPHAEL CORRINO, historical archives

After the abortive attempt to ensnare Jaxson Aru during the spice exchange, Baron Harkonnen retreated to Arrakis. He had done what the Emperor required of him; he had dangled himself as bait. Several Sardaukar and numerous rebel henchmen had been killed in the operation, but Jaxson had managed to escape, slippery as an eel.

Almost a third of the contraband spice load had also been destroyed in the battle, strewn into the Heighliner's cavernous hold, packages burst.

The Baron had been debriefed—sternly and disrespectfully, he thought—by the ranking Sardaukar officer, but the bungled operation was entirely due to Sardaukar ineptitude. None of the blame should fall on the Baron's shoulders, and he would make certain that Emperor Shaddam understood that.

For that, Count Fenring might be able to help.

Rather than heading to the comfort and security of his Carthag headquarters, he went under diplomatic escort directly to the older city of Arrakeen, where Fenring awaited him at the Residency.

He met the Count and Lady Fenring on an enclosed balcony, where they sat together overlooking the line of palm trees—a monument to human hubris in the desert environment. Not long ago, Count Fenring had invited him here to watch as those palm trees were watered with the blood of smugglers, scapegoats who had borne the blame for illicit spice shipments.

Fenring lounged in his seat, glancing behind him as if he still expected his strange Mentat to be there. "Hmm, Baron, I understand your little trap did not go as, ahhh, planned."

Servants brought a tray of iced pomegranate juice, which was either imported to Arrakis at extraordinary expense or produced from fruit grown in Lady Fenring's private greenhouse. The Baron sipped the sweet beverage, with its subtle layers of flavor. The deep red color reminded him of the sapho juice Piter de Vries drank to enhance his Mentat abilities. Self-consciously, he wiped his lips, not wanting his mouth to be stained.

"Jaxson Aru proved to be exceptionally resourceful. Even the Sardaukar were unable to capture him. I barely got out with my own life."

Lady Fenring feigned dismay, but her eyes remained as hard as aquamarines, showing none of the sympathy or concern that her voice expressed.

Fenring shook his head. "The Emperor will not be pleased that Jaxson got away, but I expect his Sardaukar will score enough victories in the end. They are, ahhh, presently engaged in a punitive eradication of other rebel sympathizers. There have already been great battles on the main worlds of House Londine, House Tull, and House Ellison, with more to come."

The Baron found the information fascinating. "The Sardaukar claimed they have another plan to track the rebel leader down to his base of operations. Maybe they will find other traitors there, as well."

The ferret-like man narrowed his dark eyes. "When the Sardaukar overran Cuarte and ransacked Lord Londine's records, we learned that Duke Leto Atreides did recently visit there. It seems he is one of the rebels—exactly as you suspected, my dear Baron."

Delighted to hear this, the Baron sat up straighter. "No doubt he is part of their bloody plans, and means to overthrow House Corrino. You cannot trust his honorable façade." He took a deep drink of the juice, imagining that it contained Atreides blood.

"From the Issimo III recordings, we already saw evidence that he was working alongside Jaxson Aru." Fenring stroked his chin. "I admit, it is not what I expected from the Duke of Caladan." He reached over to touch the back of his wife's hand, and she gave him a loving smile in response. "My dear Margot thought highly of the Duke's concubine."

The Baron frowned. "Not all is as it seems."

"Ahhh, indeed," Fenring agreed.

"Now House Atreides will fall along with the rest of the rebellion," the Baron insisted. "Duke Leto has only one bastard son as an heir, and there will be nothing left after we grind the Noble Commonwealth out of existence. Once the hated Atreides are exterminated . . ." He drew a deep breath to calm the anger in his voice.

Fenring's gaze was intent enough to dissect him. "Do go on, Baron. What are you scheming now?"

The fat man's plump lips formed a cruel smile. "Just imagining that if Duke Leto is disgraced, perhaps even executed for his crimes . . . if House Atreides were to collapse, then the fief of Caladan would be open. What a delicious irony if Emperor Shaddam saw fit to transfer its administration to House Harkonnen."

"A reward is not deserved until Jaxson Aru is brought to justice, hmm?" Fenring said. "Nevertheless, remind me at an appropriate time, and I'd be willing to suggest it to my friend Shaddam."

❧

MOLLIFIED, EVEN THOUGH his plans were more tangled than he would have liked, the Baron took a swift transport back to Carthag. The military and industrial stronghold made him feel more content, more in control.

Rabban had prepared for his return by laying out a banquet of his uncle's favorite food and drink, sparing no expense. Household servants skittered along the table, making preparations.

As soon as he saw the shadow of anxiety and the sweat on his nephew's brow, though, the Baron knew something was wrong. As he loomed at the head of the banquet table, staring across the extravagant spread, the delicious aromas turned sour in his nostrils. "Tell me what happened, Rabban."

"Enjoy your meal, Uncle. Rest and relax. You've been through a harrowing experience."

"I might relax more if I can inflict a 'harrowing experience' on someone else." He pressed himself closer to his muscular nephew. With his suspensors, he raised himself a few inches higher so that he towered above Rabban. "What have you done? How have you failed me?"

"Not I, Uncle. I made no mistakes at all!"

"I'll be the judge of that. Now, tell me what it is you are concealing!" He recalled the fiery wreckage of Orgiz. So much melange lost. . . . "Has there been more spice piracy? How did you let them slip through your fingers?"

"Not here—the problem occurred on Lankiveil. The Atreides launched a rescue operation and got their man Halleck back."

"Atreides? On *Lankiveil?*" The Baron's eyebrows shot up. "They took our captive! How did they even know he was there?"

Rabban shook his head. "I don't know. It was a commando operation led by their warrior Mentat."

The Baron grimaced. "Old Thufir Hawat—I've heard stories of his abilities. Too bad he works for the Atreides. But he is beyond his prime and doddering. How could he be a threat?"

"He was enough of a threat to single-handedly kill several of our guards and take away the prisoner, destroying my entire interrogation facility in the process." Rabban darted to the banquet table, grabbed a goblet, and gulped down cool water. He wiped perspiration from his brow and turned back to face his uncle. "We tried to slay them both, rather than let them get away, but . . ."

"But they still escaped." The Baron's mind raced as consequence after consequence fell like dominos. "And if Halleck gets back to Caladan—or worse, Kaitain!—he will explain how we prevented him from delivering Leto's message to Emperor Shaddam! He would reveal everything that Duke Atreides meant to do, and I—I will be the one blamed! They will think I am guilty!"

"We could deny finding any message," Rabban muttered. "It will simply be Halleck's word against ours."

"Don't be a fool. We have motives, man! We are known to loathe the Atreides, so even the suggestion that we blocked such crucial information will tarnish my reputation. Shaddam will believe that the Duke is not the twisted traitor we have made him out to be, rather that he was actively working to bring down Jaxson Aru from inside the movement—and we Harkonnens tried to stop him!"

Raging, the Baron flung the platters of food up in the air and smashed dishes against the wall. He whirled to punish his nephew, only to find that Rabban was already retreating out the door—falling back, no doubt, to one of the distant spice-harvesting operations until his uncle's murderous temper cooled down.

The Baron stood amid the culinary devastation in the hall and searched for a way to salvage this disaster.

A noble leader always faces difficulties in choosing a marital partner—not only during the selection process due to political and economic ramifications, but afterward, when the realities of a personal relationship come to light.

—Landsraad marriage annals, commentary

During the rough flight back over the open sea, Paul monitored the speed, air currents, and fuel-charge consumption. The partially repaired aircraft thrummed, coughed, and rattled through the air, but he concentrated on the controls, *willing* the flyer to hold together until they reached Castle Caladan.

After the escape, the Muadh had helped Sinsei, even as her symptoms grew worse. Duncan struggled along beside Paul, still fighting off the ailar, and they had rushed to the site of the flyer. The villagers possessed no cure or treatment for the unfamiliar Tleilaxu poison, and Paul knew the young woman's only chance would be with Dr. Yueh. He had to get her back there.

Yar Zell and his companions eased Sinsei on board. Thankfully, the repairs had been complete enough, and Paul had faith in his own piloting abilities.

Now, as he flew at the maximum speed the craft could manage, he monitored every warning light, every mechanical wobble and hesitation.

Duncan was still groggy, but even so, he managed to say in a rough voice, "Keep us stable, Master Paul, all the way across the sea. Stay steady . . . good job."

Paul accepted the rare compliment. "Thank you, but I'm only doing what you taught me."

"Don't rely solely on your instruments. Use your eyes, ears, sense of balance and direction. Human elements are primary, and instruments are secondary, but they should work in tandem."

No land was in sight on the blue horizon, and Cala City was still hours away. The comms were down. He glanced to the rear compartment, where Sinsei lay shivering and groaning as if trapped in nightmares.

Duncan groaned in sympathy. "She looks as bad as I feel." He reached back to touch her wrist, checking her pulse. "The ailar will work its way out of my system, but she needs a Suk doctor. Now."

⫘

AFTER THEY LANDED safely and rushed to the castle infirmary, Paul learned about events that had occurred during his brief time away, but at the moment, his main concern was Sinsei.

In the medical office, Dr. Yueh tended the new patient, asking quick, clipped questions about who she was and what had happened to her. Duncan slumped into a seat, struggling to regain his strength, while Paul gave agitated answers. He calmed himself, using Bene Gesserit techniques that his mother had taught him.

The Suk doctor looked at Sinsei's pale face, touched her skin. "Her body temperature is lower than normal, but her other vital signs are stable." He inspected the inflamed wound on her arm. "Only a shallow cut, but sufficient. I have seen Tleilaxu poisons before."

Paul felt clear worry for her. "Will she be all right?" He forced himself to give the doctor room to work.

Yueh pulled out an analytical poison snooper and placed it close to the young woman's head. Frowning, he went to a cabinet that contained more vials. "Fortunately for her, the concentration was very low. The poisoned edge just nicked her." He produced the appropriate powder and returned to administer the drug. "This should be an acceptable counter-toxin, and will stimulate her metabolism." He stepped back, watching the patient, and nodded slowly. "Over a period of days, she should come out of this. The Tleilaxu poison is designed to make its victim suffer a long and excruciating death while they gloat. Her body went into a deep coma in reaction. Think of a sea diver who goes to great depths, but must return slowly to the surface, a little at a time."

Paul took her cool, limp hand, looking into her slack face. Even like this, dirty and battered, she still looked beautiful to him.

Swaying on his seat, Duncan groaned. "I require your services, too, Yueh."

"Come with me." The doctor led the limping Swordmaster to another room, where the infirmary held a filtration and dialysis machine to scrub the drugs from his system.

Paul remained with the unconscious Sinsei, talking to her in a soft voice, even though he doubted she could hear him. Her hand was warm now, and dry.

Realizing how hungry he was, he called for dinner to be brought into the infirmary, and ate at her bedside. Before long, Yueh joined him, though the doctor seemed to have little appetite. He explained in detail about Duke Leto's brief visit and how he had rushed off to intercept the rebels again, and also about Thufir's urgent mission to rescue Gurney from the Harkonnens.

After more than an hour, Duncan emerged from the side chamber, swaying as if he suffered from a massive hangover, but he was grinning. "Filtration is finished. Never felt better."

Paul leaned closer to Sinsei's bedside. "I wish she would come out of this."

"Give it time, young Master," Yueh said. "The treatment is already working."

Picking at the food on his dinner tray, Paul finally set the meal aside and said he intended to sleep here as well. He longed for his own soft bed, but he didn't want to leave her alone in a strange place. Sinsei was so different from the other girl who kept haunting his dreams.

He and this young woman had been thrown together under strange circumstances. Even if she came from Kaitain, and her father had worked as a scientific researcher, Paul knew the two of them could never be together. Duncan would chuckle at his youthful infatuation and remind him that he was the Duke's son, the heir of Caladan. He had obligations to House Atreides and the Landsraad, and personal entanglements like this would have to go by the wayside as dead ends from a political standpoint.

Paul remembered the tangled considerations when his parents and Thufir Hawat had attempted to find worthy matches for him. His mother's actions during that discussion had led to the terrible rift between her and Leto. Paul's heart felt heavy with the thought, and he wondered where his mother was now.

But he could still care about Sinsei, after what they had been through together.

He slept on a cot that Yueh had arranged. He fell asleep and did not dream of the mysterious young woman in the desert, but rather of Sinsei in the jungle, smiling sweetly before she turned and walked away from him.

❧

ONCE PAUL KNEW that Sinsei would recover, though slowly, he spent the next several days focused on his responsibilities as the Duke's heir and the steward of Caladan. He worked on ducal business in his father's office even without the detailed briefings from Thufir Hawat. It took him quite some time just to absorb all the changes that had occurred.

But when he received a notice from Dr. Yueh to come to the infirmary, he ran down the corridors, holding high hopes. He let out a happy sigh as he saw the young woman sitting up, still wan and groggy. The antitoxins against the Tleilaxu poison had done their work. "You're awake!"

She looked at him with a quirk of a smile. "Always observant."

He didn't mind her teasing as he took a seat beside her. Her shoulders slumped, and he thought of the tragic, but heroic loss of her father. "I'm so very sorry we weren't able to save him. We did the best we could."

"He saved me," she said. "It was the last thing he did."

Paul said, "I will offer whatever help you need, but I'm not sure—" He paused, unable to find the right words.

"I've had nothing to do but rest and think and come to some important decisions. Though I was in a fog, I knew you were there at my side. I could hear your voice in the background. It was comforting."

Paul flushed, recalling many of the things he had whispered to her. "I wanted to keep you company, just in case."

"I am grateful for your attentions, Paul Atreides. Dr. Yueh says that I will recover my full strength very soon."

"We'll find a place for you to stay in Castle Caladan. I don't know when my father will return, but for the time being, I'm acting as Duke. I can—"

She touched his hand. "But we both know this isn't where I belong. Even before my father was taken captive, my place was with the Muadh people. There's still so much research my father left for me to do, and I can't just abandon it." She smiled. "In fact, it's even more important now. There is so much I want to do to help them recover from what Marek did."

Paul straightened, determined. "And I'll send an Atreides force down to the jungles to wipe out all the fields of barra ferns. We'll purge the land so the Muadh can use it again the way they want."

Now Sinsei genuinely brightened. "That would be a good thing. Thank you. We can all work together to restore the sacred Muadh mountain."

Paul felt happy, and a sense of relief. "I like the sound of that."

❧

THAT NIGHT, IN his private quarters, Paul dreamed, and for the first time in more than a week, he saw the desert girl again. Now there were two moons shining behind her, casting light across the sands.

The greatest trainers can teach important skills, but the best instructor of all may be pain.

—Swordmaster Teachings of Ginaz, banned curriculum

Time changed all definitions. The twisted Swordmaster Egan Saar had his mission from Feyd-Rautha Harkonnen, and if he simply waited and watched long enough, he could redefine his previous failure on Caladan as a mere setback. Saar had made his commitment, sold his services—and killed a hapless, useless victim in a Caladan inn. He did not intend to make such an error again.

He had gone to Elegy, on the trail of the real Jessica, confident he could assassinate her under the eyes of her new nobleman . . . but the Sardaukar had already obliterated that world. She was surely dead, along with the traitorous nobleman. Too late.

But he still intended to inflict a painful, soul-shattering blow against Duke Leto Atreides. At this point, it was a matter of honor for Saar. He no longer had any interest in payment; he would do this for himself . . . no matter how long it took.

Leaving Elegy, he made his way back to Caladan, the homeworld of House Atreides, where he would lie in wait and make plans. The first time, he'd come here disguised as an unobtrusive merchant, a seller of trilium. He had listened to gossip about House Atreides, and when he found the "Duke's concubine" alone and vulnerable, Saar had acted too soon. He had never imagined that he'd killed the wrong woman, a false concubine.

Failure, embarrassment, humiliation.

Now he was back in Cala City, once more in disguise. Jessica, the real concubine, was already dead. Instead, he would kill the Duke's son, Paul. That would certainly satisfy Feyd.

This time, the twisted Swordmaster made his moves with more caution and discretion. He chose to play a different role, one even less visible than a lowly merchant. After using a succession of false identities, he secured work as an ordinary agricultural laborer on a large farm outside of Cala City. In addition to harvesting work, he spread manure, pulled weeds, and worked his fingers from blisters to calluses, all the while observing and planning.

Now, as he picked crops shirtless under the baking sun, Saar thought of how hard he had sweated and how much pain he had endured at the Swordmaster school on Ginaz. Battered and bruised by trainer after trainer, he'd reached the top of his class in personal combat. But the Ginaz School had been overrun and torn apart a decade and a half ago, forcing him to flee with his education incomplete. Saar had finished that training on his own and used forbidden techniques that no Swordmaster would have taught him.

As chance would have it, he had fallen in among the Tleilaxu, and they offered him an even more rigorous curriculum, a twisted training . . . a particularly deadly and deranged form of training. Even though they had intended to sell him to the highest bidder, Saar accepted their offer for his own purposes. When the genetic geniuses had shown him everything they knew, and when their guard was lowered, he killed two of his masters and escaped.

Afterward, he hired himself out as a mercenary fighter, earning a good living and serving no one but himself. He had accepted the recent commission from Feyd because it sounded challenging.

The Ginaz masters taught absolute honor and loyalty, but Egan Saar did not follow the teachings precisely, nor did he miss those most peculiar of all people. He had his own personal code.

Throughout the days on Caladan, he spent a lot of time working in the fields, speaking little with the other farmhands, not joining them in fellowship, and not singing the songs they all seemed to know. Nevertheless, he worked hard, fulfilled his quota, and was accepted among them.

He had quarters in one of the bunkhouses. Saar made no effort to conceal the sword and dagger that he carried beneath his traveling cloak, explaining that his father told him never to travel unarmed because of the many perils a man alone could face. He casually put his weapons under his bed, a personal space the workers considered sacrosanct. No one ever touched the weapons, and they were ready when he needed them.

Saar worked long shifts lifting flats of fresh fruits or vegetables onto the beds of groundtrucks for delivery. Because of his physical strength and reliability, he was asked to accompany the drivers to the markets in Cala City. As they rolled to the town squares, then back to the fields, day after day, he made a point of carrying his sword and dagger under his rumpled cloak for protection.

Each week, a special delivery went to the kitchens of Castle Caladan, and he knew that eventually he would be invited to ride along on that as well.

Now, shading his eyes under the bright afternoon sun, smelling the dirt and fertilizer all around him, the twisted Swordmaster looked at the castle in the distance, a towering fortress where the Atreides were so convinced of their security.

Saar smiled to himself and went back to loading melons onto the groundtruck. Within days, there would be another delivery to the Atreides household . . . and he'd add a delivery of his own.

What is the greatest bargaining chip? Money? Blood? Honor? Each has its
own value and is measured by a different standard.
—CHOAM *Negotiating Manual and Business Ethics*

Leto found himself trapped with the violent rebels inside the central fortress vault, but by his own choice. Another risk. He knew that he was the only person in a position to stop a complete disaster.

Jaxson's abrupt and audacious action of seizing his own brother had astonished even the Ur-Director. As they retreated into the lockdown with weapons pointed at Frankos and the Urdir herself, Malina had looked impotent. Jaxson's fanatical guards had swept the outside corridor, aiming their flechette pistols at the unshielded CHOAM workers, ready to mow down any desperate attempt by Malina's security forces to stop them.

Jalma yelled after them as they retreated, "You'll destroy everything we've worked for—and you'll still fail!"

Malina Aru didn't shout, yet her words cut through the air like a razor. "You are making a huge mistake."

"Oh, I've made many mistakes, Mother." Jaxson had laughed as the tremendous doors began to grind closed. "And I always manage to adapt."

The multilayered plasteel blast doors thundered shut, driven into place by brute-force engines. Meanwhile, the Sardaukar forces landed on Tanegaard, with access granted by the Ur-Director herself—and Leto was caught up in the debacle.

Jaxson paced inside the fortress vault, restless, on the verge of manic. "Now we are secure."

Leto looked around the large vault, which was three stories high and enclosed as much room as a small administrative center. It was like a reinforced building inside a building. "We have no place to go, Jaxson. The Urdir controls every CHOAM facility here. Now that you've barricaded us inside, we'll never get out alive."

Rajiv Londine grew strident with his panic. "Your own mother betrayed us! She called in the Emperor's troops, she exposed all our allies, and now she'll just fling the doors open wide." He groaned. "We'll be gunned down in here. Once the vault is breached, they'll slaughter us where we stand."

Jaxson responded with a wicked twist of his lips. "Oh, I doubt our corrupt Emperor will do anything so swift and painless. He wants us—" He paused and squared his shoulders. "He wants *me* for painful torture and then a very public execution. His own vindictive streak gives us the time we need. We have a chance."

"What chance?" Londine wailed.

"There's always a chance, so long as we do the unexpected." The rebel leader held up his memory stone again. "I have the final option, and I'm not afraid to use it, as my mother well knows. And we need to let the Emperor know just how much destructive data we have on House Corrino."

"You can't use it," Leto said, making his voice hard.

Jaxson seemed lost in thought. "I have repeaters inside this vault, and amplifiers outside. Triggering this transmission will cause financial and political ruin throughout the Landsraad. The Houses would all turn against the Golden Lion Throne . . . unless they fall upon one another first. So, you see, they dare not kill me. It will activate automatically at the moment of my death." He pocketed the stone again.

"Let me negotiate your surrender, Jaxson," Frankos pleaded. "The black archives give you leverage, so we need to use it. I can broker a sentence of exile. It is the only way you will ever walk out of here."

"The only way?" The rebel leader smirked. "That demonstrates limited thinking."

Leto wished he could coordinate something with the Ur-Director, but he could get no word out—and no one knew which side he was on.

The fortress vault was like an armored central warehouse filled with stacked cubicle containers, each one packed with thousands of shigawire spools, ridulian crystals, and etched datasheets. These were permanent analog records, including physical lists of profits, shipments, prices and purchases, illicit customers. Only the most sensitive information was stored within these coffers, sealed in the central Tanegaard vault, never to be seen by anyone outside of CHOAM.

Open areas between the stacked records vaults held tables, illuminated screens, and workstations. Now, baffled-looking CHOAM clerical staff stood up from their stations, confused by the interruption to their workday. Document runners waited to retrieve requested files to be scrutinized by solemn Mentat accountants and business-projection specialists. Leto guessed they had about a hundred additional, unintentional hostages.

Deep at the heart of the fortress vault was an even more secure bunker, a windowless cube made of impenetrable black plasteel that seemed to drink all light. The central bunker, like an administrative panic room, had one entrance where high-level CHOAM executives could wait out even a full-scale atomic bombardment. Seeing the obsidian bunker, Leto swallowed with a dry throat. But he was thinking about something, a possibility—or better yet, a potential *impossibility*. Sealed inside the impregnable fortress vault, with its double air-gapped walls and thick door, would the rebel leader even be able to transmit his data burst? Or had it become an empty threat?

Defiant, Jaxson faced the towering main vault door, several meters thick, which had sealed into its frame with them inside. A flat comm screen on the inner wall beside the enormous sealed doors now displayed Malina Aru's cold and angry face. "The Sardaukar are coming, Jaxson—a full legion of the Emperor's best, and they will never leave until they have you. Shaddam is here personally, along with his Empress. I do not intend to let them ruin my world. Speak with me now. Resolve this *now*! You must surrender—do this last thing for me!"

"And what have you done for me, Mother?" Jaxson retorted. "You abandoned your dreams of reshaping history. Our *shared* dreams! Remember what Shaddam did to Otorio—*our home*! We had the Imperium in the palm of our hand like a fragile egg, and we could have crushed it. But you didn't have the backbone to do what needed to be done. I am disappointed in you. I expected more from the Ur-Director of CHOAM."

In response, her bitter tone made it clear she did not expect him to respond to reason. "I came to a different conclusion. I had a team of independent Mentats assess your swift and violent approach, and I could not justify the swath of destruction and permanent harm you would cause. I made the logical choice."

Jaxson chuckled. "Oh, you cannot imagine the destruction I'll cause if I release all this data. I felt guilty when I first copied these records during my time here. I knew the harm it would cause you, Mother, and our great Company, even the memory of my father." He touched his face, then shook his head. "But I never expected it would come to this. Now, I see that you deserve it." He glanced at Leto and Londine. "If I die when the Sardaukar try to capture me, the data will be automatically released anyway. Maybe I should just do it under my own terms."

Still held by Jaxson's fanatic guards, Frankos squirmed. "You can't!"

The guards pressed their flechette pistols, threatening the CHOAM President.

Jaxson scoffed at his brother. "Don't tell me what I can and can't do. We aren't having a polite meeting in the Silver Needle. This is a battle for the future of human civilization!" He blanked the wall screen before his mother could argue further.

Leto ground his teeth in concern. Events had spiraled out of control, and if the Emperor had not in fact received Gurney's message, then the Sardaukar would lump him among the rest of the traitors. But he could not escape now even if he wanted to, and he refused to leave until he secured or destroyed the dangerous data archive.

His mind raced through possibilities. The ten fanatical guards would never turn against Jaxson, but there were nearly a hundred CHOAM hostages inside the fortress vault. Leto wondered if they would help him subdue the terrorist leader.

Echoing what the CHOAM President had urged, Leto said, "That database is our only bargaining chip. Don't spend it. Negotiate for our lives and future."

"I've already given my life to the Noble Commonwealth, already made my mark on history." He frowned, seemingly disappointed with Leto. "I thought you agreed with our cause."

Leto did not have to falsify his passion. "It is not so clear-cut for me! I have my son and heir, and the future of Caladan." His vision grew bright and red, thinking of Paul . . . and Jessica. "My Mentat once taught me that in the scope of a complex problem, any simple and direct solution is usually the wrong one."

Walking away from the vault doors, ignoring the hubbub of the guards and hostages milling in the open area of the huge vault, Jaxson looked harried, even confused. He snapped at his guards, as if to divert himself from quarreling with Leto. "Fan out, search all the corridors, containers, and office chambers inside this vault. Identify and count the CHOAM administrators and clerks. They will not be armed, but I want to know where they are. Find a place to keep them where they won't cause trouble." His expression softened, just a little. "Leto, help my guards find everyone and . . . see that they're not harmed."

He responded in a quiet tone, "Thank you."

Jaxson glanced at Frankos, sniffed, then spoke to Londine instead. "Rajiv, find another room where my brother will not make trouble, but don't make him too comfortable. We will likely need him. I do not know how much value the Emperor will place on the CHOAM President, but my mother will surely want her other son, her *good* son, undamaged."

Relieved by his assignment, Londine departed with two of the armed guards, pushing an indignant Frankos Aru toward the inner conference rooms, study cubicles, and storage chambers.

Still looking for a way out so he could plan, Leto followed the guards through the corridors and crannies of the fortress vault. He used the opportunity to inspect the sealed prison in which they had bottled themselves. There were numerous insulated sub-rooms, as well as open research areas with tables, shigawire readers, and crystal players.

When threatened with the flechette pistols, the appalled clerks offered no resistance. A group of research Mentats were bustled into a large meeting room, where they would be confined. The Mentats looked distracted and sheepish, as if they could not disengage their minds from esoteric calculations, even in this crisis.

As he and the guards went from corridor to corridor, chamber to chamber, Leto mapped out the intricate fortress vault in his mind. He hoped he might find some sort of secret exit, like the privacy doors hidden in Castle Caladan. But this secure redoubt was not built to facilitate a nobleman's private tête-à-têtes. This was an impregnable fortress of classified information.

During his time here as an astute student of CHOAM, Jaxson Aru had found some way to copy the black archives and get out of here, which made Leto think there might be some hidden escape hatch. He considered the Ur-Director and imagined all of her predecessors. In centuries past, would CHOAM have thought about back doors and hidden entrances? There was a narrow maintenance passage between the armored double walls of the vault. In a doomsday crisis, an Urdir would need to get in here if only to have access to the central bunker in which they could seal themselves.

If anyone knew about the vault's possible secret exits and inner intricacies, Frankos Aru might. But Leto could not find a way to talk to him alone—not yet. He would not be able to reveal the true reason he had pretended to befriend Jaxson, so he could bring down the rebel movement.

Under extreme circumstances, Leto might be forced to kill Jaxson himself, and he was prepared to do that. But even that would not stop the memory stone from triggering its dangerous data.

His alternatives were rapidly approaching zero.

⊷

EVEN THE PADISHAH Emperor had never been granted access to this CHOAM business stronghold. The Imperium and CHOAM had a tight partnership, a balance of profit and power. Shaddam knew not to upset that delicate balance.

Now, however, he had no choice but to come to Tanegaard. This was the endgame of his long-standing feud with the violent rebels. This was a personal vendetta against Jaxson Aru.

The terrorist's ally, the annoying and outspoken Rajiv Londine, had railed against House Corrino for years, and although Londine's esoteric arguments stung, Jaxson was a different matter altogether. His blatant acts had been directed at Shaddam himself! This was a mortal insult.

His Sardaukar had been highly effective at taking down the treacherous nobles, and Shaddam had been happy to receive reports of the aftermath on Cuarte, on Elegy, and more. The effort was still ongoing, one traitorous planet and then the next. But now that the despicable Jaxson himself was cornered, the Emperor intended to be there in person.

As his lavish Imperial frigate descended through Tanegaard's atmospheric shields, Shaddam glanced over at his beautiful Empress. Aricatha wore a jet-black gown, and her full lips were stained crimson. The jewels that adorned her throat only enhanced the delicate smoothness of her rich, tan skin. Her eyes were like dark stars surrounded by nebulae. Unlike his previous unsatisfactory wives, he actually enjoyed her company. "Today will be a moment in history, my dear," he said.

She glanced out the frigate's side windowport as the Imperial invasion force converged above the administrative citadel. She seemed to be drinking in details of the CHOAM center, where a huge landing area had been cleared for the Sardaukar troops. Attack ships streaked alongside the Imperial frigate like birds of prey. With a wistful smile, the Empress said, "Today will put an end to the disruption and stress that this terrible situation has placed upon you, husband. Still, I'm sure Ur-Director Aru is distraught about what has happened to her poor son."

Shaddam frowned. "Her poor son? Why would you feel sympathy for an animal like Jaxson Aru?"

"Jaxson? No, my love, I meant Frankos, the CHOAM President. He's the one being held hostage by his own brother. Even so, a mother must be devastated to see her child become a monster."

"I understand, dear. And I agree with you, though my sympathy is limited."

The Imperial fleet landed in a wave of weapons and intimidation. All CHOAM traffic and nonessential personnel had been withdrawn from the area and replaced by a besieging army. A handful of Sardaukar should have been enough to take down the rebels, but this force was enough to conquer the entire CHOAM planet—should Shaddam decide to do so.

Deadly soldiers fanned out as he and Aricatha emerged from the frigate and proceeded into the gigantic secure building. Malina Aru came forward, accompanied by her daughter, Jalma, the Countess of House Uchan. Jalma was like an echo of her mother, just as hard and just as determined.

Facing him, the Urdir was not obsequious, not embarrassed, but rather businesslike. "I already sent you the full list of conspirators, Majesty. I trust your Sardaukar have taken care of them."

"A methodical effort is in progress, one traitor at a time. But you promised to deliver your treacherous son." Shaddam felt surly, on edge. "Where is he?"

"Still a loose end. Jaxson proved unpredictable, even for me." Malina looked away. "He is desperate. He has barricaded himself inside an impenetrable vault along with Leto Atreides and Rajiv Londine. They have hostages."

"Rajiv Londine?" Shaddam was startled by the report. He already knew about the hostages, but this was new information. "I have seen reports that Lord Londine was summarily executed, along with his daughter, as part of the punitive purge on Cuarte. How can he be here? I already received word from my colonel bashar."

Malina flashed an unreadable glance at Empress Aricatha, as if trying to communicate something to her. "Apparently, your Sardaukar exaggerated their report, Sire, because Londine is definitely not dead. I have seen him myself."

"Then we'll kill him a second time," the Emperor said with a huff. He glanced at the Sardaukar officers close to him, assuming they had eavesdropped. Their faces were unreadable, none admitting to failure with Londine. Colonel Bashar Kolona's attack force was still deployed in their sequence of punitive attacks, but Shaddam would call him to account—at a later time.

The Ur-Director continued to explain, "I intended to quietly and efficiently take care of Jaxson myself, but now he has an ultimatum of his own." She explained the dangerous cache of data he held, how he could threaten so much of the Imperium. "We must proceed carefully."

As Shaddam grasped the resounding implications of the threat, Empress Aricatha spoke up. "But Duke Leto Atreides is not a desperate terrorist. I have spoken with him, looked into his eyes, and I believe I know his heart." She turned to her husband. "Perhaps I should be the one to negotiate with him? As Empress, I can work out a resolution. Is there a way to get inside?" She looked at the Urdir.

But Shaddam interjected. "Absolutely not, my dear! That's far too dangerous. I would never put you at risk."

He watched his Empress visibly harden, as if a different person had emerged inside her. "Your entire Imperium is at risk unless we find an acceptable end to this. Remember, you have been giving me more complex diplomatic duties."

Malina frowned. "She is correct, Sire, and the Empress does have the capability. Aricatha has been trained in many subtle ways."

The thought sent an odd chill down his spine. Shaddam frowned, confused. "Subtle ways? What do you mean?" What did the Ur-Director know about his wife?

Aricatha coyly stroked his arm. "As if you didn't know how convincing I can be."

Shaddam muttered, but didn't see a way that he could contradict her. He shook his head. "No. I refuse to let you act as a negotiator among those animals. Since we have a full legion of Sardaukar, the best solution may be just to level this entire complex. Kill them all, without any further trouble. I can call in a bombardment that will turn the whole area into a pool of bubbling slag."

As Malina, Jalma, and Aricatha stared at him in disbelief, he nodded to himself. "Yes, that sounds like the best solution."

Once more residing at the Mother School after the disaster on Elegy,
Jessica felt frustrated, again a nameless pawn. She didn't want to be
here. The Bene Gesserit had wrenched her away from her stable life, leaving
her no chance to resolve the break with the man she loved. And now she had
learned that Leto was part of the radical Noble Commonwealth movement—
like Giandro Tull.

Her heart sank. Though she'd had hints before, it made no sense. If Leto
was part of Jaxson Aru's rebellion, had he seen Giandro's message with Jessica
at his side? Had he actually *seen* her?

And now Giandro was dead, all of Elegy devastated. What about Caladan? The Emperor was already known to be jealous of the Duke's popularity
in the Landsraad.

The Bene Gesserit would tell her nothing. It was as if they had plugged
her ears, blindfolded her eyes, and set a gag in her mouth.

She also learned that the Sardaukar forces had decimated Rajiv Londine's
planet and killed his entire noble family, including Vikka Londine, whom
Leto had briefly courted. Was Leto involved in that, too? The Sardaukar were
on the rampage, it seemed. What if they came for Caladan? And Paul? And
she was trapped here on Wallach IX, unable to do anything to help.

Consumed by these troubling thoughts, she strode off to the vital meeting
that had been called among a select group of Sisters and Reverend Mothers.
Even though she didn't know why she, in particular, had been included, Jessica hoped to receive more information. In fact, she would demand it.

She briskly approached the opening in a sandstone hillside above the
Mother School. These inner chambers had been carved when the renegade
Sisterhood first moved to this planet ten thousand years ago. Ducking her

head, Jessica passed through the opening and walked on ornate tiles that led to the large inner chamber.

In the octagonal room, Jessica joined a group of serious Reverend Mothers in black robes. She saw that she was one of the few here who had not undergone the Agony, the terrible test of subjecting her body to a crisis of deadly poison to unlock higher physical and mental abilities. The Bene Gesserit considered Jessica a special case.

Mother Superior Harishka sat in a wooden chair flanked on either side by Reverend Mother Cordana and an enigmatic woman in a full black robe, black gloves, and a cowl over her face that concealed her identity. Even the woman's eyes were veiled by a fine lace. Jessica felt a chill, remembering how she had previously faced the enigmatic Kwisatz Mother inside her darkened isolation cell here at the Mother School.

Unintimidated, Jessica took an open seat, keeping her eyes on the three important women at the front of the chamber. About thirty others filled the surrounding benches, and they whispered, both excited and scandalized that the Kwisatz Mother would attend this mysterious but important meeting. Recalling the intense debate she'd had with the woman in the shadows, Jessica thought these other curious Sisters might not want their questions answered.

As the murmur of conversation quieted for the meeting to begin, Jessica remained alert. The ancient chamber was meant to be comforting, filled with import. In the Sisterhood's earliest days, the first Mother Superior, Raquella Berto-Anirul, and her successor, Valya Harkonnen, had struggled with a terrific schism in the order. How many vital crises had been resolved in this chamber? How often had the Sisters made a situation worse?

Jessica knew why the Kwisatz Mother was here, and felt a chill about the Bene Gesserit business to be discussed. It made her think of Paul and their intrusive designs on him. . . .

A young man emerged from a side alcove, a blond teenager who moved with smooth grace in the manner of a dancer, followed by a very tall Sister about Jessica's age, whom she didn't recognize.

The young man was Brom, son of Sister Xora . . . the woman who had betrayed Jessica here. Xora had had much in common with Jessica, since both had defiantly given birth to sons against Sisterhood demands, both had fallen in love with their men. In punishment for her indiscretion, Xora had been kept in exile at the Mother School for years, forbidden to leave, until she arranged to be assigned as Leto's new concubine to replace Jessica. It was a bitter thought, and when Xora had arrived on Caladan to claim her position, she'd been mysteriously murdered in a Cala City inn, and the assassin was still at large. . . .

Brom, though, did not know the identity of his mother, though he had been raised here at the Sisterhood school. The young man was a year older than Paul, trained among the Bene Gesserit, and Brom had actually helped Jessica, fighting to save her against the murderous Sisters Ruthine and Jiara. Brom had even tried to get Jessica off-planet, until they were caught at the Wallach IX spaceport.

Seeing him now dredged up memories inside Jessica. She caught her breath, trying to read expressions on his oval face, much like his mother's, the eyes feline and blue. He looked determined, but deeply uneasy.

Because of Brom's genetics, fathered by a Sardaukar lover, the Bene Gesserit considered him a candidate for their long-standing breeding schemes . . . a possible all-powerful Kwisatz Haderach, where so many others had failed.

Jessica swallowed. She hoped, yet feared, that her own son—the son of Duke Leto Atreides—was also one of those candidates. But she did not want Paul to become a pawn of the Bene Gesserit, as they had done to her. . . .

Now, as the Sisterhood tested Brom's potential, they would put him through a training session to be observed by select Sisters, but most carefully by the veiled Kwisatz Mother and Mother Superior Harishka. Jessica had heard rumors that they believed the confident young man was ready for the ultimate test, being prepared to attempt the Agony himself, something that even Jessica had never done.

No male had survived the ordeal with the Rossak poison. Not one. Soon, Reverend Mother Mohiam, the Emperor's Truthsayer, would come to test him.

Brom faced the silent women gathered to observe him. Though he remained rigid, his eyes flicked around the chamber, and when he noticed Jessica, he smiled softly. Harishka noticed this, and she whispered to the Kwisatz Mother. The hooded form nodded.

Brom stepped into the center of the room, where the floor was a section of polished wooden boards. The tall, silent Sister followed him, then muttered something in the young man's ear. In response, he took several quick breaths as his trainer stepped away, giving him room. Then, Brom went through a routine of precise muscular exercises, all of which were familiar to Jessica. She had taught the same techniques to Paul.

As he sought the relaxed poise and perfect balance of a prana-bindu mindset, his eyes narrowed until he was no longer looking at anything here. Instead, he seemed to see another place in the universe, and he mouthed the words, "My mind controls my reality."

Finally, with his eyes closed, Brom bent a knee and raised that foot, while perching on the other like a bird. His movement was fluid, demonstrating a state of physical and mental balance. Brom was going deeply into his own mind, seeking an inner place of serenity.

Jessica had instructed Paul in similar poses, again and again, teaching him to control every nerve, every muscle fiber, every thought. She had worked to perfect his abilities, and now as she observed Brom, Jessica noticed a subtle wavering, little more than the twitch of a butterfly wing, and slight misaligned angles of posture.

Behind him, the tall Sister flickered her fingers to send a silent Bene Gesserit message to the Kwisatz Mother and Harishka. Jessica couldn't read the message, but the pride was clear on the trainer's face. From where she sat, the veiled Kwisatz Mother sent her own secret message with gloved fingers.

The trainer tapped Brom on the shoulder, and he relaxed to stand normally again. He emerged from his trance and opened his blue eyes. As if he had reached some kind of epiphany, the young man whispered to his trainer, and to Jessica's surprise, both of them turned to her.

The tall Sister glanced over at Harishka and the Kwisatz Mother. "Brom wishes to have Sister Jessica join him here."

The two important women nodded, and Harishka gestured for Jessica to rise and join the young man. Jessica walked uncertainly with the eyes of the Sisters on her. When she stepped onto the wooden floor, she cleared her thoughts, showing no alarm or confusion. Brom looked at her, patient and expectant. His feline eyes seemed darker blue than usual.

The training Sister spoke. "Brom has reached a point where he feels blocked, but he believes you might have observed something in his movements. Your own son is also considered a candidate as a Kwisatz Haderach, so he values your advice. What is your assessment, Sister Jessica?"

Thoughts about Paul were a whirlwind in her mind. The last time she had seen him was a hushed conversation in his darkened room at Castle Caladan. She'd slipped into the back ways, knowing the danger of the Bene Gesserit assassins sent to kill him. . . .

Now she offered a formal answer. "I see subtle differences in Brom's movements in comparison with my son's. Being raised here at the Mother School, Brom has received more focused training. I am impressed with his abilities."

The training Sister stood off to one side. "Then why is he asking for you?"

As Jessica searched for an answer, the young man blurted out, "I know Sister Xora was my mother! I also know that she is dead—killed by an assassin on Caladan."

The admission made Jessica feel hollow. "I'm sorry . . ." How did Brom know either of those things?

When he paused, no one filled that silence with an explanation. No one moved.

"Mother Superior told me." Brom looked at Harishka, ignoring the Kwisatz

Mother. "And I mourn her loss. I have been here at the Mother School all my life. I saw her, but I never knew her." He hung his head. "She seemed no different to me from any other Sister."

"I'm sorry," Jessica said again. "But why do you ask for me? How can I help you?"

When he faced her, his face suddenly flushed. "I never knew Xora—but I know you, Jessica, and I feel close to you."

The training Sister said, "We must push him to the next level, to prepare him . . . for the Agony test."

Jessica took Brom's hand and closed her eyes. His hand was warmer than expected, since his inward prana-bindu journey should have dropped his body temperature, slowed his metabolism. Accepting her touch, the young man flinched, more obviously nervous now—but trusting her to guide him.

Jessica used her own training to drop into a meditative state and travel into her mind's eye, where she replayed events in her memory, observing Brom as he went through his motions. And she did notice something he'd done wrong.

When Brom first perched on one foot, he had quivered, a flicker of doubt and hesitation for only an instant, but that indicated he had not been in the perfect state of physical and mental harmony. When facing the Agony, even that instant of weakness and uncertainty could prove fatal. His initial breaths had been a bit shaky. She recalled that Paul had made similar mistakes, but he had overcome them on his own. He was younger than Brom, but in some ways better.

Was Paul the Kwisatz Haderach? Was Brom?

When she had grasped Paul's hand like this after similar exercises, his grip had been cool and steady, as if he had mentally become a stone eons old, rather than an uncertain boy. Now, in her own trance, she thought of Paul's calmness and sense of eternity and tried to compare where Brom had gone a few moments ago.

In an odd vision, she imagined Paul and Brom looking at each other across space and time, staring hard into each other's eyes, both facing the same ultimate challenge, but only one of them—or neither—could be the Kwisatz Haderach. One of them would surely fail.

Though she was his mother, she realized that Paul was not necessarily the better candidate, but that he had reached a waystation on the journey sooner. Should Jessica tell Brom where he had gone wrong? Should she give him the advice he needed—and would even that be enough?

In the vision, Paul turned to look directly at Jessica, drew close to her, and mouthed the words, *Help him, Mother. Give him what he needs.*

The statement jerked Jessica out of her trance and back into the octagonal chamber. She bit back a gasp, but she could not be the one to convey the message that she herself did not understand.

When she opened her eyes, she was no longer looking at Paul, only at Brom.

"Did you notice anything?" the young man repeated. "How can I do better? How can I succeed?"

Jessica's vision glazed over. If both he and Paul were candidates for the long-awaited Bene Gesserit savior, then her own son was Brom's rival. But Brom had helped her, and she would help him. The difficult answer came to her like a bright star in the cosmos.

Though I am not this boy's mother, I must help him.

Any other course of action would not be honorable. If Paul truly was the Kwisatz Haderach, he should get there on his own.

No matter what she did here, she was in fact helping Paul. Jessica was conflicted about whether or not she wanted her son to be the One. It would be a dangerous and terrible journey. *But Paul is already on that journey, and so is Brom. The road does not disappear simply because one stops walking.*

Jessica saw Brom's imploring gaze, and she realized that this young man, Xora's son, truly wanted to meet his potential and become the Kwisatz Haderach.

At last she answered honestly, "What I noticed is so subtle that others might not consider it important, but the way you gathered your quick breaths, moved and stood on one foot, entered and left your prana-bindu trance—I will do what I can to help you."

Brom turned pale and swallowed hard. "I must learn everything and practice. I have been instructed to take the Rossak drug tomorrow . . . and I am fearful."

Jessica whirled and looked at the Kwisatz Mother. "So soon? Are you sure?" The veiled woman nodded.

Taking a deep breath, Jessica returned her focus to the young man beside her. Was he ready for that ultimate test? "Our Litany Against Fear will calm you and make your mind open and receptive to what I teach you."

He gave a slight nod, and she set to work.

Of all the people around Duke Leto, three are unquestionably loyal: his son, Paul; his concubine, Jessica; and his physician, Yueh, who underwent Imperial conditioning in the Suk school to guarantee his unimpeachable behavior.

—Early report from a Harkonnen operative

To Paul, Dr. Yueh seemed to be a lonely and quietly reserved man. His father had noticed it, and now the young man had come to the same conclusion on his own.

The Suk doctor was also a very tired man, looking haggard as he joined Paul on the high ramparts of Castle Caladan just outside the weapons room. From here, they could gaze out on the Cala City Spaceport in the distance while they awaited the return of Thufir Hawat and Gurney Halleck. Thufir had transmitted a report as soon as the scheduled Heighliner had arrived in orbit. Both men were battered—but safe and alive!

Thufir and Gurney had made their way to Caladan via a roundabout route until they were finally home. After learning a preliminary report about what had happened to Gurney on Lankiveil, Yueh stood ready. Soon enough, with the warrior Mentat and the weapons master returning to their duties, Paul could feel in better control in his uneasy position here. Even so, the people he wanted back more than anyone were his father and mother.

Now in the early afternoon, the flagstones of the rooftop deck were still damp from a rain squall. The stones were worn in places from centuries of foot traffic, and water pooled in the ruts. There was little wind, an anomaly for this time of day, when breezes customarily came in from the sea.

Waiting, he and Yueh both looked out to the headlands and the coastline, the drop-off beyond the battlement wall to the surf below, and then off toward the spaceport near Cala City. The shuttle had already landed, and he couldn't wait for the transport to arrive.

Yueh seemed preoccupied on the cold rooftop, and Paul said, "Thank you for helping Sinsei and Duncan, and for taking care of so much while I was down in the jungles. I had hoped for a quiet, normal week."

"It all seems very empty here. So many people gone."

"My mother is on assignment with the Bene Gesserit," Paul said, and cautiously ventured, "Like your Bene Gesserit wife, Wanna."

The Suk doctor looked sad and angry, and he muttered, "The Sisterhood has a way of intruding on our lives, doesn't it?"

Paul looked down and saw a groundcar rolling toward the castle, and he knew that Thufir and Gurney would be inside. His joy at having his mentors and advisers return washed away his reserved mood. He would celebrate this little victory. "There they are—and it's one step closer to bringing Caladan back to normal! Let's go down and meet them."

Even Yueh managed a smile. "Of course, young Master. Back to normal."

By the time he and the doctor made their way down from the ramparts, Duncan had blustered into the receiving room off the courtyard, bringing his two companions from the spaceport. Paul ran into the room, barely able to control his excitement. "Gurney!" He rushed forward, then faltered when he noticed the discolored bruises on the weapons master's face and hands. His fingers were wrapped with healing tape, as was his head. Paul's tone changed. "Gurney!"

"Young pup. I apologize for my appearance . . . and tardiness."

Paul hugged the muscular man anyway, pulling back when Gurney grimaced. He spun to call for the doctor. "Yueh can help. We'll get you to the infirmary."

Obviously exhausted, Thufir said, "I patched him up as best I could."

"Good work," Yueh clucked as he inspected the bandaged hands and fingers. "But we can improve on it. And I shall apply additional cellular therapy."

Paul was chilled by the thought of the torturous pain the weapons master must have endured. Gurney dismissed it, though, with a chuckle. "I plan to play my baliset again within a week."

The Suk doctor seemed skeptical, but his patient was determined. "You should be in bed recuperating. And Duncan Idaho, too." He frowned at Thufir Hawat, the old warrior Mentat, and said, "I should inspect you as well. It seems that the greatest Atreides defenders are all battered and bruised."

While Yueh checked his patients, Paul insisted on hearing all about the rescue and escape, as well as the appalling crimes the Harkonnens had committed. Gurney and Thufir took turns, fleshing out the tale of how Piter de Vries and Harkonnen spies had captured Gurney and brought him to Lankiveil to be tortured, where they discovered Duke Leto's implanted message crystal.

Paul simmered as he absorbed the information. "They prevented my father's truth from reaching the Emperor! Now, he's out there with the rebels, in danger, and even the Sardaukar don't know his true loyalty." His cheeks burned with indignation.

Gurney looked around the chamber. "Where is Duke Leto now?"

Yueh answered, "He is with Jaxson Aru, hoping to prevent him from making another spectacular attack."

Duncan growled, "If Emperor Shaddam imagines our Duke is one of those terrorists, it puts Leto in grave danger."

"And us as well," Thufir said, drawing his brows together.

Gurney held up his forearm, showed the scar where the crystal had been cut out. "The Harkonnens still have the message."

"Unless we can get some other proof, send the Emperor a new message," Paul said, thinking fast. "My father also gave me a recorded testament in case something should happen to him. It's in my bureau, but I haven't listened to it. Surely it also records his intentions."

The Mentat agreed. "We could dispatch that to Emperor Shaddam, with our own words of explanation. It might at least make him reconsider any rash action against Caladan." He paused a moment, and his eyes went blank as he concentrated, recalling the Spacing Guild schedule. He touched the comm, contacting the Cala City Spaceport for the schedule, then said, "Our Heighliner will be in orbit for hours longer, unloading and loading."

Paul felt a wash of relief. "Good, then we can dispatch our message right away. We will gather the documentation we need, hire a bonded courier to Kaitain."

Despite the discolored bruises on his face, Gurney looked energetic again. He paced around the room with his rolling gait. "Is there some other proof? The Emperor will think we're making excuses now that evidence points to the Duke."

Yueh looked back and forth, as if he were hunted, but he said nothing.

"The Duke's reputation has to count for something," Duncan said. "No one in the Imperium can believe Leto Atreides would try to overthrow the Corrinos and tear apart Imperial civilization." He snorted in annoyance.

Then an alarm sounded inside the castle, a distant warning, and Thufir ran to determine its source. Duncan and Gurney fell into a tense fighting stance. The Swordmaster strode over to a display case on the wall and removed an antique sword from its hook.

Gurney said to Paul, "Young Master, best be ready with your own personal shield. Get your blade."

Thufir bounded back, moving with remarkable speed. "The spaceport sounded the alarm. Ships are coming down without warning from the Heighliner—massive numbers. Military vessels. We may be under attack!"

They hurried together to the lift that took them back up to the ramparts, and when they emerged together to look toward the spaceport, Paul felt bracing sea air in his face. All five of them spoke little.

At the spaceport less than a kilometer away, they could see a pulse pattern of lights, alarms signaling a call to arms. Thufir touched the comm in his ear, demanding a report.

Gurney squared his shoulders, looked to the sky, and quoted, "We may bemoan our circumstances, but the hand of God has directed us to where we are required to be."

Paul heard the rippling roars of ships—many warships—tearing down through the atmosphere, leaving ominous gray streaks like claw marks as they decelerated. Hundreds of military vessels. He shaded his eyes, tried to make out any markings on the hull, any colors.

"Those are Imperial ships," Duncan said.

Paul recognized them at the same time. "Filled with Sardaukar."

There is a special form of violence that comes from justified desperation.
—Landsraad Court, ethics division

As the cordon of Sardaukar tightened around the Tanegaard stronghold, Leto saw a wild gleam in Jaxson's eyes, like crackles in heated glass. The terrorist leader paced frenetically. "They cannot penetrate CHOAM defenses. In this fortress vault, we are safe."

"Safe . . . ," Leto said. "I would not use that word."

The CHOAM administrative hostages had been rounded up and confined in secure conference rooms or barricaded storage closets. The bureaucrats and accountants were easily cowed by the armed rebel fighters.

Leto still tried to break through the man's fanaticism. "We can offer to surrender your memory stone for certain guarantees." His voice grew more heated. "We must consider damage control, an alternate plan."

Jaxson whirled on him. "I always have a plan." His hands strayed to his pockets.

Leto considered throwing himself upon him and wrestling him down, trying to seize the memory stone before Jaxson's guards killed him. But that was too uncertain, and the rebel leader could trigger the data release with a twitch. Leto would not get a second chance. "This is not a plan, it's just suicide. And it will not accomplish your aims."

"I'm holding the CHOAM President hostage—that's worth something. Surely my mother will want to protect at least one of her sons."

Through the external imagers, they watched thousands of armed Sardaukar march into the Tanegaard citadel. An imposing fleet of attack ships cruised over the administrative buildings, as if they might level the city on a whim. Leto was certain that Malina Aru would never allow that, but in a power struggle between CHOAM and the Imperial throne, who would win?

If Shaddam ever suspected that the Ur-Director herself was involved in the Noble Commonwealth rebellion, would he even hesitate to annihilate this place? After what the Emperor had done to other suspected rebel planets, his ruthlessness was undeniable. But outright war between CHOAM and the Imperial throne? That could be as bad as the release of the black archives.

Leto had no confidence in a rational or peaceful solution. Not from Jaxson, and not from Shaddam.

Rajiv Londine stood in the nondescript clothes he had donned as a disguise, and the normally dapper nobleman looked almost unrecognizable. His eyes flicked back and forth. "President Frankos is secure in his own holding cell, a reinforced filing room that was not designed for comfort. He can't get out." He brushed back his steel-gray hair, but it still looked rumpled. "Use him as a bargaining chip—threaten to execute the CHOAM President if the Sardaukar do not back off. What good is an important hostage if you're not willing to use him?"

Leto felt a flush of alarm. "That would escalate the situation dramatically."

Laughing, Londine gestured to the screens that showed the military force arrayed against them. "Escalate it how?"

"We won't kill my brother—not yet," Jaxson said. "My mother knows he is here, and that is enough. She knows full well what the black archives contain. The Sardaukar will exercise a certain amount of restraint, for now."

Perturbed, Leto raised his voice. "But what is your endgame, Jaxson? They'll find some way to breach these vault doors or some other way to enter. They have the Ur-Director's full cooperation, and she might be able to grant them emergency access. We should surrender on our own terms and make certain the Noble Commonwealth is not forgotten. That is our only alternative right now."

"Oh, they'll never forget me," Jaxson said. "We've always got one final statement to make."

The rebel leader wasn't even trying to find another solution. He had already made up his mind, willing to throw the Imperium into complete upheaval. Leto needed to smash the memory stone, no matter the cost, but Jaxson, as if sensing something, moved away from him whenever the Duke drew close. He seemed to be staying as far away as he could from the others.

With a jerk of his head, Jaxson flashed a glance at Londine. "Rajiv, go check on dear Frankos. Make certain my brother is ready for whatever awaits him. Tell him I am still deciding his fate."

❦

IN ACCORDANCE WITH the Emperor's demand, Ur-Director Malina Aru briefed the Sardaukar commanders and even Empress Aricatha, who insisted on being there, on the structure and defenses of the fortress vault. For her own part, Malina very much wanted Aricatha present, since the sweet Empress had been secretly molded and indoctrinated by CHOAM with the best psychological coaches, manipulators, and seduction trainers. Even Shaddam did not know his wife's connection with the Urdir. And in the end, despite her crown, Aricatha owed her loyalty to CHOAM.

For the tense briefing, Malina called in five Tanegaard subdirectors as well as architectural chiefs who provided maps and blueprints of the facility, so the besieging force could inspect and make plans.

"There must be some way in, Urdir," Emperor Shaddam declared. "With all the security on this planet, you should have planned for such a hostage situation! How can we extract that murderer without costing more lives?"

Malina shook her head coolly. "Having a simple way in would defeat the entire purpose of our security." She indicated the mammoth vault doors that had sealed shut. "It would take nearly a planet-killing attack to break through that barrier. If Jaxson decides to trigger his data transmission, it will deal a death blow to commerce and security throughout the Imperium. You must not take it lightly, Sire."

"Can't you just increase shielding around the vault and block any possibility of transmissions? That would render Jaxson's entire threat of the black archives inert."

Malina gave the Emperor an impatient look. "If only it were so simple, Sire. He has booster circuits, and CHOAM has embedded communication circuits to prevent a person sealed inside from being cut off. We could not be certain of blocking them all."

Grumbling, the Emperor looked closer at the hologram blueprint of the large central vault. "I just want this over with." At the very center was another cube the size of a small room, but it was entirely blank, an inner blackout zone. Shaddam thrust his finger deep into the image. "And what is this? You have no data about your own vault?"

Malina struggled to quell her impatience. "That is an even more secure core bunker with yet another layer of armor and shielding. It is designed to be impregnable even to atomic attack."

"If this fortress vault is your greatest security," the Emperor huffed, "why do you need something even more protected deep inside?"

She gave him a hard smile. "There is always a need for deeper security, Sire."

Aricatha looked down at the diagram, deep in thought. "Have we had word from Leto Atreides? He could be the key to our negotiations."

"Why are you so enamored with the Duke of Caladan?" Shaddam snapped. "He is obviously a traitor like the others."

The Empress shot him a hard look. "Because he might solve this for us, if you give him the chance."

"We know Leto's been in league with the Noble Commonwealth all along," Shaddam said. "He was with the terrorist leader on Issimo III giving relief supplies to those pathetic colonists. We know he visited Cuarte and left only days before our Sardaukar forces arrived. He was on Nossus at the rebel head-quarters and fled with Jaxson to here. He's inside the vault with the madman right now! How much more proof do you need?"

Aricatha raised her chin. "Proof that I can believe."

Malina herself did not understand the motives of Leto Atreides. When she'd spoken with him on Nossus, he did seem to be different from her son's other radicals. Her CHOAM Mentats had pinpointed the fact that he didn't belong in the same category with them. Maybe there was hope.

The Empress wiped her brow and claimed weariness, saying she was un-settled from their rushed journey from Kaitain. In synch with her, the Ur-Director offered to share a small meal with her, in a place where she could rest. Emperor Shaddam seemed perfectly happy to have both of them leave, so that he and his commanders could discuss strategy.

Malina wanted to be away from them as well, so that she and her dedi-cated Aricatha could discuss their real strategy. The Empress could provide her with options she hadn't had before.

Holton Tassé followed the Ur-Director and the Empress, though Malina did not want the aide-de-camp's company. She easily got rid of Tassé by send-ing him off to bring refreshments.

As soon as they were in the private room, knowing they might not have long, Malina chose to be efficient with her time. The Empress, so proud and confident when she accompanied Shaddam, now looked at the Urdir, await-ing the instructions both of them knew would come.

Malina gathered some of the paraphernalia she had prepared while mull-ing over the possibility. She set a small curio box of what looked like costume jewelry on a small bloodwood table between them, then activated a projector that displayed a far more detailed diagram of the fortress vault.

"Of course there is a secret way in," Malina explained. She rotated the three-dimensional hologram and showed a narrow service access in one of the rein-forced double walls. "The vault is secure, but there is a gap between the inner and outer walls on the east side, a narrow passage barely a meter wide to mitigate emergency lockdowns and to allow egress for anyone trapped inside."

"And therefore I have access," Arieatha said, her tone worried. "But what am I going to do?"

"You'll enter and become a hostage, one that Jaxson cannot turn down."

The Empress was not argumentative, just curious. "And what will that accomplish?"

Malina opened the curio box and rummaged around in the jewelry, the glittering baubles and small gems, looking for something that would not draw too much attention. First she selected a brooch and set it aside, then decided on a white gold ring, expensive enough not to be out of place, yet not so flashy as to draw attention. She held it up and peered through the center of the ring. "This. Wear the ring and hope you get close to Jaxson."

Aricatha accepted it, tested the ring on her fingers, found that it was the right size for her forefinger. "And what does it do?"

"Even Ixian technology is not perfect, and CHOAM knows the flaws to exploit. We sell few of these because hardly anyone knows of their existence, and Ix pays us a premium to keep them off the market."

Aricatha twirled the ring on her finger; it was somewhat loose.

The Urdir continued, "It is a *burst*. If you touch your ring to the memory stone, it will release an energetic pulse to disrupt the data matrix. Any information stored inside will be scrambled, and rendered useless."

Aricatha studied the ring, an unremarkable piece in comparison with her other jewelry. "And how will I get close enough to Jaxson to touch his memory stone?" She raised her eyebrows. "You don't believe I can seduce your son?"

Malina chuckled. "I doubt that. But once you are inside the vault, you will have to find a way . . . or maybe even find an ally."

By the time Holton Tassé arrived with a tray of refreshments, Malina and Aricatha were standing up to leave.

⁂

THE FACE DANCER hurried off, struggling to maintain the persona of Lord Rajiv Londine. In his earlier guise as Chief Administrator Rodundi, he had spent much time studying the nobleman, knew his mannerisms and personal recollections. It had been surprisingly easy to assume the man's identity after the massacre on Cuarte, and fabricate a story of how he had escaped. The relieved rebels had accepted him on Nossus without a single doubt.

But it was going to be a challenge to get away from this last-stand bunker. He stayed alert for opportunities, trying to find a way not just to survive, but to protect the Tleilaxu cause. He was in a position to tip the balance one way or the other. The planned fracturing of the Imperium into an independent commercial commonwealth would likely not occur now—at least not by the straightforward means Jaxson Aru hoped for. But the Face Dancer was flexible, and observant.

The anonymous CHOAM clerks and office workers might serve as effective bargaining chips, but they were too weak and insignificant to accomplish much. As Rajiv Londine, however, the Face Dancer could move more freely, even here.

He approached the chamber where an angry, impotent Frankos Aru was held. The tall, erudite man was the benevolent face of CHOAM, but now he looked haggard, kneading his hands as he sat on a hard bench inside his holding room. Only one of Jaxson's guards stood at the door, but the CHOAM President was not a man prone to brawling. Frankos would not try to battle his way out against a trained soldier. Now the guard acknowledged Londine, and let him pass.

Seeing him, Frankos glanced up from his misery and retorted, "I do not wish to speak with you unless you are here to free me. My brother is insane. Surely you are rational enough to know that he cannot win."

"Winning can be defined in many ways, and we must be open to whatever comes." With an unsettling smile, the Face Dancer looked Frankos up and down as he imagined how he might assume his identity. Would there be more advantages to becoming the CHOAM President?

He pondered possibilities.

❧

YEARS AGO, BACK on Caladan, a fishing boat had been swamped in a storm at sea, and Leto had participated in the dangerous rescue of the surviving crew members. He remembered the precarious balance of the desperate men in an unstable lifeboat while razorfish circled, sensing the blood. The eight survivors were twice the boat's rated capacity, and the men crowded on the sides in a delicate dance of weight and balance. If one person shifted, the other side of the boat rocked and threatened to fling another man into the sea. Even a sneeze or a shudder could disrupt the equilibrium and bring ruin down upon all of them.

Leto felt their current situation was much like that tableau.

The Sardaukar forces outside the vault were at a standoff, yet ready to unleash wholesale holocaust upon the trapped rebels. Jaxson was poised to release the black archives that would plunge the Imperium into a civil war. Everyone inside the fortress vault just waited for something to change. But Leto had decided to do something.

He stalked through the tension-drenched air, searching for alternatives. He might be able to find a way out if he merely wanted to escape, possibly free the CHOAM President, even a few of the clerical hostages at the same time.

But that would do no good unless he could secure and neutralize the memory stone. Even with the thick, reinforced walls, Jaxson seemed convinced his transmission would succeed, and Leto didn't doubt that he would have had a backup, multiple repeaters or amplifiers.

It was clear Emperor Shaddam would not negotiate, and even President Frankos was not powerful enough to force any sort of compromise.

According to the chronometers, it was late night, but he couldn't sleep. He made his way to the CHOAM executives' holding area, and found himself in the unwelcome company of Rajiv Londine.

The fidgety nobleman sniffed. "I know my daughter was truly attracted to you, Leto Atreides. Such a shame that it turned out like this. But now we are allies in desperation, are we not?"

"We are not allies—although we'll probably die together, massacred by Imperial forces."

As they walked the outer perimeter of the warehouse-size vault between barricades of armored data containers, external motion sensors triggered an alert on one of the vault screens. Leto studied the readings. "There's apparently a narrow access passage on the eastern wall. Someone moving in the gap."

Londine pressed close. "Is it Sardaukar? Some kind of commando strike? We need to get to shelter! Tell Jaxson!"

"No, just one person." Leto noticed Rajiv looking at him strangely, but felt no danger from him. He must just be afraid, and looking to Leto for some semblance of security.

The alert screen showed little detail, only a blip, a single source of movement. Leto identified a nearby hidden door reinforced by security systems, deep in the shadows of stacked data containers. Someone would have to know to look for it there.

He enhanced the image, saw a dark-haired woman working her way through a passage that was barely wide enough for a person to pass. She darted ahead, as if she had training as an assassin. Then Leto was startled to recognize her. "What is the Empress doing here, alone and without a guard escort?"

Londine hurried to the door, his eyes alight. "If she is trying to get in, we have to intercept her, take her captive!"

Leto frowned. What was Shaddam's plan? Was he sending her as a spy? Or was this an impulsive act on her own part?

Londine began to operate the security controls as if he were a master of the intricate systems. Leto was surprised that this man understood the access routines of the CHOAM data fortress.

When he managed to open the small and narrow entrance, Empress Aricatha stood before them as if she had expected them to find her. Seeing Leto, she became businesslike. "I have come to put an end to this. I shall negotiate, as your direct liaison, and the Emperor will listen if I am with you." She raised her chin and said, "I assume you'll want me as a hostage until we can resolve this dispute."

Londine seized her by the arm and pulled her inside the fortress vault.

Too much thinking weakens a person who is about to undergo the Agony. Excess thinking equates to worry, and worry equates to failure.

—Bene Gesserit admonition

I n the desert dream, a dark-haired young woman stood high on a rock escarpment, profiled against moonlit dunes. Something churned out there under the sand, an undulating shape that crossed from right to left. Then it vanished, an unseen behemoth that dove deep, like a great sea monster.

Nighttime, but stiflingly hot. Two moons . . . A terrible mysterious purpose.

Jarred out of the dream in her dim dormitory quarters, Jessica threw the blanket to the floor. She woke sweating and trembling, terrified of what she had just seen. She didn't understand, but believed that it had something to do with her son's future. She sensed death all around him. . . .

As she shook off the lethargy of sleep, she understood the pressure that had driven her to those dreams. It wasn't Paul who faced the imminent danger, but the other young man. Brom.

After seeing Xora's son in his intense private training, she knew he had been well prepared but was not yet perfect. Nevertheless, the Kwisatz Mother had determined it was time, and Mohiam was on the way here from Kaitain. Jessica felt a need to release her own tensions. Brom, who reminded her so much of her own son, was about to undergo a test that even some Bene Gesserit Sisters did not survive. Was it arrogance on the part of the Sisterhood, or hope?

Or desperation?

She wasn't sure how confident Brom felt, but the Mother Superior was giving him no choice. Tomorrow, he would face the Agony.

Needing to burn restless energy, Jessica donned exercise clothes and set off on a trail that circled the school complex. The rising sun shed low light on the pathway as she moved first at a brisk walk and then at a steady run. She had not jogged in almost a year, so she set a moderate pace. Under an overcast sky, a light drizzle of cool rain misted her face, but her exertion kept her warm. She experienced a momentary soreness in one quad, but it faded, and the exercise made her feel better, more energized and ready for her day.

The advice Jessica had given Brom was subtle, suggestions that only someone with experience in Bene Gesserit ways would understand. The intense young man had listened carefully, taking the advice to heart. He seemed to absorb the details better from her than from the stern training Sister. She knew he was clever, a fast learner, and determined, but he also had an independent streak, which she appreciated, although he probably caused consternation among his proctors.

Brom had little time left to perfect his training. Reverend Mother Mohiam would arrive on Wallach IX tomorrow morning. And the same day, he would face the his greatest test.

At a steady run, she sprang over a fallen branch, still worrying about Xora's son as if he were her own. In the Bene Gesserit sense, because children were raised and trained at the Mother School—as she herself had been—Brom really *was* her son, just as he was the son of all the Sisters.

In contrast, Paul had been raised under Duke Leto and trained with the best minds of House Atreides to be the heir of Caladan. She and Leto had discussed the possibility of having another child, but for now, all they had was Paul. And he did *not* belong to the Bene Gesserit order!

When she considered the idea from the Mother Superior's perspective, she understood Harishka's intense interest. In having a son instead of a daughter, Jessica had made a bold move—not due to any deep machinations, but for Leto's sake after he had lost his other son, Victor. And now that Paul had shown indications of his special nature, his abilities intrigued the Sisterhood.

For millennia, the order had administered a careful breeding program, shepherding one genetic line after another, combining them in exactly the right ways, breeding for the ultimate human who would bridge space and time, a male Bene Gesserit with incredible powers.

Mad old Lethea had demanded that Jessica and her son be killed to prevent disaster from being unleashed on the universe. But Harishka had decided against the former Kwisatz Mother's demented ravings. The Mother Superior knew Paul was special . . . as did Jessica.

Breathing hard, she stood off to the side of the trail. Two other Sisters walked past, talking in low voices as they glanced at her, then moved on.

Her dire situation here after the massacre on Elegy, as well as the crisis Brom was about to face, and knowing the responsibilities that hovered over Paul, all made her see what she had not previously seen. Jessica began to believe what she did not believe before.

She had not been wrong to bear a male child, despite the admonishments from her Bene Gesserit superiors. She might have been doing as Fate dictated, fulfilling a larger purpose. And she no longer even had Paul, since the Sisterhood had broken her family, her relationship with Leto, and her home. She would continue to insist on being released . . . although she didn't even know what remained for her on Caladan.

Paul was in danger from so many directions . . . and she had been relegated here to Wallach IX, asked to help another woman's son survive the testing.

JESSICA HAD EXTENDED her greatest hope and support to Brom, but she had difficulty quelling her fear. She herself had never faced that critical ordeal to become a Reverend Mother.

And she wondered if she would ever make that terrible transition herself, consuming a fatal dose of an awareness-spectrum narcotic, converting it . . . She didn't know if she even wanted to try. She had already reached a high station as the Lady of Caladan, the bound concubine of the noble Duke Leto Atreides, and she had never wanted more.

As a young Acolyte, Jessica had seen other Sisters writhe in turmoil during the Agony. Many survived, while others perished in horrible, nightmarish spasms. They had screamed as their insides churned and their brains raced out of control. Such a terrible ordeal!

How could Brom possibly succeed against such a powerful poison, when all other male candidates had failed?

I'm afraid he's not ready.

What is the value of a human being? What is the cost of a tragic loss? And
what are the most painful ways to make a person pay?

—Suk medical school, political archives

As he and Londine escorted Empress Aricatha toward the front of the sealed fortress vault where Jaxson paced and fumed like a caged animal, Duke Leto felt sickened by the risk she had taken. What did Aricatha expect to accomplish? Yet he admired how she stood vibrant with poise and grace, showing not even the tiniest flicker of fear. His mind whirled, trying to think of how he might possibly leverage her presence to turn the tables on Jaxson Aru. It seemed unlikely, but he would not give up the effort.

Just before they reached the giant, sealed doors, Leto spoke to her in a low voice. "I will do my best to protect you, Majesty, but these are impossible circumstances."

Aricatha faced forward, but replied out of the corner of her mouth, "I know you are a man of reason, Leto Atreides. Let us hope you are not the only one."

"Alas, Empress, I may be." He had so much else to tell her. If Emperor Shaddam had never received his message from Gurney, then she might be his only hope to save his reputation, and his life.

Rajiv Londine strutted ahead into the open area, where Jaxson intercepted them, grinning in surprise at the sight of her. His sparkling eyes flicked from side to side. "Ah, the lovely Empress! I am so pleased you can join us for our little social gathering. A pity that your husband wants to obliterate us all."

Her voice was as brittle as a shard of glass. "And it's a pity that you want to tear apart an Imperium that has lasted for ten thousand years. My husband will not negotiate with you, and wants to level this city as a warning to any future rebels. The CHOAM Ur-Director objects to that solution, so she has forced a measure of restraint. For now."

"Ah, my dear mother always has my best interests at heart . . ." Jaxson chuckled, then narrowed his eyes. "And such interesting details I have learned about you, Empress Aricatha." He brought out his memory stone, threatening her with it. "I'm certain Shaddam Corrino would like to know . . ."

Huffing, Aricatha turned away from him, looking at Leto instead. "My husband loves me, but I came here against his wishes because I believe in diplomacy, and in finding common ground—especially in desperate circumstances." She glanced over her shoulder. "I do not know you, Jaxson Aru, but Duke Leto Atreides is an honorable man. I believe he would prefer an alternative to wholesale slaughter."

"Jaxson, we should talk with her, work out a sanctuary agreement," Leto said. "Maybe you can retire far outside the boundaries of the Imperium. And I . . . I can just go home to Caladan."

"Where you will continue to suffocate under the oppressive Corrino Imperium?" Jaxson retorted. "I think not! And what home does Lord Londine have to go back to? Cuarte is a charred ruin. What about House Tull, with Elegy eradicated? And what about all those other planets crushed by the vindictive violence of the Corrino Emperor? Has he destroyed Caladan yet?" He stepped aggressively close to Aricatha, but she avoided meeting his gaze. "Does your husband truly think we should let bygones be bygones?"

She responded with a hard expression, "No, we won't simply forget. I was there myself at Otorio, and later at the Imperial Palace when you crashed the treasury ship. All those innocent victims . . ."

"Innocent victims?" Jaxson snorted. "Perhaps we should compare scores. Your husband's record is far worse than mine. So many Landsraad Houses with dark secrets . . ."

"Let me see that memory stone you are using for blackmail," she said.

"Seeing it will tell you nothing about the information it contains." He glared at her. "But I think you know what it contains, Empress."

"Bloodshed begets bloodshed," Leto said, then gave her an appreciative look. "If you are here with us, Empress, the Padishah Emperor will exercise restraint. Maybe, just maybe, cooler heads will prevail."

Smiling, Jaxson nodded to himself. "Her presence does indeed alter the parameters. My brother, Frankos, is not nearly so attractive a hostage, nor of such value to Shaddam Corrino. You are enough of a bargaining chip to change the paradigm."

Taking the Empress by the arm, he guided her roughly to the imaging wall beside the big vault door, with Londine following like a sycophant. Leto tried to think of how he could whisk her back to the hidden exit. When he had taken this risk, he'd known what he was in for. He had made his own choices, and so had the Empress. Aricatha was a shrewd woman, with a greater depth than a simple ornamental Empress, but she was doomed to be a pawn if she stayed here.

Slipping his arm through hers in a mocking gesture, Jaxson activated the imagers. The Empress stood stiffly beside him, her expression stormy. The rebel leader smiled as their images were projected on the outside screen. "Shaddam Corrino! I have a surprise guest. Maybe now we shall have a more open conversation?"

⚮

THE SARDAUKAR PRESENCE in the CHOAM administrative citadel was oppressive to Malina. Although their military was not directed toward the Urdir or any Company employees, still they did not belong here. No Imperial force had ever set foot on Tanegaard before, not by invitation, and certainly not as a besieging army.

Malina cursed Jaxson for his provocative actions. She should have been able to take care of this herself, quietly and conveniently, but he had made this an untenable situation, had driven them to this impasse, which would end in death and destruction. Now her main question was how to limit the disaster that her son would cause. She hoped Aricatha could find a way to neutralize his copy of the black archive.

When the external comm screen activated outside the fortress vault, the image showed Jaxson standing next to a cool Empress Aricatha, she knew that matters had taken a dramatic turn. Malina saw her carefully concealing any sign of a smile. Leto Atreides was also there, on the edge of the field of view.

Surrounded by his highest-ranking officers, Emperor Shaddam paled when he saw his wife staring out at him. Like a heavy returning tide, a flush rose in his cheeks. He seemed apoplectic as Jaxson began to talk.

The Emperor turned his glare toward Malina, as if she were personally responsible. "How did my Empress get inside the vault? You said there were no other entrances!"

The Atreides Duke was a wild card. Although she had a good opinion of him, in this scenario, she doubted Leto had the power or the opportunity to do what was necessary. Unless Aricatha herself could use the burst from her ring.

"If he harms her, I swear I will vaporize this entire complex," Shaddam said. "I don't care if Jaxson tries to release his blackmail data. House Corrino can survive it." He sniffed. "Your son certainly will not."

"Neither of my sons, Sire—not Jaxson, nor Frankos," she said quietly, then stepped closer to the screen, as if Shaddam were not there at all. "Jaxson, let us discuss terms, but you must release the Empress and Frankos. I will find some way to keep you here on Tanegaard, but there is no chance you can win."

Facing her, Jaxson offered his maddening smile. "Oh, Mother, that depends on how we define *winning*. If I drive a dagger through the black heart of the Corrino Imperium, would that not be a win, even if I don't survive? Oh, the things I have learned about them!"

Inside the vault, Leto Atreides spoke insistently to the rebel leader. "There are always ways to de-escalate tensions—"

Jaxson brushed him away, as if dealing with an annoying fly that buzzed too close. "Soon enough I'll just put an end to this. For now, however, if you value your beloved Empress, Shaddam Corrino, then withdraw your Sardaukar troops and retreat to orbit—or better yet, leave the Tanegaard system. Then I'll know you're serious about keeping this woman alive."

Jaxson gave a sarcastic tilt of his brow, knowing he had just provoked the Emperor. "Or I can kill her in front of your eyes if I don't like what you're doing." Grabbing Aricatha by the arm, he shoved her over to Londine, and then the screen went blank.

Shaddam howled.

❧

THOUGH LETO TRIED to convince him to keep his mind open, Jaxson ordered the Empress to be taken to a secure data chamber next to Frankos, and Leto escorted her, accompanied by one of the rebel guards.

When they arrived at the door, the CHOAM President looked out of his own holding room and groaned upon seeing that Aricatha was also a captive. "Now my brother will be emboldened to have you as a bargaining chip. He'll be even more dangerous."

"I still hope for a viable solution," the Empress answered in a brave voice, but neither Leto nor Frankos were convinced. Watched by Jaxson's private guard, she entered the austere chamber, retaining her dignity. "We just need to find something that Jaxson wants."

Leto glanced at the guard. "Leave us. She is secure here."

Now that Malina Aru had revealed herself as the Emperor's source of inside information, Jaxson was no longer looking for a traitor hidden among his loyalists. Leto was free of suspicion now, safe for the time being—a laughable idea considering the situation. With his fury directed toward his mother, Jaxson assumed that his last-stand companions were all loyal to him and ready to die.

When the guard hesitated, Leto snapped, "Have I not proved myself? I was there at Nossus. I flew here to Tanegaard. Go ask Jaxson if he distrusts me now." Uncertain, and then straightening, the guard backed off.

Leto stood inside the door to her holding chamber, looking at Aricatha. He dropped his voice to a whisper. "I wish you had not come here, Empress. I will do all I can to keep you safe."

"It may not be enough." She stepped closer, searching his expression. Questions swirled through Leto's mind, and Aricatha seemed to reach a decision. Her whisper was husky. "I'll have to trust you, Duke Atreides, because you're more likely to find the opportunity than I am. I want you to get close to Jaxson, where you can touch the memory stone."

Leto drew a quick breath. "Empress, I have been trying to take it away from him, but it is triggered automatically. If it is taken from his person, the data will be released. If he is killed, the data will be released. What are my options?"

Aricatha slid a plain white gold ring from her forefinger and held it up to Leto. "This," she said, and explained exactly what he could do with it.

❧

NO OUTSIDE LIGHT penetrated the thick-walled fortress vault, and only chronometers told the people whether it was day or night. To Leto, the time and the tension seemed endless. After Jaxson's taunting message, he had cut off all communication with the outside, ignoring repeated demands from Emperor Shaddam and the Ur-Director.

Leto squeezed his fist, feeling the white gold ring on his little finger. No one would notice it, and if he could just get close enough to the memory stone . . . Now the stakes had grown even higher. He would move quickly to overpower Jaxson, kill him if necessary, and burn out the memory stone before it could transmit its barrage of data.

But the rebel leader's anxiety, even paranoia, grew more frayed by the moment, and he kept one or more of his fanatical guards with him at all times. Leto still saw no chance to make his move, but he only needed a second. . . .

And then Rajiv Londine disappeared.

The large fortress vault was a labyrinth of warehoused data, windowless offices, and small office chambers, as well as the enigmatic inner bunker cube. Jaxson had only ten armed guards to watch the entire area, thus it was not immediately apparent that Londine was nowhere to be found. But when Jaxson summoned him for a parley with both Frankos and the Empress, the nobleman did not appear.

Searchers went among the hostages, then raced up and down the corridors between stacked containers, the sealed chambers, looking everywhere for the Cuarte nobleman. Suspicion lit behind Jaxson's eyes again, and Leto could feel the heat rising from the increasingly frantic rebel leader as he exclaimed, "Rajiv has been with us all this time! Did he abandon us now? Did he find some way to escape?" He appeared angry and baffled.

Leto remembered that the nobleman had seemed unusually familiar with the small emergency egress door. Did he have some special knowledge? "Perhaps Londine was not as loyal as you'd thought. That man kept many secrets from us."

The rebel leader wiped perspiration from his brow. "Where would he go? I need every person for this last stand, to witness my final victory!"

His private guards searched the fortress vault, and Leto accompanied them, feeling his uneasiness deepen. Jaxson hunched over, staring up at the towering blast doors as if they might fall in on him.

Outside, Emperor Shaddam continued demanding to see Aricatha, all the while issuing impotent threats.

❦

THE FACE DANCER had taken on the appearance of one of Jaxson Aru's private guards, so that he could disappear.

He had accompanied the rebel leader and the Duke of Caladan during their escape from Nossus, and now he was trapped along with them inside the Tanegaard redoubt. But "Rajiv Londine" was already a known target, sure to be slaughtered by the Sardaukar as soon as they breached the barrier.

As a shape-shifter, he could have melted in among the CHOAM hostages, becoming a nameless clerk or administrator, but if the situation collapsed, then those captives would be lambs in a slaughtering pen. His best option was to become a guard for now, able to move about unrecognized, unremarked.

Quickly, after killing one of Jaxson's fanatics and shifting his own features, he donned the guard's uniform and discarded the Londine disguise. Within moments, the Cuarte nobleman simply vanished as if he had never existed.

The Face Dancer waited for the absence to be noted, after which he would take advantage of the turmoil.

Searchers spread out inside the huge vault, rushing from chamber to chamber, interrogating the CHOAM hostages—none of whom had seen anything, of course. Looking like no more than a guard, the Face Dancer curtly promised to go check on the important captives, Empress Aricatha and CHOAM President Frankos.

Outside the makeshift cells, he relieved the man on duty and sent him running off to help in the search for Rajiv Londine. Then he took the man's place outside the door, staring ahead and refusing to hear the demands of Frankos or the Empress. For now.

Settling into his new identity, he waited in silence, until finally making his most important move. All alone in the vicinity, he unsealed both of the holding rooms and peered in at the urgent, confused expressions of the captives. "Now we have our opportunity," he told them in a hoarse whisper. "You must listen to me carefully. Follow instructions without hesitation, or you will never escape."

Frankos looked at him in disbelief. The Face Dancer said, "I've infiltrated this movement. I am loyal to the Emperor, and now it is my duty to see that you get away."

Aricatha looked troubled, but then she nodded to herself. "Yes, I can leave now. I've done what I can."

The Face Dancer said, "From the side egress hatch, you will make your way along the narrow passageway. Come, we must get to the exit while the others are distracted. I have created a diversion."

Frankos ducked out of his cell, looking from side to side. "We need weapons, in case we have to fight our way out."

"There'll be no fighting. I can take you." The Face Dancer indicated the flechette pistol and long dagger at his side. "These will be sufficient."

The two remained quiet and professional, understanding what was at stake. Both knew how to think and act quickly, and they understood their peril. The "guard" gestured, and they followed him, ducking among the high data vaults, taking side passages as they made their way to the perimeter and the hidden emergency door.

The Face Dancer's highest priority was to make certain the plans of his Tleilaxu people did not fall apart. Details of the conspiracy and cooperation were almost certainly contained within the black archives Jaxson was using as his insurance policy. If his Masters were tied to Jaxson Aru's violent foolishness, then the entire Tleilaxu race would pay the terrible price. He needed to make sure he could deflect any investigations that might expose his people's involvement, and thus he had to be in a position to influence decisions and divert attention.

For that, he could not afford to be trapped among the doomed rebels inside this vault. Frankos Aru had seemed to be an option, but now he had a better alternative.

Breathless and furtive, the group reached the camouflaged doorway, its outline making only a faint mark in the thick plasteel shielding. As before, he placed his palm against a control plate on the wall, altered the lines and whorls of his hand so that his identity matched what the CHOAM scanners recognized, and the door unsealed. Frankos Aru stared with bright-eyed amazement, then nodded with relief as the door slid open.

The Face Dancer nudged the CHOAM President forward into the narrow passage. "Run ahead down the access corridor—we'll be right behind you. Before long, the sensors will detect you, but get away before Jaxson can send anyone after you. Once outside the vault, the Sardaukar will intercept you."

The motion sensors registered the intrusion, and indicators lit up inside the fortress vault, as well as outside where Shaddam and the Imperial forces were watching. The Face Dancer yelled at Frankos, "Go!"

The CHOAM President cast a final glance back at the Empress and then bolted into the narrow space between the vault walls, hurrying ahead. Aricatha turned to the Face Dancer, her expression warm. "Thank you for your service and loyalty. It will be rewarded."

The Face Dancer nodded. "Yes, it will be." He had only a second to make his move.

Like a viper striking, he slipped out his dagger and drove it into the back of Aricatha's neck, severing her spinal cord. He pushed the point up through the back of her skull and into her brain—an instantly fatal blow that spilled very little blood. Her eyes bulged, but she wasn't even able to gasp as she fell into a puddle of flesh in her Imperial gowns.

⁂

LETO RETURNED TO the front of the fortress vault to report, feeling as confused and unsettled as Jaxson Aru. "Rajiv Londine is nowhere to be found. The search was thorough." Two of his guards stood next to him, tense, their hands on flechette pistols.

"But how could he hide? Did he escape?" Jaxson demanded. "Has he betrayed me?"

Leto refused to speculate. He glanced from one guard to the other. Jaxson was preoccupied and agitated, but Leto could not overpower both of the guards and take the memory stone in time. He kept his voice even. "We searched the entire vault, but you have only ten guards, and there are many nooks and crannies, data-storage containers stacked high, sealed cabinets. If Rajiv is deliberately trying to elude us, he could have slipped inside one of them."

The rebel leader breathed harder, as if the very idea had pushed him closer to the edge of madness.

External alarms suddenly rolled out with menacing, throbbing sounds. Jaxson rushed to the wall screen, where he saw that someone had operated the hidden egress hatch. "The Sardaukar must be trying to enter through the passageways! Send everyone to hold the vulnerable point." He narrowed his eyes. "We'll massacre them as they try to push their way in!"

On the imaging screen, Leto saw a blip that showed movement—someone rushing through the narrow access passageway, fleeing *toward* the Imperial forces.

❧

BEFORE THE FACE Dancer could finish and take care of the loose ends, Frankos Aru surprised him by running back. "Come, you need to go with me. If we're all together, I—" His mouth dropped open, and he sucked in a wheezing gasp.

Seeing the Face Dancer crouched over the woman's body, the blade protruding from the back of her skull, Frankos shrieked, "Empress!" He bolted away like a startled pigeon down the narrow passage.

The Face Dancer looked up from his crouch, shifted his reaction. Opening the hidden exit would draw attention both from the trapped rebels and from the Sardaukar outside the vault. He had only seconds. The sensors had already been activated.

He dragged the Empress's body back into the shadows of the data containers and began to assume her identity.

A true leader must possess the communication skills to convey his positions and inspire his people. Such skills can also be used as effective weapons against enemies.

—DUKE PAULUS ATREIDES, journal entry, shortly before his death

As the Sardaukar punitive force came down to Caladan, warship after ominous warship bristling with weaponry, Paul remembered receiving word about Emperor Shaddam's massacre against Dross only a few months ago. He'd been sitting at his father's desk, reviewing reports, when he learned that the Sardaukar had wiped out Duke Verdun's holdings because the nobleman was suspected of having rebel sympathies. Duke Verdun's daughter, Junu, had been suggested as a marriage candidate for Paul, though he'd never met her. Now the girl was dead along with all of them—slaughtered by a Sardaukar force much like this one.

And Paul had to face the massive assault without Leto, and without his mother. Yet he was not alone.

His father, the Duke of Caladan, had only "joined" the Noble Commonwealth to topple the rebellion from within, although to an outside observer, Leto Atreides would have appeared to be a fanatic just like the others. His message to Kaitain had not been delivered, thanks to the Harkonnens.

Emperor Shaddam does not know the truth.

Standing beside him on the high rampart, Thufir Hawat reached a similar conclusion in a flash of Mentat thought and began shouting orders. "Activate House shields! We must protect Castle Caladan."

Shading his eyes, Paul stared at the military ships descending toward the ancient Atreides castle, the spaceport, Cala City.

Gurney Halleck drew his sword, wincing as he wrapped his bandaged hands around the hilt. "We'll be overrun, my Lord. House Atreides forces are strong, but they cannot withstand a Sardaukar invasion. Our locals are ready to defend their homes, but it will do no good."

Duncan Idaho bounded into the rooftop weapons room and emerged with a fresh blade in each hand. Paul said, "Even you could not have come up with this training scenario for me, Duncan."

"Trial by combat—the best kind, and the worst. We'll keep you safe, Paul."

"It's not a matter of keeping *me* safe." Feeling like a captain obligated to go down with his ship, Paul scanned the coastline, the shoreline city, and the docks. Bells rang in the streets. "What about all my people? We have shields around the castle, but not the town. Not the fishing fleet or the docks. Who am I to hide here behind a barrier, if the rest of Caladan is in flames?"

Thufir's voice was cold and implacable. "You are the ducal heir, my Lord." The answer seemed sufficient to this loyal fighter.

They rushed from the battlements and returned to the main level of the castle, where they entered the Atreides battle-command center. The warrior Mentat could monitor all the communications from Atreides forces stationed within the castle as well as out at the spaceport and in the town. Dr. Yueh joined them, deeply troubled; his fingertip touched the diamond tattoo on his forehead.

A flurry of reports came in from security personnel and spaceport administrators, overlapping messages of alarm and cries for help. The Sardaukar force had requested no landing clearances, filed no flight paths, and the local air traffic scurried to get out of the way like a flock of startled birds.

Gurney rallied the household guard, passing out arms and sending them to strategic positions by the barricaded gates, while others stood watch on the ramparts. The heavy pentashields turned the air a blurry amber color, but Paul could still see hundreds of attack vessels bristling with weapons and marked with Corrino insignia.

"Not even the courtesy to announce themselves or issue an ultimatum," Duncan said. "I'd like to teach them some manners." He held his swords impatiently.

"I believe they intend to teach *us* a lesson, Duncan," Paul said, running through alternatives. "They believe that my father is a low-life traitor who colluded with Jaxson Aru's terrorists." His heart sank, but he intended to face the danger head-on. There would be no running from this fight, and even if he had the opportunity to escape, Paul would not do it. Nor would Duke Leto have done so. "We just have to convince them otherwise."

He looked at the other men in the chamber, confident in their advice and abilities, but still, he wished his parents were here—not so he could hand off the responsibility, but so they could develop a solution together.

"Shaddam wants to send a message written in smoke and blood," Gurney said. "We will hold them off as long as we can, and fight to the last man."

Thufir presented his Mentat assessment. "The Sardaukar will want us to watch them level the spaceport and the town. From here behind our shields we will be helpless as we see the smoke of all the fires."

"This is a punitive strike, and we must convince them they're wrong," Paul said. "Explain what my father is actually doing. We were going to send a message to the Emperor, but now we must make our argument here, as a defensive battle plan." He grasped at the slenderest thread of hope, remembering what he had been about to do just before the Sardaukar invasion began. "I'll get my father's farewell recording, his last testament to me. He must have talked about his real plans, revealed his true purpose! We can show it to the Sardaukar commander."

"Will such a message be sufficient to stop an angry military force?" Yueh sounded uncertain. "They have Imperial orders."

But Paul clung to the possibility. "If we can get our information to the commander, maybe he will reconsider, or at least delay." The young heir was already heading out of the room, remembering where he kept the recording hidden in a bureau drawer among other clutter.

"I wish we had a more definitive message," Thufir said. "A clear document of explanation, with evidence."

"The Harkonnens have it," Gurney grumbled, touching the inflamed scar on his arm where the message crystal had been embedded.

Yueh remained silent, as if weighed down by more than fear for his own life. Paul glanced at the Suk doctor, tried to read his expression, but had no time for that. He had to retrieve the personal message his father had left for him.

As Paul rushed out of the war room, he shouted over his shoulder, "Contact the landing force and get a message to the Sardaukar commander! Tell him Paul Atreides, acting as Duke of Caladan, wishes to speak with him, face-to-face."

Outside, though muffled through the thrumming shields, he heard the first explosions along with the faint clamor of fighting and screams from the village. He ran to his room.

Paul's quarters were quiet and cool because he had left the windows open to the fresh breezes, though now he smelled the distinctive ozone of the powerful shields that blurred the air. He raced to his antique wooden bureau, which was topped with boyhood keepsakes—lumps of coral, polished stones from the shingle beach, shells that he had gathered in the tide pools beneath the castle cliff. He yanked open the top drawer and rummaged among commemorative solari coins, a little glass carving of a whale, a piece of green ribbon his mother had given him.

He had kept his father's message there, recorded on a shigawire spool.

Duke Leto had pressed it into his son's palm, telling him to listen to it if anything should go wrong. "It explains my mission," Leto had said.

Paul moved the papers aside, the keepsakes and colorful paraphernalia that he had once considered treasures, though he rarely looked at them.

His heart sank. The message spool was gone!

He ransacked the drawer, then looked in his other drawers, but he clearly remembered placing the shigawire spool *there*. An icy streak ran through him as he looked everywhere in his room, then went back to the top drawer. Maybe someone had moved it? He could not imagine who would do that.

His father's message was not here! The record that would show the Sardaukar commander what the Duke of Caladan truly intended. It had been Paul's only hope, and worse, a last remnant of his father.

THE ORDERS CAME directly from the Emperor, and Colonel Bashar Jopati Kolona would follow them without question. He realized, however, that as commander, he was always granted his own interpretation, so long as he completed the mission.

He had devastated Cuarte as ordered, and House Verdun's world of Dross a couple of months before that. He knew that other Sardaukar forces had struck Elegy, home of House Tull, though they had been wiped out by a pseudo-atomic explosion. That debacle had impressed a heightened level of wariness upon further Sardaukar strike forces.

After leaving Cuarte, Kolona had carried out his orders on two other planets, destroying House Mumford and House Vok, both rebel sympathizers. Caladan was his last assigned target, but this particular planet gave him great pause. Jopati Kolona had both a blood feud and an honor obligation with House Atreides.

Old Duke Paulus Atreides had schemed with—or been coerced by—Emperor Elrood IX to wipe out House Kolona and take over the world of Boorhees. That disaster had thrown young Jopati Kolona and his brothers into captivity, then onto harsh Salusa Secundus, where they were tormented, tested, and indoctrinated into the Sardaukar way. Only Jopati had survived.

A disaster because of the Atreides.

Later, though, a young idealistic Duke Leto had done everything possible to rectify the situation, surrendering Kolona holdings, finding long-lost heirs to rebuild the noble family. Witnessing those actions, Jopati Kolona had glimpsed the heart of the Duke, and now he found it difficult to fathom that the same man would join the animals who had brought bloodshed and fire upon the Imperial Museum on Otorio or crashed the treasury ship into the palace. No, that did not sound like Duke Leto Atreides at all.

But Colonel Bashar Jopati Kolona had his orders, his own Sardaukar code of honor, and Shaddam's vengeance was not an insignificant thing.

Kolona's fleet washed over the small Cala City Spaceport like an ocean storm. More than a hundred troop carriers set down on the landing fields and even in public plazas of the quaint capital town. Uniformed Sardaukar emerged from the carriers, wearing body shields and carrying weapons, prepared to carry out a massacre—just like on Cuarte. It dismayed Kolona to see how many of his comrades were grinning.

His fighters swarmed into the spaceport control tower and the terminal facilities, taking hostages, replacing the controllers in the operations center. He received reports that soldiers in the town had already slaughtered a hundred civilians who foolishly tried to defend their homes. The people of Caladan seemed recklessly patriotic, not intimidated by Sardaukar! His heart was heavy because he knew the Emperor wanted him to lay waste to all this, just as he had done on those other planets.

Now, from the base ship at the landing field, Kolona looked up at the impressive and imposing castle on the headlands that overlooked the sea. It was blurred, and shimmered, distorted from view.

One of his subcommanders delivered a brisk report. "Castle Caladan is protected behind heavy pentashields. We won't easily breach them." The man's brow furrowed. "I suspect, though, that if we burn the city down and destroy the spaceport, Duke Leto Atreides may come out to face us."

"You are probably right," Kolona said, still uneasy, "but we don't even know if he is there. He may be off with the rebels."

"Leaving his people vulnerable and without a leader?" the subcommander asked, doubtful.

To his surprise, a comm officer ran up with another message. "We have a transmission, sir—from the castle."

Curious, Kolona played the message. An earnest-looking teenager announced himself as Paul Atreides, the son of Duke Leto, demanding to speak with the Sardaukar leader. The colonel bashar listened, gauged the sincerity of the boy, and then reached a decision. This was the excuse he needed. "Call off further destruction for the time being. Have our soldiers stand down until I give further orders."

His subcommander was taken aback. "We have never done that before, sir. We have been informed of the specified outcome of this mission."

Kolona turned to glower at him. "Question my orders at your own peril."

"Yes, Colonel Bashar."

He looked again at the shimmering high castle and tried to imagine what was happening inside. "Prepare an envoy ship. I will go there myself."

⤬

YUEH SAW HIS opportunity, and felt damned by it.

While Castle Caladan went into full defensive lockdown, he retreated to his offices, the small infirmary and adjacent laboratory chamber. Now, though, he huddled with his obligations, the crushing threat that Baron Vladimir Harkonnen hung over his head.

Earlier, fearing it would come to this, he'd slipped into Paul's quarters and taken the final message Duke Leto left for his son. Although Gurney Halleck, Thufir Hawat, Master Paul, and even Yueh himself could attest to what Leto intended to do, their words would not be seen as proof, merely some story concocted in the face of certain defeat. Yueh knew that these Sardaukar operated under the assumption the Duke was a traitor. Therefore, his family, his holdings, his people were forfeit.

This was exactly the scenario the Baron had hoped for, an opportunity for Yueh. The Suk doctor was to ensure the downfall of House Atreides. Right now, he could do that simply by hiding the last message Leto had left for Paul, as well as the far more important speech he had recorded with Yueh during his brief stop here. All the doctor had to do was keep them hidden. No one else knew about Leto's last recording. By staying silent, he would achieve what the Baron demanded.

If the Harkonnens were true to their word—which was by no means certain—then at least he would save Wanna, dear Wanna . . .

But Yueh himself would be dead, and while he was not so craven as to place his own life above all other things, he also knew his inaction would cost House Atreides everything, along with Paul and the rest of Caladan.

Wanna . . .

He held the two vital recordings and closed his eyes, trying to block out the outside world.

Every great dream reaches its conclusion, sometimes in resounding success, sometimes in crushing disaster. Ultimately, it does not matter because history will forget all of it.

—Annals of Leto II, God Emperor

After so many hours of helplessness, Shaddam reacted to the alarms and sensors with a surge of hope. The emergency exit had been breached from within. "There's movement! Is Aricatha coming out?"

The Sardaukar were already breaking through the perimeter tunnels and flooding into the narrow access passage. In moments, they had seized one fleeing prisoner and dragged him back out. The man was tall and lanky, normally professional, but now President Frankos Aru looked fearful, sweaty.

Malina Aru rushed toward her son. Her expression showed surprised disbelief. "You're safe!"

Frankos looked at his mother as if he didn't recognize her, and he swung toward Shaddam in shock and horror. "No one is safe! Empress Aricatha—" He struggled to find words.

Shaddam grabbed the CHOAM President by the front of his tunic. "What about Aricatha? Where is she?"

"Dead," Frankos moaned. "One of Jaxson's guards murdered her—a dagger in the back of her neck. Empress Aricatha is dead!"

Shaddam felt his legs go weak. After all the decisions he had made as Padishah Emperor, after the populations he had doomed and the punishments he had inflicted, this felt like a mortal blow to him. "Aricatha . . . dead?"

Malina pulled her son away. "Are you certain, Frankos?"

"I saw it. Aricatha has been murdered!"

Shaddam turned to his Sardaukar commanders as vengeful fires boiled up inside of him. "Then so is Jaxson Aru and this entire damned place. Nothing will stop me now."

THE FANATIC REBEL guards rallied from the high mezzanines and ran through the maze of stacked records containers to converge at the hidden emergency exit. By the time Leto and Jaxson joined them, they found a rumpled and agitated Empress Aricatha. Her fine gown was disheveled. The clips that had maintained her coiffure were scattered on the floor, and her loose hair hung down over her neck.

As the guards held her, Jaxson shouted in her face, "How did you break free? Who escaped?"

Aricatha straightened to look at him. "Your brother is gone. Lord Londine wore the uniform of one of your guards, and he said he was going to get us out." She yanked her arm from the guard. "Obviously, I didn't manage to get away."

Leto moved to intercede, fearing that Jaxson would just kill her right there, but both men were just as confused by what had happened. The rebel leader glared at her, looked at Leto, then turned away in disgust. "Now Frankos and Londine will tell them about our situation here. We don't have much time."

"We never did," Leto said. "We could have negotiated a deal with Aricatha here." He ran a thumb along his smooth ring, thinking he understood why she had stayed behind. He glanced at her, but she didn't meet his gaze.

Jaxson strode away, his shoulders slumped as he wound his way back toward the giant plasteel doors that stood at the front of the fortress vault. "I'm out of options. There is only one more thing I can do."

Leto jogged after him, and the guards brought Aricatha as well. She said, "There is always something else you can do, if you are brave enough to see it."

Jaxson stood by the towering doors, a man alone. An army powerful enough to destroy the entire world waited on the other side, as well as an infuriated Padishah Emperor. He spoke coldly. "Leto, my loyal friend, take the Empress out of sight. Hold her until I call for you both." He snapped at his guards. "Monitor the emergency egress point and make sure that we aren't breached from the perimeter." He was panting hard. "I will stay here, for what must be done."

The guards sprinted off, and Leto pulled Aricatha back from the front vault doors, but he could think of no place where she would be safe. He didn't dare leave the rebel leader alone.

He thinks I am his loyal friend. Leto worked that through his plans. "Jaxson, you have the Empress, you have the black archives. Use them as tools— accomplish something, build something that you want! Don't just destroy because there's no turning back."

"We passed that point a long time ago." Jaxson faced the comm screen, as if gathering his courage before he activated it. He withdrew the memory stone from his pocket and held it in his palm as if it were a pet scorpion.

"Now might be our last chance," Leto whispered to her, and she glanced at him with a strange light in her eyes.

Leto had to overpower the man, use the burst ring, which would destroy the dangerous device. He had to act now.

Before he could move, Shaddam's image appeared on the wall screen, a storm of terrible power. "You will be destroyed for what you have done, Jaxson Aru! I will grind the world around you into atoms. I wanted you to know that before you die."

Jaxson could not speak a word before the comm screen went blank. A horrendous pounding began on the doors as if starships were crashing against the thick barriers.

Leto watched Jaxson stare in confusion. He blinked, then looked down at the memory stone in his hand. He raised it up, and something inside of him changed.

The two guards standing near Jaxson tensed. Both wore fatalistic expressions.

No matter what happened, Leto had to stop the rebel leader, even if the guards were likely to kill him. He pulled away from Aricatha, building up speed. "Please tell Shaddam I was never a traitor."

He bolted forward, head down, and the ominous pounding masked Leto's rushing footsteps. He opened his hand, making sure the white gold ring was clear. Another external explosion distracted the guards, but Leto knew they could turn their flechette weapons at him in an instant. He just needed to reach the rebel leader, touch the memory stone.

He thought of Paul, knew this was a lesson the boy would learn. The next Duke. . . .

One of the guards saw him, and his expression crumpled into rage. He raised the weapon—but Aricatha moved with a speed Leto could not process. She struck the guard, grabbed his arm, wrenched it so hard that it made a ripping snap as the forearm dislocated from the elbow, and the needle pistol dropped to the floor.

Staring at the vault door, Jaxson turned at the last moment. His mouth opened in surprise—just as Leto collided with him like a battering ram. Jaxson coughed out, unable to speak.

Leto seized his hand, slapped his own palm down, struck the black memory stone. He felt a sizzling pop in his fingers, like a swirl of electricity, and the smooth object heated in a flash.

Leto tackled Jaxson to the floor, and the memory stone clattered away, bouncing across the hard surface of the vault. It glowed with a spiderweb of hot red lines.

Astonished, the rebel leader threw himself at Leto, tearing at his face. Leto punched him hard in the stomach, knocked the wind out of him. Jaxson retched.

The Duke was used to blade fighting. Thufir, Duncan, and Gurney had trained him to duel using speed and finesse, but this was just a brawl. Jaxson pounded him, scratched at his eyes. Leto struck him hard in the chin, while Jaxson tried to break free and grab the memory stone. Even he looked astonished and terrified.

Aricatha threw herself on the second guard as if she were a wolf taking down prey. Leto wondered how she had learned to fight like that.

Jaxson kicked him away and got to his knees. He whipped out a glistening dagger and slashed, but Leto danced back, conscious of every second, then dove for the memory stone on the floor.

The rebel leader came after him, but Leto rolled on his back, brought his legs up, and kicked Jaxson in the abdomen. His dagger clattered to the floor, and he crumpled, stunned.

Aricatha had somehow subdued the second guard, snatched his flechette pistol and his knife. With a quick burst of deadly needles, she killed the guard and his companion.

Leto scrambled for the memory stone, saw that its obsidian star-studded surface glowed orange. Had it been disrupted by the burst from the ring, or was it activating to transmit? In a desperate move, he stomped on the device with his heel, then again, seeing crazed patterns appear on its smooth surface. The black stone continued to glow with internal workings.

"Use this!" Aricatha said, and tossed him the guard's heavy knife. He caught the weapon, turned it around, and smashed with the thick butt of the hilt again and again like a hammer.

Jaxson wheezed in despair.

Finally, the memory stone cracked, then shattered into fragments. Leto struck with the knife hilt three more times until the pieces themselves broke into smaller fragments.

At long last, wrung out and shaking, he slumped back, not caring what happened to him now. Two of Jaxson's fanatic guards were dead, but others were coming. Aricatha stood over them with her flechette pistol. The sounds of the Sardaukar battering at the vault door hinted at the incredible machinery they were using to breach the barricade, but so far the CHOAM defenses held.

The Empress came over to stand at his side. "You stopped it, Leto. You saved me—you saved all of us."

Still coughing and groaning, Jaxson picked himself up, sucking hard to fill his lungs. He gave Leto a look of agonized disappointment, saw the ruined memory stone with horror, and he staggered deeper into the vault.

Leto felt drained, without the energy to pursue Jaxson and fight him further. It was time to turn him over to Imperial justice—as he had intended to do all along. He had done what was necessary, expecting to be cut down by a rain of deadly needles, and now he knew his next step.

He and Aricatha had to act before the rest of Jaxson's fanatical house guards arrived. "Stand with me, Empress." He heard people shouting from behind him in the vault, rebel guards rushing to stop him at all costs.

"We are all dead if we don't get out of here soon," Aricatha said, struggling with the comm controls, but the screen on the wall remained blank. "This is our only means of communication with the outside, but Shaddam has severed contact. Something triggered him into reckless violence."

The booming, explosive percussions continued, and the Sardaukar were surely close to ripping open the vault. Why would Shaddam so coldly endanger his beloved Empress? Given his apparent outrage, he might even unleash atomics just to level the vault, and Leto doubted the Ur-Director could stop him.

"We have to prevent him from making a further mistake." Leto ran to the main controls for the gigantic vault door, trying to find a way to bypass them. But Jaxson had locked them in, and the Duke didn't have the necessary CHOAM access. "I'm not familiar with these controls." He tried to find an emergency release so he could swing open the enormous barricade and let the Sardaukar in.

Aricatha stepped next to him. "Let me try this." She placed her hand on a reader, paused as she went into deep concentration. To Leto's surprise, the identity routine thrummed, and recognized her. "I am the Empress after all," she explained with an odd quirk of a smile. "Once I married Shaddam, my access should have permeated through the high-security levels in the Imperium, for emergency situations—such as this. I hoped that CHOAM would follow the same protocols."

The idea seemed unlikely to Leto, yet he could see the lights activating on the panel. The massive doors vibrated as the inner machinery broke the seal. Outside, the imposing blows stopped as the titanic vault began to open.

Leto heard shouts—from behind them. Two of Jaxson's guards saw what he and the Empress had done, but they could not prevent the breach now. The heavy doors swung wider.

Standing beside Aricatha, Leto noticed a stain on the back of her dress. Was that blood?

As the Imperial soldiers stormed into the vault, he quickly placed himself in front of the Empress, afraid the Sardaukar would simply blast indiscriminately at anyone inside the chamber.

An avalanche of uniforms and weapons surged in, and Leto raised his hands in surrender. He barely had time to breathe. The battle cries were deafening, and the drawn blades looked like a forest of knives. He remained frozen, nonthreatening, protecting Aricatha.

"It's the Empress!" a soldier yelled. "Empress Aricatha! *She's alive!* Tell the Emperor. Seize Duke Leto Atreides."

Leto expected to be slaughtered outright, but Aricatha spoke up, somehow managing to be heard over the din. "The Duke of Caladan is under my protection! Any person who harms him will face my husband's wrath!"

The Sardaukar's rough handling became only slightly gentler as they took him and Aricatha out of the vault.

❧

AFTER BEING ARRESTED, Leto was brought before the Padishah Emperor Shaddam IV, bruised and battered, but Aricatha never left his side. "He saved me, my love," she insisted. "Leto is not one of their rowdy band; he merely played along. I told you we could negotiate with him."

"Yet he was in there with the terrorist leader, who remains at large." Shaddam trembled with emotion, but not all of it was anger. He seemed astounded to see Aricatha. "Frankos Aru said that you were murdered! He saw it with his own eyes."

Aricatha blinked, then laughed. "I assure you, I am not even a little bit murdered. Can't you see?" She spread her hands, then changed the subject. "Did you capture Lord Londine?"

Now the Emperor glared at his Sardaukar captains who shook their heads. "Only Frankos Aru emerged."

"Londine must have found another way out, then," Aricatha said, unconcerned. "There were other emergency side passages in the vault walls." She sniffed. "Londine seems to have a way of slipping away from your Sardaukar."

Ur-Director Malina Aru strode up, looking at Leto. A flush rose to her cheeks. "I understand that you helped get Frankos released, and for that, I am deeply grateful." She shook her head. "I debriefed him myself. The accounts are confusing and contradictory."

"The fog of war," Leto said. "I doubt we'll ever know the clear and final answers."

The Urdir regarded him with an enigmatic glance. "Jaxson has lost his memory stone, but he is still in there. He will not be easily pried out, although I will offer whatever assistance I can."

"He has nowhere to go, nowhere to hide," Shaddam said. "Do not expect me to show him any mercy."

Malina gave the Emperor a withering look, and Leto could tell the relationship between the two had deteriorated. "By now, I'm sure Jaxson has taken refuge in the core bunker, the most secure chamber on Tanegaard. You may try to break inside, Majesty, but I doubt you will succeed."

She turned and left, striding into the fortress vault.

DEEP WITHIN THE impenetrable core bunker, Jaxson Aru huddled, a small, lonely figure in the heart of the great CHOAM citadel. When he retreated for this last stand, his bodyguards had fallen back with him, but they remained outside. They would guard him to the end, though they would surely fail. Jaxson knew what the Sardaukar could do.

Duke Leto had smashed the memory stone, destroying Jaxson's greatest bargaining chip, but the black archives weren't all lost. He had kept some in reserve, and Shaddam Corrino did not know what Jaxson was capable of.

This cube-shaped bunker was layered with thick plasteel and lead shielding. Not a single crack. No dust speck, not even a photon could enter or escape. He could only hope now. Feeling very much alone, Jaxson touched the earring, comforted by its smooth curve.

Leto, his trusted ally, had truly betrayed him in the end. Perhaps the Duke of Caladan had been a spy all along, but Jaxson had refused to see it. Now it might be too late, all too late.

Was everything lost?

A person's greatest weapon is not sword or shield, but is instead reputation, the life he has led, the good deeds he has performed. If those things cannot protect him, then he has already lost the battle.

—DUKE LETO ATREIDES, letters to his son

Caladan's skies were clear and mockingly blue, but from Paul's vantage on the curtain wall above the castle's great gates, he could see the smoke in Cala City—though admittedly less than he had expected. Shrieking gulls swirled above as if annoyed that galactic politics disturbed their daily routine.

Feeling dismal, even from this distance Paul could see that the spaceport had been overrun. A small Corrino escort flyer lifted from the besieging fleet and headed toward the castle.

Next to him on the wall, Thufir Hawat shaded his eyes. "Your message was received, my Lord. Frankly, I am surprised they are responding by sending an envoy."

Paul felt a surge of hope.

"I'll be more surprised if he listens," Gurney said, holding his blade at his side. The bruises on his face made him look fierce.

As the armored Sardaukar ship crossed the headlands from the spaceport, Paul heard distant small *pops*, saw glimpses of people hidden in the underbrush and then a rain of tiny projectiles. Villagers using hunting weapons. They were firing upon the envoy ship from the ground!

"What are they doing? They're fools," Paul said.

"They are trying to protect their Duke," Duncan said, pressing his lips together in a grim smile. "Well intentioned, but yes, a hopeless effort."

The envoy ship paused and hovered over the hunters, who scrambled for cover in the underbrush. As the Imperial vessel descended on suspensor engines and then landed, a side door opened, and four armed Sardaukar boiled out, dropping to the ground. They sprinted forward, and in a flash, they had butchered the Caladan hunters who had the audacity to fire upon them. Paul felt sick anguish for everyone who died.

"This is bad news indeed, my Lord," Thufir said.

"Not how I wanted to begin our negotiations." Hiding behind a strong pentashield while the rest of his world remained vulnerable did not sit well with him. He knew what his father would do, and what he had to do now. "Thufir, drop the house shields and open our doors for this envoy."

Gurney and Duncan both shouted in dismay. The old Mentat turned to him. "I strongly advise against doing that, my Lord."

"I hear your advice, and I make up my own mind," Paul said. "If they turn their full force against us, the shields might hold for some days or even weeks, but it only buys us time . . . and pain. The Emperor's forces will not go away." He drew a breath, straightened. "No, I prefer this gambit. If we are going to lose, we may as well lose it all."

Thufir hesitated, then bowed in acknowledgment and hurried off.

Paul glanced at his other two companions. "We'll have a few minutes. Clean yourselves up. Let's make an impressive appearance."

Even if he had no solid proof of what he was going to tell them.

Before long, the shimmer in the air faded and the background hum of the shield system drifted into silence, leaving Castle Caladan exposed to the legion of vengeful Sardaukar. By now, the four Imperial commandos had returned to the envoy ship, leaving the hapless dead hunters in the underbrush. The small craft resumed its approach to Castle Caladan as if nothing had happened.

Like a man braced for his own execution, Paul went down to the main courtyard and stood at the gates to meet the Sardaukar commander. Once again, he felt that sense of terrible purpose, and it changed something inside. At this very moment, facing a mysterious and inexorable future, he had a strange sense of security. He felt that he had important things to accomplish, and this was not his moment to die.

The Sardaukar envoy ship landed in the receiving ground in front of Castle Caladan. Paul stood at the gates, staring straight ahead as a military officer disembarked. Wearing the rank insignia of a colonel bashar, he stalked forward with four other Sardaukar behind him. Some had blood on their uniforms.

The officer spoke in a gruff voice. "I am Colonel Bashar Jopati Kolona. You called me here, I presume to deliver your unconditional surrender. The situation is hopeless for you and for Caladan." His brow furrowed, and he added, "Your civilians fired upon us."

"They were protecting their world from outside invaders," Paul countered. "Your Sardaukar landed on Caladan without permission and attacked—a surprise attack. I would say they had just cause to defend their homes, and they did their best to try to protect us." He calmed his voice. "But they acted without orders, and for that, they paid with their lives."

Kolona worked his jaw, then gave a small nod. He ran his gaze up and down the young man's slight form. "You are the son of Duke Leto Atreides?"

"Yes, and with the aid of my advisers, I speak for the Duke of Caladan in my father's absence."

The Sardaukar officer's face darkened. "And we know Leto Atreides has joined the radical movement and has been seen in the company of the rebel leader, Jaxson Aru. He participated in an unsanctioned rescue operation on Issimo III, thereby embarrassing the Padishah Emperor. His involvement has been documented, and Emperor Shaddam IV commands that all of the traitors must face annihilation to stand as a lesson for anyone else who would do harm to the Imperium."

Paul's expression was brave rather than distraught. "But my father is not one of the rebels, so your orders do not apply here." He felt confident, and could see that the words took Kolona by surprise.

"We have incontrovertible evidence."

"No, you have assumptions, and so-called evidence can be misinterpreted. The Sardaukar have been hunting for the core rebels for some time, without success. My father infiltrated the movement with a plan to bring it down. He weakened the underpinnings of the Noble Commonwealth, exposed some of their members. He remained in such a dangerous position for the purpose of bringing Jaxson Aru to justice, a man you could not catch."

With calm detail, using the methods of persuasion his mother had taught him, he explained about the communiqué Gurney had carried, how he was intercepted by the Harkonnens, who had intentionally prevented Emperor Shaddam from learning of the vital plan.

Gurney stood beside him as he recounted this, looking angry. He held up his scarred arm.

"An interesting story," Kolona said. "But it shows your imagination rather than proof."

"Is Atreides honor not proof enough?" Paul asked. "The entire Landsraad knows about Duke Leto Atreides. They call him Leto the Just. Which version of the story do you believe, now that I have told you the facts?"

Kolona looked deeply disturbed. "Words are insufficient."

Paul felt cold, not knowing what else he could do. The recording was gone, and even so, he couldn't be sure it would be convincing enough to countermand Imperial orders. "True words should be enough. Bring a Truthsayer—I will face her and tell what I know. All of these men will say the same." He gestured to Thufir, Duncan, and Gurney stirring behind him, all ready to give their lives for Paul in case the Sardaukar attacked.

"We Sardaukar have no Truthsayers among us," said the colonel bashar.

"We can wait," Paul said. "Truth is a matter of vital importance."

Then from behind them, scurrying out the castle gate, came Dr. Wellington Yueh. "I have proof! I have the words of the Duke himself." He held a tight shigawire spool between his fingers. "This is a message Duke Leto recorded for his son before leaving. It is his last testament. You will agree that the Duke would not lie in what he thought was his last message to his son."

Yueh had also brought a player, which he activated to display Leto's somber message, a private recording that he had thought would be seen only by Paul. The young man's heart broke as he looked at his father's face and listened to his sincere explanations, his hopes and dreams for his son, and his sadness about the loss of Lady Jessica.

"Where did you find it?" Paul asked.

"It was misplaced with good intentions, for safekeeping." Yueh didn't explain further, though Thufir looked on him with suspicion.

After listening, Paul said, "You may have your soldiers, Colonel Bashar, but this recording is my shield. It tells the true mission Duke Leto is on."

Kolona remained deep in thought. "It is cause for consideration, though I doubt Emperor Shaddam will be convinced. His anger is . . . significant."

"There is more," Yueh interrupted, "and I believe this will put an end to it." He held a second shigawire spool. "Duke Leto returned briefly to Caladan before he went off for his final gambit with Jaxson Aru. By then, we had evidence that Gurney Halleck had been intercepted, that the Emperor might not have received the Duke's communiqué of explanation. And so he recorded this additional message, which I was to keep secret except under the direst circumstances. I was to offer it as his full legal deposition."

Paul spun to him in surprise. "I did not know of this!"

"I . . . I could not use it until now." Yueh looked ashamed. "I sincerely hope this will make up for my hesitation."

Forestalling other questions, he played the Duke's full video recording, and with each part of the explanation, Paul watched the officer's stony expression falter. Details fell into place, each declaration made sense, and when the second recording ended, Paul felt warm tears streaming down his face.

Duncan burst out, "Given this evidence, you must reconsider, Colonel Bashar! Knowing what you know, you cannot let your Sardaukar obliterate Cala City."

"At least interrogate the damned Harkonnens!" Gurney said.

Thufir Hawat said in a firm voice, "Colonel Bashar, an attack here would go against the Sardaukar code."

Duncan stood holding both of his swords as if ready to strike Kolona down at the slightest provocation.

Yueh looked greatly shaken, but Paul felt profound relief. "Thank you, Dr. Yueh. I'm glad you found the recordings. You provided the necessary details."

Finally, the colonel bashar nodded to himself. "Given this new information, my orders are subject to change. The Padishah Emperor commanded us to eradicate all rebels, and it is no longer certain that Leto Atreides is truly one of the rebels. Few Sardaukar officers would be receptive to such new information, but I . . . I have personal experience with your father. I know his sense of honor. His past actions do not match the Emperor's assumptions or accusations."

He straightened. "I must bring this new information back to Kaitain and seek further guidance from the Emperor. Of course, it will be checked for authenticity, but I suspect it will pass any tests." Then Kolona's expression grew dark and stormy. "And we must also speak to Baron Harkonnen." He spun on his heels and went back to his envoy craft, where he issued orders for the Sardaukar invasion force to stand down and to return to their dropships.

As the envoy craft rose on its suspensor engines, Paul felt weak. He swayed until he found a stone bench to sit on. Dr. Yueh rushed to his side to check him out, but the young man's reaction was merely surprise and relief.

Duncan and Gurney looked at Paul in admiration, while Thufir Hawat nodded to himself. The Mentat spoke to Paul. "Young Master, you took a risk in facing the Sardaukar down like that. I'm sorry I doubted your decision. The Duke will be quite proud of you."

Love and loyalty are powerful forces. It is a pity that we don't always recognize them for what they are.

—CHOAM UR-DIRECTOR MALINA ARU, "Letter to my *two* children"

The original builders of the CHOAM administrative citadel on Tanegaard had incorporated proven methods of defensive security, ranging from brute-force barricades to electronic shielding and detailed surveillance. The fortress vault itself should have been impregnable, and the core bunker was an ultimate sanctuary to be used only in extreme crisis.

But because the Company's inner workings operated as much on politics and hidden obligations as on profits, Urdir after Urdir had also ensured that there were back doors and escape hatches to allow them to conduct their bribery or blackmail, their machinations, their covert treacheries.

Malina knew all of those back doors.

The main fortress vault was filled with angry chaos as Sardaukar forces surged inside after the great doors were opened. They seized Leto Atreides, rescued Aricatha, freed the CHOAM hostages. Two of Jaxson's fanatical guards had already been killed—supposedly by the Empress herself—and the rest fought to the death in front of the sealed core bunker. They did not survive long.

But the core bunker would not be easily breached. It had been designed as a final shelter, an armored shell in which a person could survive the gravest military assault. The shielding was supposedly impenetrable, but that would be little consolation for the person huddled inside. Any refugee who resorted to such a desperate measure was probably doomed from the moment they entered the chamber.

Malina wished she could have taken care of her disruptive son in a cleaner, more private fashion, but Jaxson never did anything in the most convenient way—nor had his father. Both of them were maddening agents of chaos. Brondon had been an inept fool, and Jaxson was overtly malicious, defiant. How dare he use the black archives to threaten the entire Landsraad, the Imperium—and CHOAM!

Malina had to take care of him herself.

Sardaukar occupied the large vault, bringing powerful weapons and tools, battering rams, explosives, and lascutters. They worked relentlessly at the enigmatic black cube in the middle of the chamber. The air was filled with sparks and smoke, shouts and the noises of destruction. In the past hour, they had barely made a scratch, but Shaddam would never relent. They would continue without respite—and without CHOAM permission—until they tore open a hole and exposed Jaxson. Days or weeks from now.

The bodies of the slaughtered rebel guards had been dragged away, leaving smears of blood on the scuffed floor and giving the Sardaukar and the Imperial engineers more room to work. Her aide-de-camp Holton Tassé stood distraught, observing the operations and unable to make them stop.

Malina waited next to him at the sidelines, her brow deeply furrowed. He turned to her. "Ur-Director, you must command them to stop!"

"They need to finish." She didn't approve, but she knew it was the truth. "And it ends with Jaxson."

Jalma and Frankos came to join her, all three of them agitated. "Why does he have to do this?" Jalma said in a deprecating voice. "It only emphasizes his failure."

The CHOAM President felt bitter. "Our brother has an extraordinary talent for making a situation worse at every turn."

Jalma looked at their mother. "Is there no way you can contact him inside there, and convince him to surrender? Surely he knows this is over."

"Jaxson knows," Malina said, "and he knew it some time ago. He actually attempted to trigger his cache of disastrous data, which would have ruined us all." Her voice was hoarse with disbelief. "Fortunately, Leto Atreides prevented that. He destroyed the memory stone, and Jaxson's last bargaining chip." She looked at her son and daughter . . . her only children, as far as she was concerned. "Stay here and remain visible, both of you. Let the Emperor and his Sardaukar see you, but tell them I prefer to be alone with my thoughts in this time of grieving."

Holton Tassé looked to her for further instructions, but she offered him none.

Frankos gave a solemn nod, though his shadowed eyes were filled with questions. "Yes, Mother."

Jalma asked in a low voice, "What are you actually going to do?"

As Malina left the vault, she called over her shoulder, "As I said, it all ends with Jaxson."

She retreated to the Ur-Director's primary offices in the upper levels of the Tanegaard fortress, her own sanctuary. The aide-de-camp tried to follow, but she dismissed him. Inside the room, she opaqued the windows and locked the doors, then took a moment to calm herself, collect her thoughts. This was her last gambit.

She went to the back of the room, faced the blank wall, and found the access plate. The wall opened into a labyrinth of concealed passages, a secondary network inside the already intense security of the Tanegaard citadel.

When she entered the dark passage, a suite of sensors detected her movement, identified her, and consequently deactivated the deadly countermeasures. No one but the Ur-Director could move through these hidden ways without being annihilated. Glowplates illuminated the way ahead. By design, in an absolute emergency, the Urdir could move swiftly from the primary offices down into the final bunker. Even Jaxson didn't know about this back door.

The narrow passage ended in a small chamber, rounded at the ends like an upright coffin. She entered, arms at her sides, and the capsule dropped like a bullet down to a level beneath the fortress vault. The walls of the capsule and the chute were plasteel shielding mixed with a baffling foam that deadened any sound. Not even the best Sardaukar sensors could detect her movement throughout the building.

When her emergency capsule came to a rest one level beneath the bunker vault, she emerged, smoothing her business attire. From above, she could still hear the faint syncopation of the unending Sardaukar pummeling against the bunker.

She walked along the muffled passage, which took her to a narrow staircase leading up to the level above, where a smooth gray wall blocked her way. The staircase appeared to go nowhere, a secure barricade that blocked further movement. She had reached her destination.

She took a deep breath to calm herself, gathered her thoughts. Above and on the other side lay the sealed bunker.

Microscopic scanners were studying her. She touched her palm to the smooth plasteel surface, where detectors not only mapped her palm and fingerprints, but analyzed the chemistry of her perspiration and studied her DNA with technology that would have astonished even the best scientists on Ix or Tleilax.

When the system recognized her, a rectangle of hair-fine lines appeared in the metal barrier. Malina pushed against it, and the wall section turned on a central pivot to give her access. She stepped inside the core bunker. Because the mechanism was so smooth and silent, her desperate son did not at first hear her with the background uproar of Sardaukar trying to break in.

"You have truly ruined everything, Jaxson," she said.

He spun about like a panther ready to spring, then nearly collapsed with amazement and relief. "Mother, you came to save me!"

"I am here to speak with you."

His eyes were bloodshot. "But if you found a way in, you can lead me to sanctuary, hide me from my enemies. There must be thousands of secret places on Tanegaard. Or . . . or we can go to Tupile. I can stay there. Emperor Shaddam will never catch me."

"Oh, I intend to let him catch you because this needs to be over," Malina said. "You disrupted my carefully orchestrated resolution of the crisis. That was the only way to save our family reputation and CHOAM business, and keep moving forward with the goals of the Noble Commonwealth. But you thought only of yourself and your petty goals. Dramatic gestures instead of common sense! Now you have left me with just one option." She hardened her voice. "And I have had enough."

His expression darkened. "I did what I had to do, Mother."

She shook her head. "I was willing to risk a great deal, push the boundaries, undermine the corrupt Corrinos—but you went too far by stealing precious data from secure Company records. The black archives were never your plaything. You shifted this conflict from remaking the Imperium and created a situation where CHOAM would be destroyed. You made it *about me!*"

Jaxson looked cowed. "I would not have needed to use the black archives if you'd been by my side. We could have built a Noble Commonwealth together."

When she stepped closer to him, he seemed to shrink away. The sealed core bunker had efficient filtration and recirculation, but the air still smelled hot and close. The tang of Jaxson's perspiration was clear. The thundering against the bunker door suggested that the Sardaukar might break through, possibly sooner than she expected.

"You no longer have your insurance because Leto Atreides destroyed your memory stone. That option is no longer on the table."

Jaxson's anger and defiance had transformed into despair. He hung his head. "I thought Leto was my friend, and he turned against me. I offered him power and influence after he saw the true corruption in the Imperium. He claims to be a man of honor, but played politics like any other noble. He wasn't worthy to be one of us."

"One of us?" Malina placed her hands on her hips. "You are no longer one of *us*. You have no way out. No alternative. Let me end this."

Jaxson touched his earring, like a worry stone. "I have one more trick, Mother. I always do." He squeezed the earring, bending the pattern-etched iron until it began to glow with an internal source.

A cold shock swept through her. "What are you doing?"

"The memory stone wasn't the only copy of that data. The worst of the information is encoded here, more densely packed—a Richesian data coil with a transmitter. I compiled the most damning records about the Corrinos." He took his hand away and looked at his fingertips. "How many families they betrayed and destroyed, how much of the Landsraad they have already turned against one another."

The earring continued to glow and then faded back to dull metal. He let out a sigh of relief. "I just released it, the greatest treacheries, the business betrayals, the blackmail and corruption. I'd guess it affects about three-quarters of the Houses of the Landsraad. They will be outraged at House Corrino. They'll fall upon one another like wolves."

His smile seemed wistful and vicious at the same time. "It's too late, Mother. I've sent the transmission, and it cannot be recalled. The signal will be picked up by repeaters and sent on and on." He slumped back, knowing he had just used the final weapon in his arsenal. He removed the earring and tossed it with a faint clatter on the floor. "You cannot stop it. Someone will hear. I have many amplifiers on Tanegaard, and the signal is already out there."

Malina listened to him without moving. Any remaining spark of love for her son had just been extinguished. She forced a tight, intimidating smile. "Are you sure about that?"

He looked back at her like a petulant boy, crossed his arms over his chest. "You will never put the genie back in the bottle. There's nothing you can do."

"There's nothing I need to do. Remember where you are—inside the most heavily shielded bunker, which is itself within the fortress vault of Tanegaard. I already intensified all the scrambling fields, both above- and belowground. You are surrounded by meters of plasteel and lead, airtight, insulated, completely impenetrable—inside and out." Malina gave him a maddening shrug. "Your transmission went nowhere. It died inside here with no one to hear it. And you have no threats left."

Appalled, he looked at her, trying to find words to scream. Tears sparkled in his eyes, and one ran down his left cheek.

She continued, smug and withering, "Your last desperate act failed, just like everything else you've tried. I have come to a conclusion, son. We must be rid of you—it is our best and only option. You would continue to cause too much damage across the Imperium, kill too many people . . . and corrupt our cause."

"My cause is your cause!" he shouted.

She shook her head, lecturing him like a stern teacher. "The cause of the Noble Commonwealth was to reshape the Imperium into something better. Through careful and patient work over the past century, we already undermined Imperial power a great deal. There are cracks in the Landsraad, pervasive mistrust of the Corrinos. The Imperium will crumble sooner or later—but not in the way you intend. You would *break* it and leave only rubble. And that serves neither CHOAM's purposes, nor my own."

The pounding outside the vault grew louder. A huge boom in the thick plasteel indicated the Sardaukar were using even heavier explosives. The wall began to glow a deep red. She and Jaxson could both see that it would fail soon.

"Unless you do as I say, you are going to be captured, Jaxson, and Shaddam will make a grand spectacle of torturing and executing you." She added a little more warmth to her voice. "Poor boy, I know you think you'll be brave and can withstand it, but Imperial torturers are experts, and they enjoy their work. No matter how strong you think you may be, they will break you, make you whimper and grovel. You will plead and sob before a vast audience." She shook her head in dismay. "I could not bear to watch it."

Jaxson bent his legs and slumped to the floor, just sitting there like a broken doll. Showing a hint of mercy, she touched his shoulder, stroked his thick, curly hair. His features, due to the Tleilaxu facial cloning, still made her think of her dead husband. But Jaxson was not him; the resemblance was only superficial. "Consider this, my son. Wouldn't it be better . . . if you just took care of this yourself?"

"Too late for that, Mother."

She reached into a pocket of her business suit, withdrew a package wrapped in transparent polymer film. It crackled as she pulled it out. Inside were two dried curls of plants, brown and bent like a scorpion's stinger.

"These are barra ferns, the exceptionally potent variety. The toxic ailar. I think it's a fitting end." She pressed the packet into his sweaty hand.

When he looked up at her, his eyes were like a little boy's, and filled with pain. She recalled when he'd been young and eager, not yet fallen off the appropriate path. Salvageable. But not anymore.

"Wait, I can escape with you," he pleaded, his voice like a pitiful little child. "Take me! You can save me, Mother."

She stepped away. "I'm trying to save you in the only best I can. Find the courage to do what you have to do, the only path of honor you have left."

He stared at the packet as if hypnotized, and she slipped back to the hidden exit out to the corridors. Even if he followed her, the security systems would vaporize him. He wouldn't go farther than a few steps.

"Helping you escape would not be a wise business decision," she said.

He pulled out the two curled, dried ferns as the outer wall turned brighter red. Sparks began to shower inside as the Sardaukar cut through. She watched Jaxson hold the poisonous ailar in front of his face.

Malina pushed through the pivot plate and sealed the door behind her. She knew she would never see Jaxson again. She'd given birth to him, and nurtured him throughout his life—and that included this final act of kindness.

Now I only have two children, she thought.

Even if my brother is my enemy, he is still my brother. This complicates things.

—GLOSSU RABBAN, Count of Lankiveil

When he saw his uncle's anger over the rescue of Gurney Halleck and all the repercussions it might bring down on House Harkonnen, Rabban realized that simply retreating to a desert spice crew would not be long enough nor far enough away.

As the Baron raged about how Halleck's revelations could inflict irreparable damage, Rabban found pressing business back on Giedi Prime. He hurried away from Arrakis without notifying Carthag operations; necessary paperwork was misplaced, but it would be filed automatically days after his departure. He hoped his uncle would cool down by the time he returned to Arrakis.

Once he was safe on Giedi Prime, the burly man headed for Harko City. His half brother, Feyd, had been left in nominal charge, and he would be insulted if Rabban shouldered his way into the Harkonnen business there. Despite his youth, Feyd was dangerous, scheming, and focused on his own advancement. But Rabban could handle him; worst case, he could pummel some respect into his weaker brother.

He emerged from the transport craft and strode at the front of his escort troops. Traveling faster than fanfare, they passed among the towering blocky buildings. Rabban gazed up at the steam chutes and smoky exhaust stacks, the darkened windows of one-way glass. He smelled the rich air and remembered how much he preferred this place to the desert planet.

He wore a deep blue military uniform and a cape trimmed in gold, attire that marked his noble status. At the main headquarters—home—he passed through towering doors with his head held high, his shoulders braced. One of his bodyguard troops bellowed out an announcement of his arrival. "All hail Glossu Rabban! The Count of Lankiveil!" He felt like a conquering general.

Feyd-Rautha glided out to meet them, but the young man was not impressed. He stood before his brother, wiry and whip-thin, his face twisted in a sneer. "Your demeanor smacks of arrogance to me, and more than a bit of ignorance. You come slinking here with your tail between your legs after being humiliated. I'm surprised our uncle didn't simply execute you on Arrakis."

Rabban swung his open hand without warning and cuffed Feyd on the side of the head. The young man reeled but did not fall. In a flash, he whipped out a long stiletto and held it in front of him. Feyd's voice was like splintered ice. "I will allow that one blow to welcome you home, but if you make another move, I'll slice you to ribbons and decorate my quarters with the pieces."

Rabban's guards tensed, ready to fight. Giedi Prime troops came forward, watching the tableau, but taking no sides. Rabban glared at the fighters spread out in the gigantic hall, all wearing Harkonnen colors. He felt a moment of indecision, wondering where they would cast their allegiance if this developed into a full-blown internecine conflict.

After a tense moment, he decided he didn't want to know. "I will call an administrative meeting to make sure that Harkonnen business has not been damaged while you were left in charge."

"You can look at the records, brother," Feyd said in a mocking voice, "though I doubt you will understand them. Intricate concepts have never been your strong suit."

Rabban snorted. "Our uncle has not yet announced his choice of na-Baron after the challenge he issued." With a laugh, he turned away. "Yes, one prisoner slipped through my hands, after being thoroughly tortured and interrogated, but I remain the obvious winner of our challenge. You, little brother, proved to be nothing more than a popinjay with empty talk. What have you accomplished?"

Feyd's eyes narrowed into weapons as sharp as the stiletto he held. "You don't know what you're talking about."

Rabban strode past him under the looming sculptures that had watched over Harkonnen business for generations, huge griffins that seemed at once whimsical and deadly. He turned to look back at Feyd. "I single-handedly destroyed the moonfish industry on Caladan. The Atreides bankers are wailing into their empty accounts."

"No one cares about *fish*!" Feyd called after his brother's back as Rabban stalked down the corridor. "Our uncle said to strike a *personal* blow against Duke Leto, something that would crush his soul. You think he will weep with misery over some moonfish floating belly-up?" He stalked after Rabban. "Letting Halleck escape is an embarrassment and a disgrace. Worse, it'll make Duke Leto Atreides look like a hero if he helps to bring down the rebellion. I can see it now: the Duke receiving rewards, while we are censured." His voice oozed with disdain. "You struck a painful blow indeed, my muscle-headed brother—a blow against House Harkonnen!"

Rabban whirled. "Our uncle made himself indispensable to the Emperor by setting a trap for Jaxson Aru, even if the Sardaukar botched the capture. So what if Halleck claims that we roughed him up on Lankiveil? Emperor Shaddam doesn't take part in noble family squabbles." He bunched his muscles and turned to glower at the younger man. "And what have you done with our uncle's challenge? You not only failed—you never even made an attempt. Or was your failure too embarrassing to admit to us?"

Feyd offered a dark chuckle. "As I said, intricate details are not your strong suit. There are wheels within wheels, clever plans within plans. True pain takes time to set up and inflict. I've already struck against House Atreides, even killed the Duke's new concubine . . . although that was just for practice. My operative is in place, and I trust him to complete his mission. The Atreides may think they are safe now, but just when they least expect it, the blow will devastate them." Feyd laughed louder now, while Rabban just stared at him, simmering in rage.

Every human faces daily testing, but not everyone is faced with tests of the same magnitude, or danger.

—MOTHER SUPERIOR HARISHKA to a selected group of Sisters

Brom insisted he was ready for the supreme test. He had to be.

Jessica had done the best she could for the young man, but she remained worried. This would be the most crucial ordeal Xora's son had ever faced, and she feared the Sisterhood was rushing him, eager to test their potential Kwisatz Haderach.

Though only the highest-ranked women knew the implications for their long-standing breeding program, the rest of the Mother School could feel the tension in the chill air. Jessica's old teacher Reverend Mother Mohiam had arrived from Kaitain to administer his test. Seeing her, Jessica had acknowledged the old woman with only a cool nod. Their relationship had been strained since Mohiam tried to grind her under the Bene Gesserit bootheel for her intractable behavior.

But Jessica refused to let past enmity distract her now. The Emperor's Truthsayer and Mother Superior Harishka were far more concerned with Brom and his potential.

The small, cold sun was directly overhead. Sitting outside on a stone bench near the Raquella statue, Jessica watched Mohiam, Cordana, and two other Reverend Mothers cross the main square from the administration building. She knew they were heading for the Lost Chamber. And why.

By now, Brom would be in the private underground room. He had spent the previous night preparing, meditating, building himself up to the proper mindset. He would use the techniques and subtle fine-tuning she had shown him.

The young man was not arrogant or overconfident. He had been raised among the Bene Gesserit and taught their special skills, just as Jessica had done her best to impart to Paul. Through the intricate labyrinth of coincidence and genetics, Brom had certain qualities . . . as did her own son.

She winced to recall the vitriol and fear spouted by mad old Lethea, who insisted that Paul was too dangerous, that he must be killed. If Brom passed their test and served the role the Sisterhood had anticipated for millennia, then no one would need to be concerned about Paul. *The Kwisatz Haderach.* . . .

Sitting on the bench, she held on to her hopes, but she had been forbidden to see him beforehand, supposedly to eliminate distractions at his crucial moment when so much was at stake. He had to be utterly focused on every cell in his body, every thought in his mind.

He had asked Jessica to be there for support, to witness his ordeal, but Mohiam had flatly refused, and the Mother Superior concurred. No one who had not herself endured the Agony could be present. Brom would have to do this alone.

All alone.

No male had ever succeeded before. Did Brom finally have the genetic makeup that was required, after countless generations of subtle guidance?

Did Paul?

As she waited outside, isolated and cold, Jessica concentrated on her breathing, ignoring the sharp chill in the air. She gazed up at the statue of the first Reverend Mother, her beatific face carved from marble. Though Raquella Berto-Anirul had lived ten thousand years earlier, her features were presumably accurate in this rendition, preserved through Other Memory. Raquella had been poisoned, and though she had survived, she emerged changed. That had started millennia of Bene Gesserit training and transformation. Now, though, the heroic-looking statue offered Jessica too little comfort. Fatigue and dread seeped through every bone and muscle of her body.

She couldn't stop thinking about the emotional and physical rigors Brom would be going through.

Hearing the approach of footsteps, she looked up and saw the kindly face of Cordana, who also approached the Lost Chamber. The Reverend Mother said, "I will be there, and I will bring your support with me. He will know you strengthen him."

"Thank you," she said. But it wouldn't be the same. "I don't think he is entirely prepared."

The bent-backed woman frowned. "Will he ever be? Are any of us? That is what the test proves."

She kept thinking of Paul. What would they do to him next?

Cordana lowered her voice. "You've had some sort of premonition?"

Jessica shook her head. "Just an observation. He has had all the training the Bene Gesserit could give him. But still . . . the poison. Others have died."

"And others have not." The Reverend Mother clucked her tongue against her teeth. "Maybe he'll transmute the poison and emerge on the other side at a higher level—a much higher level. Mother Superior has high hopes."

Jessica straightened. "What does Mohiam think? She's administering the test."

"Reverend Mother Mohiam has spent little time with the boy, but knows that he possesses the genetic markers and behavioral characteristics we have long sought. He is our best hope."

"Our best hope," Jessica said. "He was nice to me from the beginning. He—" She paused.

Cordana conceded, backing away. "He reminds you of your own son, I know. Perhaps your child won't need to be tested after all . . ." She walked away with her odd gait brought on by a contorted back, to join the others inside the hill.

Jessica watched more Reverend Mothers heading into the isolated chamber.

She gazed toward snow-covered mountains in the distance. Tears stung her eyes, and she felt no inclination to use Bene Gesserit skills to drive them back. She would rather experience and accept her emotions. They made her feel alive.

Brom deserved to have someone care about him.

THE WOMEN WERE silent and somber as they took their seats. Brom stood in an alcove, comforted by the shadows but fighting back his uneasiness. He looked at each of their faces, searching for Sister Jessica. It was almost time for him to begin the terrible ordeal. Why wasn't she here?

He centered himself, concentrated on his preparations. He did not need Jessica to be there watching. He felt self-sufficient, and ready. The Mother School taught it was a weakness to rely on others, and another weakness to fall victim to emotions.

I must not fear. Fear is the mind-killer. . . .

Jessica had helped him, and he even thought of her as his good friend. They were bound by shared questions, shared struggles. He had been grateful for her advice, the help in fine-tuning his skills, but he had also learned to observe subtle changes in a person's face and mannerisms. In looking at Jessica's expression after Brom's training sessions, listening to her words and tone, he knew she worried about him, afraid that he was not ready for this.

Fear is the little-death that brings total obliteration.

He steeled himself and went through the entire Litany Against Fear as calmly as he could, then gave himself more personal advice. *I must be strong. I must retain what Jessica gave me to succeed.*

Reverend Mother Mohiam came up to stand before him and stared with bird-bright eyes. "Your time is now."

Brom followed her out into the octagonal chamber.

Where the fear has gone there will be nothing. Only I will remain.

⟤⟥

THE ROOM WENT quiet except for the occasional coughs of the older women. Harishka sat silent, and Mohiam could tell that the Mother Superior was barely breathing.

Mohiam leaned over the platform where Brom lay supine, eyes closed. His body was rigid, motionless, but with her heightened senses, she could feel him thrumming with barely-controlled fear. In one hand she held a vial of clear liquid, the Rossak poison, collected on the planet where the fundamental roots of the Sisterhood had begun so long ago. A variant of this potent chemical was used to enhance Truthsaying abilities. The poison killed anyone who was not prepared with every fiber of their being. Mohiam remembered her own Agony well, one of the worst and most glorious moments of her life. She would not change her ordeals or their consequences. She was the Emperor's eminent and trusted Truthsayer.

And this young man might be the Kwisatz Haderach, at last. How remarkable it was for her to live at such a time, after centuries upon centuries of careful planning and guidance . . . and *waiting*.

Brom, the son of ambitious Xora, needed to consume the Rossak drug and then process the deadly toxin through his body, convert it to a harmless agent, and reach the other side with his mind and metabolism fundamentally changed. Mohiam had seen many talented Sisters try, and fail. And they swiftly vanished from memory.

But if Brom was indeed the Kwisatz Haderach. . . .

She spoke softly, giving him instructions rather than reassurance. He kept his eyes closed, but the lids flickered. He did not resist when Mohiam parted his lips and emptied the small vial into his mouth. He grimaced, possibly from the awful taste, possibly from the knowledge of what it was. He held the liquid in his mouth for a long moment before gathering the courage to swallow.

He opened his eyes and shot a sharp, wild glare in her direction, then looked into infinity and smiled, finally closing his eyes again, and stopped trembling. He mouthed the familiar words of the Litany.

Hoping desperately that Brom would emerge on the other side of this test to become the male Bene Gesserit who could bridge space and time, Gaius Helen Mohiam held her breath.

In less than a minute, Brom's body grew entirely still. Then to her horror, blood began to seep from his eyes, ears, nose and mouth. The young man made a very faint cry of pain, followed by another.

Leaning over him, Mohiam realized he was trying to scream, but could not make a sound.

Then the horrible convulsions began.

Every Swordmaster must be prepared to fight to the death. The Ginaz combat skills will serve you well, but your thinking skills are of equal importance. Analyze your opponent in minute detail. That is how you win. And that is how you kill.

—A lesson from the Ginaz School

In the castle library, Paul fidgeted as Duncan made him watch a training filmbook about personal combat. In a monotone voice, the instructor lectured about the mathematics of why a blade needed to be slowed to penetrate a personal shield. Late-afternoon sunlight peeked around blinds half-drawn over the open windows. He could still hear the outside sounds, though the day was winding down. His thoughts were not on the lesson. It seemed too . . . normal for the circumstances.

After the Sardaukar fleet had withdrawn from Caladan, the people trembled with joy, and terror. The Imperial troops had landed indiscriminately and caused great damage, a show of force, and when they departed, they left scars on the spaceport and many damaged sections of Cala City.

According to the best estimates, 115 people were dead, including the foolhardy hunters who had tried to shoot down the envoy ship. Others had been murdered in the town out of callous cruelty. Paul had asked for a list of casualties, and he read over every one, thinking of the victims, remembering their names. It was what Duke Leto would have done.

The Sardaukar commander had taken copies of his father's two important recordings, and to ensure that the word did get to Emperor Shaddam immediately, Thufir had made four additional copies and dispatched them to Kaitain along different space routes. This time, no Harkonnen interference would prevent the word from being delivered, and Shaddam Corrino *would* know the full truth.

But Paul still had received no word from his father, and in these days of tension and unrest, the news that traveled around the Imperium was haphazard and unreliable. Paul received troubling reports of other attacks by Sardaukar forces against well-respected noble families also accused of collusion with the violent rebellion. The names of the targeted planets were scattered, contradictory, and unverified.

At least Caladan was not among them.

Jaxson Aru had long been marked for death, but the man kept eluding Imperial pursuit. Paul knew his father was with the rebel leader, and the Sardaukar continued to hound him. Leto Atreides was in graver danger than ever before. All of the reports that came to Caladan were weeks old.

Paul also knew that his father's efforts to infiltrate the Noble Commonwealth had drawn a target on Caladan. For that reason, the colonel bashar and his ruthless Sardaukar forces came to inflict terrible damage on the good people.

One hundred fifteen dead—innocent men and women who had nothing to do with a violent rebellion, nothing to do with his father's plans. The Duke of Caladan would never have wanted that, and yet his people had paid the price.

Despite the sadness he felt, Paul realized that the situation could have been so much worse, that the casualties could have numbered in the hundreds of thousands, including every retainer who served House Atreides, every person who lived in Cala City or the surrounding lands. The ancient castle would have been turned to rubble if the colonel bashar had refused to listen.

Despite their grief and the succession of memorial services, the people of Caladan did find reason to celebrate. The town held a parade of thanksgiving, and the reef market was crowded with customers. Paul heard that dozens of new weddings had been announced.

The sense of relief also enfolded Castle Caladan. With his mother and father both gone, Paul had felt a palpable gloom and tension for so long. Knowing that the threat of Imperial retribution was now gone, however, he could breathe an easy sigh.

Even the old warrior Mentat was sleeping the full night through. Gurney Halleck spent more time in Dr. Yueh's infirmary getting himself patched up again. His bruises were fading, and with therapy, he was regaining the full use of his fingers—enough, he vowed, to play the baliset again in no time.

The House Atreides forces relaxed, the soldiers remembering what it was like to live on peaceful Caladan and to serve a Duke who was well liked by his own people. Paul and everyone else began to let down their guard.

"You're not paying attention." Duncan nudged him in the arm.

"I've seen this filmbook before, and we've trained in this exercise."

"Training never stops, nor is it ever the same no matter how many times you think you have learned a thing. You just endured a huge lesson on the front lines, facing down a Sardaukar commander! And I admit you performed exceptionally well."

"I had to," Paul said, knowing how rarely Duncan Idaho issued compliments. "I didn't want to be a spoiled dukeling who lost a planet while his father was away."

"It was a desperate time for you to be in charge, Paul. But let's not forget about the danger your father is in, wherever he is."

"Or my mother . . ." Paul gazed toward the sunlit windows. When Jessica had slipped back here to protect him, shortly after Xora was murdered in the inn, she had revealed her new assignment to Elegy. He was hoping for any word from her, but information was unreliable and slow.

Duncan shut off the filmbook with a snort. "You know I will do whatever I can to help, just tell me what you want me to do."

Paul went to the window, opened the shade. He looked out into the courtyard and saw supply vehicles coming in through the back, making deliveries to the kitchens. It was late in the day, and shadows stretched across the open area. "Right now, I need you to be my friend, Duncan."

"That is a mission I will undertake."

<hr/>

THE PRODUCE DELIVERY vehicles rolled through a service entrance on the expansive castle grounds, then through a thick copse of trees in the rear open areas that led up to the kitchens. Today they'd been late, not arriving until nearly dark. And that worked out well for Egan Saar.

The twisted Swordmaster performed his duties as before, riding beside the driver, going through the motions. This was his third delivery to the castle, and by now, he knew what to expect and how to plan. Mentally, he made a list of vulnerabilities.

After unloading the groundtruck's bushels of vegetables, the gruff driver relaxed as he turned the vehicle around and drove back, keeping only one hand on the controls. The low western sun was in his eyes as the vehicle entered the copse, where shadows and leaves blocked the view. The driver shifted his position to see better and let out a weary sigh.

In the passenger seat, Saar whipped out his long dagger and stabbed the man deep in the side of the chest, then two more times rapidly, even before the blood began to spout. As the dying man twitched and jerked, the Swordmaster easily pulled the slow-moving vehicle off the road into the trees just inside the castle grounds. He wiped off his dagger, slipped it back into its sheath, and covered his sword with the dirty cloak as he slipped away on foot. He had all the time he would need.

Sprinting through the copse, he proceeded back toward the kitchens, where the castle staff let him in, having just seen him with the vegetable delivery. The vehicle was parked on castle grounds, so there was no more castle security. The workers were still unloading and sorting the produce, chattering away about a big celebration feast now that the Sardaukar were gone and Caladan was safe again.

Saar wore a calm half smile as he moved among them, distracted as if he had simply forgotten something. He bustled down a corridor outside the kitchens, where one shift of the staff had sat down to an early dinner. Intent on their conversations and their meal, they did not notice him.

Saar had a diagram of the castle etched in his mind, and every movement was clear as he slipped up a service stairway to the top level. Ever since the Imperial invasion, Paul Atreides had made a habit of spending time in the evenings up on the ramparts, where he could look out to the city and spaceport, and the ocean just below.

An armory chamber served as weapons storage on the roof, where Atreides fighters could take shelter against the ocean wind and fog, although as twilight set in, Saar saw that the night would be bright and clear. A good time for a killing.

The door to the weapons room was closed tightly, but unlocked—foolishly, he thought—although he could have broken in regardless. Carrying his own blade, Saar ducked along the wide ramparts, where he found a place to crouch among crates of supplies under a tarpaulin. He folded his lithe body into the shadows where he could see anyone approach along the open ramparts.

He was inside the castle now, and he could wait.

⸎

PAUL AND DUNCAN ate dinner with Thufir and Gurney in the main dining hall, which seemed much too large for them. The servants outnumbered them by far, and the head chef was pleased to serve several variations of fresh vegetables that had just arrived from outlying farms. Although Dr. Yueh had withdrawn, preferring to rest, Paul enjoyed the meal with his friends and advisers, but his stomach remained knotted as he waited for some word, any word at all, about his father or his mother.

As their meal came to an end, Gurney enjoyed a tankard of kelp beer, but Duncan declined, saying he preferred to keep his mind and reflexes sharp. Restless, Paul rose from his chair in the dining hall, glanced up at the mounted bull's head, and signaled the Swordmaster. "Let's go up into the night air. Maybe we can burn off some energy with a little swordplay."

Duncan grinned. "It's a cool evening, but I think we can keep ourselves warm."

"You'll feel warm with shame after I beat you," Paul teased, bounding out of the dining hall. Duncan followed him.

Out on the open ramparts at the top level of the castle, the brightest stars shone out. Pearly-white water curled around the base of the cliffs directly below the castle walls.

They strolled toward the weapons room to select dueling swords for their evening's romp. Duncan pulled open the door, activating the interior glow-globes that shone against the gloom. Paul entered after him, flexing his arms and discussing which blades they should use.

Duncan suddenly paused, whirled, and shouted, "Look out!"

Paul sensed someone sprinting silently toward them. He saw the silvery flash of a drawn sword, and a figure racing across the rooftop. Duncan grabbed Paul by the arm and hauled him inside the weapons room as he kicked the door shut after them. The barrier crashed into place just as the pursuer slammed into it, but Duncan didn't have enough time to lock it.

"Who is it? Duncan—"

"Don't know. How in the Seven Hells did he get in here?" The man outside pounded on the door, worked the latch. Duncan lunged toward the rack of swords in the armory, grabbed the first blade, and tossed it to Paul just as the attacker knocked the door open.

Paul caught the sword, wrapped his hand around the hilt, but Duncan was even faster, charging like a bull and slamming into the stranger. Both raised their swords and crashed together in the doorway. Duncan's momentum drove the other man back outside.

Paul saw that the intruder had a thicket of black hair, shaved temples, and flinty eyes. He wore a patched brown cape, and moved with shocking speed and fluidity.

Duncan attacked like a storm, asking no questions, just protecting Paul. He clashed swords and battered his opponent, who seemed mockingly confident. The attacker easily countered each strike, even shifted his weapon from hand to hand, depending on what Duncan did. The man parried and moved away smoothly, like a jungle predator.

"So whom do I kill first?" he asked in a husky voice. "The Atreides Swordmaster, or the Atreides heir?"

Duncan held his own. "Not just a Swordmaster—I'm a Swordmaster of Ginaz."

The attacker snorted. "That is not enough. I could say the same, but I am more."

They moved farther onto the open rooftop where they would have more room to fight, and Paul followed, holding his own blade and ready to help. Angrily, Duncan gestured him back to safety, but Paul refused to hide. He would strike if he saw an opportunity.

Something about their foe's movements made Paul's skin crawl. His blade work was masterful. Duncan matched him in every way, but Paul sensed that this opponent—a Swordmaster in his own right?—was holding something back.

As Duncan drove the other man across the battlements, his rival danced out of the way, weaving, leading him. With his own blade raised, Paul darted in silently to harass the attacker from the side, forcing him to change tactics and deal with a second fighter.

At first, the stranger looked annoyed, and swished up his patched cloak to catch the point of Paul's sword, nearly disarming the young man. Paul tightened his grip and yanked his weapon away as Duncan charged into another whirlwind of swordplay.

The attacker deflected Duncan's offensive, and when he was backed closer to the wall, he sprang up onto the wide crenellations, where he had the higher ground. The other Swordmaster reveled in his position, high above the sea at his back, looking down at the two men who came for him.

"Paul, keep your distance," Duncan warned, gesturing him back.

"I have no intention of doing that." The young man kept looking for an opening.

As if taking the words as an invitation, the attacker sprang down and charged toward Paul, slashing and hammering with his sword. The young man used all of his training to parry the blows, to guard himself, but this man was a rampaging brute, raining down blow after blow. Paul could barely hold on to his weapon, and his arms shook with each impact.

Duncan threw himself into the melee with a roar of anger. His energy surprised the arrogant assassin, which forced him to divert attention to his own defense. Perspiring with the effort, the attacker slashed at Duncan even as he was pressed back against a low point in the crenelated rock wall.

Paul didn't know who this assassin was, or who might have sent him, but the man's intent was obvious. He had assumed he could easily kill Paul and even defeat the great Duncan Idaho. But the stranger could not have taken the measure of the ducal heir, not yet.

While fighting Duncan, the intruder snatched a dagger from a sheath at his waist. He flung the knife at Paul with expert aim, but the young man managed to slash it out of the air with his sword, sending the blade clanging across the paving stones.

Duncan roared as if the attack were a personal insult, and he hammered at the other man.

Paul took that moment to plunge in, wildly thrusting with his sword, and his sharp tip struck the assassin's shoulder, cutting into the meat of the muscle.

The attacker recoiled against the low wall, more in surprise than pain. "Blood—"

Duncan needed only that fraction of a second, and he lurched one step closer. The assassin raised his sword to counter a strike, but Duncan didn't use his sword. Instead, he struck out with his other arm, slamming the flat of his hand into the center of the man's chest. The blow knocked him backward, and the momentum sent him off balance.

In the space of a heartbeat and an indrawn breath, he was over the low wall, falling backward into the abyss. Paul caught only a glimpse of his astonished expression as he plunged down over the cliff. He didn't even scream as he plummeted to the crashing surf.

Paul and Duncan both ran to the edge and stared down, but they couldn't see the enemy's body in the darkness among the rocks and crashing waves.

"I thought you would just run him through," Paul said.

"A sword isn't the primary weapon. The Swordmaster is." Duncan peered down the cliff. "A shove at the right moment proved sufficient." His expression darkened as he turned back to face Paul. "You put yourself in danger! You should have gotten to safety and left him to me."

Paul sniffed. "I used everything you taught me, every move and every trick."

They stood in the open night, catching their breath, never letting their guard down in case there was another intruder. Finally, Duncan clapped him on the shoulder. "And you are barely fifteen. Imagine standing against you as a grown man!"

An explanation, if believed, can change the course of empire. One must simply survive long enough to deliver that explanation.

—Landsraad Court, prosecution records

Leto was detained inside the Tanegaard administrative citadel, which Emperor Shaddam had made into a temporary Imperial headquarters. He was held under heavy guard like a valuable prize, isolated from all others. Sardaukar operatives and Imperial officials moved through parts of the building, closely watched by CHOAM security.

Every one of Jaxson's personal guards had been slaughtered. The supposedly impenetrable core bunker had finally been breached, but the terrorist leader was not found alive. Lord Rajiv Londine, another Noble Commonwealth traitor, was nowhere to be found despite the extensive search parties.

Leto felt a growing dread as he realized he was the only living prisoner from the radical rebellion. The only witness, the only participant. With no other scapegoats at hand, Shaddam would feel compelled to make him the figurehead for Imperial justice.

From inside his holding cell, Leto demanded answers of his own, especially anxious about what had happened on Caladan. Even more than his concern for his own life, he feared that a Sardaukar force had decimated his home, just as they had done to Cuarte and those other rebel worlds. Had Castle Caladan been reduced to a pile of rubble? Was Paul still alive? Even with Empress Aricatha speaking on Leto's behalf now, he feared it would take too long to resolve the issue.

Sardaukar would not delay.

He shouted from his holding cell, called for Emperor Shaddam and demanded the opportunity to speak, but although he yelled himself hoarse, the door guards acted as if they were deaf.

When Shaddam and Aricatha finally came to see him hours later, the Padishah Emperor was angry and restless, and his fine Imperial garments looked disheveled. The Empress, on the other hand, seemed refreshed and vibrant, as if she had spent the day strolling in a pleasant garden. Her dark eyes held an odd light, as if something were just the tiniest bit off about her, but she gave Leto a radiant smile.

"Don't be angry with him, my love. We owe this man our lives. He accomplished what we could not. He defeated Jaxson Aru, and saved me."

Outside the holding cell, more Sardaukar arrived as if Leto suddenly posed an increased threat.

Shaddam remained unforgiving. "My Empress used all of her favors to convince me that I should hear you out. She was very persuasive." He glanced at the beautiful woman on his arm. "But I agreed only with the knowledge that I can still execute you if I am not satisfied with what you have to say." For a moment, he looked more confused than indignant. "You are my cousin, Leto Atreides. Why would you betray me? I have done you many a fine turn. My favors were not enough?"

"I'm aware that you are missing some vital facts, Sire. Jaxson Aru tried to recruit me into his rebel movement, and I pretended to go along. I felt that if he trusted me, I could work my way into his inner circle. I could expose his vulnerabilities and leave him open to Imperial justice. That was my intent all along."

Shaddam remained skeptical. "Any captured traitor could make up a fanciful story like that."

Leto raised his chin. "I dispatched a courier more than a month and a half ago with exact information about my mission. My man Gurney Halleck carried an implanted message for delivery to Kaitain."

"I received no such message."

"No, you did not, because Halleck was intercepted by Harkonnens, taken to Lankiveil as a prisoner, and tortured. I believe by now a rescue operation has freed him from their clutches. If he survived, my man can vouch for what I say."

"Why was this not brought to my attention beforehand? This is of vital Imperial interest," Shaddam demanded.

Fighting back bitter anger against the Harkonnens, Duke Leto responded only in a cold, hard voice, "I have repeatedly conveyed the Baron's attempts to disgrace and destroy House Atreides. I filed a formal complaint when one of their attacks destroyed our moonfish industry and brought great financial harm to Count Fenring's investment. You dismissed it all as a mere family squabble."

Shaddam flushed as he recalled the matter.

Aricatha stepped close to Leto. "I can vouch for him, my dear. I saw how the Duke was desperately working from within the fortress vault, trying to find a way to overthrow Jaxson Aru. Leto himself destroyed the memory stone that held the terrible data we dared not release. He saved us all."

Shaddam rumbled and fumed, but it was clear that Aricatha was softening his anger. "He saved *you*, my dear, and eliminated the black archive data. That goes a long way toward Imperial forgiveness." She leaned closer. "Remember, he saved both of us on Otorio, too. You should reward a nobleman like him, not punish him."

The Emperor regarded the Duke with narrowed eyes. "And when my Sardaukar arrive at Caladan, they will find proof of your intentions?"

"I hope so, Sire," Leto said. "I left a detailed message with my Suk doctor, who has Imperial conditioning. Dr. Yueh should be an unimpeachable source."

The Emperor grimaced as if taking a bite of poison. "I will see what Baron Harkonnen has to say about why he kept vital information from me. If it is true, he will pay for this—have no doubt of that."

"Sire," Leto said, his voice breaking just as his heart was, "if you already sent Sardaukar to attack Caladan, please stop them before irreparable damage is done."

Shaddam made an aloof gesture. "It is probably already too late. The second wave of Sardaukar forces should be well underway, finishing up after the initial assault."

"Then I must go there myself! Please send me on an Imperial escort ship to Caladan. I have to help my people. I have to . . . I have to see what's left." He thought of Paul and everything he held so dear.

Aricatha touched the Emperor's arm. "It is what we should do."

"If Caladan has been damaged in error, then I, the Padishah Emperor, promise to make amends," Shaddam said. "House Atreides will not suffer any losses." His voice became more of a growl. "Although House Harkonnen may soon forfeit one of their most valuable assets for what they have done."

Leto was too focused on the urgency in his mind and heart, knowing he had to find the swiftest Imperial ship home. He had Shaddam's permission, which would cut through all the regulations and bureaucracy. He needed to be on his way to Caladan.

❦

THE THICK DOOR to the supposedly impregnable inner bunker lay in ruins. Plasteel blocks were twisted, their edges rounded from molten cuts. Oily smoke hung in the air, mixed with the smell of burning. With incredible brute force, the Sardaukar had torn through the fortress vault.

Malina Aru felt heartsick to see the wanton destruction the Imperial forces had caused . . . the destruction *her son* had caused.

When they had breached the final bunker door, the Emperor's soldiers expected to encounter resistance, in a grandiose suicidal move from Jaxson Aru, like what Viscount Tull had done on Elegy.

Instead, they found Jaxson dead, his body sprawled on the bunker floor, one hand curled around a dried nub of barra fern. The potent ailar filled his mouth and his system, and he had died like so many others who had used the drug he himself had distributed.

Official Imperial history would call it a coward's way out, that the terrorist leader had been afraid to face Imperial justice, though Malina knew it was the safest way out, the best end for all of these tangled schemes. In the end, she'd told him that suicide was "the only path of honor" he had left, and he'd grasped at that straw, and taken it. Of course, in reality she'd seen no honorable course left for him, not after the terrible things he'd done, for which there could be no redemption.

She sighed, and struggled to think of good things about him. Maybe he'd seen his death as an honorable way to reduce the damage to the Aru family. But the tangled workings of his mind no longer mattered. Her son's death would allow her to sweep this inconvenient nightmare under the rug and continue her subtler work.

As Urdir of CHOAM, she invoked her clout to force her way into the recaptured fortress vault. She brought Har and Kar with her, and now the spinehounds padded along at her side, both of them strong, faithful. Their molten-copper gazes darted back and forth, their lips curled to show fangs as if they were ready to attack the Sardaukar. They could smell the blood and fire in the air. She soothed them with a code word.

Together, they picked their way through the blasted gap into the bunker. Her heart skipped a beat as she saw Jaxson lying on the floor. She had known intellectually that he was dead, and had seen images of other ailar victims, so she should have been prepared. His death had not been swift or painless, but it had been necessary.

Sardaukar troops moved about securing the vault, but there was little for them to do. Jaxson posed no further threat, and the rest of the violent rebels had been eradicated. The Imperial officers looked at the Urdir, ready to challenge her presence, until they realized who she was. Malina did not flinch, maintained a steely expression. The two spinehounds growled, and she walked forward, making up her own mind.

The soldiers' voices dropped to a murmur as Malina stood over the body of her son, gazing at his face, his matted hair, trying to remember the person he had once been, some of the good things about him. Her vision blurred and she could barely retain her balance, but she had to make sure no one saw how it affected her. The spinehounds both whined. Har cautiously stepped forward and bent down to sniff Jaxson's body. Kar gently licked a dead hand.

Malina kept staring, probing, but she did not recognize him—had not recognized him for some time. She had tried, and she had hoped, but he had turned into an absolute stranger. His altered face reminded her of Brondon, with remnants of Jaxson, but they were both gone now. Deeply flawed men, both of them failed.

She would grieve for Jaxson, and lament what she'd been forced to do, but she also had to use her influence to repair the damage he had done. She was the Ur-Director.

Malina spoke a soft command to the spinehounds and turned to walk away with her pets. The air was redolent with blood and smoke, and she needed to find privacy and sanctuary before she could deal with all the clamor inside her heart.

We work and plan for so long, seeking the loftiest of goals, and then have our hopes dashed. Again and again.

—The Despair of the Kwisatz Mother,
entry in the breeding records

Following Brom's tragic death, the Mother School was in an uproar. The high-level Sisters showed emotions that the Mother Superior would have curtailed under normal circumstances, but Harishka herself seemed just as deeply affected.

A deep sadness, disappointment, and sense of failure permeated the compound, even though most of the Sisters did not know the significance of what had happened. Testing a male was extremely rare, and Brom had lived his entire life in the school complex. The young man had been an unexpected birth, an outlier rather than a planned data point on the long skein of tangled bloodlines, and yet they had allowed themselves to hope for the chance.

Jessica knew all the reasons, but her grief was more personal. Even though she'd had a deep sense that Xora's son would not survive, that he wasn't ready, she felt numb. Could she have trained him better, or averted the testing? And would it have made any difference? A rogue talent nurtured by Bene Gesserit training, Brom had been born outside of the careful Kwisatz Haderach breeding program . . . just as Paul himself was not part of the Sisterhood's original plans. The very existence of Brom, and Paul, was fraught with danger.

You were ordered to bear only Atreides daughters!

She deadened her sadness, made her thoughts cool and unemotional—the way the Bene Gesserit wanted them to be. She had learned the penalty for disobedience. In her austere quarters now, she sat by the window and gazed out at the gray skies. A flock of birds flew south, the V shape of their formation dark against the sky.

She heard a rap at the door, and a robed, veiled woman glided inside without being invited, as if she ruled the school complex. Jessica rose to her feet as a chill ran through her, wondering what the Sisterhood would do next. The last time she faced the Kwisatz Mother alone had been in her dark isolation cell.

More women entered behind her with a rustling of robes—Mother Superior Harishka, Reverend Mother Cordana, and even Reverend Mother Gaius Helen Mohiam. The Kwisatz Mother's face remained hidden, but the stern expressions of the other women made Jessica wary. Sure that they wanted something, she gave a cautious, formal bow.

The mysterious veiled woman said in her ageless voice, "Do you know why we are here, Sister Jessica?"

An ominous feeling settled over her. Her life, once serene and happy with her family, had fallen to the lowest level when they recalled her from Caladan. She had been pulled away as punishment, and as a way to prove herself. The Sisterhood considered her, and her son, to be mere pawns. Paul had been threatened by the ravings of old Lethea, and she herself had been assigned to another nobleman, who was now dead and all his holdings vaporized.

Reverend Mother Cordana had given her hope that her penance might be over, that she would be allowed to return to Caladan, to rebuild what had been damaged. But Jessica had lost hope that any new schemes of the Sisterhood would be to her benefit. She kept her eyes down. "No, I do not know."

The Kwisatz Mother stepped closer until she stood just in front of her. Jessica found the strength to look at the veil, imagining the hidden eyes.

"We have spent hundreds of generations mapping the bloodlines of humanity for one purpose. We are finally reaching the culmination, but like the myriad eddies of a river current at the delta before it reaches the sea, we cannot see the precise end in the midst of variant possible futures. Genetics is not an exact science." She bowed her hooded head. "We must follow our plan, but also be willing to take risks, to test unexpected opportunities."

"Like Brom," Jessica said, and the words felt thick in her throat.

"Brom was a viable candidate to become the one we have long sought, but his bloodline became a dead end," the veiled woman said, "punctuated by his death."

Mohiam, Harishka, and Cordana remained silent, letting the other woman continue.

"We are close, very close. I did not expect it to happen during my watch, but I will meet my obligations, as we all must." She bowed her hooded head. "This is not about one woman filling one role. It is about the thousands of years it took to get to this place in our breeding history. It involved the efforts of so many of our Sisters, the trials and tribulations. We thought we might have found a viable shortcut, to skip a step, but this morning, that hope ended."

Jessica nodded, thinking of the young man not as a data point, but as a person. "I know. This is a sad day."

She tried to envision the Kwisatz Mother behind her mask and robes. Was she ancient, like Lethea, or a wise and healthy, much younger woman?

Harishka stepped closer to join the conversation. "Sometimes optimism is a weakness, and we placed too much hope in Brom. We were impatient, and now the Bene Gesserit must step back and look at the expanse of time. We reassessed the complexities of our program, explored the genetic pieces . . . picked up some loose ends we had dropped."

Jessica tried to fathom why they were here. Something to do with Paul, she felt certain. "What loose ends?" *Paul is alive,* she thought. *What do they intend to do to him?*

Mohiam and Cordana loomed nearby like great black predator birds, as if to intimidate her. Jessica felt smothered by how close they all were.

"We can go back to our original plan," the Kwisatz Mother said.

"You want to return to Caladan and your Duke, don't you?" Harishka said in a tantalizing voice. "After all you have been through."

Jessica stiffened. "I demonstrated my loyalty to the Sisterhood." She found greater strength. "I did everything you asked."

"There is only one way that might be possible," the Kwisatz Mother whispered through her veil.

"What else do I have to do?" Jessica asked, reining in her hope and also demonstrating strength. She stared around at the dark-robed women. "That's why you're here, isn't it—because you want me to do something? Didn't I prove myself with the assignment to House Tull?" Her anger and fear increased, but she did not raise her voice. "Does this involve my son as another potential candidate? Are you going to force him to take the poison, no matter how young he is? So he dies like Brom?"

Now Cordana smiled. "Why, no! You suggested the alternative yourself, child, when we spoke together at Viscount Tull's estate. Your Duke wanted a son, and you gave him one . . . but it may not be too late to prove your value to the Sisterhood."

Jessica caught her breath.

"We wanted daughters, but both you and Xora bore sons without permission," Mohiam said. "Now you can correct your own mistake."

"Your son's potential may still be worth considering, like Brom's," interjected the Kwisatz Mother. "But we can salvage our bloodlines in another way and correct the course of the breeding paths. We were too impatient with Brom."

"Too impatient," Cordana agreed. "With tragic consequences."

Mother Superior Harishka spoke in her severest tone. "If you return to Duke Leto Atreides, you must give us exactly what we require: an Atreides daughter."

Jessica caught her breath. She realized she might have some leverage with these women, but this was not an impossible request. They needed an Atreides daughter from her, by Leto . . . but that could only happen if they let her go back to Caladan. Back home. And yes, it was something she could do. Paul was their only son, but they had considered having another child. Leto would be pleased with a daughter—and so would she.

"So that is how you would have me prove my obedience."

Jessica saw them nodding, and she thought, *I do love Leto.*

She knew they could see this in her expression, even if she didn't say it out loud. "Maybe I can salvage our relationship, go back and earn his forgiveness and trust." She paused. "Then I would bear an Atreides daughter."

I can return to Caladan! To Paul! To Leto!

"Now go and *love* your Duke," said the Kwisatz Mother with a faint edge of sarcasm.

Suddenly, they had given her what she wanted most, and Jessica's joy swelled. But even though the Bene Gesserit had released her, she thought of Leto. Had he seen the subtle message she included on the recording she'd made beside Giandro Tull? What did he think of her?

Just because the Sisterhood had commanded her to go back did not mean that Leto would have her. . . .

Stepping off the Imperial ship at the Cala City Spaceport, Leto looked up at the milling crowd there to greet him, saw Paul at the head of them—and could think of nothing else but his son.

The young man sprinted toward him. Though still small in stature, he looked more mature and much more serious now, as if the weight of responsibility had aged him by years in only the past month. Even so, he was an exuberant son swept up in a joyous reunion with his father.

Leto had been raised formally by Paulus and Helena, learning his place in the Landsraad, his role as the future Duke of Caladan, but they had shown him little warmth. Although he had a close bond with his own son, Leto had never allowed himself wild displays of emotions, which had always been frowned upon when he was a young man.

But not now. He swept Paul up in a crushing embrace, lifting him off the ground. Paul pounded him on the back of his shoulder. "Father, you're home. You're safe!"

"We're all safe now," Leto said. "The rebellion is over, and I honestly think we can find normal days again."

Thufir Hawat stepped up behind them, stiff-backed. Gurney Halleck rolled up to them, predatory and full of deadly energy. He seemed happy to see his Duke, but he also carried a shadowy sadness and shame. "I failed you, my Lord." Some of the bruises were still plain on his face. "I did not deliver your message to Emperor Shaddam, as commanded."

"I know, Gurney, and you paid a terrible price for it."

"Not a high enough price, my Lord, considering the pain I caused. That one failure nearly led to Caladan's complete destruction . . . and your own."

Duncan Idaho joined them, looming over Paul. The Swordmaster's presence made the young man seem smaller and more compact. "There'll be enough time for beating yourself up later, Gurney. What none of us counted on was the sheer genius and persuasive powers of this lad here." He clapped a hand on Paul's shoulder. "Your son faced down a Sardaukar legion and talked a colonel bashar out of following his orders."

Paul flushed. "We were all there together, Father. I only used what you taught me. Your own reputation is what carried the day, as well as the recording that you gave Dr. Yueh."

Leto felt pride—not just in his son, but in the staunch steadiness of his trusted advisers and comrades. He glanced around. "And where is Yueh?"

The Suk doctor approached through a throng of Atreides guards as more Caladan people pressed forward to see the return of their beloved Duke.

Paul motioned the doctor forward and said, "Dr. Yueh showed them your message. Their colonel bashar said he'd had favorable dealings with you before."

Not sure what Paul meant, but deciding it didn't matter now, Leto swept the young man up in another hug. "I just want to revel in being home again . . . and moving on with our lives. Emperor Shaddam has granted me complete absolution from any alleged crimes, but so much damage has already been done to some of the Great Houses and their people . . . irreparable damage."

A blur crossed his vision like mist rising from Caladan's seas. Jessica must have been one of those casualties, along with Viscount Tull, Vikka Londine, so many others. The radical conspirators themselves might have warranted the harsh retribution, but Jessica hadn't deserved what happened to her. She had just been a pawn assigned to some Landsraad nobleman to further Bene Gesserit schemes.

Paul followed his father to the waiting groundcar. Leto saw the sparkle in the boy's dark eyes, but also a flicker of sadness, as he clearly missed his mother. Would Paul's life ever return to normal? No, not without Jessica.

Then Leto realized that Paul had no inkling of what had happened on Elegy. Here on Caladan, he would have received only sporadic news, maybe unverified reports of the other Sardaukar massacres. Did he even know that Jessica had been assigned to Viscount Tull? Events had happened so quickly.

As they rode along, the weight and responsibility of leadership slammed like an asteroid into his conscience. Paul had not asked for such terrible responsibility so that his father could go off on a dangerous mission, nor did he deserve having it forced on him. The young man had already lost his mother once when the witches called her away, and now he would lose her all over again. She could not possibly have survived the annihilation of Elegy.

Yet as they approached the imposing edifice of Castle Caladan, Leto took a moment to regard the soaring walls, the turrets, the weight of history. He clung to the momentary good feelings. Leto was home now. Despite all the

other tragedies, he was buoyed in the knowledge that they were back together, that *this much* at least was right with the universe. For now, that would
have to be enough.

The rest would resound throughout their lives later, when it all sank in.

⤝

THE NEXT FEW days were torture as Leto explained all the details to his son,
unfolding and revealing everything he had done after being caught up with
Jaxson Aru. He'd been swept in the maelstrom of the radical movement, trying
to maintain his camouflage while holding his own code of honor. Though he
had prevented more bloody massacres, and even helped the colonists on Issimo
III, Leto now wished he could have done more.

But Leto was most heartsick about the rest of the story he had to tell about
Jessica and what had happened on Elegy.

Then, in cool analytical words, he tried to explain. "When the Bene Gesserit revoked your mother as my concubine and transferred her to Wallach IX,
they had other plans for her. I cannot say whether she resisted the orders, but
when sent to another nobleman, she performed her duties as assigned." He
steeled himself, but could not lift the weight of his words. "As I would have
expected of her."

Paul's face was tight. "I know my mother loved you, sir. She loved *us*."

Leto reached over to touch his son's hand. "Love isn't always a strong enough
defense when you are up against an irresistible force. Your mother was assigned
to Viscount Giandro Tull, and the Sisterhood would not let her refuse. She
went where she was commanded and served her role." He forced the next words
out. "Impeccably, I assume. That was always the way your mother did things."

Paul's expression darkened, but the news did not seem a surprise to him,
which puzzled Leto.

Behind him in the castle room, Thufir Hawat's gaze darted from side to
side, then sharpened as the realization struck him. "Viscount Tull, my Lord?
Of the planet Elegy?"

Paul straightened in shock. "You said that Elegy was destroyed by the
Sardaukar, everything wiped out! Were there no survivors?"

"I wasn't there, so I cannot say," Leto said. "But the odds of your mother
surviving that onslaught are very slim."

Paul tried to stay strong, but Leto saw tears welling up in the boy's eyes,
before he looked away and gained control of them.

Gurney and Duncan were both outraged. Duncan said, "So the Lady Jessica became a victim because of Viscount Tull's betrayal?"

"How do we measure all the threads of betrayal?" Leto asked. "Remember, I played my role in all this, too."

He set up a ridulian crystal player on the table, then inserted the crystal fragment into the slot. Taking a deep breath, he activated the message that Tull had sent with his shield-nullifier prototypes. Leto had watched the recording only three times himself because it was too painful, but now his son deserved to know. These were possibly the last images of his mother ever recorded. No matter what Jessica had done, Paul still had a right to see them.

"Viscount Tull provided weapons for the Noble Commonwealth," he explained. "He sent this message to Jaxson Aru on Nossus, while I was there. Your mother doesn't speak on the recording, and I cannot read her expression." Leto swallowed. "But you can see her. Judge for yourself."

He replayed the recording, observing the emotions on his son's face as he watched. Behind them, Thufir, Gurney, and Duncan also listened. When the message was over, Leto muttered, "She seemed so cold, as if masking her true thoughts. She was good at that."

"Father, don't look at her facial expression," Paul spoke in a rush. "Watch her *hands*."

Leto kept studying Jessica's eyes on the image, her oval face, the hair that was shorter and darker than he remembered. "Her hands?"

"Look at them!"

Although Jessica kept her arms at her sides, her back straight and stiff, her right hand was twitching, her fingers moving. Now he saw it.

Thufir Hawat came closer, studying, and he arched his eyebrows. "Master Paul is right. Those are not random gestures, my Lord."

Leto paused the recording, wound it back, and played it again. His heart began to beat faster. Now he recognized the subtle but special coded movements, the secret gestures known only to his tightest inner circle. "That's Atreides private language. Jessica is using the slightest of movements."

He watched the bend of her index finger, the twist of her wrist, the flick of her thumb—words and concepts.

Do not be deceived.

Bene Gesserit orders.

Mutual cooperation.

Political necessity.

Leto had to watch the play of her fingers three more times, not because he didn't understand it, but because he wanted to make sure.

I love you, Leto.

Paul read it, too. He shot a glance at his father. "She might have been assigned as Tull's concubine, but she never gave her heart to him."

"I had hoped for as much, Paul," Leto said. He stared at the last images of the Lady of Caladan. "And now I know."

He could not dredge up more words about this, and left them unspoken. Regardless of her true feelings, Jessica would have been with Giandro Tull when the Sardaukar forces swept their fire and slaughter across Elegy, when the pseudo-atomic explosion annihilated the capital city.

Her message made all the difference in the world to Leto's heart, yet she was still forever lost to him.

❧

AS WORD SPREAD throughout the Imperium that Shaddam's interdiction of Caladan had been lifted, Guild Heighliners returned to the world, and commerce began to thrive. To those with only a shallow understanding of events, life seemed to return to normal.

A courier shuttle delivered a sealed, secure package to Castle Caladan— not for the Duke, but for his son, Paul Atreides. As the contract-service courier entered officiously to deliver her message cylinder, the young man was working on his studies in the sunlit receiving room of the castle. Nearby, Leto sat at a large desk, preparing to meet supplicants. It had been far too long since the Duke had met with his people.

After acknowledging the delivery and dismissing the courier, Paul picked up the cylinder, turned over the burnished platinum surface, saw the seal. He felt the hairs prickle on the back of his neck.

From the desk, Leto offered him a curious glance. "Who is sending you such a formal message, Paul?"

"The Bene Gesserit." With his thumbprint, he deactivated the identity lock and opened the container. He withdrew a message from Reverend Mother Cordana. "Why would she write to me?"

Leto felt the burning ember in his heart. "No one knows what schemes the witches are working. If they knew that I had fallen in among the Noble Commonwealth, they might have thought I'd never return. That message could have been in transit for days. They may think . . . they may be trying to influence you."

Paul scanned the message and sat back, his eyes open. He looked thunderstruck. "Father, it is the best news ever!"

After he had endured so many setbacks and emotional blows, Leto wasn't sure how to judge what his son would consider good news. He wasn't at all prepared for what Paul said next.

"She is alive! The Bene Gesserit rescued her."

Leto snatched the message and scanned the Reverend Mother's words. "'To Paul Atreides, son of the Lady Jessica and Duke Leto Atreides. It is my duty to inform you that the Sisterhood withdrew your mother just before the attack on the holdings of Viscount Giandro Tull, to whom she had been assigned as concubine. Jessica is safe with us on Wallach IX.

"'You may hear other disturbing reports. Do not believe them. Jessica is still sworn and oathbound to the Bene Gesserit Order. Take heart in the knowledge that she is alive.'"

Too often the eyes see what the heart wants to see, regardless of logic.
—*Mentat Handbook*, analysis of sensory input

After the embarrassing debacle, CHOAM Ur-Director Malina Aru was in a rage. Although more tightly focused and rationally driven than Jaxson during his reckless actions, her anger was just as deadly.

Her daughter, Jalma, had already booked passage from Tanegaard on a swift ship, claiming urgent business back on Pliesse. Frankos called it a cowardly retreat while he stayed to face their mother; Malina was sure he would also have slipped away if given the chance.

After the Emperor's invasion force finally departed, leaving CHOAM to clean up the damage, Tanegaard began to settle back to normal. Nevertheless, the fortress world was like a victim trying to recover from an assault. Even when the wounds healed and the scars faded, the damage would still run deep and remain for a long time after so many Sardaukar and Imperials had been inside the administrative citadel.

Now, in her privacy-screened conference room, the Urdir and the CHOAM President met to discuss the future of the Company and of the Imperium. Malina's spinehounds looked thin and shaken, their spiky silver fur ruffled and matted. Har and Kar whined more than usual, clearly unsettled, as if they didn't comprehend how their human master could allow such turmoil. The shaved fur on Kar's abdomen was a reminder of mortality, and Malina felt it herself.

As he sat across from her, Frankos looked pale and confused. He fiddled with his fingers, frowning, and when he looked up at Malina, he spoke in a quiet voice as if he were a child who had just been scolded. "We should insist on having Jaxson's body returned to us. Even after what he did, he deserves a proper, if unceremonial, disposition of his enemies." Frankos shook his head. Clearly, he wanted to divert the subject of the conversation. "Maybe we could even put him at the site of our Otorio estate. I think he would like that."

"It does not matter," Malina said, then let out a sad sigh. "I loved him in my own way, tried to save him, and also tried to save CHOAM. I couldn't accomplish both, and the outcome is still not entirely certain with respect to our reputation."

Frankos was more agitated than she'd expected. "But if we don't do something, Emperor Shaddam will use Jaxson's body as a . . . a spectacle."

"As a lesson, and we have to grant the Emperor that," Malina said, hanging her head. "There are other terrible prices we will have to pay, so be prepared to face them. Letting yourself be taken hostage was inexcusable. That made the circumstances far worse."

"It wasn't my choice, Mother."

"Everything is a choice. You weren't alert enough. You knew what Jaxson could do, and you stumbled right into his trap."

He flushed. "As did you, Mother. You lured him here, and now Tanegaard has been . . . ravished. If Leto Atreides hadn't destroyed the memory stone in time, all of that damaging data would now be propagating throughout the Imperium."

Malina did not mention the backup earring that Jaxson tried to use. Her dark eyes flashed. "And you almost triggered a different catastrophe. That wild story—some nameless guard murdering Empress Aricatha! Shaddam nearly unleashed planet-burners on Tanegaard! And all because in your panic you thought you saw something."

"I saw it," Frankos insisted, "even if I can't explain it. My adrenaline was pumping, but I saw Empress Aricatha clearly with a knife in the back of her neck. I saw the blood and saw her fall—and then I ran."

Malina pursed her lips. "And who was this murderous guard? You looked at the corpses of Jaxson's allies, but you could identify none of them as the one. Empress Aricatha has been thoroughly checked by Suk doctors." She scoffed. "They would have found a fatal wound in her neck, but there is not even a scratch there."

Frankos fumed, obviously frustrated. "It must have been some trick of Jaxson's. He used ingenious holograms on Otorio, and again on the palace fountains before the treasury ship crashed into the Promenade Wing."

Malina placed her elbows on the table. "You're suggesting the Empress you saw was just a hologram all along? A trick? That makes no sense. Why would Jaxson want you to witness her apparent murder?"

Frankos toyed with his fingers again. "You said it yourself, Mother. After I escaped and told the Emperor what I saw, it drove Shaddam over the edge."

"But why would Jaxson want that? Open war between CHOAM and the Imperium?" Malina sighed. "Who can explain any of his actions? He was volatile and reactive." She reached down to soothe Har and Kar. "Fortunately, Shaddam is happy to have Aricatha back. She's got him wrapped around her finger, and with my influence on her, she will keep him diverted from vengeful thoughts . . . for a time."

The Urdir was worried, though, because she had heard nothing from Aricatha. Before the Imperial entourage departed, Malina had sent a coded message to request an immediate meeting, since the two of them had much planning to do, particularly damage control. But the Empress, who had been so carefully trained and planted in her role, never answered, as if she was ignoring her obligations to CHOAM . . . or had forgotten them.

"There's one last thing you must do." Malina prepared herself for the hard announcement. "CHOAM will increase security and effect all necessary repairs here, but we must make a strong statement to the Imperium at large. Soon enough, Shaddam will conclude that there has to be a price to pay. Therefore, we need to offer him a price under our own terms."

"What further price? Jaxson is the responsible party, and he is already dead. All blame falls on his shoulders."

"That is not painful enough, my son." She gave Frankos a warm, maternal pat on the back of his hand, and he flinched at the uncharacteristic gesture. "You must resign immediately as CHOAM President, but without accepting any blame. Cite family reasons."

He stiffened. "Why? Why must I resign?"

"Because you are the most obvious sacrifice. You were only a figurehead anyway, and you will still have your power and family wealth. We will find *something* for you to do."

His expression fell, and Malina thought he might even cry.

She continued, "In order for an Aru to remain the Ur-Director, another Aru must step down as President. That will mollify Shaddam, and someday, you will be groomed to take my place."

Frankos was pale and trembling, but he spoke no words. He would accept her instructions, no matter how much it hurt him. He was a good son.

❧

DRESSED IN HIS formal Imperial finery, Emperor Shaddam felt powerful and respected, ruler of the known universe. And with the lovely Aricatha at his side—especially after the terrible scare when he thought she'd been killed—he felt invincible.

He had been invited to the Landsraad Hall to hear an important speech. Politically, Shaddam was required to be there, and for once, he didn't disagree with the obligations of his office. He would approve the formal motion, and he had an announcement to make of his own.

It had taken him a long time to understand and accept Leto Atreides's explanations of what he had done among the rebels and inside the fortress vault. Seeing Aricatha alive and safe, he'd felt a tremendous debt of gratitude toward the Duke of Caladan, though it was not quite enough to offset the damage and embarrassment Jaxson Aru had caused. Still, his trusted Empress had spoken so highly of Leto. . . .

Shaddam had feared the revelations were too late, since Sardaukar punitive forces had already been dispatched to rebel worlds, including Caladan. Again, Leto's luck and grace, as well as the verbal skills of his son, had saved the Atreides holdings when Colonel Bashar Kolona reconsidered his orders. The very idea upset the Emperor, although when he reviewed the recordings Leto had made, he admitted that the proof was strong enough to warrant a review. Now the Duke was celebrated across the Landsraad. Shaddam had mixed feelings about that now, as he had felt before, fearing it would erode his own popularity.

Today, the escort through the Imperial city provided full pomp and ceremony as he and his Empress made their way from the palace to the Landsraad Hall. Because the nobles were in full session, the colorful flags of their Houses flew from tall poles up and down the grand boulevard, waving in the lazy, climate-controlled breeze.

Inside the Hall, representatives from countless Great and Minor Houses filled the tiers of seats. The news that the Noble Commonwealth movement had been eviscerated, the traitors caught and punished, and the hostage Empress saved caused great cheer. Even though many nobles continued to grumble about the harsh Imperial punishment inflicted on suspected conspirators, they were also quick to reaffirm their loyalty to House Corrino, hoping such gestures would appease the Emperor.

A loud fanfare played at the Hall's pillared entrance. He and the Empress strolled regally up the marble steps and through the enormous doors as if they had simply come here from a walk through the palace gardens. When they entered the main chamber, though, a hush fell across the crowded hall, and the governmental proceedings paused.

Shaddam had arrived a few minutes late, by design. The Emperor and Empress settled into their ostentatious chairs that overlooked the proceedings. The two sat side by side with all the noble representatives gazing up at them, exactly as it should be. Although the Landsraad was supposedly independent of Imperial interference, for thousands of years, their cooperation had been entangled.

Wearing a generous expression, Shaddam waved to all the nobles. "Continue, please. We apologize for making you wait."

Now a nobleman walked out into the illuminated speaking circle, where voice amplifiers would pick up his every word. He was an older man with dark hair and a face that was like a garment that had been washed too often by tragedy. He wore loose indigo garments and a dark blue cape trimmed with silver. When he turned, his cape swished aside to reveal an empty sleeve pinned to his chest. The one-armed Archduke Armand Ecaz had taken center stage. A hush fell over the Landsraad Hall.

"I am here to speak on behalf of my friend Leto Atreides, the Duke of Caladan. He has gone home to be with his people, rather than coming here to receive accolades, because that is who Leto is. Nevertheless, I am here to call for recognition of his service. On Otorio, after the first attack by the heinous Jaxson Aru, Leto Atreides saved the Emperor, the Empress, and many other nobles during those desperate hours." Archduke Ecaz drew in a deep breath. "I was one of them."

The nobleman turned to face a different section of seats. "Later, even as countless investigators scoured the galaxy to find the terrorist leader, Leto Atreides was the only one who managed to infiltrate the deadly rebels. He helped bring them down, and for a second time, he saved the life of our beautiful Empress Aricatha."

With his one hand, Ecaz gestured up to the Imperial box, and the Empress rose to her feet, smiling graciously and bowing. She received a tremendous round of applause. After a moment of hesitation, Shaddam rose to stand beside her, accepting the applause as his due.

"Therefore, I, Archduke Armand Ecaz, propose before the assembled Landsraad that we officially acknowledge the services of the loyal Duke of Caladan. He is a man of the greatest honor and integrity, of immense worth to the Imperium."

The crowded nobles murmured, then applauded. Though Shaddam was pleased by what Leto had done, he was somewhat soured to hear so much adulation.

The one-armed nobleman turned back to the Imperial box, raising his voice. "Emperor Shaddam, we ask that you find a way to reward House Atreides."

The Corrino ruler had already been considering this, trying to decide whether to offer the Duke a new noble title or a large sum from the Imperial treasury. Leto was so popular that the Emperor couldn't deny him the gesture. Aricatha had discussed various possibilities with him.

The Duke of Caladan had indeed done a remarkable thing and taken huge risks, knowing that if his mission failed, the name of House Atreides would be forever blackened. Because of an ancient family feud, the Harkonnens had intercepted a vital message to him—*to him!*—and used it for their own aggrandizement, rather than for the good of the Imperium. That venal action had caused incalculable harm, and Baron Vladimir Harkonnen and the whole damned noble family needed to pay a price—a high price.

The Padishah Emperor could think of only one thing that was significant enough to accomplish both aims.

Amplifiers picked up Shaddam's words so that the entire Landsraad Hall could hear him. He was smiling as plans unfolded in his mind. "I assure the whole Landsraad that House Atreides will receive an appropriate measure of gratitude." He spread his hands wide. "By this action, we shall demonstrate our love and honor for the noble Duke of Caladan."

Love is a tactic to be used only by the most expert practitioners.
—Bene Gesserit training manual

Under the bright sunshine of the Cala City Spaceport, Duke Leto stood at the ramp, preparing to board the Atreides frigate. Along the perimeter of the field, repairs were underway as busy construction crews erased the marks from the brief Sardaukar occupation. Gurney Halleck and Thufir Hawat had already boarded, but Leto inhaled a few last breaths of the salty air.

Paul, with the ever-alert Duncan Idaho at his side, watched the Duke, dressed in his formal green-and-black jacket. Leto stepped forward and took his son by the shoulders. "I know you want to go along with me to Wallach IX, but confronting the Bene Gesserit will take all my grit and imagination, along with the faculties of my Mentat." He nodded to Thufir, who stood above at the frigate's hatch.

"And my sword, m'Lord," Gurney added, standing beside Thufir. The scar rippled on his jawline and cheek.

Leto said, "If it comes to using your sword against the Bene Gesserit, we've already lost." He turned back to Paul. "No, I intend to look the Mother Superior in the eye and make my demands."

"The lad has already proven he has the heart of a Duke, my Lord," Duncan said. "And I will be here with him to keep Caladan safe."

"Duncan and I have our own work to do here." Paul straightened his shoulders, leaned closer to his father. "Promise me you'll resolve things with my mother . . . that you'll bring her back."

"I will have an explanation, Paul, and a satisfactory one." His eyes stung. "And I intend to bring Jessica home. There is no way the witches can stop me."

CASUAL UNAUTHORIZED TRAVEL to the Mother School was not allowed. Leto Atreides had never attempted to arrange Heighliner passage to the Sisterhood's homeworld, but now he had no choice—not if he meant to rebuild his life, his home, and his heart. He had to do it for Paul, for Caladan, and for himself.

In making arrangements with the Spacing Guild, he had invoked Shaddam's name and influence, calling in a favor that even the Emperor didn't know he'd granted. A Guild representative with an oddly distorted and unreadable face stared at him for a long, cadaverous moment before allowing the Atreides frigate to be routed through to Wallach IX.

Once the Heighliner arrived above the cold, gray world, cargo ships, transport shuttles, and diplomatic yachts dispersed out of the cavernous hull. Thufir Hawat piloted the Atreides craft down into the cloudy atmosphere, rebuffing increasingly insistent demands on the comm for identification and a statement of purpose. Not until the Bene Gesserit landing-zone control activated defensive emplacements did the Duke finally respond.

He didn't let Thufir or Gurney answer on the comm. This was his own discussion, his own demand, and the witches would damn well hear him out. He activated the pickup and spoke sharply. "I am Duke Leto Atreides, and I have come from Caladan to reclaim something you took from me. The Lady Jessica, my bound concubine."

The Sister stared back at him with a bland expression. "She is no longer your bound concubine. Her contract was rescinded, and we sent you a new concubine. Be satisfied."

Leto sniffed. "I did not request a new concubine." He drew a breath through narrowed nostrils. "And in any event, that one is dead."

The woman on the screen raised her eyebrows. "Why should we grant you any concubine at all, if you cannot protect them?"

Throughout the conversation, Thufir continued to take the frigate in a steep descent, slipping through the clouds. Below them the Sisterhood school spread out among rolling hills, a complex of buildings with terra-cotta roofs.

"We are landing," Leto insisted. "And I will see your Mother Superior to arrange for Jessica's return to me."

⥿

IN THE MOTHER School's receiving hall, the old woman sat in an imposing chair, glowering out at this upstart visitor who had demanded to see her. The Bene Gesserit were not inclined to grant frivolous requests—unless it served their purposes.

Jessica had to pray that was the case here. She had already made her bargain with the Sisterhood—to let her return to her role as the Duke's bound concubine, but before the Sisterhood could make their own arrangements, before they could press him to take her back, Leto had come here! Demanding exactly what the Bene Gesserit wanted in the first place.

She waited in an alcove concealed behind a dark curtain, but through the fabric, she could see the receiving hall and hear every word. The Mother Superior could never understand how Jessica's heart swelled to see him, the only man she had ever loved.

He has come here for me!

Leto marched in like a conquering general, as if he had just invaded Wallach IX and assumed control of the world. The sight of him after so much time and emotional distance made Jessica's breathing increase. She had so much to explain to him, so much she needed to reveal—how the Sisterhood had forced her to go against everything she believed . . . everything Leto loved about her. But she had done it to save him, his reputation, and their son—that much he could never know.

More than a week ago, Reverend Mother Cordana had explained to her in a hushed but excited voice about the events on Tanegaard, how Jaxson Aru was dead, that Leto's involvement in the rebellion had been revealed for what it was. He had saved Empress Aricatha—and was the hero she always knew he was.

For the time being, the Duke of Caladan held more Imperial influence than ever before. And now he had come back for her.

As he entered the Mother School, she had been told to remain in hiding in the alcove behind Harishka. Jessica had already agreed to their terms, and she would not let them use her as another pawn. She knew full well what leverage she had, the price she had to pay. And thinking of how much she loved Paul, she firmly believed that a child—a daughter by Leto—was an acceptable cost for returning her to her family.

The Duke's face was full of confidence when he stepped up to present himself to Mother Superior Harishka. Even from her hiding place, Jessica knew what he was thinking. Her heart was pounding. She had not only observed him for so many years through the eyes of a Bene Gesserit, she had studied him because she loved him deeply, and that provided her with an even more intense power of observation.

Leto spoke up, without any formalities. "You took Jessica from me, Mother Superior, and I will have her back. I wish to restore her contract as my bound concubine. She is an *Atreides*." He was like an angry bear, and he would get what he wanted. Jessica knew that Harishka would make it what *she* wanted, too.

The old woman leaned forward in her blocky chair. Her facial muscles struggled to form a smile but couldn't seem to remember how. "We gave Jessica to you in the first place, Duke of Caladan. Are you aware that she has been reassigned?"

Jessica felt a flush in her cheeks. Why was Harishka prodding him?

"I know about Viscount Tull, and that he is dead. But I also know Jessica is safe, and here." He glanced at the curtained alcove, as if sensing she was there, and worked his jaw. "And I know how you withdrew her from Caladan, took her from my service. I know the reasons you gave and the lies you told." He stepped even closer, as if to intimidate the old woman. "I know the truth."

He stood steadfast, and Jessica studied the slight movements of his face, the posing of his body. She felt a rush of warmth go through her—he had seen her message, her finger movements!

Harishka laughed again, but Jessica detected a hint of uncertainty there. "Perhaps we have other plans for Sister Jessica."

"You made your point," Leto said to Harishka, not using her title. "I just saved Empress Aricatha on Tanegaard and helped put an end to Jaxson Aru's rebellion. And don't forget, I also saved your Reverend Mother Mohiam on Otorio. If I were to ask the Padishah Emperor, I believe he would grant my request to reinstate Jessica's contract with House Atreides. He would not deny me this."

Jessica struggled with her impatience, realizing that the Mother Superior had calculated the benefits of making Leto push for the result that the Sisterhood wanted anyway. Harishka was just playing with him—and Jessica had had enough of the games. He would feel like a hero for bringing her back, but she did not need tricks to repair their relationship. She needed honesty.

Against Harishka's specific instructions, Jessica pushed aside the dark hanging and stepped into the receiving room where Leto could see her. His gray eyes snapped toward her, and when his face lit up, she knew it wasn't a lie.

"Duke Leto, the Sisterhood will allow me to return to Caladan." Jessica wanted to throw herself into his arms, but instead, she glanced at Harishka. "It seems that I have more work to do for House Atreides."

Jessica controlled her emotions, but she hoped Leto could see the delight on her face. She knew he would get what he wanted, so would she, and so would the Bene Gesserit.

Still seated, the ancient Mother Superior pressed her hands together, fingers steepled. "There is no need for threats, Duke Leto. Jessica has performed well, and has proven her dedication to the teachings of the Sisterhood. We have no further need to keep her away from her son, her Duke, and her contented home on Caladan. We happily release her to you." She smiled at Jessica, suddenly remembering how to be benevolent.

"Go with this man to the place where you belong. Once more you shall be the Lady of Caladan."

After his father departed, Paul understood what was important for Caladan. He and Duncan had loose ends to tie up. At the head of an Atreides strike force, they would go back to the southern jungles, not on a training exercise, but for retribution and restoration.

Three large troop carriers crossed the sea, flying through the night and following the same route he and Duncan had taken earlier. The hawk crest was prominent on every aircraft hull, and they flew like birds of prey.

Though Paul and the Swordmaster rode in the lead aircraft, dressed in Atreides colors, neither of them took the controls. This troop carrier had more sophisticated instrumentation than the nimble flyers the young man was accustomed to piloting, although he still watched the crew work.

Each carrier held eight hundred troops—more than the operation would need, but the Atreides soldiers remembered full well the high casualties they had suffered when they eradicated Marek's northern barra fern plantings. Even though they knew the drug lord was now dead, Paul intended to take no chances. The Tleilaxu might already have sent a replacement and an increased defensive force.

As they flew, Duncan swore he could wipe out all the fields single-handedly, after what Chaen Marek had done to him and to Sinsei's father.

But Paul looked at him with a hard smile. "You may very well be sufficient for the job, but I'll take more satisfaction from an overwhelming attack."

Dawn colors splashed across the sky as the Atreides force neared the Southern Continent. Ahead, Paul saw the coastline, the highlands, and the jungles ahead. He identified the volcanic range and the looming mountain the Muadh considered sacred. This time, they would steer clear of the reefs and any dangerous manta birds.

Small scout craft raced ahead, identifying clearings on the slopes that were broad enough for the large vessels to land in. Suspensor engines allowed the aircraft to land even in the rugged jungles, and after the carriers came to rest, armed troops swarmed out. In the sky above the morning mist, more scout craft raced ahead to reconnoiter the barra fields and ailar-processing complex. The scouts opened fire on the armed sentries scrambling to defend the operations center.

After softening the mercenary defenses, Atreides troops disembarked and swarmed out, rushing the last distance through the jungles to the fern-growing areas. Troops trampled the neat rows of curling ferns that poked out of the rich soil, from delicate pale-green fronds to more robust speckled species. Black smoke twisted up into the morning air as they incinerated the crops.

The Atreides troops met with little resistance. Chaen Marek's most dedicated underlings had remained, harvesting and packaging the ailar, but others fled into the jungles. Some of the hardened mercenaries fought to the death, and the Atreides fighters eliminated them. The bunkers and laboratories in the caves were all destroyed.

Beside Paul, Duncan paced restlessly as he watched the Atreides troops engulf every vestige of the drug fields. He drew his sword, impatient. "I prefer not to let others do such work."

"Then let's go fight them," Paul said. "There must be some operatives still in those facilities. Consider it part of our training exercise."

"It's more important that I stay with you and prevent you from being harmed." He seemed frustrated with the answer, but adamant.

"If I'd been afraid to take risks here, I would never have rescued you."

Duncan just snorted. "All right, we'll work together to burn some ferns and be happy with that."

Paul and the Swordmaster used incendiary hoses and destroyed rows of the genetically modified ferns. The air stank of smoldering vegetation, but he was glad to know the hated Caladan drug was being obliterated. Ailar would no longer spread among these people, or other customers in the Imperium, and the Atreides reputation would be restored. He ground his teeth as he torched another row.

He thought of the peaceful Muadh, not just the tribe that had welcomed him and Sinsei in these jungles, but also the Archvicar and his pundi rice farmers in the north. The people used ailar for their rituals, but it had been sacred, careful, and rare, done only with ferns they themselves harvested in the wild.

Chaen Marek and his operation had ruined that.

As he looked at the orange flames in the fields as well as the structures burning inside the cave headquarters, he thought of Old Mother and her

Muadh tribe. The villagers would be concerned about so much destruction on their revered mountain, but he intended to send in foliage-restoration teams after the strike. The illegal drug fields would be gone, and in a few months, the area would be pristine again with native plants. The Muadh could have their sacred wilderness peace once more.

As Duncan relished every row of ferns he burned, Paul mused aloud, "This is just a microcosm of a cleansing that's occurring across the Imperium. The Noble Commonwealth revolution is unraveling, and mop-up operations are taking place on planet after planet."

His companion let out a gruff laugh. "Well, now, aren't you the philosophical one."

"I am seeing the bigger picture, as well as our small part in it. And I hope that my father succeeds with the Bene Gesserit and brings my mother back home. The Duke and his lady, and our beautiful Caladan home—I would give anything for it to be restored."

"So would I, young Master."

The Atreides forces completed the bulk of the operation by midday. Paul was exhausted, but felt a sense of grim satisfaction. He and Duncan commandeered one of the scout flyers to make an inspection overflight, and this time Paul took the controls.

Atreides teams ran along the edge of the burning fields to spray fire-retardant foam that would prevent the flames from spreading into the jungle. Banking to the left, Paul glided high above scattered ground troops that continued to hunt down fleeing drug workers. A handful of mercenaries fought back. Some surrendered, many more died.

From the copilot's seat, Duncan watched in cloudy silence. "That ailar we destroyed would have been worth a king's ransom. Your father pretended to cooperate with Jaxson Aru, but I doubt he ever dreamed that the Caladan drug was funding so much violence."

"It's not anymore," Paul said.

Curious, he extended the range of the inspection and located the dry mountainside clearing where he had made a hard landing last time. Using suspensor engines, he settled the scout craft onto the scrub brush. On the slopes and flatlands below, the drug eradication continued to mar the jungle, adding black soot to the hazy sky, but here they were far enough away for an uninterrupted moment.

Duncan released the cockpit hatch and emerged while the young man wound down the engines and powered them off. "What did you expect to see from up here, Paul?"

"Not expecting, but hoping." As he stepped away from the craft, he saw figures moving on the fringe of the jungle. Smiling, he waved as he strolled forward to meet the others.

The Muadh villagers had come through the jungle, avoiding the burning fern fields. Paul felt happy to see them again, under better circumstances. Old Mother had made the trek herself, and now she led a group of her people out into the clearing.

"You are destroying parts of our jungle," Yar Zell scolded, standing protectively beside the village elder.

Paul bowed in respect. "Mostly the parts that don't belong here. The drug fields will be gone; the evil men are ousted. You'll have your jungle back again. We're replanting only native vegetation."

"I have every confidence it will all be restored," Old Mother said.

"I can help guide the full-scale reforestation," said a young woman, hidden by the thickets. "There's still much research to do."

Sinsei Vim emerged from the jungle, scuffed and bedraggled, but she was smiling and even appeared relaxed. She ran toward Paul, and they embraced.

Duncan gave the Muadh a hearty greeting. "Let me express my great appreciation for what your people did for me. Master Paul here could not have rescued me without your help. Now we're returning the favor by eradicating that scourge from your jungles."

Paul leaned into the cabin of the scout craft and transmitted a message, calling in another flyer. "Not only that, Sinsei—Dr. Yueh helped me prepare other things you will need." He looked up in anticipation, and soon heard the hum of a small cargo transport gliding over the treetops. Sinsei watched with a puzzled expression.

As the cargo transport landed near the scout flyer, its bay doors opened, and Paul motioned for the young woman to accompany him inside. "A mobile biological research facility, everything you need to analyze the flora and fauna in this region. You can continue your work here."

Her eyes grew moist with happiness. "I wish my father could have been here to help." She lifted her chin proudly. "I am left to do what he would have done."

The research station was as large as a medium-size groundtruck. Workers rolled it out of the cargo hold. Excited, Sinsei stepped inside the mobile station, while Paul watched her inspect doors and compartments, appreciating the scientific supplies and instruments. Her brown eyes lit up. "This is exactly what I need!"

"It's exactly what Caladan needs," he added. "And the Muadh as well."

Old Mother came up to them, leaning on the arm of the warrior Zell. She looked at the complex scientific devices without understanding. "We are happy that we will be left alone, no longer harassed." She touched her fingertips to her chest and extended them, as if drawing on invisible threads. Paul remembered that the Muadh Archvicar had used the same gesture. "We shall forever be grateful to the Atreides, to our Duke."

Paul chuckled, feeling a flush. "I'm not the Duke! There is time enough for that. Right now, I'm just the heir."

Duncan patted him on the back. "Ha, just the ducal heir! One day, this young man will be a great leader, like his father."

After exchanging warm goodbyes, Paul found another excuse to hug Sinsei, but they did not kiss. He and Duncan climbed aboard the scout flyer to rejoin the Atreides mop-up operation. The Swordmaster piloted this time, and from the air, Paul watched the group of people, and especially the lovely Sinsei, who was waving up at him.

As the craft skimmed over the jungle toward the smoke of burning fields, Paul's thoughts turned to the other mysterious young woman, who was once again beginning to haunt his dreams. . . .

The rise and fall of great powers throughout history should terrify every person who aspires to Imperial leadership.

—CROWN PRINCE RAPHAEL CORRINO, *Memoirs*, volume 3

The discovery of hidden Harkonnen financial transactions and the Baron's direct involvement in the black-market spice channel was eye-opening to Count Fenring—and infuriating, considering the fat man's repeated, lying denials.

As he pored over the numbers that proved House Harkonnen's malfeasance, Fenring had much to ponder. He needed to consider how much pain he should recommend that the Emperor inflict, not only on the Baron himself, but also on the CHOAM Company. Too much punitive action would create a dire threat to the stability of the Imperium, but the culprits had to pay somehow.

After defeating the violent rebels, the Imperium was left stunned, its foundations cracked. One more sharp blow could well shatter the whole construction, and then Jaxson Aru's dreams of anarchy would succeed after all. Fenring couldn't allow *that*.

No, he thought, wrecking CHOAM and basic interstellar commerce would not be a good idea, nor would it benefit Count Fenring or his friend Shaddam. True, the Ur-Director was involved in the black-market spice scheme, but Fenring saw the rigid boundaries of law as a bit more flexible than the Emperor did, based entirely on practicalities, rather than the absolutes that were so important to the throne.

Even though the incriminating data was complex and encrypted, he decided to expunge Malina Aru's name from the records before he forwarded them to Imperial Mentat accountants, and before providing his recommendations to the Emperor.

He had discovered the corrupted financial dealings by scouring information stolen from the CHOAM vaults in Tanegaard during the distraction of the lockdown there. It wasn't the black archives, but dangerous data nevertheless. Fenring hadn't even needed his eccentric Mentat to analyze the numbers. He'd had enough of Grix Dardik.

Humming to himself, he stroked a fingertip along his lower lip as he studied the ridulian crystal sheets that his spies had delivered to him. With a razor-tipped stylus and then a lascutter, he burned and chipped parts of the crystal, destroying the records in the appropriate places. "Damaged during the conflict on Tanegaard"—that would be the excuse he'd give for the portions he'd redacted. He left the remaining information intact, the numbers in all their damning glory. House Harkonnen could take the entire blame.

In the matter of Baron Vladimir Harkonnen, Fenring's sense of justice was defined by his indignation. The Baron had lied to him, tricked him, and that deception had strained Fenring's friendship with Emperor Shaddam. For that, he had in mind a different approach to resolving the matter of House Harkonnen.

He reminded himself that Rabban, no doubt under orders from the Baron, had also decimated the Caladan moonfish industries as part of a family squabble, which cost Count Fenring a fortune. Yes, the Harkonnens needed to be put in their place.

Taking the now-damaged ridulian crystal that contained the proof for Shaddam, he checked his appearance in the mirror and thought wistfully of the lovely Margot waiting back in Arrakeen. He wished she were here now as a sounding board, but he knew Margot would agree with his decision. The two of them were so mentally attuned. Rehearsing his words, he went off to meet the Emperor. . . .

In the grand throne room, Shaddam was glad for any excuse to interrupt the endless stream of whining supplicants, demanding nobles, and dissatisfied trade ministers who insisted on better terms. Without being announced by Chamberlain Ridondo, Fenring glided up to the throne and whispered in Shaddam's ear. The Emperor called an end to the day's meetings and followed his lifelong friend to a side chamber with privacy doors and security locks.

Concealing his smile, Fenring presented the damaged ridulian crystal sheet and paused while Shaddam scanned the information. He knew the Emperor wouldn't understand what it meant, but he allowed him some time, to make a show of it.

After a moment, Fenring spoke up. "Sire, in the turmoil on Tanegaard, when the Sardaukar placed Jaxson Aru under siege, one of my, ahhh, operatives took the opportunity to . . . ahhh, obtain some rather sensitive information. CHOAM would be unhappy if they knew we have access to this."

Now, Shaddam raised his eyebrows as he looked across the small table at Fenring. "I am listening."

"CHOAM keeps their commercial transactions highly secure, but this . . ." He tapped the crystal sheet and illuminated the numbers, names, dates, and specific transactions. "This is highly relevant, hmm. CHOAM never expected outsiders to see such accounting."

"I'm sure it must be relevant." Shaddam looked down at the document again. "What do you think we should do?"

Fenring gave an obsequious smile. "We have both been, ahhh, victims of a clever deception. Remember the spice thieves who had such an extensive operation on Arrakis, the ones who rebuilt the Orgiz spice refinery? They were not a front for the Noble Commonwealth rebellion after all. It was, in fact, a secret operation created by Baron Harkonnen himself. He was the one selling spice behind your back and keeping all the profits."

Fenring watched shock play across the Emperor's face. "What is this, Hasimir? How?"

"The Baron provided extensive shipments of melange to a customer base of his own, reaping lucrative profits while hiding them from you, Sire."

Shaddam's face reddened, then purpled. "How? We know that Jaxson Aru was trying to obtain a large shipment of spice to fund his rebellion."

"Yes, hmm, but blaming him was just a cover, and a clever one. The Baron had been doing the same thing for a long time. I suspect that he destroyed the Orgiz refinery himself because I was on the verge of discovering his operations."

Fenring waited as the Emperor absorbed the information, then said, "And the Baron also blocked vital information about Duke Leto's bold infiltration of the radical movement. Imagine if you had only, ahhh, known about the Duke's honorable plans earlier! But the Baron concealed that from you, setting up his rival to fall." He huffed. "It was a vindictive, personal slight—which caused great harm to the Imperium. And now this illicit spice business . . ."

Shaddam paced the room in his elegant white robe that was trimmed in scarlet and gold. The Count was wise enough to remain silent and let his friend complete the convolutions in his own mind.

Finally, the Emperor said, "House Harkonnen must be punished—and more than fines or censures." He scanned the crystal sheet again as if he could now understand the numbers and diagrams. "The Baron has earned my wrath, in more ways than one! Now he deserves something even worse than I had planned. Summon Colonel Bashar Kolona again. It is time to use Sardaukar force on another planet. Arrakis."

UNDER THE DUSTY yellow sky, Shaddam emerged from the overwhelming force of troop carriers and sentinel ships that had landed across the Carthag spaceport, disrupting all air traffic. Intimidating Sardaukar craft overwhelmed the Harkonnen headquarters.

Shaddam was glad to flex the muscles of his private army. After the punitive attacks on rebel worlds and the siege of the CHOAM citadel on Tanegaard, the rest of the Imperium would already learn a significant lesson. On Arrakis, though, the Emperor could not let his Sardaukar damage the spice industry. Melange operations were far too valuable, and far too essential. This Imperial dosage of pain would come in another way.

Baron Harkonnen would not soon recover from this defeat, although he would likely hate the Atreides all the more. That could be used. Shaddam summoned the Baron. . . .

The flustered fat nobleman rushed to the Carthag spaceport accompanied by his thick-brained nephew, Count Glossu Rabban. There were onlookers in the terminal, but Shaddam didn't send them away. This would be public, very public.

The Baron looked hastily dressed with a dark cape across his massive shoulders and an untucked tunic that barely covered his suspensor belt. "Sire, we were not expecting you here on Arrakis! You should have informed me. You deserve an honor guard, a grand reception."

"I deserve *honesty*," the Emperor retorted, "not treachery. I was convinced that you and Count Fenring had taken care of the black-market spice operations here. I believed you!" He watched the Baron's corpulent face turn pale. "I must compliment you—it is not easy to fool Hasimir. But we have CHOAM records that prove *you* were the one selling illicit spice, not the handful of smugglers you offered as scapegoats. And not the Noble Commonwealth rebellion, not Jaxson Aru. *You* were keeping the profits, through secret black-market deals."

Taken aback, the guilty man raised his hands, then lowered them weakly. He opened and closed his mouth.

Shaddam cut off any response. "Don't offend me with your denials."

The Baron's dark-eyed gaze flicked over to Rabban, who stood just as nonplussed.

Surrounded by Sardaukar, the Emperor Shaddam Corrino drew himself up, as terrible as his title could make him. "You already earned my great disapproval for how you blocked vital information sent to me by Duke Leto Atreides. And now this!" He sniffed. "*This!* Only one punishment is appropriate and sufficient."

The Baron glanced back at all the crowds observing in the terminal, and stammered, "Sire, perhaps we should resume this discussion in my private headquarters? You and I can speak candidly, so you have all the facts."

"I have all the facts necessary. I am the Padishah Emperor." As his emphatic words echoed across the hushed crowd, the Baron wisely did not respond. Shaddam had devised an excellent solution for this debacle.

Empress Aricatha had insisted that he find some way to reward Leto Atreides, and this was also the perfect twist of the knife to hurt Baron Harkonnen. Yes, he was concerned about the popularity of the Duke of Caladan in the Landsraad, and this move would only make him seem like more of a hero. Shaddam suspected that the nobles admired the Duke more than their Emperor. That would have to be carefully watched, and dealt with, if necessary.

For now, this was the right thing to do. The people certainly liked Duke Leto more than they liked the Baron.

"For your crimes and indiscretions, I hereby rescind your siridar-governorship over Arrakis. House Harkonnen will no longer be the chosen noble family to run my spice operations."

The fat man was appalled, sickened. "Sire, there must be a way for me to make up—"

"Silence!" Shaddam's expression tightened, but he felt the joy building inside him. "Instead, I grant the fief of Arrakis to House Atreides. Your dear friend Duke Leto will take your place here." He raised his hand, looked out at the blocky industrial buildings the Harkonnens had built in Carthag. As he considered the distant dunes, the stark mountains, the harsh heat, the miserable conditions, Shaddam realized this was not exactly a reward for his Atreides cousin, but no one could dispute the magnitude of the gift.

At his command, Sardaukar now filled the streets of Carthag, intimidating the Harkonnen soldiers with a force that was ten times what they could resist.

The Baron acted as if he had received a mortal wound. Beside him, Rabban looked about to blurt out the wrong things, but his uncle silenced him with a glare because any response would only make things worse. The Baron said, "Please, Sire, I beg you to reconsider."

"I have already considered the matter in great detail, and you are fortunate I allow you to keep Giedi Prime, and that I do not insist on financial reparations. As for Arrakis, House Harkonnen will be given time to prepare and withdraw. I warn you to leave a fine welcome for House Atreides as the new governors of Arrakis. I have spoken."

He knew his commands were provocative, and the more he thought about it, the more he liked playing the two rival Houses off against each other, which would occupy and distract them—and perhaps more.

Shaddam could always change his mind. After all, he was the Emperor.

Opportunity can be a dangerous thing.

—DUKE PAULUS ATREIDES,
commentary on the Boorhees occupation

After the operations on the Southern Continent, it would take a long time before Castle Caladan felt like home again to Paul.

When the Atreides frigate returned from Wallach IX, Paul and Duncan rushed to the spaceport to welcome it, not knowing whether or not Duke Leto had been successful. A fist of anxiety squeezed Paul's heart. One did not simply bully or manipulate the Bene Gesserit.

But when the frigate hatch opened, Duke Leto emerged with Jessica on his arm. Even though the Duke often masked his feelings, this time the happiness on his face was there for everyone to see.

Crowds had gathered outside the landing zone, and when they saw Lady Jessica back on Caladan soil, they sent up loud applause. Seeing his mother, Paul did not need to hear the thunder of happy cheers, whistles, and laughter. He'd felt elated the moment he set eyes on her again.

Leto extended his free arm, and Paul moved forward to join his parents. The Duke raised his voice to the people. "Welcome home, Lady of Caladan!"

With his mother and father back together, and such strong and loyal advisers as Duncan, Thufir, and Gurney, House Atreides was strong again. The Duke had resolved not to pursue his aspirations of playing Imperial politics to enrich and improve the fortunes of his family. His independent mission to prevent Jaxson Aru from continuing his destructive attacks had been done without promise or reward, but because it was the right thing to do.

The Imperium had changed to the core in the wake of Jaxson's rebellion, enhancing political instabilities and social unrest. After the Otorio disaster, the status of House Atreides had shifted and grown as the Landsraad filled the numerous empty representative seats. Duke Leto's brave actions had altered how he was viewed in the eyes of the noble houses, although they had already respected him greatly. Then, while he was suspected of treachery against the throne, his fortunes dropped, and with his latest heroics they went back up again, to a new, higher level.

For himself, Paul had faced great turmoil and emerged stronger, although he expected it would still take a considerable amount of time for him to grow into his role as a future Duke.

His father had been tragically thrust into that position at around Paul's age . . . and now that Paul had turned fifteen, he, too, carried a great burden and responsibility. He had faced down the Emperor's Sardaukar, had obliterated the last of the ailar fields in the jungles. The idea of ruling a planet had never felt so clear to him as it did now, or so heavy. Paul wondered how his father managed to carry such weight on his shoulders, and wondered if he himself would ever grow accustomed to it.

What mattered most to him was a smaller, but far more intimate thing. His mother had returned from the Bene Gesserit. His parents were together, and that made all feel right with the world.

What he really wanted was to be quiet and content, and lead a normal life. He'd experienced more than enough changes for a while, and hoped the waters of Caladan would remain calm.

Unfortunately, his hopes would not come to pass.

⤸

WHEN THE UNEXPECTED Imperial decree arrived, Leto was finally getting back to the business of being the Duke of Caladan.

The first two days after his return home were a fog to him, thanks to Jessica's presence. The two of them had long, earnest conversations, learning what it meant to love each other again. Jessica was warm and open now, more passionate than she had been in a long time. She said she had never forgotten how deep her feelings were for him, and he felt the same about her.

They talked. They made love. They dined together in lavish, intimate banquets served by happy kitchen staff. They took romantic walks along the cliffs and watched the fog rolling out below. With Paul in tow, they strolled among the busy stalls in the reef market, and Leto purchased anything that caught Jessica's eye. She accepted the simple gifts as mementos of him, wishing that she'd had more such reminders while she was captive among the Bene Gesserit.

Though Leto's heart was whole again, he couldn't act like a young, love-struck schoolboy. He had to rule his people. So, he read his daily briefings, met with his advisers, and consulted with his Mentat, while also asking Jessica for her recommendations so they could be strong together, the Duke and his lady.

Seated across the table in his private study, the two of them reviewed projections and damage reports of the ruined moonfish industry, assessing the operations that had suffered such losses. After the harm Rabban had caused, the CHOAM contracts would now never be fulfilled. The market had collapsed. He and Jessica shared ideas about how to mitigate the disaster, but no viable solution appeared. It did not seem possible they could ever rebuild the moonfish industry on Caladan.

Then it became an irrelevant question.

An officious-looking courier in Corrino colors insisted on hand-delivering an embellished message cylinder. One of the household staff looked annoyed as she explained to Leto, "This man wouldn't trust us, my Lord. Said he could not rely on the castle staff and needed to see you in person!" She made a noise of disbelief.

The Imperial courier ignored the servant and stepped forward, extending the ostentatious cylinder. "By order of the Padishah Emperor, his majesty Shaddam IV, this decree is of legal standing, irrevocable, and generous. After you read it, I will relay your gratitude to the Emperor."

The courier placed the cylinder directly into Leto's palms. Curious, he turned the tube in his hands. With the abundance of jewels, etched designs, and encrusted gems, he couldn't at first fathom how to open it.

Jessica helped him, and when finally the long, ornate document rolled out, Leto spread it on the table beside the moonfish reports. The paper was covered with precise calligraphy. After his recent deeds, Leto thought that Shaddam might issue some sort of proclamation, maybe name a street or building on Kaitain after him, even grant him a small planet.

But this . . . he had not expected this.

"We need to tell Paul," Jessica said.

"I need to inform all the people of Caladan." Leto should have been overjoyed, but this breathtaking reward made him uneasy. The benefits of the Arrakis fief were obvious, but he wondered about the strings attached, invisible though they may be. "I will summon the troops."

The courier waited, and despite Leto's mixed reaction to the news, he told the man to pass his gratitude on to the Emperor, then dismissed him. The man bowed and hurried away.

Later, when Leto stood before a regiment of the Caladan army that had gathered in the great courtyard of Castle Caladan, he surveyed the crisp uniforms, the green-and-black banners flying high. It made him think of the proud history, of twenty-six generations of Atreides that had ruled this beautiful ocean world. The arrayed troops stood at attention as a moist breeze whipped around them. The banners snapped back and forth on high poles.

With Paul on one side of him and Jessica on the other, Duke Leto faced the wind. Jessica looked regal, no matter that she was just a concubine, a *bound* concubine. She was as elegant and impressive as any noblewoman Leto had seen in the Imperial Palace. She had restored the natural color of her bronze hair and adorned it with a pearl-studded clip he had bought for her at the reef market. The breeze pulled a few strands loose so that a rebellious lock of hair drifted across her brow.

He spoke into the anticipatory silence. "People of Caladan, loyal soldiers of the Atreides army." Leto paused, drew a deep breath. "His Imperial Majesty Shaddam IV has sent us an important decree, and our lives are all about to change. This is considered to be a tremendous reward for House Atreides."

He didn't know if anyone would notice how he had parsed his words.

Duke Leto smiled and nodded, as if convincing himself. "The spice melange is the most valuable commodity in the known universe. It is found on only one world, the desert planet Arrakis, a hard place to be, even if it does exude wealth. Arrakis is a necessary place, for without spice, there would be no Guild Navigators, there would be no Imperium."

Everyone listened closely, not sure what he was about to say.

"House Harkonnen has ruled Arrakis for eight decades, and they have now been removed. The Padishah Emperor has granted the fief to us! Arrakis is ours! House Atreides has been granted the siridar-governorship and oversight of all spice-harvesting operations."

There was a collective gasp, and a sudden burst of cheers, followed by muttering and confusion. The ranks of soldiers looked up to their Duke expectantly, but did not appear entirely happy.

Leto had a feeling of foreboding, but he could never decline such an incredible gift. "We will be leaving Caladan!" His shouted words sounded like a death knell.

He should feel joy even just imagining the wealth and power that would now belong to House Atreides, but he could not change his unsettled feeling. "We must pack up and prepare for our new responsibility—our new adventure!"

As the cheers grew louder, Leto looked down at his son. The young man seemed troubled, but proud. Paul stood at attention beside his father, ready to face and accept this new turn in his life.

Why do certain people take on greater and greater challenges that require supreme efforts to accomplish? One has only to look at the opposite type of person, one who attempts little in life, to answer this question. It is the difference between a leader and a follower, but they have a symbiotic relationship because one cannot exist without the other.

—PAUL ATREIDES, private journals

Circling over the lush green pundi rice paddies just after dawn, Duncan landed the 'thopter near the Muadh village. It was just the two of them, and they had no scheduled business with the Archvicar or the people. Paul had another challenge in mind, before all of House Atreides departed for Arrakis.

In the shadow of the stark Arondi Cliffs, the 'thopter's articulated wings beat more slowly as the systems shut down. The early-morning shadows stretching out from the rock uplift were long and ominous. The air was still, the day would be hot, and already the pundi rice farmers had gone out to wade in the terraced paddies, singing Muadh chanties.

Duncan had insisted on taking the controls for the short, smooth flight up from Castle Caladan, and as the two emerged from the aircraft near the base of the cliff, Duncan made no attempt to conceal his disapproval. "This is unnecessary and foolish, but I suppose it is stuck in your mind."

Paul stood beside him in the cool air, looking up the face of the sheer cliff. "I'm glad you knew enough not to talk me out of it."

"Wouldn't have worked."

The young man stretched, limbering himself up for the ordeal he was about to face, then reached into the cockpit and removed his pack and climbing gear. Some of the Muadh villagers had seen them and were watching, shading their eyes in the low light of sunrise. The bearded Archvicar came out of the wooden temple and approached, but Paul was not here to meet with any of the villagers. He turned instead to the imposing cliff that called to him.

In a firm voice, Paul said, "And you're not going up with me like you did when I ascended the sea cliffs. It's too dangerous."

Duncan snorted. "Try to stop me."

"You tend to distract me, and that's dangerous. You may be big and strong, but I'm nimble and better suited for this." He adjusted his straps, cinched the fit tighter. "You already checked my pack and ropes after I did the same myself, so you know my equipment is good. Now . . . trust me."

They walked toward the enormous slabs of talus that had sloughed off the stone edifice that towered over the flat landscape. All around, boulders had piled up like an ascent ramp to the cliff face.

"This rubble holds the bones of many fallen climbers," Duncan warned.

Paul scoffed. "I don't intend to join them."

Again, the Swordmaster made a gruff grumble. "None of the other victims *intended* to fall."

"You aren't bolstering my confidence, Duncan."

The big man planted his hands on his hips and looked up at the high stone wall before them, its face fractured with cracks and angled planes where rock had fallen. "Very well, I will stop objecting and give you my wholehearted support."

Paul looped a long coil of rope over his shoulder, rubbed powder on his hands, and kicked the toes of his climbing shoes against a rock to fit them properly. "Wholehearted, or half-hearted?"

Duncan laughed. "*Wholehearted*, Master Paul. I want you to succeed." He hesitated, then said in a smaller voice, "And I know you will."

Paul focused his thoughts and centered his mind on the approach, marking his line up the cliffs. This ascent would require all of his skill, but he had the equipment, the physical and the mental strength—the latter of which was the most difficult part.

According to family stories, his grandfather Paulus had attempted to climb the Arondi Cliffs when he was younger. He had not succeeded, but he had survived, and the ordeal had frightened him enough that he had never attempted it again. But Paulus Atreides had not been blessed with a Bene Gesserit mother who shared training with him. In his mind, he heard the Litany Against Fear in her voice.

Paul had studied images of this particular cliff face, so he knew the routes up, and the names of climbers who had fallen to their deaths here. Human beings, in their ambitious and competitive nature, continued to accept the challenge.

In dreams, half dreams, and waking moments, he'd envisioned this ascent, and now he was ready. Though Paul knew how to use carabiners, slings, and other climbing gear—and had them in his pack to keep Duncan happy—he preferred to rely solely on his sure hands and feet, and on a climbing rope.

The rock face was higher than the sea cliff on the top of which Castle

Caladan stood, and significantly more difficult than the outcropping he and Sinsei had climbed to reach Chaen Marek's base. With all that practice, he was more than ready for this.

With a clear mind and the full certainty that he could accomplish the ascent, Paul left Duncan and scrambled up the boulders and talus slabs to reach the real cliff. He found a few cairns left by other climbers, even a staging area where they had checked their equipment. Some discouraged people must have turned around here.

Paul began ascending, sure-footed. His shoes had perfect grip on the rough stone, his hands found stable holds. He looked up, not down, intent on his route. So far, the cliff was not as treacherous as he'd expected, but he did not allow hubris to intrude on his thoughts any more than doubt.

Below, Duncan would be watching him, likely joined by other villagers, maybe even the Archvicar himself.

Paul wedged his body into a deep crack between rocks and worked his way higher, until he reached a narrow ledge, a minimal place for a brief rest. He had memorized the line upward, knew every part of the climb, and now he remembered what was above him. The rock was dry and firm, and the rising sun warmed his back enough to take away the chill in the morning shadows. The pack was snug against his shoulders.

He did not let himself feel relief that the ascent had been smoother than expected. He was surprised that Duncan had not been more resistant. He used his upper-body strength to heave himself up to the next ledge, then finally had to resort to the rope, tying a sturdy boating knot like his father had taught him, and then he hooked it above him, on an outcropping.

Just as he acknowledged his success, his left foot slipped and he dropped a few terrifying feet. The rope braced him, and he managed to grab a handhold while jamming his heel into another cranny. His racing heartbeat set off a percussive drumbeat in his ears. He'd burned his hands on the rope.

Calming himself, Paul made his way over to a spot wide enough to sit, where he paused to gather his thoughts.

On impulse, he ventured to look down, seeing how high up he was, facing the fear of the long plunge. From this vantage, he could see the simple dwellings of the Muadh village, the lush green rice fields, the silvery canals. Directly below, by the rubble of rock and debris at the base of the cliff, he saw the ornithopter, and Duncan among the Muadh spectators looking up at him, including the Archvicar in his brown-and-green robes. They would all be worrying about him, afraid he might fall.

But he would not fall. He inhaled a long, slow breath. With deep reverence, Paul whispered the opening lines of the Litany Against Fear of the

Bene Gesserit, which left him feeling clean and pure, all doubts and fears washed from his mind.

Here on the narrow ledge, he took a moment to open his pack and review the available tools and equipment. Paul had thought the pack was a little bulkier than he'd expected, and when he moved aside the pitons and carabiners and energy-dense food wafers, he was angered to find a small suspensor ball inside, set to activate automatically.

Duncan had checked the pack last, and he must have slipped the safety device inside, using the low-setting field to lighten his load during the climb— making the challenge easier. And the suspensor had been set to activate to full power if Paul slipped.

No wonder Duncan had conceded so easily, knowing that Paul carried a secret fail-safe device. Indignant and determined, Paul removed the globe and tossed it off the edge of the cliff, watching it float slowly toward the onlookers like a soap bubble, bobbing and moving in slight breezes. Duncan would be upset seeing it, but Paul did not intend to use the assist.

Now, with renewed determination to prove himself, Paul continued to climb, working from memory as well as careful observations of the cliff's topography. He made his way higher, somehow more relaxed now. He barely even noticed the difficult parts.

This was the greatest physical challenge he had ever attempted, though he wasn't sure if it was the biggest mental challenge. Now he imagined what he must look like from below, a tiny figure on a massive slab of rock, a young man trying to conquer something much larger than he was. Oddly, the faster he went, the more sure-footed he was. He would not fall.

Near the top, the cliff face became less steep, as if in reward for his great exertion, and he followed the slope to the top of the huge rock formation. The summit was a surprise and a relief, and even something of a letdown. He stood there panting, drinking in the panorama. He could see the Muadh village, the expansive pundi rice paddies, the groups of workers, the irrigation canals. Beyond the fields, he saw forests, lakes, dark foothills, a gray haze of coastline.

Now that he stood alone and triumphant, he felt closer to this world. Beautiful Caladan.

He hated to leave this planet, his home. Distant Arrakis would be such a different place. . . .

He heard a whirring hum and turned to see the small Atreides 'thopter rising from the back of the Arondi Cliffs. Duncan expertly piloted the craft and found a place to land on the rocky expanse of the summit.

Paul was disappointed that his moment of peace had been broken, but he was glad to see his friend. He had planned to descend the cliffs as well, taking a different and simpler path down, using ropes, but Duncan swung himself out of the aircraft and motioned him over. "You proved yourself, lad. I'm proud of you."

"I didn't need the safety suspensor," Paul said. "I made the climb the way I wanted."

The Swordmaster's dark eyebrows drew together. "There's a difference between needing something and knowing you can rely on it. That doesn't mean I don't respect your skills, but you can always rely on me."

Paul smiled and came closer. "I know that, Duncan."

The other man urged him to the 'thopter. "Now come with me. You've climbed the Arondi Cliffs, but you have other tasks and challenges back at Castle Caladan. You're the ducal heir, and you have a new world to prepare for—and another one to leave behind."

Feeling the weight of responsibility, Paul lowered his head. "I know."

"And all that packing to do!" Duncan said. "You'll have to do it yourself. Don't expect me to help you put clothes in boxes. I'm leaving on the next Heighliner, a one-man advance team ahead of the rest of House Atreides."

Paul felt alarmed. "Leaving? Where are you going?"

"To Arrakis. On a mission for the Duke." He clapped his hand on the young man's shoulder, and they both boarded the 'thopter. "But I will see you there, have no doubt of that."

Paul took one last look at the breathtaking expanse of Caladan. This might be his last cliff, but he knew he had other heights to climb.

Throughout the history of our breeding program, we have sought the elu-sive Kwisatz Haderach, but one candidate after another has disappointed us. A failed candidate is alive today, a man to whom we never adminis-tered a formal test, but we dropped his name from consideration after a deep analysis of his bloodlines. He remains useful to us though, and serves as the Emperor's assassin . . . Count Hasimir Fenring.

—Notations made by the late Lethea,
a disgraced Kwisatz Mother

Two paths forward remain," said the veiled woman. "Two possibilities on the same genetic path. Sister Jessica is the crux of both of them. She will not let us down this time."

Shut inside her private office, Mother Superior Harishka leaned across her desk to look at the Kwisatz Mother. Down the long, dark table sat Cordana, her elbows on the wooden surface, and Reverend Mother Mohiam, who had once been Harishka's closest adviser and now filled that role again. All of the women had been served strong tea, but the Kwisatz Mother did not lift the covering on her face, and her cup sat untouched.

"Jessica has always been a challenge," Mohiam said. "If not for the poten-tial she holds, if we did not need her to bear us another Atreides child . . ."

"The correct Atreides child," Harishka said. "A daughter."

"I believe we can count on her now," Cordana said. "She did what we asked on Elegy, and she's made her commitment to bear that child. She is an independent woman, but is still a true Bene Gesserit Sister."

Though all of the women in the room knew a great deal about the science of the breeding program, the possibilities and hopes of it, they did not speak of this. They knew the details of Jessica's parentage, although the girl had been raised here on Wallach IX with none of that knowledge.

Mohiam wrapped her hands around her teacup, as if wrestling with de-cisions and loyalties. "Emotions made her weak, but her training and her obligations—especially now—make her . . . reliable."

"Xora was on a parallel path, and her son met the criteria," Cordana cau-tioned, shifting in her chair. "What can we learn from all of this?"

"Xora and Brom are dead," said the Kwisatz Mother. "We can learn that they both failed us."

"If Jessica bears a daughter for us, we can get our program back on track.

That Atreides girl can mate with a Harkonnen, and their offspring will be the culmination of thousands of years of planning." The Kwisatz Mother's long sigh rustled the veil in front of her face.

"And Ruthine wanted to kill Jessica and the boy because of Lethea's ravings," Cordana snorted. "If that had happened, we would have been set back by generations."

"We are Bene Gesserit," the veiled woman said. "We always have options."

"It will take time," Harishka warned. "Jessica has not even conceived a daughter yet. Then the child must mature and bear another child, by a Harkonnen, who may—*may*—become the all-powerful male we seek. It will not happen in our lifetimes."

"We Bene Gesserit are not afraid of time," the Kwisatz Mother said.

Harishka slid her teacup aside. "Brom failed to meet expectations, but there is another possibility, available to us sooner than a new Atreides daughter and yet another generation of waiting. Even Jessica in her foolish hope knows that her son may be what we need."

"Waiting carries risk," Mohiam said. "Jessica almost didn't survive on Elegy, and Leto Atreides faced near-certain execution from the Emperor. An unknown assassin even went after the boy Paul. All three survived, but we could lose everything. If we wait."

Cordana looked at the gathered women. "Are you suggesting we should bring Jessica's son here and prepare him for the Agony? Protect and train him at the Mother School, as we did with Brom?"

"A premature suggestion," the Kwisatz Mother said with a gruff undertone. "We do not even know the true potential of this Paul Atreides. But he should be interviewed, inspected . . . tested."

Harishka pursed her lips. "I don't believe Jessica has prepared him well enough for the Agony. She's been away from him for months."

"Not the Agony . . . not yet," said the Kwisatz Mother. "Give him the gom jabbar."

A hush fell over the room.

The Mother Superior turned to the veiled woman with another question. "I have a concern. This Kwisatz Haderach—if we succeed in creating him after all these generations—do you think we'll be able to control him? Or will he be accountable to no one? Will he be dangerous?"

The answer lay not in words because no one had any reply. The answer lay in their silence, broken only by the sounds of Reverend Mother Mohiam rising to her feet.

"I shall leave for Caladan immediately," said the Emperor's Truthsayer as she moved toward the door. "I will examine this Paul Atreides for myself."

ACKNOWLEDGMENTS

Special thanks to those who have helped us take a great journey through Frank Herbert's spectacular universe. Our literary agents John Silbersack and Robert Gottlieb; Tom Doherty and Christopher Morgan at Tor Books; Kim Herbert and Byron Merritt at Herbert Properties LLC, who are dedicated to maintaining the Frank Herbert legacy; and, of course, our wives Janet Herbert and Rebecca Moesta, as always.

ABOUT THE AUTHORS

Jan Herbert

BRIAN HERBERT, the son of Frank Herbert, wrote the definitive biography of him, *Dreamer of Dune*, which was a Hugo Award finalist. Herbert is also president of the company managing the legacy of Frank Herbert, and is an executive producer of the motion picture *Dune*, as well as of the TV series *Dune: The Sisterhood*. He is the author or coauthor of more than forty-five books, including multiple *New York Times* bestsellers, has been nominated for the Nebula Award, and is always working on several projects at once. He and his wife, Jan, have traveled to all seven continents, and in 2019, they took a trip to Budapest to observe the filming of *Dune*.

KEVIN J. ANDERSON has written dozens of national bestsellers and has been nominated for the Hugo Award, the Nebula Award, the Bram Stoker Award, and the SFX Readers' Choice Award. His critically acclaimed original novels include the ambitious space opera series The Saga of Seven Suns, including *The Dark Between the Stars*, as well as the epic fantasy trilogy Wake the Dragon and the Terra Incognita fantasy epic with its two accompanying rock CDs. He also set the Guinness-certified world record for the largest single-author book signing, and was recently inducted into the Colorado Authors' Hall of Fame.